BEASTS
OF
PREY

PENGUIN BOOKS

UK | USA | Canada | Ireland | Australia
India | New Zealand | South Africa

Penguin Books is part of the Penguin Random House group of companies
whose addresses can be found at global.penguinrandomhouse.com.

www.penguin.co.uk
www.puffin.co.uk
www.ladybird.co.uk

First published in the USA by G. P. Putnam's Sons, an imprint of
Penguin Random House LLC, 2021
International paperback and exclusive Fairyloot edition published in
Great Britain by Penguin Books 2021
Paperback edition published in Great Britain by Penguin Books 2022

001

Design by Marikka Tamura

Printed and bound in Great Britain by Clays Ltd, Elcograf S.p.A.

The authorized representative in the EEA is Penguin Random House Ireland,
Morrison Chambers, 32 Nassau Street, Dublin D02 YH68

A CIP catalogue record for this book is available from the British Library

PAPERBACK ISBN: 978–0–241–53254–6
EXCLUSIVE EDITION ISBN: 978–0–241–54386–3
INTERNATIONAL PAPERBACK ISBN: 978–0–241–53256–0

All correspondence to:
Penguin Books
Penguin Random House Children's
One Embassy Gardens, 8 Viaduct Gardens, London SW11 7BW

PENGUIN BOOKS

BEASTS OF PREY

Dedicated to the roots of the tree from which
a flower blossomed.

THE GREATER JUNGLE

THE AMAKOYAN SEA

NORTHERN PASS

Lake Msitu

EASTERN PASS

WESTERN PASS

Heart of the Jungle

SOUTHERN PASS

NO-MAN'S-LAND

LKOSSA

The Tusks

THE LESSER JUNGLE

FORBIDDEN FRUIT

ADIAH

Baba says only wicked things happen after midnight, but I know better.

I hold my breath, relieved the front door doesn't creak as I nudge it open and relish the evening breeze on my skin. This late, its scent is distinct, a sharp blend of ozone and pine. I glance over my shoulder. In the next room, my parents are fast asleep; Mama's snores are gentle, my father's thunderous. It's easy to envision them, two brown bodies curled against each other under a threadbare blanket, both worn out from a hard day's work in the harvesting fields. I don't want to wake them. Perhaps in the repose of their dreams, their daughter is different, a responsible girl instead of one who sneaks out. Sometimes I wish I *was* that responsible girl. I hesitate a second longer before slipping into the embrace of night.

Outside, the air is temperate, the rolling gray clouds overhead thick with the promise of monsoon season, but Lkossa remains a city bathed in silver moonlight, more than enough for me. I weave through its empty roads, darting between the flickers of sconce-lit streets, and pray I don't run into one of the patrolling Sons of the

1

Six. It isn't likely I'd get in trouble if the city's anointed warriors caught me, but they'd almost certainly make me turn back, and I don't want to. It's a rare pleasure to walk here without whispers following in my wake, and there's another reason not to be sent home yet: Dakari is waiting for me.

I note the new cloth banners decorating most of the city as I trek north, braided together in ropes of green, blue, and gold— green for the earth, blue for the sea, gold for the gods. Some hang limp from laundry lines as thin and worn as thread; others are nailed clumsily to the doors of modest mud-brick homes not so unlike my own. It's an endearing effort. In a few hours, once the dawn breaks anew, citizens will gather to begin their observance of the Bonding, a holy day in which we celebrate our connection to the gods of this land. Vendors will peddle amulets for the reverent and give away pouches of throwing rice for the children. The recently appointed Kuhani will offer blessings from the temple, and musicians will fill the streets with their discordant symphony. Knowing Mama, she'll make roasted sweet potatoes drizzled with honey and sprinkled with cinnamon, like she always does on special occasions. Baba will probably surprise her with a small gift he saved up for—and she'll probably tell him he shouldn't have. I ignore a small pang in my chest as I think about Tao, wondering if he'll stop by our house like he normally does for holidays. I'm not actually sure he will this time; Tao and I haven't been speaking lately.

The city darkens as I reach its border, a wide dirt clearing a few yards wide that separates Lkossa from the first of the Greater Jungle's towering black pines. They seem to watch my approach with an immemorial regard, as stoic as the goddess said to dwell among them. Not everyone would dare to venture here—some believe the jungle isn't safe—but I don't mind it. My eyes search the expanse in anticipation, but when I realize I'm alone, I have to quell a fleeting disappointment. Dakari had said to meet him at this exact spot just after midnight, but he's not here. Perhaps he's running late, maybe he's decided not to—

"Songbird."

My heart stutters in my chest at the familiar nickname, and a dull flush heats my skin despite the evening chill as a figure peels away from one of the nearby pines to step into better light.

Dakari.

It's hard to make out all his details in the night, but my imagination can fill in the gaps just fine. Half his face is dipped in moonlight, tracing along the sharp cut of his jaw, the easy bend in his broad shoulders. He's taller than me, with the lean build of a runner. His golden-brown skin is several shades lighter than mine, and his hair, raven-black, is freshly cut in a top fade. He looks like a god, and—judging by the cocky grin he gives me—he knows it.

In a few confident strides, he closes the gap between us, and the air around me immediately fills with the smell of him: steel and dirt and leather from his apprenticeship in the forges of the Kughushi District. He gives me a once-over, visibly impressed.

"You came."

"Of course." I make myself sound at ease. "We said just after midnight, didn't we?"

"We did." His chuckle is low, almost musical. "So, are you ready to see the surprise?"

3

"Are you kidding?" My laugh echoes his own. "I've been waiting for this all day. It had better be worth it."

"Oh, it *is*." Abruptly, his expression turns more serious. "Now, you have to *promise* to keep this secret. I've never shown anyone else."

This surprises me. Dakari is, after all, attractive and popular; he has lots of friends. Lots of *girl* friends, specifically. "You mean, you haven't shown anyone at all?"

"No," he says quietly. "This is really special to me, and I . . . I guess I've just never really trusted someone else enough to share it."

At once, I straighten, hoping I look mature, like the kind of girl who *can* be trusted. "I won't tell anyone," I whisper. "I promise."

"Good." Dakari winks, gesturing all around us. "Then, without further ado, here it is!"

I wait a beat before frowning, confused. Dakari's arms are extended like he's about to take flight, his expression absolutely jubilant. Clearly, he likes whatever he's seeing, but *I* can't see anything at all.

"Um . . ." After a few more uncomfortable seconds, I break the silence. "Sorry, am I missing something?"

Dakari glances my way, eyes dancing with amusement. "You mean you can't feel it around us, the splendor?"

The moment the words leave his lips, there's a thrum deep in my core. It's like the first pluck of a kora string, and it reverberates through my entire body. And then I understand, of course. Foreigners call it *magic*; my people call it *the splendor*. I can't see it, but I sense it—a great deal of it—moving just beneath the dirt like ripples in a pond. There's far more here than I've ever felt practicing with the other darajas on the temple's lawns.

"How . . . ?" I'm afraid to even move, to disturb whatever this strange wonder is. "How is there so much of it here?"

"It's a rare, natural occurrence, only happens once a century." Dakari's eyes are closed like he's savoring a forbidden fruit. "This is why the day of the Bonding is so special, Songbird."

I look around us, astonished. "I thought the Bonding was symbolic, a day of reverence for—"

Dakari shakes his head. "It's far more than a day for symbolism. In a few hours, an immeasurable amount of splendor will rise to the earth's surface. The power will be glorious to behold, though I doubt most people will be able to feel it the way *you* can." He throws me a sly, knowing look. "After all, few darajas are as gifted as you."

Something pleasant squirms inside me at the compliment. Dakari isn't like most people in Lkossa. He isn't scared of me, or of what I can do. He isn't intimidated by my abilities.

"Close your eyes." The words are less a command and more an invitation when Dakari says them. "Go on, try it."

I follow his lead and close my eyes. My bare toes wriggle, and the splendor responds as though it was only waiting for me to make the first move. It tingles as it flows through me, filling me like steeped honeybush tea poured into black porcelain. It's *divine*.

"Songbird." In my new darkness, Dakari's voice is barely audible, but I hear the emotion in it, the *want*. "Open your eyes."

I do, and the breath leaves my body.

Concentrated particles of the splendor are floating around us, sparkling like diamonds turned to dust. I feel a million of their tiny pulses in the air, and in the moment their collective heartbeat finds my own, I also feel a distinct sense of connection to them.

5

The red dirt at my feet shifts as more of it rises from the ground, dancing up my limbs and seeping into my very bones. A current of its energy runs the length of me, intoxicating. I instantly crave more of it. Beside me, something tickles my ear. Dakari. I hadn't noticed him moving closer to me. When he leans in and one hand finds the small of my back, I barely resist a shiver.

"Imagine what you could do with this." His fingers interlaced with mine are warm, his lips soft against my cheek. I think of them, so close to my own, and forget how to breathe. "Imagine what you could make people *see* with this kind of power. You could show everyone that the splendor isn't dangerous, just misunderstood. You could prove they were wrong about everything, about *you*."

You could prove they were wrong. I swallow, remembering. The memories come in an onslaught—the brothers of the temple and their scoldings, the children who run when they see me, the gossiping elders. I think of Mama and Baba back home in their bed, fast asleep. My parents love me, I know, but even they whisper to each other when they think I'm not listening. Everyone is afraid of me and of what I can do, but Dakari . . . He isn't afraid. He's believed in me all along. He was the first person to really see all of me. In his eyes, I'm not a girl to be chastised but a woman to be respected. He understands me, he *gets* me, he loves me.

I love *him*.

The splendor before us has taken clearer shape now, forming a towering column of white-gold light that seems to stretch into a realm beyond the sky. It emits a low hum. I could touch it if I reached out. I start to, when—

"Adiah!"

6

A different voice fractures the peace—one full of fear—and I tear my gaze away from the splendor. Dakari's hand tightens around mine, but I pull away and search the clearing around us until I find a skinny boy in a dirt-smudged tunic. His short dreadlocks are bed-tousled, and he's standing yards away with the city at his back, holding his knees like he's been running. I didn't see him arrive, and I don't know how long he's been here. His eyes are wide with horror. He knows me, and I know him.

Tao.

"Adiah." My best friend doesn't call me Songbird—he uses my real name. His voice is hoarse, desperate. "Please don't touch it. It's . . . it's dangerous."

Tao loves me too, and in a way I love him back. He is smart and funny and kind. He's been like a brother to me all my life. I hate hurting him. I hate that we haven't been speaking.

"I—" Something catches in my throat, and Tao's words echo in the space between us. *Dangerous.* He doesn't want me to touch the splendor because he thinks it's dangerous. He thinks *I'm* dangerous, just like everyone else does. But he doesn't understand, he doesn't get it. Dakari hasn't said anything, but now *his* voice fills my head.

You could prove they were wrong.

I realize I can, and I *will*.

"I'm sorry." The words leave me, but they're swallowed by the sudden roar of the splendor. The column has grown bigger and louder; it drowns out Tao's reply. I watch the light of it illuminate his face, the tears on his cheeks, and try to ease that same pang in my chest. My friend knows I've made my choice. Perhaps it doesn't matter now, but I hope one day he'll forgive me.

I close my eyes again as my fingers reach to brush the closest fragments of the splendor. This time, at my touch, they course through my veins in an eager, heady rush. My eyes open wide as they consume me, the wonder of it so enthralling that I barely register the pain until it's too late.

PART ONE

A ROARING LION KILLS NO PREY.

CHAPTER 1

GOOD SPIRITS

The hut reeked of death.

It was a nauseating smell, both fetid and sickly sweet, thick in the dusk as it filled Koffi's lungs. A quarter hour had passed since she'd last moved; her legs were stiff, her mouth dry. Every so often, her stomach twisted, threatening revolt. But it was no matter; she kept still as stone. Her eyes were fixed on what lay mere feet from her across the worn dirt floor—the victim.

The boy's name was Sahel. Koffi hadn't worked with him in the Night Zoo long, but she recognized his bare face, mahogany brown like her own, framed by tight black curls. In life, he'd had a crooked smile, an obnoxious braying laugh not unlike that of a donkey. Those things had abandoned him in death. She studied his lanky frame. As was Gede practice, most of his body was shrouded, but dried blood still stained the white linen in places, hints of the gruesome wounds beneath. She couldn't see them, but she knew they were there—the scratches, the *bite marks*. From the darkest corners of her mind, a chilling image grew vivid. She imagined Sahel stumbling through a jungle, clumsy, oblivious to what waited for him among the vines. She envisioned a grotesque creature stalking forward in the moonlight, tongue darting between serrated teeth as it eyed easy prey.

She heard the scream.

A violent shudder racked her body then, despite the muggy heat. If the rumors she'd heard earlier were true, Sahel's manner of death had been neither a quick nor a painless affair.

"Kof."

Across the stuffy hut, Mama was on her knees beside Sahel's body, staring at the tattered blanket before it. On it were six crudely carved wooden figurines of animals—a heron, a crocodile, a jackal, a serpent, a dove, and a hippo—one familiar for each god. The oil lamp to her right bathed one side of her face in lambent light; the other was cast in shadow. "It's time."

Koffi hesitated. She'd agreed to come here and offer parting rites for Sahel, as Gede custom called for, but the thought of getting any closer to the corpse unnerved her. At a sharp glance from Mama, however, she moved to kneel with her. Together they let their fingers brush each of the figurines before folding their hands.

"Carry him." Mama whispered the prayer. "Carry him to his ancestors in the godlands."

Their heads were still bowed when Koffi asked the question in a murmur. "Is it true?"

Mama cracked a wary eye. "Koffi . . ."

"Some of the others were talking," Koffi went on before her mother could stop her. "They said others were killed, that—"

"Hush." Mama's head snapped up, and she swatted the words away like tsetse flies. "Mind your tongue when you speak of the dead, lest you bring them misfortune."

12

Koffi pursed her lips. It was said that, to pass into the next life, one of the gods' animal familiars—represented by the figurines before them—carried each soul to the god of death, Fedu. Each soul then had to pay Fedu before being carried on to paradise in the godlands. A soul with no money to pay for passage was doomed to walk the earth as a lost spirit for all eternity. Like Koffi, Sahel had been a beastkeeper indentured to the Night Zoo, which meant he'd had little money in life and likely had even less in death. If faith held true, this meant his misfortunes had only just begun, whether she minded her tongue or not. She had started to say so when the hut's straw-thatch door opened. A stout woman with salt-and-pepper cornrows stuck her head inside. Her simple tunic was identical to theirs, gray and hemmed just below the knee. At the sight of them, she wrinkled her nose.

"Time to go."

Mama gestured to the figurines. "We're not finished—"

"You've had ample time for this nonsense." The woman waved a dismissive hand. She spoke Zamani, the language of the East, like them, but her Yaba dialect gave her words a sharp, clicking quality. "The boy's dead, praying to toys won't change that, and there's work yet to be done before the show, which Baaz expects to begin on time."

Mama gave a resigned nod. Together, she and Koffi stood, but once the woman had left again, they both looked back to Sahel. If not for the bloodied shroud, he could have been sleeping.

"We'll return and finish our prayers later, before they bury him," said Mama. "He deserves that much."

Koffi tugged at her tunic's frayed neckline, trying to temper a moment's guilt. Everyone else in the Night Zoo had already offered

13

prayers for Sahel, but she'd begged Mama to wait. She'd blamed chores, then a headache, but the truth was, she hadn't wanted to see Sahel like this, broken and hollow and devoid of all the things that had made him real. She'd built her own kind of walls to protect herself from the near-constant reminders of death's presence here, but it had crept in anyway, intruding. Now the idea of leaving Sahel to lie here in the dirt, as alone as he'd been in the last grisly seconds of his life, unsettled her. She thought again of what she'd heard other beastkeepers whispering earlier in the day. People were now saying that Sahel had waited until late last night to make a run for it. They said he'd gone into the Greater Jungle hoping to find freedom and instead had found a creature that killed for amusement. She winced. The Shetani's murderous reputation was frightening enough, but it was the fact that the monster had evaded capture for so many years that set her on edge. Misunderstanding the look on her face, Mama took Koffi's hand and squeezed.

"I promise we'll come back," she whispered. "Now come on, let's go." Without another word, she ducked out of the hut. Koffi glanced back at Sahel's body a final time, then followed.

Outside, the sun was setting, cast against a bruised sky curiously fractured by strange black fissures amid the clouds. Those fissures would fade to a gentler violet as monsoon season drew nearer, but they'd never truly disappear. They'd been there all Koffi's life, an indelible mark left by the Rupture.

She hadn't been alive a century ago when it had happened, but elders deep in their palm wine still spoke of it on occasion. Drunk, voices slurred, they recalled the violent tremors that had splintered the earth like a clay pot, the dead who'd strewn Lkossa's streets in the aftermath. They talked of a relentless, blistering heat that had driven men mad. Koffi, and every other child of her generation, had suffered the consequences of that madness. After the Rupture, her people—the Gedes—had been dwindled down by war and poverty, easy to divide and regulate. Her eyes traveled along the cracks in the sky, weaving overhead like thin black threads. For a second, she thought she felt something as she surveyed them . . .

"Koffi!" Mama called over her shoulder. "Come now!"

Just as quickly, the feeling was gone, and Koffi kept on.

In silence, she and Mama whisked by mud-brick huts crammed along the Night Zoo's edge; other beastkeepers were getting ready too. They passed men and women dressed in shabby tunics, some nursing freshly bandaged wounds from encounters with beasts, some marked by more permanent injuries like old scars and missing fingers. Each carried a quiet defeat in their hunched shoulders and downcast eyes that Koffi hated but understood. Most of the Night Zoo's workers were of the Gedezi People like her, which meant the show would go on this evening, but Sahel's absence would be felt. He hadn't had real family here, but he'd been one of them, bound to this place by bad luck and bad choices. He deserved more than quick prayers in a run-down hut; he deserved a proper burial with token coins placed in his palms to ensure he made it to the god-lands. But no one here could afford to spare any coin. Baaz made sure of that.

A chorus of shrieks, roars, and snarls filled the eventide as they reached the crooked wooden post marking the end of the beastkeepers' huts, trading red dirt for an expanse of green lawns filled with cages of every size, shape, and color. Koffi eyed the one nearest her, and the eight-headed nyuvwira snake met her gaze, curious. She followed Mama's lead around cages of white pygmy elephants, chimpanzees, a pair of giraffes grazing quietly in their paddock. They passed a dome-shaped aviary full of black-and-white impundulus, barely mindful to cover their heads as the birds beat their massive wings and sent sparks of lightning into the sky. Baaz Mtombé's Night Zoo was rumored to hold over a hundred exotic species within its confines; in her eleven years of contracted service to it, Koffi had never bothered to count.

They moved quickly between other enclosures, but when they reached the grounds' border, her steps slowed. The blacksteel cage kept here was separate from the others, and with good reason. In the dying light, only its stark silhouette was visible; what it contained within was veiled in shadow.

"It's all right." Mama beckoned even as Koffi instinctively faltered. "I checked on Diko earlier today, and he was fine." She approached the cage at the same time something in its corner shifted. Koffi tensed.

"Mama—"

"Come now, Diko." Mama kept her voice low as she withdrew a rust-speckled key from her pocket to insert into the massive padlock. In answer, there was an ominous hiss, slick as a blade. Koffi's toes curled in the grass, and from the cage's shadows a beautiful creature emerged.

His body was reptilian and sinewed, entirely adorned by iridescent scales that seemed to hold a thousand colors captive each time he moved. Clever citrine eyes danced back and forth as Mama tinkered with the lock, and when the beast flicked his forked black tongue between the bars, a smell like smoke tinged the dry air. Koffi swallowed.

The first time she'd seen a jokomoto, as a little girl, she'd thought they were creatures spun from glass, fragile and delicate. She'd been wrong. There was nothing delicate about a fire-breathing lizard.

"Get the hasira leaf out," Mama directed. "Now."

At once, Koffi pulled three dry, silver-veined leaves from a drawstring pouch at her hip. They were exquisite, shimmering with white resin that left her fingertips sticky when she pinched them. Her heartbeat hammered as the door to the jokomoto's cage swung open and his head swiveled. Mama covered her nose with one hand, then raised the other in warning.

"Steady . . ."

Koffi went stock-still as the jokomoto bolted from his cage and slunk toward her on long clawed feet. She waited until he was within a few yards of her before tossing the leaves high into the air. Diko's eyes caught them, and he lunged, impossibly quick. There was a flash of pointed teeth, a merciless crunch, and then they were gone. Koffi stuffed her hands back into her pockets quickly. Jokomotos weren't native to this part of Eshōza; they were creatures from the western part of the continent, said to be children of Tyembu, the desert god. At roughly the same size as a common monitor lizard, Diko wasn't the largest, fastest, or strongest animal kept in the Night Zoo, but he *was* the most temperamental—which also made him the most dangerous. One wrong move and he could set the entire place ablaze; it was all too easy to recall the nasty burns on beastkeepers who'd forgotten that. Her heartbeat only settled after the hasira leaf's power took effect and the lurid yellow glow in his eyes slightly dimmed.

"I've got it from here." Koffi was already moving behind Diko

17

with a leather harness and leash snatched from a nearby post. She stooped down, and the moment she fastened its worn straps under his scaled belly and tightened them, she relaxed. The flimsy binds were a silly thing to take comfort in—they'd do nothing if Diko's mood soured—but he was subdued, at least for now.

"Make sure those binds are secure."

Koffi looked up. "Done."

Pleased, Mama bent to give Diko's snout a demonstrative pat. "That's a good boy."

Koffi rolled her eyes as she straightened. "I don't know why you talk to him like that."

"Why not?" Mama shrugged. "Jokomotos are spectacular beasts."

"They're dangerous."

"Sometimes things that seem dangerous are just misunderstood." Mama said the words with a strange sadness before patting Diko again. This time, as if to affirm the point, he gently nudged her palm. This seemed to cheer her back up. "Besides, just look at him. He's in good spirits tonight."

Koffi started to argue, then thought better of it. Her mother had always had a strange empathy for the Night Zoo's inhabitants. She changed the subject.

"You know, that was the last of the hasira leaf." She patted her empty pouch for emphasis. "We're out until more is delivered." Even now, wisps of the leaves' cloying fragrance still suffused the air. Inadvertently, she caught a lingering whiff of it, and a pleasant thrum tickled the edges of her senses.

"Koffi!" Mama's voice turned sharp, cleaving through that

momentary bliss. She was still holding Diko's leash, but frowning. "You know better. Don't breathe it in."

Koffi shook herself, unnerved, then fanned at the air around her until the smell was gone. Plucked from shrubs along the Greater Jungle's border, hasira leaf was a sedative herb potent enough to knock out a mature bull elephant when consumed; it wasn't wise to inhale its fragrance at close range, even in small quantities.

"We should get moving." Mama's gaze had locked on an illuminated tent set across the Night Zoo's grounds; other beastkeepers were already heading toward it with animals in tow. From here, it was no larger than a candle's red-gold flame, but Koffi recognized it—the Hema was where tonight's show would be held. Mama glanced her way again. "Ready?"

Koffi grimaced. She was never ready for shows at the Night Zoo, but that hardly mattered. She'd just moved to stand on the other side of Diko when she noticed something.

"What's wrong?" Mama asked, noting Koffi's raised eyebrow.

"You tell *me*." Now Koffi squinted. Something was off about her mother's expression, but she couldn't quite tell what. She studied it harder. The two of them looked similar—shoulder-length black twists, broad nose and full mouth framed by a heart-shaped face—but there was something *else* about Mama tonight. "You look . . . different."

"Oh." Mama looked uncharacteristically flustered, there was no doubt about it. Then Koffi named it, that foreign emotion in her mother's eyes. Koffi was embarrassed to realize the thing she hadn't recognized was happiness.

"Did . . . something happen?"

Mama shifted her weight from foot to foot. "Well, I was going to wait until tomorrow to tell you. After what happened with Sahel earlier, it didn't seem right to discuss it, but . . ."

"But?"

"Baaz pulled me aside a few hours ago," she said. "He calculated our debt balance, and . . . we're almost paid off."

"What?" Something like shock and joy erupted in Koffi. Diko snorted at the sudden outburst, sending tendrils of smoke into the air, but she ignored him. "How?"

"Those extra hours we took on added up." Mama offered a small smile. She was standing straighter, like a plant coming into full bloom. "We only have two more payments left, and we could probably pay those off in the next few days."

Sheer disbelief coursed through Koffi. "And after that, we're done?"

"Done." Mama nodded. "The debt will be paid, interest and all."

Koffi felt a long-held tension within her release as she exhaled. Like most things in the Night Zoo, the terms and conditions held by its indentured workers only benefitted one person. Eleven years of service with Mama had taught her that. But they'd won, beaten Baaz at his own wretched game. They were going to *leave*. It was so rare that beastkeepers managed to pay back their debts—the last one who'd managed it had done so at least a year ago—but now it was their turn.

"Where will we go?" Koffi asked. She could barely believe she was really posing the question. They'd never gone anywhere; she barely remembered a life outside the Night Zoo.

Mama closed the gap between them and took Koffi's hand in hers. "We can go *wherever we want*." She spoke with a fervor Koffi had never heard before. "You and I, we'll leave this place and start over somewhere else, and we'll never, *ever* look back. We'll never return."

Never return. Koffi considered the words. All her life she'd longed for them, dreamed of them. Hearing them now, however, they felt strangely different.

"What?" Mama noted her changed expression immediately. "What is it?"

"It's just . . ." Koffi didn't know if they were the right words, but she tried. "We'll never see anyone here ever again."

Mama's expression softened with understanding. "You'll miss it."

Koffi nodded, quietly angry with herself for doing so. She didn't necessarily love working at the Night Zoo, but it was the only home she'd ever known, the only *life* she'd ever known. She thought of the other beastkeepers, not quite a family, but certainly people she cared about.

"I'll miss them too," said Mama gently, reading her thoughts. "But they wouldn't want us to stay here, Koffi, not if we didn't have to."

"I just wish we could help them," Koffi murmured. "I wish we could help all of them."

Mama offered a small smile. "You're a compassionate girl. You lead with your heart, like your father."

Koffi shifted uncomfortably. She didn't like being compared to Baba. Baba was gone.

"Sometimes, though, you can't lead with your heart," said Mama gently. "You have to think with your *head*."

A horn's brassy trumpeting split the air without warning, its summons rising from the distant Temple of Lkossa to reverberate across the Night Zoo's lawns in long, sonorous notes. They both stiffened as the sounds of newly agitated beasts filled the ground around them, and Diko bared his teeth in anticipation. The city's saa-horn had at last announced nightfall. It was time. Again, Mama's eyes flitted from the Hema to Koffi.

"It's almost over, little ponya seed," she said softly, a touch of hope in her voice. She hadn't called her that in years. "I know how hard this has been, but it's almost over, I promise. We're going to be okay."

Koffi didn't answer as Mama tugged Diko's leash to lead him toward the massive tent. She followed but kept a step behind. Her eyes cast wide, holding in their gaze the final remnants of a sky the color of blood. Mama's words echoed in her mind.

We're going to be okay.

They would be okay, she knew that now, but her thoughts still lingered on something else, *someone* else. Sahel. He wasn't okay— he'd never be okay again. She couldn't help but think of him then, of the boy with the crooked smile. She couldn't help but think of the monster that had killed him and wonder who it would take next.

CHAPTER 2

FROM THE ROOT

In the years before his disappearance, they'd called Satao Nkrumah mad.

Later, his colleagues would suggest that the telltale signs of decline had lurked just beneath the surface, quietly ravaging the scholar's mind like moss on a rotting tree. The symptoms had become increasingly apparent over time: fits, erratic mood swings, worsening amnesia. But when old Master Nkrumah, age eighty-seven, had begun referring to the Greater Jungle as "her," *that* had been the last straw. Caretakers had been procured, intervention plans arranged. An assembly of well-intentioned people had marched right up to the elderly man's front door one rainy afternoon to escort him—by reason, or by force—to a facility for proper care. They'd discovered an unsettling surprise.

Satao Nkrumah had vanished.

He'd left his modest home with nothing but the clothes on his back. He hadn't even taken his journal, which would later become prized for its unrivaled accounts of the Zamani Region's natural history. Search parties had yielded nothing, and after several days, rescue efforts had been suspended.

Decades later, Lkossan academics still occasionally spoke of old Nkrumah, musing over his infamous demise and disappearance. Some believed silver-haired yumboes from the depths of the Greater Jungle had spirited the old man away and still danced with him barefoot by moonlight. Others held a more sinister opinion, sure that some malevolent creature had dragged him from his bed. Of course, these stories were just that, a collection of myths and folktales. Ekon Okojo, who was *not* an academic, knew better than to believe in myths and folktales—they lacked accreditation—but there *was* one thing he believed in with certainty.

The Greater Jungle was an evil place, and it could not be trusted.

Sweat rolled down the back of his neck in beads as he marched, focusing on the steady crunch beneath his sandals instead of the eerie black-trunked trees to his immediate right. *Five hundred seventy-three steps exactly, a good number.* He tapped his fingers against his side in a steady rhythm as he added to that count.

One-two-three. One-two-three. One-two-three.

Goose bumps stippled his bare arms despite the heat, but he did his best to ignore them too, and continued his counting.

One-two-three. One-two-three. One-two-three.

He'd prayed to the Six that he wouldn't be assigned a patrol shift tonight, but it seemed the gods either hadn't heard him or hadn't cared. It was nearly dusk now, the time when Lkossa's blood-orange sun fell behind the trees and set their silhouettes ablaze, the time he *least* liked to be near the jungle. He swallowed hard, tightening his grip on the leather-hilted hanjari tucked into his belt.

"We found the last body earlier."

Kamau was walking beside him, shoulder to shoulder, his hawkish gaze trained ahead. He seemed unbothered by the adjacent jungle, but he did look fatigued. "It was an old woman, prone to late-night wandering."

Ekon drew in a sharp breath. "How bad?"

"Bad." Kamau shook his head. "We had to wrap what was left of the remains in a blanket just to get her to the temple for cremation. It . . . wasn't pretty."

The remains. Ekon tore his gaze from the trees, fighting a sudden wave of nausea. For his part, Kamau's expression remained stoic. Most people said that Ekon and Kamau, seventeen and nineteen respectively, looked more like twins than like older and younger brother—both had skin the color of rain-soaked earth, umber-brown eyes, and coiled black hair tapered on the sides in Yaba fashion. But their looks were where their similarities ended; Kamau was more muscled, while Ekon was of a leaner build. Kamau favored a spear; Ekon preferred books in his spare time. And there was another visible difference between them tonight.

Ekon's kaftan was clean. His brother's was bloody.

"Didn't see you at dinner last night," Ekon noted, trying for a distraction.

Kamau didn't answer. He was staring at a shrub of silver-veined leaves clustered near the roots of a nearby tree. When his gaze lingered, Ekon cleared his throat.

"Kam?"

"What?"

"I . . . asked where you were last night."

25

Kamau frowned. "Father Olufemi had some work for me to do, confidential." He glanced at Ekon's fingers, still drumming at his side. "You're doing that weird thing again."

"Sorry." Ekon closed his hand in a fist, forcing his fingers to still. He couldn't really remember when he'd started doing it, the counting, just that it was something he couldn't help. It was impossible to explain, but there was something calming in the habit, a comfort he found in the trifecta of it.

One-two-three.

Three. *Three* was a good number, as was any number divisible by it.

He let the new count in his head fill the awkward silence that followed. It was easier to think about numbers than to think about the fact that Kamau hadn't actually answered his question. There'd been a time when he and his brother had shared everything with each other, but that was happening less and less lately. When it became clear his brother wasn't going to offer anything else, he tried again. "So . . . there are still no new leads? No witnesses?"

"Are there ever?" Kamau kicked at a pebble in frustration. "It's the same as always. No tracks, no witnesses, just bodies."

A shiver ran through Ekon, and a solemn quiet settled between them like dust as they continued on. It had been nearly a full day since the Shetani's latest victims had been recovered along the jungle's edge. By now, it should have been less shocking—the beast had menaced Lkossa longer than Ekon had been alive—but in truth, it was impossible to get used to the carnage left in its wake. Somehow, the pools of blood in the dirt always managed to be horrific, the mutilated corpses ever-sickening. Ekon's stomach churned at the thought of the mortality report he'd read a few hours ago. Eight victims. The youngest one this time had been a little boy, an indentured servant no older than twelve, found alone. Those were the kinds of people the beast seemed to always pick—the defenseless, the vulnerable.

They rounded a bend in the path where the sunlight had not yet withdrawn. At once, Ekon tensed. To his right, the jungle's trees still loomed like sentries; to his left, a barren expanse of russet dirt stretched several yards wide between the city's edge and the jungle's border to create a no-man's-land. It was a familiar place. As small children, he and Kamau had come here to play when they were feeling brave or reckless. They'd fashioned sticks into fake spears and pretended the two of them alone could defend their city from the creatures of the Greater Jungle, the monstrous beasts of legend. But those adventures were a thing of the past; times had changed. Now when Ekon looked into the jungle's snarl of trees, roots, and vines, he remembered no legends.

He remembered a voice.

Ekon.

Ekon started. Every time he heard his father's voice in his head, it was slurred like that of a man who'd drunk too much palm wine.

Please. Ekon, please.

It wasn't real, Ekon knew that, but his heartbeat still quickened. He started to drum his fingers again, faster, trying to use the counts to center himself and quell what he knew was coming next.

One-two-three. One-two-three. Don't think about it. One-two-three. One-two-three.

It didn't work. The corners of his vision began to blur, growing hazy as an old nightmare returned to him. He felt himself slipping, struggling to separate reality from memory, the immediate present

27

from the distant past. In his imagination, he wasn't at the jungle's edge anymore, he was *in* the jungle now, hearing everything, *seeing* everything, things he didn't want to . . .

Ekon, please.

And then he saw the body, soaked in dark blood. He heard a menacing rustle in the leaves just before a putrid smell soured the air—the smell of something long dead. He saw a shadowy figure weaving between the trees, a monster.

It all led back to the monster.

In protest, his lungs seized, and then Ekon forgot how to breathe at all. The trees seemed to be reaching for him now, gnarled black branches outstretched like claws, hungry . . .

"Ekon?"

As suddenly as it had descended, the opaque haze in Ekon's mind receded, returning him to the present. He was back at the jungle's edge, his father's voice was gone, and Kamau had stopped walking. Concern creased the skin between his brother's brows. "You okay?"

"Uh, yeah." Ekon shook himself, brushing away the remnants of the nightmare like a cobweb. "Just . . . thinking about tonight."

"Ah." The brief bemusement vanished from Kamau's face, replaced with a look of knowing. "You're scared."

"No."

"It's entirely understandable," said Kamau smugly. He made a show of stretching, and Ekon resented how much bigger his biceps were. "Some consider the temple's rites of passage to be the most difficult in all Eshōza. Of course, *I* didn't find them too challenging . . ."

Ekon rolled his eyes. Two years ago, his brother had become

eligible to join the Sons of the Six, the city's elite warriorship. His rites had gone so well that, immediately after his initiation, he'd been promoted to a kapteni, a captain, despite his youth. Now Kamau was a well-respected warrior, a man. In their people's eyes, Ekon was still just an unproven boy.

"Hey." As though he could hear Ekon's thoughts, Kamau's expression turned rueful. "Don't worry, you're going to pass."

"Don't you have to say that?"

Now Kamau rolled his eyes. "No. And I certainly wouldn't bother to if I didn't mean it." He punched Ekon in the arm. "Just loosen up a little, okay? Relax. You've stayed out of trouble, you know your scriptures better than anyone, and . . . your spearwork's *nearly* as good as mine. Plus, you're an Okojo, so you were basically born for this."

Ekon felt as though he'd swallowed a kola nut whole. *Born for this.* For generations, every male Okojo had served the Sons of the Six, a longer tradition than that of almost any other family in Lkossa. That legacy was fortified, respected; it left little room for ineptitude.

"You'll make our family proud." Kamau studied his sandals. "And I know Baba would be proud too, if he were still here."

At the mention of their father, Ekon flinched. "Thanks." He paused before speaking again. "Look, Kam, I know I'm not allowed to know what's going to happen beforehand, but can't you—?"

"Nope." Kamau was already shaking his head, a renewed grin tugging at the corners of his mouth even as he tried to look serious. "The rites change each year at the presiding Kuhani's discretion, Ekkie. It'll be Father Olufemi who chooses yours. Even *I* don't know what it will be."

The imaginary worms wriggling around in Ekon's stomach settled momentarily. He was still nervous, but knowing that he wouldn't have to do whatever Kamau had done during *his* rites of passage was a small comfort.

They reached the end of the patrol path and stopped. Just yards away, the edge of the Greater Jungle unfurled before them. Kamau looked up, and Ekon followed his brother's gaze to take in the silver-white stars beginning to speckle the sky overhead. In their quiet luminance, the scars left from the Rupture almost disappeared. Almost. The illusion didn't fool him.

"We'd better get going," said Kamau. "It's nearly time."

Ekon didn't admit it aloud, but the more distance they put between themselves and the jungle's border, the better he felt. With each step away from it, the tension in his shoulders eased. Gradually, the evening air filled with the familiar din that was the city of Lkossa, the sounds and smells of home.

Along its dirt-swept streets, grocers stood posted beside stalls of fresh fruit, haggling down their final sales as shops prepared to close. Ekon tallied each one. He counted fifteen different merchants waving wax-dyed textiles through the air and a pair of boys stooped over a wooden oware board as they stopped their game to wave enthusiastically at Kamau when they saw his hanjari's gilded hilt. A huddle of young women—*four* young women—giggled behind their hands when they passed, eyeing Kamau appreciatively, and Ekon tried to temper an old stab of jealousy. As a boy, he'd been used to people giving Baba this kind of attention when they saw him in uniform, but with Kamau it was harder. Ekon wanted that respect and admiration for himself, to be noticed without trying.

Almost there, he reminded himself as his fingers drummed at his side. *After you pass your last rite of passage tonight, you'll become a Son of the Six, a warrior, and a man. It'll be your turn.* Even in the privacy of his mind, that promise felt like it belonged to someone else.

The streets quieted as they neared the road that led to the temple, but just before it, Kamau's expression hardened.

"Halt!"

At once, the street's bustle died, and apprehensive gazes lifted. Even Ekon stopped in confusion. There were, by his count, only eighteen people on this particular road. He searched a moment, then found what Kamau already had. He'd miscounted.

The little girl standing a few yards from them had dark, sunken eyes, a tangle of uncombed black hair framing her gaunt face. She wore a threadbare tunic, one sleeve hanging off her too-sharp shoulder, and the skin of her legs and feet was visibly dry and cracked. For a moment, Ekon didn't understand her frightened expression as she stared back at them, but then he saw her bulging pocket, the tremor in her hands. She had the distinct look of someone who'd just been caught.

"You!" Kamau started toward her, and Ekon's heart sank. "Remain where you are!"

A single beat passed before the girl tore down the street.

"Stop!" Kamau broke into a run, and Ekon did too. No one else in the street moved as they wove between people in pursuit. The girl veered right, then disappeared into a forked alley. Kamau growled in frustration. "These passages connect." He started down one and pointed Ekon in the opposite direction. "Take the other!"

Ekon obeyed without hesitation, ignoring the small pang of pity

31

in his chest. The girl had looked so young, scared. He didn't know if she'd actually stolen anything of value, but that didn't matter. She'd disobeyed a direct order from a Son of the Six. If she was caught, she'd be caned. He shook his head, pushing emotion away to refocus. The girl had led them into the Chafu District, Lkossa's slums, a rougher part of the city. His hand flew to his hanjari as he ran. He wouldn't make a fool of himself here by getting jumped or ambushed.

He turned a corner, expecting to find Kamau. Instead, he stared down an empty alley.

"Hello?" His call went unanswered, echoing eerily against the grimy mud bricks. "Kam?"

"Afraid not, young man."

Ekon whirled. An old woman was sitting cross-legged against one of the alley's walls, nearly camouflaged in its filth. Her hair was white and cottony, and her skin was brown and uneven in texture like roughly hewn wood. A tarnished amulet hung from a cord around her neck, though it was too dark to distinguish its details. She offered Ekon a gummy smile as they appraised each other, and he fought a shudder—she was missing several teeth.

"How strange . . ." The old woman dragged a finger across her bottom lip. She was speaking Zamani, but her dialect had an almost musical lilt. She was a Gede, and of the Gedezi People. "I don't usually see Yaba boys in this part of the city."

Ekon drew himself up to full height. "I'm looking for a little girl, have you seen—?"

Ekon.

Ekon went stock-still, unnerved. For a second, he thought he'd heard . . . but . . . no, not here. It couldn't be. He was too far away

32

from the jungle now for Baba's voice to follow him. He'd never heard it at this distance. It wasn't possible. He cleared his throat.

"Ahem. Have you—?"

Ekon, please.

This time, Ekon's jaw snapped shut. He didn't resist the shiver that ran the length of him.

No. He looked right, in the direction of the jungle, as his fingers danced at his side. *No, not here, not now . . .*

"Does it call to you often?"

Ekon started. He'd almost forgotten about the old woman entirely. She was still sitting before him, but now her expression held amusement.

"I—" Ekon paused, trying to process her words. *"It?"*

"The jungle." The old woman readjusted, rocking from side to side as though swaying to an inaudible tune. "It calls to me too sometimes. I couldn't tell you why, magic is a peculiar thing, as are the things it touches."

A chill skittered up Ekon's bare arm like a spider; his mouth went paper dry. "There . . . there's no such thing as magic," he said shakily.

"Is *that* what you think?" The old woman cocked her head like a bird and rubbed a thumb against her amulet. She was studying Ekon much harder now. "How curious, *very* curious . . ."

Every instinct in Ekon's body told him to run, but suddenly that felt impossible. Something about the old woman's voice, her *eyes*, held him fast. He stepped toward her, tugged like a fish helplessly hooked on a line—

"Ekkie?"

Ekon looked up, the strange trance instantly broken. Kamau was

33

approaching from the other end of the alley, lit sconces mounted on the wall throwing his frown into sharp relief. "What are you doing?"

"I—" Ekon looked to where the old woman had been sitting. She wasn't there now. Strangely, he found he had trouble even recalling her likeness. It was as though she hadn't existed at all. Unnerved, he faced Kamau, trying to keep his voice steady. "I . . . couldn't find the girl."

"Me neither," said Kamau. "But we don't have time to keep looking. Come on."

They walked in silence until they reached the two gilded pillars marking the start of the Takatifu District, and Ekon stood straighter. The city of Lkossa was a collection of neatly ordered sections, but the temple's district was different. It was the only part of the city that maintained a curfew; after sunset, it was closed to the public. They made their way up its winding path, and even from there he could already discern the temple itself. Of course, it was home, the place where he lived, but tonight it seemed different. Its massive dome, capped over white alabaster stonework, seemed determined to hold every one of the stars' glittering lights in its reflection. The breeze lifted, and he smelled the cloves of prayer incense emanating from its arched windows and parapets. Just as he'd expected, when they got closer, he made out two figures standing at the top of the main stairs with their backs turned away. Fahim and Shomari—his co-candidates—were waiting for him. It was time.

"When we meet again, you'll be an anointed Son of the Six." Kamau stopped beside him at the base of the stairs, keeping his voice low. "We'll be brothers in spear, just as we are brothers in blood." He made the proclamation without a trace of doubt. Ekon swallowed. His brother had faith in him; he believed in him.

Just like Baba once believed in you, said a cruel voice in his mind. *He trusts you, just like Baba did.*

Ekon shoved that voice away as he nodded.

"Be strong." Kamau nudged him forward before receding into the night. "You can do this. And remember: Kutoka mzizi."

Ekon started up the stairs, the words echoing in his wake. *Kutoka mzizi* meant "from the root." The old family adage was a reminder of where he came from and the expectations that came with that. Kutoka mzizi.

Baba had been the one to teach him and Kamau those hallowed words when they were small. He should have been here to say them now.

But Baba wasn't here. Baba was dead.

Just before he reached the landing, Ekon glanced over his shoulder. Kamau was already gone, and from here the Greater Jungle on the opposite side of the city was little more than an ill-shapen smudge against the obsidian night, too far away for its voices to reach him. Still, as he turned back around, Ekon couldn't ignore the feeling that—from within its depths—something was watching him, and waiting.

CHAPTER 3

The SMALLEST RESISTANCE

No matter how many times she'd faced it over the years, Koffi had always dreaded the Hema.

She gnawed on her bottom lip, unease rising as she watched its crimson folds flutter in the breeze, noting the violating way its central pole impaled the maiden night sky like a gilded spear. Her steps dragged as she and Mama moved to join the queue of beast-keepers waiting to enter it with their assigned beasts.

Almost over, she thought. *This is almost over.*

Once, in another era, she supposed the massive tent might have been considered grand, even impressive to some. But time had taken a visible toll; tears in the seams hadn't been mended, and rust coated most of the metal stakes hammered into the grass to keep it secure. Attendance at the Night Zoo had, like many things in Lkossa over the years, steadily declined, and it showed.

"Smile," Mama reminded her, guiding them to their place in line as several of the other beastkeepers took cautionary steps back. Koffi twisted her mouth to form a half grimace she hoped would suffice. Baaz required all beastkeepers of the Night Zoo to look cheerful during shows, and notoriously punished those who didn't. With a shiver, she thought of the whipping post, not so far from here. The cruelty of it—the bizarreness of being forced to look happy about handling creatures who could kill you as soon as look at you—was one thing she *wouldn't* miss about working here.

"Don't forget to check Diko's harness," said Mama. "Make sure it's secure before we—"

"Hey, Kof!"

Koffi looked up, a genuine smile tugging at her lips now. A boy of about fourteen was approaching them fast, surrounded by a pack of wild dogs. He had bright, intelligent brown eyes and a permanently cheeky grin.

"Hey, Jabir."

Upon seeing the wild dogs, Diko hissed, his multicolored scales rippling as he eyed them. Mama pulled him away with a disapproving look. "Jabir," she said sternly, "those dogs are supposed to be on leashes."

"Meh, they don't need them." Jabir's smile didn't falter. "They're well trained."

"Didn't one of them poop in Baaz's slippers the other day?"

Jabir's mouth twitched. "Like I said, they're well trained."

A real laugh bubbled in Koffi's throat, followed by a shot of unexpected pain. Jabir was her closest friend at the Night Zoo, like a brother to her in some ways. She watched him drop to his knees to play with his dogs. Leaving the Night Zoo would mean leaving him too; she didn't relish having to tell him the news, but she had to. It would be better if he heard it from her.

"Jabir," she started tentatively. "I need to tell you some—"

"Did you hear about tonight's visitors?" Jabir smirked the way he usually did when he was about to gossip. One of his jobs at the zoo was to run errands for Baaz, so he always had news first.

"No," said Koffi, momentarily distracted. "What about them?"

"It's some merchant couple visiting from the Baridi Region," he said. "Apparently, they're pretty rich. Baaz is angling for a patronage. I saw them coming in. The old man seems okay, but the wife walks like she's got a stick up her—"

"Jabir!"

Koffi snorted as Jabir offered Mama a sheepish smile. His words lingered in her mind, and she looked around as more beastkeepers gathered. She hadn't noticed before, but far more animals were out of their cages tonight, and the grounds did look like they'd gotten an extra bit of grooming. If this merchant couple *did* agree to a patronage, it would add not only prestige but new revenue for the zoo. Baaz would be especially anxious tonight.

A dulcet chorus of voices suddenly rose from the inside of the tent, beautiful and harmonic. At once, all three of them stilled. Those were the Night Zoo's indentured musicians; their song meant the show had officially commenced. It took only seconds for a thunderous percussion of goatskin drums to join the singing, and instinctively Koffi's own heart attuned to their pounding cadence. She looked up when the musical overture ended, and in its place an anticipatory silence weighted the air.

"Excellent!" said someone inside the tent. "A lovely performance from our choir!" Koffi recognized that booming showman's voice—*that* was Baaz. "If you enjoyed that, Bwana Mutunga, you're sure to marvel at the beauties I have in store for you tonight. Though, of course, they'll all pale in comparison to your lovely wife. Bi Mutunga, words could never do your radiance justice . . ."

Koffi barely managed not to roll her eyes. Baaz was using *Bwana* and *Bi*, the more formal honorifics of the Zamani language, clearly trying to impress. The Hema's canvas was too thick for Koffi to discern anything from outside, but she heard what sounded like two sets of hands offering polite applause as the musicians exited the tent. *Two, only two guests.* Baaz would have told them that this was part of their "exclusive" experience, but she knew better; no one else had showed up. Canceled shows due to lack of attendance seemed to happen more and more often lately. After a moment, her master spoke again.

"Now, as I'm sure you've both heard, my spectacular Night Zoo boasts the widest array of specialty creatures in the region, the likes of which you've never—"

"Just show us the animals," said a heavily accented female voice. "We do not plan to be here all evening."

There was an awkward pause. Then:

"Of course! Right away, Bi Mutunga! May I now present, without further ado, the Parade of Beasts!"

It was a cue, and no sooner had Baaz spoken the words than he was pushing open the Hema's front entrance flap. Koffi tensed on principle at the sight of him.

To his credit, Baaz Mtombé certainly *looked* like the owner of a "spectacular" Night Zoo; everything about him seemed larger than life, like a caricature. He was a mountain of a man with deep oak-brown skin and a mane of thick black and blond dreadlocks that stuck out in every direction. With his red dashiki and fake-silk slippers, he looked jolly, if not slightly overdressed. Koffi knew better than to believe the ruse.

"Move!" He beckoned the first beastkeepers in line as they struggled to guide a pair of silverback gorillas into the tent by their harnesses. "Just as we've rehearsed, *big smiles*!"

The line ahead of them began moving into the tent, and Koffi swallowed. There was nothing to be afraid of, really; shows were the same every time and this one would likely be one of her last. Still, she was oddly nervous. All too soon, she, Mama, and Diko reached the Hema's entry. She tried not to inhale Baaz's spicy cologne as they ducked past him, and then they were inside.

If the outside of the Hema reflected what the old tent had once been, the interior clung to its former grandeur with a desperate grip. Its decor was slightly dated, furnished with old animal-print throws and well-worn chaises. Carefully arranged candlelight gave the place a flickering golden glow while also hiding some of the more stubborn stains in the rugs, and the heady scent of palm wine just barely masked the stench of animals past and present. A massive statue of a peacock carved from turquoise was arranged in one corner, and in the center, an open space was designated as a stage. A well-dressed couple sat before it, waiting on a plush red divan.

The man looked old enough to be Koffi's grandfather. His skin was dark and wrinkled, his cropped hair nearly white. He wore a plum-colored dashiki Koffi knew at once was expensive despite its subtlety, and he exuded the air of someone senior and refined. Beside him, his wife was the opposite, uncomfortably young and gaudy. She seemed partial to the color green, because she was covered in it from her wax-print dress to the glittering jade beads clacking at the ends of her box braids. She pinched her nose as Koffi and Mama entered the tent with Diko, and an embarrassed heat crept up Koffi's neck. Jabir followed behind with his wild dogs, and Baaz came in last.

"Ladies and gentlemen!" He said the practiced words as though he were addressing millions instead of an audience of two. "For your delectation and delight, I present to you the many creatures of my spectacular Night Zoo! Tonight, we will take you on a journey through the wilds of the southern marshlands, the ferocities of the Greater Jungle, even specimens procured from the farthest reaches of the western wastes. First, the *guiamala*!"

Koffi relaxed a little as she and Mama moved to a space against the tent's walls while two beastkeepers ushered the camel-like guiamala to its center. They walked it in circles several times, letting the merchant and his wife admire the shiny black spikes running down the length of its back, each one sharp enough to draw blood.

"From the Kusonga Plains," Baaz narrated, "the guiamala is an herbivore and can survive weeks without water. They're graceful creatures, and the story goes that a western princess once used the spike of one for a *love potion* . . ."

Koffi let Baaz's stories about the Night Zoo's creatures—some true, most fake—blend together as more animals were summoned one by one. He told a particularly gruesome story about the silverback gorillas when they were called up next, then shared a folktale about impundulus when a young male beastkeeper came forward with one perched on his arm. She held her breath as the shrieking hyena was brought forth—when unmuzzled, its cackle could paralyze the human body—but fortunately, Baaz did *not* suggest a live demonstration. Soon enough, he was looking to Jabir.

"And now for a special, local treat," he said proudly. "May I present Jabir and his Lkossan wild dogs!"

A surge of pride ran through Koffi as Jabir stepped forward with his fluffy brown dogs and offered both a smile and a cordial bow to the Mutungas. While she didn't care much for the Night Zoo's shows, Jabir took them in stride, a natural performer. He raised a hand, fingers dancing through the air in a complicated array of signals, and at once the dogs stilled. Koffi smiled. Jabir's expertise was in nonverbal commands; he could train almost anything with them. He pointed two fingers, and the dogs began to run around him in a perfect circle; a closed fist then directed them to rise to their hind legs and yip. Bwana Mutunga chortled as one of the dogs faced him and bent its forelegs in an unmistakable bow while another hopped adorably in place. Koffi felt another pang. *These* were the moments she'd miss.

Jabir demonstrated a few more tricks before clapping his hands and signaling for the dogs to stop and sit. He offered a deep finishing bow while the merchant applauded.

"Well, well!" said Bwana Mutunga. "That was quite impressive, young man!"

Jabir grinned before herding his dogs offstage and letting Baaz resume his position.

"One of the zoo's up-and-coming stars!" Baaz said, beaming. "And there's more yet to see! For our next act—"

"My love."

Koffi glanced up to see the merchant's wife, Bi Mutunga, fanning the air with a distinctly impatient expression. She addressed her husband. "It's getting late. Perhaps we should return to the caravan."

"But . . ." Baaz's voice faltered. "But surely you'll stay just a little longer? I haven't even given you the full tour of the grounds yet, an exclusive offer for patrons only—"

"Ah, I'm afraid my younger, better half is right, Baaz." Bwana Mutunga gave his wife a doting look. Like her, his accented words had the thick, choppy cut of a Baridian, a northerner. "I have business at the temple tomorrow morning. Perhaps we could discuss a patronage next time . . ."

Baaz wrung his hands, anxious. "But you haven't even seen our grand finale yet!" He addressed the merchant's wife. "I think you'll be particularly interested in this one, Bi Mutunga. If I could just have ten more minutes of your time—"

"Five." Bi Mutunga's expression didn't change.

"Perfect!" Baaz clapped his hands, at once revitalized. Koffi knew what was coming next but still jolted when her master's eyes shot to her. "May I now present Diko the jokomoto!"

Just keep calm. Koffi willed the words as she and Mama led Diko forward together. She held his leash, but Mama stayed at her side, there for backup. *You've done this a hundred times,* Koffi reasoned. *Easy, just like you've always done . . .*

Slowly, they guided Diko around the perimeter of the stage. In the candlelight, his scales shimmered in an almost-mesmerizing way. Though she didn't dare look up, she heard the merchant's soft sighs of awe.

"What an *exquisite* creature," said Bwana Mutunga. "Baaz, where did you say this one was from?"

"Ah." There was renewed excitement in Baaz's voice. "Jokomotos

come from the Katili Desert of the west; they're exceedingly rare beasts these days—"

"Speaking of *beasts*," Bwana Mutunga interrupted. Koffi chanced a look at him as she and Mama made another lap. "Is it true that the Shetani got one of your keepers, Baaz? I heard it went on another rampage last night, killed eight people."

Koffi faltered in her steps as a hush fell over the tent. She knew without looking that every beastkeeper in the vicinity would have stilled at the mention of Sahel, waiting to hear Baaz's answer to the question.

"It's . . . true." Baaz kept his tone light. "But the boy did *choose* to run away. He was a fool to leave my generous protection."

Koffi's free hand curled into a fist, but she kept walking. For the merchant's part, when Koffi looked at him, he was chuckling into his tea.

"That would be quite an addition to your show, would it not?"

Koffi saw unmistakable longing flash across her master's features. "Well, a man can dream," he said wistfully. "But I think I'd have to barter my soul for such an acquisition."

"I must admit . . ." The merchant balanced the porcelain cup on his knee. "That abomination has been something of a boon for my business."

Baaz's eyes brightened. "Remind me again what you said you traded in, Bwana. Priceless jewels? Fine textiles?"

Bwana Mutunga gave Baaz an indulgent look. "I *didn't* say, but it's neither," he corrected. "My specialty is in administrative supplies—quills, papyrus, Baridian ink—the Temple of Lkossa alone constitutes a quarter of my business, what with all the books and maps they house there."

44

"Naturally." Baaz nodded as though he knew all about such things.

"I used to have to price match against my competitors," Bwana Mutunga went on. "But now most of them fear traveling to Lkossa, so I have the monopoly! It's been a blessing!"

Baaz's expression held visible greed. "Well, Bwana, let me be the first to wholeheartedly congratulate you on your . . . *prosperity.*"

Koffi fought to hold her stage smile in place, but it felt more and more like a scowl. The Shetani was no blessing to the people of Lkossa; it was a menace. Anyone who saw such a monster as good was no better than dirt, in her opinion. She thought of Sahel, how small he'd looked in his shroud. He'd run from the Night Zoo and into the Greater Jungle because he'd felt like he had no choice. Some people wouldn't understand that—Baaz had called him a fool—but she knew better. She knew that poverty could be a different kind of monster, always lurking and waiting to consume. For some, death *was* the kinder beast. Not that men like these two understood that.

"I wonder, Baaz . . ." Bwana Mutunga was now leaning forward in his chair. "Could we . . . have a closer look at the jokomoto?"

Baaz perked up. "Of course!" He turned to Koffi and her mother. "Girls, bring Diko over for our guests to see."

At his words, Koffi froze. Usually, they just paraded Diko around the stage a few times, so *this* was a break from the routine. Instinctively, she met Mama's eyes, but her mother didn't look worried. She nodded, and together they guided Diko toward the merchant and his wife, stopping a foot in front of them.

"Fascinating." Bwana Mutunga moved his teacup to a side table

45

as he actually stood to examine Diko. At the sudden motion, the jokomoto tensed but didn't move.

Easy, boy. Koffi kept her eyes trained on Diko, willing him to behave himself. *Easy does it . . .*

If Bwana Mutunga was impressed, his wife was decidedly not. She inhaled, then wrinkled her nose again. "It *stinks*," she declared. She pulled a small perfume bottle from a bag at her side and sprayed into the air aggressively. In the confines of the tent, the scent suffused the air, sharp and tangy. Diko hissed low, and Koffi's throat went dry as she suddenly noticed something near his neck.

One of the loops to his harness had come undone.

"I—" Koffi reached for the loop, then stopped herself. Mama had told her to make sure the harness was secure, *twice*. If Baaz saw that it wasn't now . . .

"Ugh!" Bi Mutunga fanned faster, waving her perfume around. "Honestly, the smell is absolutely—"

It happened fast, but for Koffi it seemed to take a century. She watched one of Diko's yellow eyes flick in her direction before he suddenly lunged, jaws snapping at Bi Mutunga's sandaled feet. His teeth caught the hem of her dress. She screamed, reeling back so violently, she flipped right over the back of the divan. Mama gasped, and Koffi's heart sank. Quickly she pulled Diko away. He calmed down again almost immediately, but it was too late.

"It . . . it *attacked* me!" Bi Mutunga jumped to her feet before her husband could get to her, tears and kohl streaking her face. She stared down at the embroidered hem of her dress, now in tatters, then looked to her husband. "My love, it tried to *kill* me! Look what it did to my clothes!"

No. Koffi's thoughts tangled together, unable to process what had just happened. This was very, *very* bad.

The merchant took his wife in his arms and held her a moment before jabbing an accusatory finger at Baaz. "You assured me your show was safe, Baaz!" he said angrily. "I was told this was a professional establishment!"

"B-B-Bwana." Baaz, usually cool under pressure, was stuttering. "I—I offer my humblest, most sincere apologies. The next time you come, I assure you, this won't—"

"The *next* time?" Bwana Mutunga's brows rose, incredulous. "My wife is traumatized, Baaz. We're never setting foot in this wretched place again. To think we even *considered* supporting it . . ."

"Wait!" Baaz's eyes went wide. "Wait, sir—"

He couldn't even finish his sentence before the merchant took his wife by the elbow and steered them out into the night. Koffi listened to their footsteps until they faded. For a long moment, no one in the Hema moved. She glanced up to see that the other beastkeepers' eyes were all fixed on either her or Baaz. It was he who broke the silence.

"You didn't secure him."

Baaz's voice was dangerously low. No longer was he the jolly owner of a spectacular Night Zoo; now he was just Baaz, her master, glaring at her. *"Explain yourself."*

"I . . ." Koffi hated how small her voice sounded. She searched her mind for a decent answer but found none. The truth was, she *had* no good answer. She hadn't secured Diko's harness because she'd forgotten. Mama had reminded her, twice, but she hadn't done it. Her mind had been elsewhere, so distracted by the idea of leaving . . .

47

"You *will* pay for this." Baaz's words cut through her thoughts like a knife. "You'll go to the whipping post, and a fine will be added to your debt—the sum of the two tickets I just lost. By my calculation, that's about six months' worth of your wages."

Tears stung Koffi's eyes. The whipping post was bad enough, but the fine . . . six *months'* wages. She and Mama would have to stay at the Night Zoo; they wouldn't be leaving after all.

Baaz turned to one of the beastkeepers near him, then pointed at Koffi. "Take her out to the post now. She'll learn her lesson—"

"No."

Several beastkeepers started, Koffi included. For the first time, she looked to her mother, still standing on the other side of Diko. There was a strange resolve in her brown eyes.

"No," Mama said again calmly. "*I'm* the one who forgot to secure Diko's lead. The punishment and the fine should go to me."

Koffi drew in a sharp breath and fought a sudden wave of pain. Mama was lying. She was going to take the blame for this, even though she hadn't been the one in the wrong. She was sacrificing herself, her literal freedom. Koffi blinked back fresh tears.

"*Very well.*" Baaz sneered. "*You* can go to the post, then." He waved a dismissive hand. "Take her away."

Koffi still held Diko's leash tightly, but her fingers felt numb as she watched one of the beastkeepers grab Mama by the upper arm and offer an apologetic look. Her mother held her head high, but Koffi saw it, the slight tremble in her bottom lip, the fear.

"No!" Koffi stepped forward, her voice trembling. "Mama, don't—"

"*Be quiet*, Koffi." Mama's voice was even as their gazes met. "It's all right." She gave the beastkeeper another nod, more final, and he started to escort her out of the tent. With every step, Koffi felt an acute internal pain.

No.

It wasn't right, wasn't *fair*. They'd been about to leave and be *free*. Now that glimmer of hope was gone, and it was *her* fault. Koffi ground her teeth and stared at her feet, determined not to cry. This Night Zoo had stolen many things from her in eleven years; these tears would not be one of them.

Her lungs strained as she took in a deep breath and held on to it fiercely. Blood roared between her ears in protest, her heart pounded harder, but she refused to let the breath go. It was the smallest resistance, a losing battle from the start, but she relished the gesture. If she could control nothing else in her life, for a few seconds she would control this, the very breaths she took. A distinct sense of triumph filled her body as she finally exhaled, releasing the pressure in her chest.

And then, beside her, something shattered.

CHAPTER 4

FAITH ᴀɴᴅ FORTITUDE

The eyes of two young men flicked to Ekon as he reached the Temple of Lkossa's landing.

Twenty-seven steps, divisible by three, a good number.

He moved into his place at the left end of their line without a word, but the boy nearest him still chuckled low. He was almost as tall as Ekon, built like a stack of boulders, but his long, narrow face had the twitchy likeness of a meerkat. After several seconds, he nodded Ekon's way.

"Nice of you to finally join us, Okojo," said Shomari.

Ekon didn't answer, fixing his gaze on the front doors before them. They were carved from aged iroko wood, as unforgiving as steel. Any minute now, the city's saa-horn would sound and they would open. Then the rites would begin. He let his fingers find a new rhythm at his side.

One-two-three. One-two-three . . .

"So . . ." This time, Shomari made a point of jabbing an elbow into Ekon's ribs hard, messing up his count. "Where were you?"

"We're not supposed to be talking, Mensah," Ekon said through his teeth, hoping his use of the boy's surname was enough of a hint.

"Let me guess." Shomari's black eyes grew flinty. "You were holed up somewhere reading the ancient ramblings of some crusty old master. Tuh, I'll bet the ladies *love* that."

"Your *mother* loves it," Ekon muttered.

At the other end of the line, Fahim Adebayo snickered. Shomari gritted his teeth, as though he meant to fight, and for a second looked as though he might try it, but then he seemed to think better of it and stared ahead. Ekon barely resisted a smirk. As the sons of prominent Yaba families, he and Shomari had grown up together, but that didn't mean they liked each other. In recent months, their once somewhat-cordial rivalry had changed drastically. The old rivalry was still there; it just lacked the cordiality.

A moment of silence passed among the three of them before Fahim cleared his throat. He wasn't tall like Ekon, or burly like Shomari, and his face still held a softness that didn't allow him to ever really look serious. "What do you think he's going to make us do?" he whispered. "For the last rite?"

Shomari shrugged too quickly. "Dunno, don't care."

It was a lie, but Ekon didn't bother to call the bluff. Deep down, he knew they all had good reason to be afraid. Mere weeks ago, they'd stood on these very steps crowded among fourteen other Yaba boys who, like them, had spent their whole lives dreaming of becoming Sons of the Six. Now they were the only ones left. The reality of it should've been exciting—if not slightly intimidating—but Ekon struggled to focus on it. He was standing before the city's most revered site, but his mind was still down in its bowels, remembering what he'd heard, the strange things the old woman had said.

Does it call to you often? . . . It calls to me too sometimes. I couldn't tell you why; magic is a peculiar thing, as are the things it touches.

He didn't know which part of the encounter he found more unsettling in recollection. On the one hand, it was frightening that he'd heard Baba's voice so far away from the jungle, but worse still, the old woman had *known* it. She'd *empathized* with him, and even said she sometimes heard things coming from the jungle too. How? How had she known? He'd never told anyone about what he heard when he got near the trees, the disturbing things hoarded in his memory. Even thinking about them now made his hands clammy. His fingers were twitching, eager to restart their tapping, when a low tremor interrupted his thoughts. His ears rang with the metallic bellow of the saa-horn up in one of the temple's towers, rattling his bones from head to toe. There was a pause, and then—as if on cue—the scrape of weathered wood against stone. The temple's front doors opened, and all three of them immediately straightened as a figure emerged from its shadows.

A corpulent man dressed in a sweeping blue robe met their gaze. Ekon tensed. There was no explicit way to know that Father Olufemi was old—his umber skin was unwrinkled, and his thin black hair was betrayed by only a few strands of gray near the temple—but something about the holy man always exuded an agelessness. As the Kuhani, he alone led the temple's Brothers of the Order, and in more ways than one, he was the city's leader. Ekon felt the shrewd evaluation in the man's hawkish eyes as he looked over each of them.

"Come with me," he murmured.

Ekon's heart pounded like a goatskin drum as they followed him into the temple.

Dozens of white prayer candles illuminated the stonework of its worship hall—one hundred ninety-two at a quick count—arranged on built-in shelves that reached all the way up to its vaulted ceilings. Wafts of burning cedarwood suffused the air with every step as Father Olufemi led them deeper inside, and Ekon knew the scent came from the offering fires the brothers of the temple kept stoked at all times. It was the smell of home. The Temple of Lkossa housed worship halls, a library, studies, even a dormitory where candidates and unmarried Sons of the Six slept when off duty. It was magnificent, reverent, and like no other place in all the city. He noted the multicolored banners folded in woven baskets, to be shared with the rest of the populace in two months. The temple was already preparing for the Bonding, a celebration of the gods; to be initiated into the Sons of the Six just before such a holiday would be a special honor.

"Line up." Father Olufemi still had his back to them, but his voice cracked through the quiet like a whip. Ekon scrambled to move back to his assigned place, standing shoulder to shoulder with his co-candidates. He balled his fists to keep his fingers from moving. Father Olufemi faced them again, eyes appraising.

"Candidate Adebayo, Candidate Mensah, and Candidate Okojo." He nodded to each of them in turn. "The three of you are the last remaining candidates eligible for warriorship this season. You stand on the cusp of joining a hallowed brotherhood, a covenant eternal and divine. There are men who would lay down their very lives for membership, and many who already have."

Ekon swallowed. He thought about Memorial Hall, a quiet corridor in the temple that bore a permanent list of fallen Sons etched directly into the stone walls. He knew about men laying down their lives for this brotherhood. His own father's name was on that list.

"You have completed five rites on the sacred passage to warriorship. Now the time has come for you to undergo your last," Father Olufemi continued. "If you are successful, you will be anointed as Sons of the Six tonight. If you are not, your journey will come to an end. Per holy law, you will not be permitted another chance to take the rites, and you may never speak of them again."

Ekon knew he should have been paying closer attention as Father Olufemi went on, but it was next to impossible now. Both excitement and anxiety warmed his skin, pumping blood hard and fast through his veins and making it harder and harder to keep still.

This is it, he thought. *It's finally happening.*

When none of them raised objections, Father Olufemi gave an austere nod. "Very well, then, let us begin."

He gestured for them once again to follow him out of the worship hall and down one of its connecting halls. Ekon kept his strides even as they ventured deeper into blackness, turning and twisting through corridors until he was sure they were lost. He'd spent the last ten years of his life here in the temple, but he doubted he'd ever know the full extent of its layout. In time, they reached a weathered door illuminated by a single sconce mounted to the wall. Father Olufemi opened the door and ushered them into a small, windowless room. Ekon stilled as he saw what was in its center.

The woven raffia basket on the floor was large and round, not unlike the ones he sometimes saw women balance atop their heads down in the market, but something about this basket was wrong.

It was *moving*.

Without a word, Father Olufemi ambled over to it, leaving

them at the door. If he was at all concerned about its contents, he made no outward sign of it as he faced them again.

"Recite chapter three, verse thirteen, from the Book of the Six."

Ekon's mind went frighteningly blank for a few seconds before the memorized words tumbled from his mouth.

"A righteous man honors the Six as he honors each breath," he said in tandem with Fahim and Shomari. *"He honors them constantly with the words of his tongue, the thoughts of his mind, and the acts of his body, for as long as he should live among gods-fearing men."*

Father Olufemi nodded. "A holy warrior, a *true* Son of the Six, must be obedient at all times. He must answer only to the six gods and goddesses of our faith, and to those through whom they speak. Do you understand that, candidates?"

"Yes, Father," they replied in unison.

"And you understand"—Father Olufemi glanced at Ekon— "that when ordered to act in the name of the Six, you must *always* obey, without question or hesitation?"

Ekon had the distinct feeling that he was teetering on the edge of something, preparing to leap into some unknown abyss. He glanced at the strange moving basket again before answering.

"*Yes*, Father."

"Then you are ready." Without warning, Father Olufemi stooped to lift the basket's lid. There was a faint sound, a stirring. He gestured for the three of them to approach. With every step closer, Ekon sensed it, a wrongness that implored him to turn back, but he forced his feet to move until he was within a foot of Father Olufemi. When he saw what was inside the basket, however, his blood ran cold.

A tangle of golden-brown snakes writhed among one another,

twisting and coiling in an indistinguishable mass. They didn't hiss, nor did they seem to notice that they had new spectators, but a chill erupted across Ekon's arms anyway. It was impossible to tell where one serpent's body began and another ended. His fingers tapped, trying to find a cadence.

Too many. Can't count. Can't count. Can't count . . .

Fresh anxiety rose in his throat, and he found he couldn't swallow it. He didn't know much about snake species, but he was almost certain he knew what *these* were. Atop their interlaced bodies, three small scraps of parchment rose and fell with their movements. There was something written on each one, but he was too far away to read them.

Three scraps, a good number at least.

Shomari moved first, reaching for the slingshot hooked to his belt loop, but with surprising speed, Father Olufemi blocked his hand.

"No."

Shomari's eyes widened with surprise, but Father Olufemi spoke before he could.

"These are eastern black mambas," he explained. "There are six of them, one to represent each of our gods and goddesses. They have been anointed by this temple, and shall not be harmed."

Ekon tensed. He didn't like where this was going at all. Father Olufemi had said there were six snakes, but he couldn't separate them in his mind, which meant he couldn't count them. *That* frightened him to his core. Every instinct in his body told him to run or, at the very least, to distance himself from them, but he found he couldn't move.

"A Son of the Six is a man of faith and fortitude," Father Olufemi went on. "Tonight, we will put both to the test. Each of your family names has been written on a piece of parchment and placed inside this basket." He pointed. "Your final rite of passage requires you to retrieve your name without being bitten by one of the snakes. We will proceed alphabetically, by surname."

New beads of sweat slicked Ekon's neck, and it wasn't from the small room's stifling heat. Frantically, he racked his mind, thinking of what he knew about black mambas. They were said to be the most venomous snakes on the continent; a single bite could kill in a matter of minutes. From his brief readings, he knew they weren't particularly aggressive by nature, but provoked . . . He looked to his co-candidates. Fahim's nostrils flared as he took hard breaths in and out through his nose; Shomari's pupils were dilated. Both were visibly shaking. As if on cue, one of the serpents lifted its head slightly from the basket to eye them with curiosity. It opened its blue-black mouth, and in the low light, venom glistened wet on its fangs. Ekon froze.

"Candidate Adebayo," said Father Olufemi. *"Proceed."*

Ekon watched Fahim shuffle toward the basket, trembling from head to toe. He started to bend at the middle, then, as though thinking better of it, lowered to his knees. The serpents turned toward him, six pairs of glittering black eyes watching and waiting. Fahim started to reach out but withdrew his hand when one of the snakes hissed. Father Olufemi shook his head.

"They are *anointed*, which means they will only bite those who are unworthy," he murmured. "You must act without fear, and you must act with *faith*."

Fahim nodded, chest rising and falling as he steadied himself. He shifted his weight, flexed his fingers, then—so fast Ekon barely saw it—snatched a scrap of parchment from the center of the basket. He stumbled backward, landing on his bottom, then held the paper up to his eyes to read the name scrawled on it. Every muscle in his body instantly relaxed, and he handed the paper to Father Olufemi, who nodded.

"Very good. Candidate Mensah, it is your turn."

Shomari was more confident than Fahim, but not by much. He circled the basket like it was prey, wary eyes fixed on the two remaining slips of paper as he tried to determine which bore his family's name. But when it came time to kneel before the basket, he shook just as badly. Unlike Fahim, he reached into it with painstaking care, sweat gathering on his upper lip as his fingers hovered over the snakes' knotted bodies. He pinched one of the scraps, then carefully withdrew his hand. Nervous laughter echoed around the room as he rose, and Father Olufemi took his slip from him. After reading it, he nodded again, indicating for him to move back and stand beside Fahim. Ekon winced when the holy man's eyes shot to him.

"Candidate Okojo, *come forth.*"

Ekon tried to swallow again but found his throat had gone dry. He counted his steps—four, a *bad* number. His legs seemed to move of their own accord as Father Olufemi gestured toward the basket a final time, then stepped back to give him space. At last, Ekon made himself look down at it. There, right in the basket's center, he could see the last scrap of parchment. The name written on it was penned in bold black ink.

OKOJO

That was it; that piece of paper was the final thing standing between him and everything he'd worked for. He lowered slowly, ignoring the stone pressing hard against his knees. At once, as though somehow aware that he was their last intruder, the mambas hissed loudly in unison, their cold eyes meeting his own like onyx plucked from a starless night sky. He remembered Father Olufemi's words, spoken only moments before.

They will only bite those who are unworthy.

He swallowed. What if *he* was unworthy? He thought of the jungle, the things he'd done—the things he *hadn't* done. He thought of the strange old woman, the secrets he held on to, and a monster—it *always* seemed to lead back to the monster. He thought of the voice that plagued his nightmares.

Please. In his mind, Baba's voice was still slurred, pained. *Please, my son.*

No. Ekon screwed his eyes shut. He made himself think of Kamau, of the temple, and of the life the two of them had made here after Baba's death. He replaced visions of the Greater Jungle with memories of scorching-hot training sessions on the temple's front lawns, the smell of rice bread baking in the kitchens, a library full of books that he could count forever and ever.

Be strong. He heard Kamau's voice in his mind, reassuring and confident as always. *You can do this. And remember: Kutoka mzizi.*

Kutoka mzizi. The words made six syllables. Six, a *good* number. Slowly, he opened his eyes again. With his free hand, Ekon drummed his fingers against his side, finding an old rhythm as he chanted his ancestors' words in time with it.

One-two-three. One-two-three. One-two-three. One-two-three.

Kutoka mzizi. Kutoka mzizi.

After tonight, everything would change. After this, he would finally belong to something, a brotherhood.

Kutoka mzizi. Kutoka mzizi. Kutoka mzizi.

In his people's eyes, in this *city's* eyes, he'd be respected as a warrior and a man. Children would look up to him; girls would notice him. He would, at last, make Baba proud, even if his father wasn't here to see it. He might make his mother proud, even if she hadn't stayed to see it either.

Kutoka mzizi.

He steadied himself as he reached for the slip, fingers extending toward the snakes. He would do it Shomari's way, slow and careful. He counted the distance as it grew smaller.

Nine inches, six inches, three—

The door flung open with a bang, so sudden Ekon was on his feet with his hanjari drawn before he'd even discerned who'd opened it. When he saw who it was, however, he lowered the blade, confused.

The young man staring back at them held a torch and wore a sky-blue kaftan dampened with sweat around its neckline. He was tall, broad, and brown-skinned, chest heaving as he fought for breath. He was a Son of the Six.

"Kuhani." The warrior pounded his fist against his chest in salute and bowed at his middle.

"Warrior Selassie, what is the meaning of this?" Ekon had never seen Father Olufemi so angry. The holy man's mouth was set in a tight line, and a large vein near his temple throbbed dangerously. "How *dare* you interrupt a sacred rite of—"

"Forgive me, Father." Fahim and Shomari exchanged a look as the warrior bowed again, lower for good measure. For the first time, Ekon noticed that he was trembling and that, when he spoke, there was a catch in his voice. "Kapteni Okojo commanded me to find you at once."

Ekon's heart skipped a beat. *Kamau* had sent this warrior? The realization put him on edge. Something wasn't right.

Father Olufemi's expression sharpened. "What's happened? Speak."

Warrior Selassie straightened from his second bow and met Father Olufemi's gaze.

"It's Baaz Mtombé's Night Zoo," he whispered. "It's *burning*."

REMARKABLE THINGS

ADIAH

"Bwana and Bi Bolaji, thank you for coming so quickly."

Standing beside Father Masego, I watch my parents slowly ascend the Temple of Lkossa's last steps and try to temper my nerves. Perhaps it's the iron gray of the afternoon sky overhead, casting gloom as it always does this time of year, but today the two of them look especially worn down and tired.

Maybe it's because I know they always are.

My parents have come from all the way across the city at the behest of the messenger boy Father Masego sent for them. A tight line replaces my baba's usual smile, and I know at once that he's in pain. Stairs like the temple's are hard on his back, which has been bent badly out of shape from all the years of harvesting work. I look to his hands, calloused and big enough to entirely envelop my own. He has dark brown skin and a rounded face; people say I take after him. At his side, my mother, wearing her gray-streaked braids in a high bun, supports him by the elbow as they finally reach the landing. Her rich copper eyes are locked on me.

Not good.

"Kuhani." Mama greets Father Masego with a small, reverent bow. My father does the same, though it's a clumsier gesture. "We were very surprised to receive your message this morning. My husband and I were at work, you see, and we're paid by the hour—"

"I do apologize for calling you away from your occupations," says Father Masego. Today, he's wearing simple blue robes, but with his white dreadlocks tied back and his trimmed beard, he still looks annoyingly regal. "However, I'm afraid that the matter was urgent."

For the first time, Mama looks from me to Father Masego. Worry pinches the skin between her brows. "Is everything all right? Has something happened?"

"Well . . ." Father Masego pauses as though considering his words. "You could say so. Your daughter was involved in an incident this morning."

I feel the old man's gaze on me but refuse to meet it.

"After conferring with several witnesses," he continues, "I thought it best for us to speak in person—immediately."

"Adiah Bolaji."

Full name. *Really* not good. This time, I can't help but wince as Mama's gaze cuts into me, sharp as a blade. Even Baba looks unhappy.

"What have you done *this* time?"

"Nothing!" I hate how high-pitched my voice sounds, practically an admission of guilt. I'm almost a teenager, but I still sound like a little kid. I look between my parents before continuing quickly. "I mean, it was an *accident*. Brother Isoke—"

"Is currently in the temple's infirmary recovering," says Father

Masego. He turns to my parents. "As I've come to understand it, he was working with Adiah and some of the other young darajas this morning when she showed a bit too much . . . enthusiasm."

"Enthusiasm?" Baba's brows furrow in confusion.

Father Masego nods. "The exercise the students were practicing called for them to summon a small amount of splendor from the earth and let it move through them, then immediately out again. Adiah summoned far more than Brother Isoke expected, and when he went to correct her stance, it seems she—"

"Oh, come on, his hair will grow back!" I interrupt in a huff. "Er . . . *eventually.*"

At this, both my parents start. Mama has to grab Baba's arm to keep him from toppling down the steps as he reels, then stares at me in horror. It's a look I've seen before, and I resent it. I also resent Father Masego for tattling on me. It isn't *my* fault the splendor in the earth comes to me so willingly; it's done so all my life. I scowl at him, wriggling my toes as I feel the pleasant tingle of the splendor in my feet. I could probably zap his stupid beard off if I put my mind to it. As though he can read my thoughts, he gives me a wary look and moves imperceptibly to the left, putting slightly more space between us.

"*Perhaps,*" he says gently, "we should continue this conversation in the privacy of my study?"

Mama lets go of Baba and takes my arm none too gently as we follow Father Masego into the Temple of Lkossa. This time of the day, most of the brothers and Sons of the Six are busy studying, praying, or patrolling. We head up a set of stairs—slowly, so Baba can keep up—and Father Masego ushers us through a well-polished wooden door. I don't really like being inside the temple, and I *especially* don't like being in the Kuhani's private study. The room is long and rectangular, but with the overflowing bookshelves on both sides, I feel caged in by it. I think of my best friend, Tao, and how much he would love it here. When he's not doing chores down in the temple's kitchens, I know that sometimes he sneaks into the library. *He* could spend an entire day with his nose in a book. Unlike me, he doesn't mind being still.

Father Masego settles into a leather chair behind his desk and gestures for my parents to take the two matching seats opposite him. I don't want to notice it, but the two of them look so painfully out of place here in their harvester uniforms. There are patches all over Baba's tunic, and Mama's work dress is stretched and slightly too big for her bony frame. For a moment, I'm ashamed of them, and then I hate myself for it. Mama and Baba have sacrificed so much for me to be here; I have no right to be ashamed. Notably, there isn't a chair in the study left for me, so I'm forced to stand between my parents as Father Masego addresses them again.

"I want to be frank with you, Bwana and Bi Bolaji." He steeples his long fingers. "Two years ago, when you first brought Adiah to me at the age of ten for evaluation, I told you that I believed she could possibly be a gifted daraja if given proper training." He looks between them, tentative. "I'm afraid I was mistaken."

The temperature in the room seems to drop instantly. I watch as Mama sits upright in her chair, and Baba tenses. In my own head, I hear a roar growing louder and louder as the seconds pass, and I try to quell the churning in my stomach. This is it, I know it. Father Masego is about to expel me from the temple; he's going to tell my parents that I'm not allowed to train here anymore. I can practically hear their hearts breaking as the reality sinks in. Two years of endless sacrifice, wasted. They would no longer have a daughter who could rise to something more than a harvester, a daughter to be proud of. Guilt lodges in my throat as I stare at the floor, and hot tears well behind my eyes.

"What I *mean* to say is . . ."

My gaze lifts. Father Masego is no longer looking at my parents, but watching me carefully. It takes everything I have not to squirm. His round, piercing brown eyes remind me of an owl.

"I now think that I have severely underestimated Adiah's potential," he continues. "I once said that I thought she *could* be a powerful daraja, but now it is clear to me that she already is. In fact, Adiah is one of the most powerful prodigies I've ever encountered in my seventy-two years. Even at the age of twelve, her abilities are extraordinary."

If the study was cold before, warmth returns to it twice as quickly. I feel relief pulsing through the air, like a heartbeat bringing life back into the room. Both of my parents relax in their seats, and where I was nervous, I now feel a distinct sense of pride.

Extraordinary.

Father Masego, the head of the entire temple and city, thinks what I can do with the splendor is *extraordinary*. I'm *not* being expelled, and I'm *not* a failure. There's still time for me to prove myself, to find a way to make my parents' lives better. Once I'm a fully trained daraja, I'll be able to earn good money and share it with them. There's a chance at a better life. There's *hope*.

"So, you believe our little girl will be . . . all right?" Baba leans forward, his expression imploring. At the sound of his quiet joy, something squeezes in my chest. In return, Father Masego offers him a kind smile.

"Indeed," he says. "I believe Adiah will be quite accomplished in a few years, once she completes her training."

Training. Like that, I'm itching to get back to the front lawns to drill. I want to practice the exercise Brother Isoke was trying to teach me earlier, and I want to get it right this time. Maybe I can—

"But." Father Masego's eyes are still on me. "Adiah, along with paying you a well-earned compliment, I do also feel obligated to give you a word of advice: 'To whom much is given, much is required.'" He taps the thick leather book on the corner of his desk. "That saying comes from scripture. Do you know what it means?"

I shake my head because, honestly, I don't. The corners of Father Masego's lips tug into a deeper smile.

"What it means," he says, "is that because you have such a distinctly strong affinity for the splendor, you're going to have to work very, *very* hard to learn how to channel it properly and safely. You're going to have to study harder, practice longer—"

"I will."

"—*and* follow your teachers' instructions during lessons." His expression turns wry. "It also means there can be no more incidents like the one this morning. Do you understand, young lady?"

"Yes, Father. There won't be." I say the words immediately, and I mean them. Father Masego annoys me sometimes, but the truth is . . . I *do* want him to be proud of me, just like I want my parents to be proud of me. I don't want to be sent away from here.

I don't want to fail.

"Good." Father Masego rises, and so do my parents. "I have the utmost faith in you, Adiah," he says. "And I believe that, one day, you are going to do remarkable things."

CHAPTER 5

INTO THE STARS

Koffi winced as something burned across her skin.

There was a thunderous *boom*, so loud it shook the entire tent, and a flash of white-gold light. It took her a moment to process the sting of fresh pain, the warm trickle running down her forearm as beasts and beastkeepers alike yelped in surprise. Her vision swam for one long beat, and she blinked several times before it came back into focus. Slowly, she took in the scene before her.

A nearby end table had toppled over; its once-white linen cover was now soiled in the dirt, part of the table was scorched black, and near her feet, the ground was speckled with something red, too bright to be blood. She realized after a pause that it was wax, *candle* wax, and when she looked closer, she saw it had gotten everywhere, even on her arm. That explained the pain, but she didn't understand what had happened. Seconds ago, that candle had been quietly flickering in its gilded candelabra; now only the tiny flames flickering on the ground remained. It was as if the candle had *exploded*. She looked around, confused. The candle had burst at the same moment she'd exhaled, but . . . surely that was a coincidence, it had to be. There was no other possible explanation, but she felt strange. Her skin— uncomfortably hot before—was now clammy, and the bottoms of her feet were tingling the way they did when she sat cross-legged too long. The longer she stared at the candle's sizzling remnants, the harder it became to ignore the question forming in the back of her mind.

Did I do that?

No, of course not. It was a preposterous idea, illogical, and yet . . . she remembered the building pressure in her chest, followed by that brilliant sense of release. A warmth had coursed through her body, rushing up her limbs, then out through her hands. Something had happened, but she didn't know what, and the longer she considered that, the more uneasy she became.

I did do that. I caused that.

Most of the other beastkeepers were still staring in bewilderment at the place where the candle had been; a few were looking around it trying to find what had caused it to combust. Koffi felt a single pair of eyes on her and looked up.

Mama.

Her mother was the only person in the Hema not looking at the ruined candle, but at Koffi. There was sheer terror in her gaze.

"Order!"

Baaz, who still stood in the middle of the tent, shouted the command at the top of his lungs, then glared at the little fires as though he meant to douse them with admonishment. "One of these days, you idiots will learn to watch where you step and quit knocking things over. Everyone will remain calm and escort the animals outside in single file." He turned to a burly beastkeeper

69

beside him. "Dosu, run to the well and fetch some water. Gwala, take Rashida to the post. I'll be out in a moment . . ."

Koffi's gaze shot to Diko, then froze. Beside her, the jokomoto had suddenly gone unnervingly still as he eyed the growing fire. There was an unmistakable look in the lizard's yellow gaze, a *hunger*. At once, Koffi dropped the lead to his harness.

"We need to get out." She practically tripped over her own feet as she backed away from him. Somewhere in the Hema, she thought she heard a gasp. "We all need to get out, right now."

In her periphery, Baaz's scowl grew more menacing. "Shut up, girl," he growled. "There's no need to—"

"I'm telling you, we need to *leave*!" Koffi's voice rose an octave, but she couldn't help it. She tore her gaze from Baaz to stare back at Diko. The jokomoto had not yet moved, and there was a subtle red-gold glow just beneath his scales. "Please." She looked over her shoulder. "Please, everyone needs to—"

Someone grabbed her roughly by the arm, and she found herself face-to-face with Baaz. His face was contorted with rage. He either hadn't noticed Diko or didn't care anymore. "I said, *shut up*," he hissed through his teeth. "This is *my* zoo, not yours. *I* decide who leaves this tent and when, not you, you foul little—"

It happened without warning. There was an earsplitting shriek, so shrill several beastkeepers dropped to their knees at the sound of it. Koffi felt Baaz release her, and she fell to the ground as the entire Hema shook again and a blaze of light filled the space. The hairs on the back of her neck stood on end as she curled into a ball and covered her head. A long scream punctuated the air, then set off a chorus of others. Head still bowed, she listened to the sounds of pounding feet and panicked animals running around her until she dared to look up. When she did, her heart stopped.

Diko.

He was now in the middle of the tent, illuminated as though he were standing over some invisible white light. Fire erupted from his mouth in horrible yellow-gold waves, scorching everything in reach. He would burn the entire tent down.

"Koffi!"

Koffi looked to her right. Jabir was standing on the other side of the tent, looking around, as his dogs surrounded him and whined. His eyes were searching as he grew frantic. Koffi had opened her mouth to call his name when one of the gorillas barreled toward her and forced her to roll out of its path. When she sat up again, she couldn't see Jabir anymore.

"Move!"

There was a stab in her ribs as someone tripped over her, toppling to the ground with another scream. She doubled over. The Hema's air was growing thicker and darker by the second, harder to breathe and more difficult to see through. To her right, the guiamala—now abandoned—trotted in nervous circles until it knocked down the tent's central pole and the whole structure gave an ominous shudder. A metallic tinkling intermingled with new screams as hundreds of the pitching stakes outside uprooted, unable to bear the tent's new strain. Koffi stared up at it in horror.

"Get *down*!"

Someone yanked her to the floor as pieces of the crimson tent began folding in on themselves, catching flame with alarming speed. A body covered hers, shielding her from the worst of the falling debris. When Koffi turned her head, her face was inches from another's. Mama. She'd somehow gotten to her.

"Stay behind me," Mama said. "Crawl!"

She gestured for Koffi to follow her across the rugs on hands and knees as the animals and beastkeepers trapped inside the burning tent continued screaming. The tent's exit had already collapsed, and more pieces of it were still caving in. Several feet away, on the other side of the tent, there was a gap where the edge of the Hema had slightly lifted from the dirt. It was a small opening, but if they could slip under it . . .

Beneath her, bits of broken glass cut into Koffi's palms and knees; plumes of smoke filled her lungs with every ragged breath she took. The fire worsened, hotter still, but she didn't stop. To her dismay, the gap in the tent seemed to be getting farther, not closer. Fresh embers danced around her face, and she waved a bloodied hand to bat them away.

Gods, she prayed, *please don't let my hair catch.*

A terrible ringing filled her ears as she opened her mouth to call out to Mama and took in a mouthful of acrid heat instead. Her mother's silhouette—still crawling just ahead of her—was growing fainter, harder to discern amid the smoke and bits of tent falling in around them. Koffi tried to take another breath, but it was only a dry wheeze. It burned. She winced again as someone stepped on the back of her feet. Any minute now, she knew her body would reach its limits. She wouldn't be able to go on.

"Kof!" Mama shouted her name from somewhere in the darkness. "Hold on to me!"

But it was already too late. Koffi couldn't see or feel anything but smoke and blood. Her head was growing fuzzy now, and the world tilted as she fell forward. She waited for the pain, the inevitable collision with the ground, but it never came. There was a loud crash as a new section of the tent imploded, another long, agonized scream. Strong arms caught her, half pulling, half dragging her out into cooler night air.

"Koffi!"

The world was still dark and blurred, but Koffi felt someone gently slapping her cheek and trying to force her upright. She blinked hard and found Mama staring down at her. "Get up! We can't stay here!"

Koffi inhaled clean air, and the world righted itself. They were outside now, mere feet from the burning Hema. No sooner had she stood than Mama grabbed her arm and broke into a sprint.

"The animals," Mama said between strides. "Help me with them!"

Koffi looked behind them. The Hema was now completely ablaze, a great fiery heap spreading fast to other parts of the Night Zoo's grounds. She heard the bleats, snarls, and shrieks of caged beasts as its searing heat reached them, and her stomach heaved.

"Quickly!" Mama pointed Koffi toward the aviary while she raced toward a pen of panicked kudus. Koffi didn't stop to think as she yanked the domed cage's door open and let the birds soar up and into the night in a rainbow of feathers. A pair of beastkeepers watched in confusion before they understood what she was doing and darted away to help other animals. Koffi freed the chimpanzees, a baby warhyppo, and then a zebra. She was so lost in the pandemonium that, at first, she didn't hear the whooping. When she did, her blood ran cold.

Warriors.

Of course, no doubt they'd seen the smoke and flames from down in the city and come to investigate. She shuddered. Lkossa's warriors, the Sons of the Six, weren't known for their compassion. Suddenly, Mama was at her side again.

"We must leave." Mama's voice was tight, eyes wide. "Now!"

Koffi jolted. "What about our debts?"

Mama grabbed her by the shoulders, her grip almost painful. *"We cannot stay here,"* she pressed. "What just happened in the tent, if Baaz realizes what you really did and what you really are, you will never leave this place."

What you really did and what you really are. The words sounded odd, somehow wrong, but Koffi didn't have time to dwell on them as Mama tore off across the Night Zoo's lawns, pulling her in tow. Her legs screamed in protest with every stride, but she pushed to stay on Mama's heels. Around her, brief images flashed by in vivid color. It seemed the rest of the Night Zoo's creatures had been freed, stampeding around the lawns, looking for escape too. Several more fires had broken out over the grounds, and the air was punctuated with the sounds of not only animals, but beast-keepers too. Koffi shuddered, her gaze sweeping the grounds' perimeter. She flinched as her feet began to tingle again, and this time she felt an internal tug just beneath her navel as something shot through her once more. She turned her head in its direction, and a wave of relief flooded through her. A giant brick wall surrounded the Night Zoo, but there was a section of the wall where creeping vines hung down in thick ropes.

"Mama!" Koffi pointed toward the vines. Following her gaze, her mother nodded and changed course. They stopped together at the base of the towering wall.

"Climb!" Mama glanced over her shoulder. They were alone there, but probably for mere seconds.

Koffi didn't hesitate. The vines formed in a curtain of deep green as she twisted one of the stalks around her bare foot and used it to hoist herself up. She reached as high as she could, but stinging pain lanced through her palms. When she pulled her hands away, the vine was stained dark with blood. Her hands were scratched from crawling over debris in the Hema.

"Hurry!" said Mama.

"My hands are cut up!"

Mama ripped two strips from the hem of her tunic. "Wrap these around them!"

Koffi obeyed and tried again. This time when she grabbed the vine, the pain was manageable. The pull below her navel was still there, urging her on as she hauled herself up the wall inch by inch. It seemed to take a century, but gradually the top came into view. The stars above twinkled through the rising smoke, and Koffi used them as her guide. *Reach,* she told herself. *Just keep reaching.*

"Don't stop!" Mama called from below. Another surge of profound relief overtook Koffi as her bandaged hands finally found purchase on the ledge, a flat stone surface just wide enough for her to heave onto and perch like a bird. She looked down, expecting to see Mama right behind her, and triumph turned to terror.

Mama was still several feet down, frantically climbing the vines and looking over her shoulder with a panicked expression. Koffi followed her gaze, trying to understand. Her throat tightened as her eyes finally found what Mama's already had.

Two young men in plain brown kaftans were running across the lawns and toward them with purpose, their silhouettes blurred against the blood-orange glow of the roaring fire at their back.

Sons of the Six, come to stop them.

"Come on!" Koffi leaned over the wall's ledge as far as she dared, fingers outstretched. "Take my hand!"

But if Mama had seen or heard her, she gave no sign of it. Her eyes were darting back and forth now like a hare caught in a trap, looking from the vines to the approaching warriors to the vines again with visible panic. She made a desperate sort of half leap, and it cost her as she slipped farther down the vines.

"Mama, please!" Koffi reached, aware that if she extended much more, she'd fall forward; as it was, her body was already teetering. Finally, Mama seemed to understand. She looked up and reached for Koffi's hand, oblivious to the small black stone hurtling her way. With a horrific crack, it connected with the back of her skull. A soft sound escaped her lips as her eyes rolled back to expose their whites, and Koffi knew what was about to happen.

"No!"

Their fingertips grazed, then came apart. It seemed to take a thousand years for Mama to fall to the ground in a crumpled heap. Koffi waited, heart pounding, but her mother didn't move.

"Got her!"

Someone shouted the words from far away, but Koffi didn't look up to find the speaker. Too-dark blood was pooling in the grass under Mama's head like a crown. It seeped into her head wrap, soaking the black twists sticking out from it. In that moment, Koffi understood. It was the terrible sense of comprehension she'd felt when Baba's eyes had closed on that cot so many years ago, when she'd realized he hadn't gone to sleep but to someplace much farther away. A slow dread clawed its way up her insides, seizing at her throat with long, vicious fingers.

No. She stared at her mother's body, trying to process it. *No, no, no, no*—

A stone collided with her shoulder, sending fresh pain ricocheting through her body and jolting her back to the present. Yet again, something tugged in her core, compelling her to turn away from the Night Zoo and toward the open fields beyond. She felt a distinct kind of tearing within her, two things at war and pulling her in different directions. The foreign feeling in her core was demanding she leave; Mama's body begged her to stay.

Mind over heart. Heart over mind.

She faced the lemongrass fields before her.

"Hey, wait!"

Koffi started and looked over her shoulder. One of the warriors was closer now, his dark eyes fixed on her with a hunter's focus. He *was* hunting, hunting *her*. She swayed on her perch, willing herself not to fall forward.

Go.

It was a single word in her mind, but it was sure, repeating itself like ripples on a pond's smooth surface.

Go.

She made the decision then, mind over heart. Her stomach lurched as she leaped from the ledge and into the stars, praying they'd catch her as she fell.

CHAPTER 6

The COLOR of MIDNIGHT

Ekon ran through Lkossa's empty streets, Sons of the Six flanking him on all sides.

Two hundred eighty-two steps from the Temple of Lkossa, he counted. *A good number.*

The cheerful din that had filled the city earlier was gone, and the few denizens still outside shop fronts did not wave or cheer as the warriors passed. It wasn't hard to imagine what their group must have looked like: a pack of uniformed men, spears, and stern faces, charging into unknown danger. He gripped his hanjari's leather hilt in one hand and tapped his fingers against his side with the other.

Two hundred eighty-four steps. Two hundred eighty-five steps. Two hundred eighty-six . . .

It didn't take long to reach the Night Zoo, though Ekon still paused as the hill it perched upon loomed into view. Of course, he'd *heard* about the zoo—every Lkossan child grew up with stories of its wonders and terrors—but he'd never actually visited it or dared to come so close. It bore an uncanny resemblance to a prison: a large, bricked-in compound with walls at least twice his height. Flickers of gold-orange flames were visible, and even several yards away the acrid stench of smoke and burning grass stung his eyes. They kept running until they'd reached the zoo's ornate blacksteel entrance gates. Kamau, positioned at the head of their group, stopped before the gates and turned. He looked every bit of a true kapteni.

"We need to move quickly," he said. "The vegetation around this area is very dry, especially the lemongrass fields. If the fire spreads to it, Lkossa proper will be decimated. We have to contain it, then extinguish it, so we'll work in groups." He pointed to several seasoned warriors. "You will join me in the search and rescue. We'll start on the south end of the zoo, and move west." He looked to another group. "You are going to be runners. You'll take buckets of water to the areas where the fire is closest to getting out and work to contain it. Don't let up for any reason—"

"Kamau!"

Ekon almost regretted speaking up as the eyes of every warrior shot to him. He couldn't discern the look on his older brother's face, so he braved the rest of his words. "Sorry, um . . . Kapteni, how can I help?"

Kamau was already looking past the Night Zoo's open gates. "There should be a well somewhere inside the zoo—city ordinance requires it. You, Shomari, and Fahim will be in charge of refilling water buckets to hand off to the runners. Make sure there's always one ready for them."

Disappointment flooded Ekon. There was no way being a bucket boy would be enough to prove his worthiness to Father Olufemi and the warriorship. He was all too aware that he hadn't actually grabbed his name from the basket of mambas in the temple before being called away, which meant that—technically—he hadn't completed his last rite of passage. If he couldn't prove himself here . . . He swallowed a lump in his throat.

Kamau gave them all a measured look. "There are indentured servants in this zoo called beastkeepers," he said. "They're mostly indentured Gedes, and no doubt, some of them will be trying to escape in this chaos. If you see one and you're able, secure them. They are under legally binding contracts and not permitted to leave the zoo's grounds. Move out!" He turned on his heels, and the rest of the Yaba warriors obeyed, following him through the Night Zoo's entrance and into the compound with whoops and war cries. As soon as he was inside, Ekon winced. It wasn't just hot here, it was sweltering. He'd never known how loud a fire could be; its roar was thunderous. All around him, people in gray tunics were running, screaming, and they weren't the only ones. The hair on the back of his neck stood on end as something shimmery and scaled barreled past him with a snarl, sending waves of heat in its wake. A few feet away, another shape, hairier, fled the growing flames. The beasts of the Night Zoo had been freed.

"Get to the well!" Kamau swung his spear in a wide arc as something horned charged at him. Ekon watched him disappear into the plumes of smoke.

Please be all right, he silently prayed. *Please be okay—*

"Okojo!"

Ekon jumped as someone shoved him, surprised and annoyed to find Shomari glaring at him. "Get moving. The well's over there!"

Ekon bit back a retort. He and Shomari ran across the lawns to the well where Fahim was already standing and started filling buckets. Beastkeepers were also desperately carrying buckets of water and haphazardly throwing the water onto the fire, but it was no use. Ekon snatched one of the buckets none too gently from a bewildered old man. His eyes shot to a large tent entirely engulfed in flames, likely the original source of the fire. Kamau was right; they had to get it contained fast.

He plunged the bucket into the well. The water was lukewarm and foul, but a runner was already racing toward him. No sooner had he passed the bucket off to him and refilled the empty one dropped at his feet than another one was coming, and then another. It was repetitive work; the muscles in his arms and lower back twinged as he stooped over and over to pass off refilled buckets and pick up empty ones. His heart lifted as he looked across the Night Zoo's scorched lawns. One of the smaller fires had already been doused, and a team of warriors was now battling the main one near the giant tent. His eyes were still searching when he saw it—saw *them*.

Two gray-clad figures were running across the Night Zoo's grounds amid the chaos, one glancing over her shoulder every few strides.

Two, a bad number.

The first woman wore a head wrap and looked old enough to be his mother, but the second could have been his age. Even from a distance, Ekon saw the fear reflected in both their faces—the fear of people running for their lives.

They were trying to escape.

Ekon glanced over his shoulder as he threw another bucket into the well, alarmed. "Hey!" he shouted. "We've got two potential escapees heading for the wall!"

Fahim was still refilling buckets as fast as he could, but at the words, Shomari looked up, eager.

"Not for long."

He dropped his bucket at the same time Ekon did, and together they broke into a run. Their strides were evenly matched as they closed the gap between themselves and the fleeing beastkeepers. The younger of the two was already at the top of the zoo's border wall. The older one was climbing up the vines to follow suit.

"They're going to get away!"

Shomari stopped, pulling his slingshot from his belt. "No, they won't." He snatched a rock from the ground, knelt, then shot with perfect aim. The stone soared across the lawn like a bird of prey, striking the older beastkeeper in the back of the head so hard she fell from the wall. Ekon flinched as her body crumpled on the ground.

"Got her!" Shomari punched the air, then shot another rock. That one hit the second beastkeeper, the girl, square on the shoulder. "One more, and she'll—"

"No!" Ekon was already running. The girl on the wall's top ledge had turned her back on them, teetering dangerously. His lungs burned as he inhaled smoke and grew dizzier, but he shouted at her anyway.

"Hey, wait!"

The girl only glanced over her shoulder. Ekon knew what she was going to do, but he still gasped when she leaped into the darkness.

"No!" Ekon stopped short just as Shomari caught up to him again. "She jumped."

Shomari swore aloud, already turning to head toward the Night Zoo's entrance. "We can still cut her off. I'll go around the back—you take the wall!"

Ekon sprang into action, charging toward the wall before he could pause to think about it. The older beastkeeper, the one Shomari had shot down, was lying in the grass unmoving, but Ekon didn't stop to look at her. He vaulted up the vine-covered wall, scrabbling to get over it as fast as he could. The world darkened as he reached the ledge the girl had been balanced on only seconds before, and he leaped as she had, landing hard in the dirt on the other side. His eyes panned, then stopped.

It had been ten years since he'd seen the four-legged creature staring back at him in the darkness, though that didn't make it any less terrifying. He drew in a sharp breath as the beast eyed him, illuminated in a horrid red-orange glow from the fires on the other side of the wall. Its body was leonine, the skin stretched across its lean frame the pale pink color of something that hadn't seen true sunlight in years. Ekon knew what it was.

The Shetani.

There was a half-second pause as it studied him, baring a row of yellow teeth crammed into a gummy black mouth. That would have been frightening enough in its own right, but the animal's teeth weren't what rooted Ekon to the dirt; it was the thing's *eyes*. They were emotionless, two black pits that threatened to swallow him whole. They rendered him immobile, helpless, as the familiar voice rose from the back of his mind. He found he could do nothing to stop it; he couldn't even make his fingers count.

Son. Baba's voice was desperate as ever. *Son, please.*

Ekon wasn't standing near the Greater Jungle's border now, but it didn't matter. It seemed the jungle's very essence had sought him out, a living nightmare purged from its most wretched depths. At once, he was a little boy again, staring at a monster as it towered over his father's body.

Please, Ekon.

In his memory, Baba's body was broken, and there was too much blood.

Please, son.

But Ekon couldn't move, couldn't help. As the Shetani held his gaze, he knew then that the creature wouldn't be the thing that killed him in the end; it would be the *fear*. After all these years, the beast still laid claim to him, ravaging his body like an incurable sickness. He screwed his eyes shut, waiting for the creature to advance and finish him, then—

"Go."

Ekon started, his eyes flying open again. The voice that had spoken wasn't Baba's, and it hadn't come from his mind. It was softer, lighter. His eyes flitted right and focused on a figure standing just a few feet from him in the darkness, still as stone. The girl. In the moonlight, he saw she had a small, broad nose, round cheeks, and a slightly pointed chin. Black twists curtained her face, stopping just past her shoulder. She wasn't looking at him, but at the Shetani, and her expression managed to be both tentative and calm. She regarded the beast as though staring at something faintly familiar. Ekon tensed, waiting for violence, but the Shetani did nothing. It seemed as perplexed as he was by the girl. A moment passed among the three of them, and then Ekon felt it. The sensation came quietly at first, a low hum, like something rumbling just beneath his feet. It grew palpable in the air, *heating* it. Then:

"*Go.*" The girl said the word again, this time louder, surer. It seemed to surprise her as much as it surprised Ekon. Another second passed before the Shetani jolted without warning, retreating into the lemongrass fields and leaving the two of them alone.

It understood her. Ekon stared at the place where the creature had been, trying to process what he'd just seen. He wanted to pinch himself, to do something to prove to himself that this was real, but he couldn't move. *It listened to her,* he realized. *She told it to go, and it . . . listened. It obeyed.*

For her own part, the girl still hadn't moved. She was staring off into the blackness, as though seeing something he could not. A long silence filled the space between them before instinct took over and Ekon closed the gap between them. His fingers locked around her upper arm, and she jumped at the sudden contact. He was shocked to find her skin was hot to the touch, almost feverish. In that moment, in that *touch*, he felt as though something was radiating from her to him, that same peculiar thrum so strong it rattled his teeth. Her wary gaze lifted to meet his, and from some detached place in the back of his mind, he noted that her eyes were exactly the color of midnight; at least, if he'd imagined such a thing could have a true color. His grip on her arm loosened, but he didn't realize he'd actually released her until she stumbled back from him and began to run. She wasn't terribly fast—he could have caught her again if he'd wanted to—but he didn't. Ekon watched until she'd disappeared into the lemongrass. A feeling like relief graced him only a moment, before a voice shattered the night.

"You let her *go*?"

Ekon swiveled. Shomari was standing feet away, having just rounded the corner of the Night Zoo's wall. His expression held indecision as he looked back and forth between Ekon and the surrounding fields. There was a terrible pause; then Shomari turned on his heels and ran.

No.

Ekon tore after him, heart thundering in his chest. The smoke in the air was thinning, the roar of the fire dulled in his ears. It seemed most of it had been put out, but Ekon didn't care now. His focus was singular. He couldn't let Shomari tell anyone what he'd just done. He'd let that beastkeeper girl go, deliberately. If any of the other warriors found out, if Father Olufemi found out . . .

He ran faster, but it was no use. Too soon, they were back inside the Night Zoo, stopping short at its well. To Ekon's horror, several Sons of the Six were already standing there, surrounding a larger group of people seated in the grass with bound wrists. These had to be other beastkeepers, ones that either hadn't managed to escape or hadn't bothered trying. Each one of their somber gazes was locked on a man wearing a cheap-looking red dashiki a few feet away.

". . . will cost thousands in damages!" the man was saying. "You must appeal to the Kuhani tonight and tell him I need immediate relief and financial aid from the temple's coffers! I'm a gods-fearing man, I pay my tithes—"

"You'll have to lodge a formal request with the temple's

Fiduciary Committee, Baaz." Kamau's words were clipped as he looked down his nose at the man with only thinly veiled disgust. "We are not responsible for the disbursement of its funds. For now, I suggest you salvage what you can. We were able to recover every beastkeeper who tried to run—"

"Not all of them!" Shomari's words split the night. Ekon watched his co-candidate step forward with a smirk. "*Ekon* let one of them go."

Every warrior in the vicinity straightened, their faces growing stony as Shomari's words sunk in. Ekon watched Fahim, standing nearby, as his eyes widened in horror. Baaz Mtombé looked nothing short of confused. The worst expression, however, was Kamau's. In two strides, he'd closed the gap between himself and Shomari and grabbed a fistful of the boy's kaftan. He pulled him so close the tips of their noses were almost touching. When he spoke, his voice was a growl.

"If you *ever* accuse my brother of such a thing again—"

"K-Kamau, it's true." Shomari's eyes lost their smug gleam as Kamau's grip tightened. "I saw him do it with my own eyes. He let one of the beastkeepers go, on the other side of the wall! She was wearing a beastkeeper uniform! I swear by the Six!"

Kamau's eyes followed Shomari's trembling finger before looking to Ekon. Gone was the rage, the instinctive protectiveness his older brother had always harbored for him. In its place was something far worse—shock.

"Ekkie," he whispered. "That's . . . that's not true, is it?"

Ekon's blood turned to ice. Another dull roar filled his ears, but this time it wasn't from a fire. His mind seemed to break into a million pieces he couldn't gather under his older brother's waiting gaze. Every instinct in his body told him to lie, but the confession escaped him before he could stop it.

"It's true."

He would have given anything in the world not to see the look that touched his brother's face just then; there were no adequate words for it. It was a collision of disappointment, disgust, and the distinct pain of watching something break, something that would never be quite whole again. None of the other Yaba warriors dared to speak; only the crackling remnants of the fire filled the silence.

"Do you mean to tell me," Baaz finally said in indignation, "that Sons of the Six now break the law without consequence?" He looked to Kamau. "Tell me, which committee should I speak to about—?"

"Silence."

Every head swiveled in the direction of the voice that had spoken, a voice Ekon wished to every god and goddess he hadn't heard. The world seemed to slow as Father Olufemi ambled across the Night Zoo's smoldering lawns. His mouth was hard-set, the skin between his brows pinched hard.

"The boy is no warrior," he said. "But he *will* be punished."

Ekon's fingers danced of their own accord, tapping hard against his leg in a frantic beat.

One-two-three. One-two-three. One-two-three.

He tried balling his hands into fists to still them, but with so many eyes on him, it was impossible. Centuries seemed to pass as Father Olufemi continued forward, then stopped a few feet his opposite. His gaze was unflinching when he spoke.

"Candidate Okojo." His voice was entirely too soft. "You have willfully abetted the escape of a legally indentured servant, and in doing so you have stolen from this man a debt fairly and rightfully owed. This is both a crime and an act of sin. There is no place for either among the Sons of the Six."

Ekon didn't look away from Father Olufemi's searing gaze, but in his periphery, he felt the other warriors watching him, their distaste palpable in the acrid night air. From among them, an unspoken sentiment seemed to grow and form into a unanimous decision. Ekon's fingers moved so fast with his counts that the joints in his hands began to ache.

One-two-three-one-two-three-one-two-three.

Father Olufemi folded his hands at the same time Kamau looked away. Ekon understood what was about to happen a second before the holy man's mouth uttered the words.

Seventeen words, a bad number.

"Ekon Okojo," he said quietly. "Effective immediately, your candidacy for the Sons of the Six has ended. You are dismissed."

CHAPTER 7

RHYTHM and FLOW

Koffi watched the fractured sky above her pale as night yielded to dawn.

For a few fragile seconds, she remained as detached as the clouds overhead, suspended in an intermediate space between nightmares and dreams, where reality couldn't reach. It didn't last long; memories of the previous night found her soon enough.

Then she remembered the *eyes*.

They were a fathomless black, fixed firmly in her mind. She remembered the sensation of falling after she'd leaped from the Night Zoo's wall, the impact as she'd landed feetfirst in the dirt and stumbled. When she'd risen, she'd come face-to-face with a monster—and not just *any* monster.

The *Shetani*.

She'd known what it was instantly. Growing up, she'd heard tales of it, but nothing that had prepared her for the truth. The creature she'd laid eyes on had been a thing built from nightmares, a mass of raw pink skin stretched tight over tendons and bone. She envisioned the knifelike teeth and bottlebrush tail, the way each of its black claws had curled in the earth as it tensed. Perhaps it had been drawn to the commotion of the Night Zoo's fire; maybe it'd come for something else. She'd been sure it would kill her, and then—

"Go."

The word had left her lips in a whisper. Yet again, she'd felt that strange tingle in her feet, a rush of something moving through her.

"Go."

She wasn't sure why she'd repeated the command; it had just come to her. And then, against all reason . . . the Shetani had *obeyed*.

She imagined its retreating figure as it disappeared into the night, and tried to recall other details. Someone had grabbed her momentarily—a boy she hadn't noticed before—but when he'd let her go a second later, she'd seized the opportunity and made a run for it. That same insistent pull she'd felt in the zoo had guided her through the lemongrass fields as the zoo's towering brick walls grew distant, and the city of Lkossa's outer slums rose to meet her. With each step, she'd fallen into a cadence, a steady drumming rhythm that began in her feet and worked its way up her ribs until her heartbeat attuned to it.

Thump-thump. Don't stop. Thump-thump. Don't stop.

The pull had led her through winding side streets rank with the stink of waste and rotting food until she'd found refuge in one particularly small alley filled with old crates she could hide behind. Now she sat there with her knees pulled up to her chin.

The throbbing ache near her clavicle when she shifted was a painful reminder of the rock that had hit her, but she bit into her lip until the threatening tears waned. She *wouldn't* cry, she determined, not here. To cry now would be to unleash something, a deluge she wasn't sure she'd be able to dam once released. Her stomach twisted as she stemmed two different kinds of pain, refusing to let either consume her. After a moment, the first subsided, but the second kind remained.

Mama was gone.

The revelation didn't come the way she'd expected it to—total and devastating. Rather, it rolled over her in waves, each one crueler than its predecessor, until it was numbing. She and Mama had come close, *so* close, to a different life entirely. She remembered the hope she'd seen in her mother's eyes as she'd shared the news that they'd be leaving.

We can go wherever we want, she'd said. You and I, we'll leave this place and start over somewhere else, and we'll never, ever look back. We'll never return.

In the end, that dream hadn't even made it over the Night Zoo's walls.

Koffi stared at her hands, still loosely wrapped in the bloodied strips of cloth Mama had torn from her own tunic to help her climb the vines. Koffi winced at the sight of them. Those two tattered rags were literal pieces of her mother, the only things she had left now. New truths took shape the longer she stared at them. Mama had understood that there was a chance they wouldn't both make it out of the Night Zoo, so she'd followed a maternal instinct and told Koffi to climb the wall first. That sacrifice had ultimately made all the difference, but it hadn't been the only one. Koffi suddenly remembered all the little moments too, the times Mama had shared her food when meals were sparse, or shared her blanket on colder nights. Even last night, before they'd run,

Mama had been prepared to take a punishment that she hadn't deserved, to give up her own freedom so that Koffi didn't have to give up hers. That was all Mama had ever done, put others before herself. She'd never seen any of that goodwill returned; she never would now.

And it's all your fault.

Koffi flinched away from the accusation in her head, from the vitriol in it. The sense of emptiness was one thing, but the blame and guilt cut through her like a knife. None of last night would have happened if she'd remembered to check Diko's harness. The exploding candle, the fire, the aftermath, it all led back to one careless mistake. She thought of the look she'd seen on Mama's face in the seconds after the candle had burst, what she'd said as they ran from the Hema side by side.

If Baaz realizes what you really did and what you really are, you will never leave this place.

Koffi focused on those words now, letting them echo in her head. Mama had known something about her, but *what*? Something significant had happened last night, a thread that interwove between her, the Shetani, and that strange feeling in her feet, but she couldn't understand the connection. A new stab of pain struck as she realized that it didn't matter. That strange feeling, whatever it had been and whatever had caused it, was gone now. That truth had likely died with Mama.

Every muscle in Koffi's body screamed in protest as she pulled herself to her feet, collecting what dwindling resolve she had left. Her feet were sore, her tunic was sticky, and she was sure the twists in her hair were unraveling, but she set her jaw with a new determination. She couldn't stay in this alley. Her mother's last gift to her had been a second chance at life, and that gift couldn't be wasted. Sitting here waiting for something or someone to happen upon her wasn't an option. She had to *move*.

Her eyes watered as she emerged from the alleys of the slum slowly, adjusting to the new morning light. Lkossa's streets, it seemed, were only just beginning to stir, filling with people leaving their homes and setting up wares for the day. Koffi found it all strange to see firsthand. This was, after all, where she was truly from—her family had once lived in the city before moving to the Night Zoo—but years had passed since she'd been here in person. It was a peculiar thing, to know a place was home without knowing it at all.

She idled through the roads quietly, trying to lay out a map in her mind. Each part of Lkossa, it seemed, had its own style and character. She passed through a street that smelled of linens and soaps, one full of strung-up meats and animal hides, and yet another filled with artisans and pottery work. With each discovery of something new or unexpected, she watched the city come to life. The red dirt beneath her feet seemed to hum, and the collective smells around her formed a fragrance of their own. She was still tired, still on edge, but something about the city calmed her. It wasn't so unlike the Night Zoo, she realized; Lkossa had its own rhythm and flow. She closed her eyes and listened to it, the droves of people pounding through the streets, a chorus of vendors calling out prices to their customers, the sounds of marching feet—

Her eyes snapped open. That *new* sound, the marching, was distinct from the rest of the city's morning din. She searched the road, tensing, until she found where it was coming from. A trio of young men had just entered from the opposite end of the street, weaving through it in single file. They wore telltale blue kaftans and gold belts, and each had a hanjari dagger looped on his belt. A few of the vendors stepped out of their way as they walked, but most paid them little attention. From her spot, Koffi stiffened. Those were Sons of the Six in broad daylight, perhaps some of the very same ones who'd come into the zoo. They looked smug, *superior*, like the kind of men who were used to holding power. Not a single one of them even looked her way as they passed, but she still ducked behind a fruit cart until they were farther down the street. Newfound anger boiled her blood as she watched their retreating backs and remembered yet another piece of the night before. Two warriors had come after her and Mama, chased them down like animals. She gnawed on her bottom lip until she tasted blood, until she could no longer see the three warriors. The sight of them had prompted an unpleasant reminder.

She was a runaway.

In fleeing the Night Zoo, she'd broken her legal-indenture contract with Baaz, the one she and her parents had signed years ago, which meant she'd also broken the law. What she'd done was considered theft and desertion, and if she was caught, she'd be caned, jailed, or worse. Instinctively she looked over her shoulder, and a fresh stab of sadness nearly winded her. Mama wasn't here. No one was. From here on, she'd have to figure things out on her own. She pressed her fingers into her temples, trying to think. *Think.* Mama had said something else to her last night, something about *thinking*. Koffi tried to pull the words from memory.

Sometimes, though, you can't lead with your heart. You have to think with your head.

Koffi resolved then that that was what she would do. She *would* think with her head, and she'd come up with a plan. She and Mama had once dreamed of leaving Lkossa, so that was what she'd do.

She was going to find a way out of here.

The sun rose higher as the morning went on, drawing heat from every crevice of the city's roads and buildings. Eventually, Koffi found a public well where she could wash. She didn't have clothes to change into, so the best she'd been able to do was a few buckets of water poured over her body, but that had at least gotten rid of the grit and the lingering smell of smoke. Only so much could be done about her hair without shea butter and a good comb, but she at least tried to redo some of the unravelling twists. She was still wringing out her clothes when she reached the end of one street and stopped.

If Lkossa had been designed like a pie—a circle cut into thick, even slices—then this had to be its center. It was like nothing she'd ever seen before. Tents in every size, shape, and color were pushed together, so close it was hard to discern where one stopped and another started. She inhaled, and her lungs filled with a thousand scents all at once. She smelled egusi soup brewing—thick with onions, tomatoes, and fresh peppers—alongside jollof rice and banku. Women with kohl-rimmed eyes flocked around carts of multicolored pots, while bearded men in extravagant garb haggled over wax-dyed textiles that shimmered in the breeze. The sight of it managed to be both overwhelming and magnificent all at once.

Koffi was so taken by it that she didn't notice anything near her until she tripped.

"Oh, excuse me, I—"

She started. She hadn't seen the person sitting on a blanket near her feet. It was an old woman, sitting before an assortment of small glittering trinkets. There were beaded bracelets, hoop earrings, and several jeweled hair barrettes, but her eyes focused on the six wooden figurines displayed in a semicircle at the blanket's center—a heron, a crocodile, a jackal, a serpent, a dove, and a hippo—icons of the gods' familiars.

"Quite all right, little one." The woman offered a small smile. Her tunic was as plain as her blanket, and tufts of white hair peeked out from the edges of her cotton head wrap. A tarnished amulet hung around her neck. "I'm easy to miss." She followed Koffi's gaze and nodded to the figurines. "You are faithful?"

"I am." Koffi swallowed a hard lump in her throat. The figurines, clearly carved from good marula wood, were so much like the ones she and Mama had prayed to only yesterday. That memory now felt like part of a different life. "They're lovely," she whispered.

"Thank you, dear." The old woman's voice held a touch of pride, and Koffi relaxed as she recognized the fluid way she spoke Zamani. This woman was Gede, like her. Out of respect, she bowed her head.

"Good morning, Auntie," she said, deferring to the respectful greeting for an elder.

"Ah." The old woman's dark eyes danced. "And a good morning to you, little bird. The gods are kind today to bring us together." She studied Koffi more closely. "You're skinny." It wasn't a question, but it wasn't an accusation either. "Are you hungry?"

"I—"

Before Koffi could answer, the old woman was digging in a bag at her side and withdrawing a wrapped loaf of bread. The smell alone made Koffi's mouth water. "I've got more than enough here, if you'd like to share?"

"Um . . ." Koffi paused. She was still feeling cautious, and more than a little wary of strangers, but . . . Mama had taught her the rule of kin. You never refused a meal offered by another Gede. Besides that, she was starving. As though she'd read her mind, the old woman split her bread in half without another word. Koffi took a seat beside her on the blanket as they ate. She barely resisted a moan. Food had never made her cry before, but this bread was so delicious that she almost wanted to. Every morsel seemed to give something small back to her, revitalizing her. When she looked up, she found the old woman was watching her.

"You seem a bit young to come to the market on your own," she noted.

Koffi sat up straighter. "I'm eighteen," she lied. "Perfectly capable."

One of the old woman's white brows rose. "Really? I'd have guessed *sixteen*, actually."

Koffi was grateful the darker hue of her skin couldn't betray her embarrassment. She pointed to the trinkets on the blanket, eager to change the subject.

"So, how much do these usually go for?" she asked.

"Oh." The old woman brushed crumbs from her lap and leaned against the building directly behind them. "I suppose it depends on the buyer. I accept payments in coin, of course, but sometimes I get offers for a barter."

"A . . . *barter*?" Koffi repeated the word. It sounded vaguely familiar, but she couldn't remember another time she'd heard it.

"It means a trade," the old woman explained. "One thing given in exchange for another thing of equal value."

Koffi stared. "You can do that here, trade one thing for another without paying money?"

The old woman smiled. "Of course you can. Anything can be bartered for, *if* you know its true value."

Koffi sat back for a moment, considering. All her life, currency had worked one way. She and Mama had worked for a daily coin allowance, which they'd then used to pay down their debt. The idea of paying for things in other ways, through *trade*, felt entirely foreign to her. She was still thinking about it as her eyes roamed over the items on the blanket, stopping on one in particular. It was a silver ring, simple enough at a glance, but the jewel at its center was exquisite. It reminded her of an opal, but brighter, impossibly prettier. At once, she felt distinctly drawn to it. For a second time, the old woman followed her gaze.

"Ah yes, the duniastone," she said knowingly. "It's a modest thing, but it does catch the eye. I've had several offers for it in the last week, though none that were worthy."

Koffi paused. "Did you say . . . *duniastone*?"

"I did." There was a glint in the woman's eyes now. "You've heard of them?"

"Sure, in stories." Koffi thought about what her mother had told her about duniastones when she was a little girl. It was said they came from the very heart of the earth itself and could only be found in . . . "You've been to the Kusonga Plains," she said aloud.

The old woman nodded. "I have."

Now it was Koffi who sat back against the wall. She'd only just left the Night Zoo for the first time since she and her parents had become indentured there, so it felt impossible to imagine something as far away as the Kusonga Plains. She was fairly sure even Baaz had never been so far west. She stared at the old woman, distinctly impressed.

"What's it like there?"

"Oh, it's beautiful," said the old woman. "There are fields of lemongrass that stretch for miles, food that tastes like paradise." She closed her eyes, wistful. "I imagine it's what the godlands might someday be like, if I am so lucky as to get there. It's truly a place of wonder." She cracked an eye open to look at Koffi. "*And* a place of magic."

Koffi scoffed before she could stop herself, then tried to disguise it as a cough. The old woman's other eye opened, and she pursed her lips.

"You don't believe in magic?" she asked.

"Well . . . no," said Koffi. "Magic isn't real. It's just something from stories."

Now the old woman looked offended. "And who told you *that* nonsense?"

"My . . ." Koffi faltered. "My mother."

"Hmph!" The old woman crossed her arms and sniffed. "Well, your mother is *quite* incorrect."

Koffi's gaze dropped to her hands. When she spoke, her voice was barely a whisper. "My mother is dead."

"Oh."

Koffi looked up and found the old woman's expression had

changed. Her face was drawn, and her eyes were full of sadness. For a moment, she seemed at a loss for words. "I'm . . . very sorry to hear that, little one," she murmured. "I know what it means to lose a loved one."

"It's—" Koffi stopped herself. She'd been about to say that it was all right because that seemed like the polite response, but it didn't feel right to say. Things weren't all right; *she* wasn't all right. She wasn't sure she ever would be. Another beat passed before the old woman spoke again.

"I'm sure your mother only told you what she knew to be true," she went on more gently. "But you should know that magic has not always been confined to the pages of stories. In another time, it was here, as real as the air we're breathing."

Koffi sat up. "It was?"

The old woman nodded. "In cities like Lkossa, it was once a part of everyday life. People used magic to heal the sick and injured, to protect our borders, and it was even part of some children's education. Yabas and Gedes alike could inherit it, and those who did were trained at the Temple of Lkossa by brothers of its order. They were called darajas."

Koffi frowned. Mama had certainly never told her any of this. She looked around and tried to envision what this city would have looked like when magic simmered just beneath its surface. Had magic sparkled, she wondered, or had it been invisible? Dangerous, or utterly ordinary? It was hard to even contemplate. "What happened to it?" she asked.

The old woman looked up and into the bustling market, as though she was seeing past it. "The *Rupture*."

"The Rupture?" Koffi repeated. "What's an earthquake got to do with magic?"

The old woman gave her a shrewd look. "No doubt you've heard the stories," she said. "Tales of tears in the earth and sky, waves of heat scorching bodies whole. I am old enough to remember it, and I can tell you, it was a terrible thing to behold."

Koffi shuddered. She'd been told the story plenty of times and ways, but that made it no nicer to think about.

"To this day, no one truly knows what caused the Rupture," the old woman continued. "But afterward, things changed in Lkossa. People stopped looking at darajas as resources and instead saw them as threats. Over the years, they became ostracized, hunted down like—"

"Like animals," Koffi finished. "So that's how magic was lost."

"Not lost." The old woman's eyes twinkled. "*Hidden*."

Koffi frowned. "Hidden?"

The old woman started rocking side to side. "Many darajas fled Lkossa when they felt it was no longer safe, but I believe there is still magic in this city, *and* those with the ability to wield it, even if they do not know it themselves."

Koffi didn't answer. She thought of what had happened in the Hema, the way it'd made her feel. She remembered the sense of release as the candle burst, the clamminess, Mama's words.

If Baaz realizes what you really did and what you really are . . .

There'd been a time when magic had existed in this city, when people had been able to use it. The idea that she could be one of those people felt impossible, but . . . She didn't have another explanation for what she'd done. All her life, she'd been led to believe in certain truths, but there were things Mama had never told her, things Mama had even hidden from her. Why? How much had she known? She stared at her hands.

"Are you feeling well, dear?"

Koffi looked up. The old woman was watching her much more intently now. It almost made Koffi uncomfortable. Slowly, she got to her feet and brushed off.

"Thank you so much for the bread," she said. "It was really kind of you."

The old woman cocked her head. "Have I upset you, child?"

"No." Koffi heard herself answer too quickly, but she didn't take it back. In truth, she barely knew what she felt. She was tired, confused, even angry. Why hadn't Mama told her the truth? Why had she left her own daughter in the dark all this time? She cleared her throat when she realized the old woman was still staring at her. "It's just . . . I'm sure I've taken up enough of your time."

"Nonsense." The woman waved a dismissive hand. "I've quite enjoyed your company, and *actually* . . ." She gestured toward the trinkets. "I could use a young person like you as an assistant, if you were interested?"

Koffi paused, caught off guard. The offer was generous, and incredibly tempting, but . . . something still stopped her. All her life, she'd relied on others to make a way for her, to help her figure out her next steps. If she was going to learn how to survive in this world, she reasoned, she'd have to start finding a way on her own.

"Thank you." She bowed her head. "But . . . I should get going."

"Very well, little one." The old woman nodded, and there was a touch of renewed sadness in her voice. "You should know that the offer stands, and I do hope the gods bring us together again someday. Take care."

Koffi looked over her shoulder a final time before heading down the market's winding roads.

If the city of Lkossa had been stirring when Koffi first ventured through its streets, it had fully risen in the time she'd taken to sit with the old woman. The roads, still packed with vendors, felt even more crowded than before, so compressed with people that it was impossible to walk without being jostled. Someone barreling through the throngs bumped her hard to the right, which caused someone else to yell at her to watch where she was going. It was no longer a beautiful rhythm and flow; the longer Koffi stayed in it, the more overwhelmed she felt. She thought back to the old woman sitting quietly with her blanket of trinkets, almost wistful. It was strange; only a few minutes had passed, but she was already finding it difficult to recall the details of the woman's face. Their encounter felt increasingly dreamlike, though Koffi knew absolutely that it had happened. She focused on the woman's words, on her job offer, and felt the bite of regret. That opportunity had been generous, but she'd said no without real consideration. Once again, she'd reacted instead of thinking things through.

Being an assistant would be good work, a voice in her head reasoned. *You'd have a steady income, maybe even a way out of Lkossa.*

The old woman had said she'd been to the Kusonga Plains before, maybe she planned to return to them; a plan began forming in Koffi's minds rapidly. *Yes.* She would go back and find the old woman, take her up on her offer. Perhaps she could learn a new trade and, just maybe, the old woman could tell her even more about magic. Someone bumped into her back as she abruptly stopped short in the middle of the road, but she didn't care. She had a plan, a way forward, *hope*. She turned on her heels to head back the way she'd come.

And then a hand clapped over her mouth.

Koffi started. A scream rose in her throat as her attacker's grip tightened, but it was muffled in the din of the crowds around her. Another large hand grabbed both her arms and pulled them behind her in a viselike grip, dragging her off the main roads. She winced as a low chuckle filled her ears, and when she took in the familiar smell of spicy cologne, her blood ran cold.

"*Hello*, Koffi," said Baaz Mtombé.

CHAPTER 8

A SCHOLAR OF DESTINY

By the time Ekon returned to the Temple of Lkossa, dawn had shrouded it in mist.

He stared at the old building, at the grand alabaster staircase gleaming in the morning light. It was composed of twenty-seven steps—in theory, a good number.

That was the *only* good thing he'd thought about in recent hours.

For the better part of the night, he'd wandered the city's empty streets, letting the count of his footsteps numb his mind.

Seventy-five thousand, six hundred and twenty-one steps—at last count.

The walking had helped him delay the inevitable for a time, but now the sun was peeking over the eastern horizon. He could avoid the day no longer.

He eased through the same front doors he'd entered the night before, but instead of following the corridor that led to the worship hall, he took a narrower side stairway up to the dormitories. They were quiet at this hour, a line of closed doors muffling the sounds of his sleeping co-candidates. He padded down the passageway to the last door on the right, then opened it with a sigh.

In truth, it had never been much of a bedroom. Wall to wall, it was only seven feet long, and there was always a faint smell of mildew in its air. The furnishings were sparse: a narrow bed, a rickety nightstand, and a secondhand trunk for clothes and books. A tightness constricted in his chest as he looked around. After today, this wouldn't be his bedroom anymore; he wouldn't be allowed to stay in the temple. Sometime this morning, while Fahim and Shomari were moved to the larger and nicer chambers befitting anointed Sons of the Six, *he'd* be moved to . . . he realized he wasn't sure. He and Kamau had essentially grown up in the temple. Their family home was gone, sold shortly after Baba's death. That house belonged to a chapter in his life that was no more, the chapter his mother had lived in. White-hot pain seared through him at the thought of *her*. He couldn't remember the details of her face anymore; he'd only been four years old when she'd left one night. In his memory, there were brief glimpses of her—a flash of copper eyes, short curly hair, a birthmark on her shoulder—but they never lingered. It forced him to cling tight to the things he *could* remember, like silver bangles catching in sunlight, a sweet scent he knew but couldn't place. What would Mama have thought, if she'd stayed to see what became of him?

Again, he heard Father Olufemi's voice.

Effective immediately, your candidacy for the Sons of the Six has ended. You are dismissed.

Each word struck like an arrow, piercing all the soft parts of his ego. He hadn't merely failed; he'd been formally expelled in front of the entire warriorship. In a single night, he'd broken a generations-old legacy for his family. He wouldn't follow in Baba's and Kamau's footsteps. He *wouldn't* prove his manhood.

He flopped down on his mattress, letting its itchy stuffing feathers poke into his back as he glared at the ceiling and tried to figure out how it had all gone wrong so fast. Each moment of the night recounted itself in his mind, blurring together like pages in a book; one in particular stayed dog-eared.

The girl.

Even now, the thought of her made Ekon's blood boil; last night's disaster had been, after all, *her* fault. But then . . . there was another feeling—uncomfortable and harder to identify. Something plucked within him when he remembered her eyes, strangely bright against the night. They'd been brown like his, but . . . they'd held something within them, a glow like two embers cooling in a hearth. He'd tried for hours to forget them, but—

You let her go.

Shomari's accusation curdled inside him like bad milk, leaving a sour taste in his mouth. *Why?* It was the one question he hadn't been able to answer as he'd walked the city's streets alone. *Why did you let her go?*

Thinking of the girl also made him think about the events that had unfolded just before he'd released her, when he'd found a very different set of eyes in the darkness. *That* pair hadn't been brown or warm—they'd been cold, black, and utterly unfeeling. They'd belonged to something he knew.

The Shetani.

He shivered. It had been ten years since he'd last seen the creature, not that anyone else knew that. He remembered the fear he'd felt the moment he'd seen it again, the way it had dismantled him entirely. Unbidden, all the old images returned. He saw flashes of the Greater Jungle with blood on its leaves, envisioned vines covered in thorns. He saw a dead body that looked like . . .

No.

Ekon shook his head, barely noticing the way his fingers had automatically started their dancing.

One-two-three.

He saw Baba's face.

One-two-three.

He saw the Shetani's teeth.

One-two-three.

He saw the girl.

His eyes narrowed. That girl, whoever she'd been, had told the Shetani *Go*, and, without hesitation, it had *obeyed*. He'd never seen anything like it. The Shetani was a primordial monster, responsible for the deaths of countless people. It should have killed them both, but it hadn't. It had done the opposite. The same persistent question ricocheted in his mind.

Why?

"Ekon?"

Someone gently rapped against the other side of his bedroom door, and Ekon sat up as it opened. A frail old man entered the room, the ghost of a smile on his withered face. His chestnut skin was wrinkled and thoroughly spotted, as though age had been welcomed as a friend instead of an adversary. Ekon flinched. In the chaos of last night, he'd forgotten all about Brother Ugo.

"I hoped I'd see you." The elderly man offered a small nod of greeting. "Moved as fast as I could from my chambers after morning prayers, but these old legs just aren't what they used to be." He lifted the hem of his robe. It was deep blue, as finely made as Father Olufemi's, but far looser on his bony frame. "You know, lately they've been mooing."

"Mooing?" Ekon's eyes narrowed. "Your legs have been *mooing*?"

"*Yes.*" Brother Ugo scratched his white beard, frowning as he examined them. "It's a curious thing. You might say I have a . . . *calf* injury." He looked up, grinning. "Do you get it? Because a baby cow is called a—"

"You can't be serious."

"Well, excuse *me*!" Brother Ugo pointed a gnarled finger at him, feigning hurt. Ekon noted with a pang that the slight tremor in the old man's varicose-veined hand was getting worse. "I recall that you used to like my jokes when you were a little boy!"

Ekon tried to swallow the hard lump rising in his throat, the renewed pain. Brother Ugo was the oldest member of the temple's fraternal order, and nothing at all like Father Olufemi. The old man had been a mentor to him all his life, a constant advocate. Ekon hung his head, embarrassed.

"I'd like a word," said Brother Ugo, more softly now. "Walk with me, please."

In silence, Ekon followed Brother Ugo out of his room and through the temple's stone-walled hallways. Their steps were slow—Brother Ugo wasn't as fast as he'd once been—but in time, they made their way to a corridor that led to the temple's library. Ekon had thought that was where they were headed—most of his childhood lessons had been there—but a hint of mischief touched Brother Ugo's eyes as he made an abrupt turn to the right instead.

"Perhaps we might try for a . . . *loftier* view, today," he murmured. He approached a nondescript door and wrenched it open. Inside,

Ekon was surprised to find that what he'd always assumed was just a broom closet actually contained a set of narrow, inclining stairs. He was more startled when Brother Ugo marched up them without hesitation. He followed. They reached a trapdoor at the top of the steps, and the old man gave it a firm push with his shoulder. A sudden shaft of golden light poured in above them, and he wriggled through the opening with unexpected flexibility. Ekon copied the gesture and stuck his head through the door. Then he froze, stunned.

The circular garden that lay before him was like nothing he'd ever seen. It wasn't large—he guessed he could lap its perimeter in under a minute—but almost every inch of it was blanketed with flowers. Lush roses, long-stemmed tulips, even a group of red-gold fire lilies in mid-bloom sprouted from the dark, shimmering soil like some piece of unworldly paradise. When he stared beyond the garden's low walls, he saw the tops of every building in the city. From this vantage point, he guessed they were at one of the highest points of the temple.

"What . . . ?" He looked around. "What *is* this place?"

"It's called a sky garden," said Brother Ugo cheerfully. He closed his eyes a moment and smiled, the very image of contentment. "According to my readings, they were once quite popular among the upper classes, though I'm sad to say they've gone out of fashion in the last century or so."

Ekon marveled at the place. When he looked closer at the ground, he saw that, despite the illusion, hundreds of tiny flower beds had been arranged to give the impression that the flowers grew straight from the stone, but it was still impressive landscaping. "I . . . had no idea this was here."

"To be fair, most people don't," said Brother Ugo. He gave Ekon a meaningful look. "And I wouldn't mind *keeping* it that way, actually. An old friend introduced this place to me many years ago, and it's since become one of my favorites in the city, wonderful for meditations *and* bird-watching!"

He ambled over to a long stone bench in the garden's center and patted a spot beside him. For several minutes, they sat in silence, side by side, before Ekon felt Brother Ugo's gaze.

"Do you want to talk about it?"

"Not really."

"Last night did not go as you would have hoped, I presume."

"It was a *disaster*." Ekon massaged his temples. "An absolute, unmitigated nightmare."

Brother Ugo's eyes flitted to the thorned white rose before them. *"Nightmares hunt like beasts of prey, vanquished in the light of day."* He looked up. "Do you know who said that?"

"You?"

"Good guess!" Brother Ugo smiled. "But no, those words come from a poem written by the esteemed poet and linguist Master Lumumba. Do you know what they mean?"

Ekon shook his head.

"It is an allegory. Those *beasts of prey* represent our worldly troubles," Brother Ugo explained. "Often, we run from painful things and hope that they will tire of chasing us. But in truth, avoiding our troubles simply gives them more sustenance, allowing them to eventually consume us whole. Only when we cast light on them and acknowledge them can they truly be vanquished, allowing our spirits to be free."

112

Ekon didn't know exactly where the words came from, only that they rose from within him and left his mouth before he could stop them. "Brother, could I ask you about something?"

Brother Ugo smiled. "Of course."

"I wonder what you know about . . . the Shetani."

"The Shetani?" The old man's voice sharpened, and at once Ekon regretted asking.

"Sorry, I—"

"No, no." Brother Ugo shook his head, even as Ekon thought he saw something in the old man's eyes imperceptibly change. "There is no need to apologize. I was merely surprised. Though, perhaps I shouldn't be. You of all people would certainly have questions about the creature. I was grieved to hear of its latest attack, such senseless violence." He leaned back slightly on the bench and interlaced his fingers. "What is it that you want to know?"

Ekon paused, considering. A part of him wanted to tell Brother Ugo everything he'd seen last night—about the old woman, the strange girl, *and* his actual encounter with the Shetani—but something held him back. Instead, he said: "I just wondered what's factually known about it, where it came from."

Brother Ugo gave him a measured look, as though evaluating, before he answered. "The Shetani's attacks began nearly a century ago, right after the Rupture," he said quietly. "In fact, much of the reason Yabas and Gedes don't get along today is *because* of the creature; both blame the other side for its terror. Over the years, there have been many attempts to find it, thwart it, even bargain with it, but none have been successful. We at the temple have done our best to keep a record of its death toll, but even that is a sometimes

113

difficult task. To my knowledge, no one who has seen the monster in person has lived to tell the tale."

Except for me, Ekon thought. *Me, and that girl.*

Brother Ugo sighed. "It is certainly a fearsome beast, perhaps one of the most intelligent predators to ever walk these lands."

Ekon tempered a sudden, inexplicable anger. It irritated him to hear his own mentor talk about the Shetani with any kind of respect or admiration. That beast, that *monster*, had taken so much away from him: first his father, and now his chance to be a warrior. If the Shetani hadn't come to the Night Zoo at all, he would have arrested that girl without hesitation and solidified his place as a loyal Son of the Six. He'd thought everything led back to *her*, but he'd been wrong.

It all led back to the monster.

"I did not intend to upset you." Brother Ugo was looking at him more carefully now, as though seeing something for the first time. "We do not have to speak any more of it, if you would prefer—"

"I *hate* it." Ekon slammed his fists hard against the bench's seat. "I wish it was dead." He heard his own anger aloud and paused. "*You* probably think I should be more disciplined."

"What I *think*," the old man said gently, "is that I have no right to judge you, Ekon. I think you are hurting. And if you want to talk about it, I'll always be here to listen."

Ekon sighed. *This* hadn't been what he'd expected this morning. If anyone had a right to be angry with him, it was Brother Ugo. His mentor had spent years molding him into the strongest possible candidate for the Sons of the Six; now it was all wasted. The words tumbled from him.

"My life is *over*."

A hint of surprise, then of mirth touched Brother Ugo's eyes. "Well, that seems generous, given your age—?"

"It's done, Brother." Ekon wanted to look anywhere else, but the old man's gaze held his. "I had a chance to *be* something, the only thing I know how to be. Joining the Sons of the Six was what I was born to do. It was my destiny—"

"Funny." Brother Ugo's white brows came together like kissing caterpillars. "I didn't know you were a scholar of destiny, able to divine the future?"

Ekon opened his mouth, but the old man continued.

"Destiny is not a single path, but many, Ekon. Some are as straight as an arrow, others twist and tangle like thread. Our duty is not to question them but to *follow* them."

"Easy for *you* to say."

The corners of the old man's eyes crinkled, amused. "I follow a path too, Ekon, one that I believe will someday allow me to fulfill my most righteous work. The journey is long, but each day is a gift. And speaking of *gifts* . . ." He reached into the folds of his robe. To Ekon's surprise, when Brother Ugo withdrew his hand, he was holding a leather-sheathed hanjari. It was a simple weapon, unadorned by any jewels or intricate designs on its wooden hilt, but Ekon's breath still caught when he saw the name carved into it.

Asafa Okojo

"This . . ." Ekon's throat tightened. He blinked hard, hating the tears that stung his eyes. "This was my—"

"Your father's," Brother Ugo confirmed. "Found on his person after . . . the accident. I've kept it for many years. In traditional circumstances, it would have gone to your older brother when he came of age two years ago, but . . ." He gave Ekon a sad smile before pressing the hilt into his hand. "You must forgive an old man's sentimentalities."

Ekon stared at the blade, feeling its new weight in his palm. It was crafted in an older style, not as sophisticated as he was used to, but he instantly felt a deep attachment to it.

"Thank you, Brother."

Brother Ugo nodded to the dagger. *"A wise man keeps his weapons sharp, but his mind sharper."* He paused, thoughtful. *"Those* words were composed by a rather excitable master of this temple called Garvicus, curious fellow. I believe Father Olufemi has several of his works in his study; he keeps the oldest volumes there. I really must inquire . . ."

Ekon let the old man's words fade to a faint buzz in the background. He was still staring at the hanjari, feeling the goose bumps on his skin. His baba had held this blade, and he'd kept it with him until the end. He didn't know whether to be awed by that knowledge or terrified.

"Ekon?"

He looked up. Brother Ugo had stopped musing and was now staring at him again. "I wonder, was there a particular reason you wanted to know more about the Shetani?"

Ekon tried to sound offhand. After Kamau, he probably trusted Brother Ugo more than anyone else in the world, but he still wasn't ready to talk about what had happened last night. So he made himself shrug. "I guess I was just . . . curious."

"Ah," Brother Ugo said sagely. "Curiosity killed the cat, but *satisfaction* brought it back."

Ekon massaged the bridge of his nose. "Is that another one of your terrible old-man jokes?"

Brother Ugo crossed his arms, indignant. "As a matter of fact, it is *not*." He paused, stroking his beard. "Though, now that you mention it, I *did* hear a rather crude one recently about a pig, a farmer's wife, and an eloko who walk into a tavern . . ."

Ekon let Brother Ugo's words about destiny and the Shetani steep in his mind as he left the sky garden and wandered the temple. By now, true morning light was seeping through its arched windows, reminding him of the time, but he just couldn't make himself return to his room to pack his things, not yet.

He didn't realize where his feet had led him until he'd reached a short corridor, darker than most. Polished sconces every few feet kept it faintly illuminated at all times, and Ekon didn't have to look at the distinctly black granite walls to know where he was.

Memorial Hall.

Involuntarily, his fingers traced along the cool stone. Nearly every inch of it was covered in tiny inscribed names. There were mostly retired warriors listed, occasionally the name of an esteemed master scholar of the temple. He searched the chronological roster until he found what he was looking for.

WARRIOR ASAFA OKOJO—*Death in Service to the Six*

Ekon looked from the name to the old hanjari now looped on his belt, and fought a shudder. Brother Ugo had said the blade was found on his father's person after the accident.

Accident was a polite way of putting it.

Baba had been found at the edge of the Greater Jungle, mauled nearly beyond recognition. Ekon tried to remember the better things, the crinkles around his father's dark eyes when he smiled, or the way his laugh had boomed like thunder. But those better things, just like the faint recollections he had of his mother, never lingered in his mind. In their stead, far uglier images plagued him. He envisioned an overgrown jungle, a body facedown in its leaves. Ekon screwed his eyes shut, trying to use his fingers to count away the rising nightmare, but it held fast. He watched Baba's body rise from the dirt, mouth open in a silent scream as a creature stalked forward, a being with wretched black eyes and blood dripping from its maw. And then Ekon wasn't seventeen anymore, he was just a little boy—a boy who'd seen everything.

A boy who'd said nothing.

"Thought I'd find you here."

Ekon turned. He hadn't heard Kamau enter the hall. His brother's face was inscrutable. In the sconces' flickering light, he noted Kamau looked even more fatigued than usual. His eyes were bloodshot, his hair was unkempt, and he smelled faintly of something sweet, maybe wine.

"I didn't get much sleep," he said, reading Ekon's mind. "Father Olufemi called for an emergency meeting a few hours ago."

"What about?"

"I can't say." Kamau's stoic expression didn't change. "It's confidential."

Confidential. There was that word again, erected between them like a wall. Ekon thought back to a different time, when he and Kamau had faced everything together. After Mama had left and

Baba had been killed, it had been Kamau who'd found them a new home at the temple. The two of them had carved out a life here, built hopes and dreams together side by side. All of that was gone now.

"I spoke to Father Olufemi about you too," Kamau murmured. "He's agreed to let you stay in the temple."

"What?" Ekon gawked. "How?"

"I reminded him that you've worked here for a decade, that you could still be of service. He said there was a position available."

"Really?"

Kamau didn't meet his eyes. "Brother Apunda is getting older, and he needs help overseeing temple maintenance, especially with the Bonding coming up in two months . . ."

Ekon didn't hide his immediate scowl. Brother Apunda, the temple's head custodian, was a stern old man who always smelled of spoiled legumes. "Kam, I really appreciate you speaking up for me," he said in earnest. "But I don't want to be a custodian. I want to be a *warrior*."

For the first time, Kamau's face held real sadness. "I know," he said. "But it was the best I could do. I'm sorry."

A silence fell between them, and Ekon looked away for a moment. When he lifted his gaze, he found that Kamau was staring at the memorial wall. Not for the first time, he wondered if his brother was thinking about the same thing *he* always thought about when he came here.

"I miss him." He thought he'd said it too faintly for Kamau to hear, but his brother slowly nodded.

"Yeah." The word was choked. "Me too." Kamau shifted his weight. "Look, Ekkie, I know how badly you wanted to be a Son of the Six, and I know you feel like you have to be one to make Baba proud. But what Baba loved most wasn't his uniform or title; it was the fact that he got to serve this city and its people." Kamau looked up. "That's something you can still do as a custodian of the temple. Working here still allows you to serve Lkossa, to be like Baba . . ."

Kamau went on, but Ekon stopped listening. His eyes had wandered, yet again, to his father's name etched into the wall before them. In his mind, only one part of what his brother had said echoed.

Be like Baba. Be like Baba.

In seventeen years, he'd wanted plenty of things—to kiss a girl, to have more time to read in the library, treats from the temple's kitchens—but the thing he'd wanted above all else had been singular; he'd wanted to *be like Baba.* He'd longed to follow in his father's footsteps, the *Okojo family's* footsteps, and to add something worthwhile to that legacy. *That* had been his path, laid out before him as straight as an arrow since childhood. Kamau had gotten to follow that path, but Ekon's path had been taken away, and not because he hadn't earned it or wanted it enough.

His path had been *stolen* from him, by a monster.

The Shetani had taken his father's life, and now, in a different way, Ekon reasoned that it had taken his too. His plans, his hopes, everything he'd spent years working for was gone because of that wretched creature. His fingers tapped out a rhythm, trying to find a new count, but it was futile. There was no way to calculate a loss of that magnitude, to enumerate that kind of pain. He'd never wear the blue kaftan, never have his name added to this wall with his father's when he someday died. His life was over before it had begun, and it was the Shetani's fault. It always led back to the Shetani. His fingers stopped their tapping and curled until he felt the fingernails digging into the flesh of his palm. He wanted that gods-forsaken thing dead, wished with all his heart that someone would—

He stilled.

"Ekon?" In his periphery, he felt Kamau's eyes on him. "You okay?"

"Yeah." Ekon had to work to keep his expression impassive. The idea slowly forming in his mind was no more than a budding sprout; small, impossible, but . . . it was *there*. He was scared to think about it, to even entertain the notion, but he found that once he'd acknowledged it, its roots dug into him, refusing to let go. He chose his words carefully. "I . . . I think I've just . . . figured it out."

"What?" Kamau frowned, visibly confused. "What are you—?"

"My rites of passage," Ekon muttered to himself. "The killings . . . I could . . . Yes, then everything would be fixed . . ." Ekon ignored his brother's arched eyebrow and started to pace. He knew it probably looked strange, abrupt, but he did his best thinking when he was in motion, counting something. At once, his fingers picked up where they'd left off. He listened to the sound of his sandals slapping against the temple's stone floor as he let the idea unfurl in his imagination.

One-two-three. It would be foolish.

Four-five-six. It would be dangerous.

Seven-eight-nine. It would fix everything.

"*Ekkie.*"

Ekon stopped short, feeling dazed. Kamau was staring at him, his expression a cross between mild amusement and genuine concern.

"Let me in," he said softly. "*What are you talking about?*"

Ekon swallowed. They were alone in the corridor, there was no one else around, but he was still almost afraid to speak the words. He lowered his voice. "I think I know a way to get Father Olufemi to reconsider my candidacy for the Sons of the Six."

At once, Kamau's face fell. No longer did he look amused; now his expression held distinct pity. He sighed, and the sound hurt more than Ekon expected.

"Ekon . . ."

"Hear me out." Ekon raised a hand, speaking quickly. He tried not to notice that Kamau was staring at his counting fingers with a disapproving frown. "I failed my final rite of passage." It hurt him to say the truth aloud, but he forced himself to do it. "But what if there's another way for me to prove to Father Olufemi and the brothers of the temple that I *am* capable?"

Kamau's frown deepened. "What do you mean?"

"I mean, what if a candidate performed an act no other Son of the Six has ever managed to do, something that improved the lives of every single person in this city? Surely *that* would make Father Olufemi reconsider."

"It might." Kamau shrugged. "But that act would have to be truly extraordinary, it would have to be something like—"

"Like killing the Shetani?"

It seemed to take Kamau a moment to process the words. Ekon watched as understanding dawned on his brother's face, as his mouth and eyes simultaneously widened in horror.

"Ekon," he whispered. *"No."*

"Think about it, Kam." Ekon closed the gap between them and bowed his head. "If I could find it, if I *killed* it—"

Kamau shook his head. "Ekon, listen to me, you can't—"

"You know, I'm not as incompetent as you think," said Ekon mulishly. "I trained in this temple, same as you."

Kamau looked pained. "It's not that, it's . . ." His words trailed off, and Ekon jutted his chin.

"Tell me."

Kamau shot a furtive look over his shoulder. "You can speak to no one of this."

Ekon nodded.

"You can't go after the Shetani because a hunting party is being assembled to do the exact same thing *as we speak*," said Kamau in a rush.

Ekon drew a sharp breath. "A *hunting*—?"

"Shh!"

He closed his mouth but repeated his brother's words in his head. *A hunting party.* For the first time in a decade, Father Olufemi was going to select warriors to go into the Greater Jungle in search of the Shetani. To be chosen for it would be an unmatched privilege, the highest distinction, an honor.

"Who's been asked to join?" It was the first question that came to him.

"I don't know all the names yet," said Kamau. "Father Olufemi is still making his selections. He wants to make sure there's a good balance of novice and experienced warriors in case . . ."

In case none of them make it back, Ekon finished the unspoken words. He nodded to his brother. "Are *you* going?" He didn't bother to ask if he was one of the ones selected.

Kamau looked uncomfortable. "I haven't decided."

"The meeting you just left, that's what it was about, wasn't it?"

Kamau didn't speak, but his eyes held the answer. "If you go into the Greater Jungle looking for the Shetani, you need to understand that you won't just be contending with what's already in there. The Sons of the Six will be hunting too, the Yaba way."

Ekon swallowed. He knew the rules of the Yabahari, his people's traditional way of hunting. *No mercy.* The warriors going into that jungle would be looking out only for themselves, and anyone else would be treated like the enemy. *He* would be treated like the enemy.

"I know the way a Son of the Six hunts," he said with more confidence than he felt. "Which means I know how to avoid them too. If I just stay out of—"

"Ekon, *listen to me.*" Kamau's voice had changed. He sounded like a true warrior now, more stoic and serious. "This is not a game. The Sons of the Six and the Shetani are each bad enough on their own, but then there's the Greater Jungle itself. You've never even been in it before."

Ekon chose not to mention that, technically, *that* wasn't true.

"Hunting for the Shetani in there won't be like the training you've done here in the city," Kamau continued. "If you make a mistake out on the sparring lawns, it costs you the match. But if you make a mistake in that jungle . . ." He paused. "It may cost you your very life."

"A price I'm willing to pay." Ekon drew himself up to his full height. Growing up, Kamau had always been slightly taller than him, but in the last year, he'd finally had a growth spurt. They were mirrors of each other now, two identical pairs of dark eyes level with each other. "You said so yourself just last night: I'm an Okojo. I was born to be a warrior. It's in my blood, same as it's in yours. It's in our roots. *Kutoka mzizi*, remember?"

Kamau shook his head. "Ekon—"

"Faith and fortitude." Ekon stepped forward. "Last night, Father Olufemi said a true Son of the Six has faith and fortitude. Killing the Shetani would prove I have both."

Kamau's expression hardened. "I might remind you that I am honor-bound to report information like this to Father Olufemi, and to the brothers of the temple."

"Kam." Ekon's voice was barely a whisper. *"Please."*

He wasn't sure if it was the plea itself or perhaps the way he said it, but slowly Ekon watched something in Kamau's expression waver. It was minimal, a single crack in an invisible armor, but it was enough. Like that, Kamau wasn't a kapteni anymore, he wasn't even a warrior; he was just an older brother. He wasn't "Warrior Okojo," he was Kam, the boy who'd once snuck with Ekon from the temple's dormitories down to the kitchens for late-night feasts of red grapes and mango juice. He was the Kam who'd first taught Ekon how to properly hold a hanjari, and who'd patiently drilled with him for days until he got it right. He was the boy who intimately knew what it had been like to lose two parents, because he'd lost them too. And he was Kam, the brother who'd never betray him.

"I won't tell Father Olufemi," Kamau said. "Unless he explicitly asks me. If he does, you need to know I will have no choice but to answer truthfully."

Ekon nodded. His brother had sworn a holy oath of fealty; this half promise was the very best he could offer him as an anointed warrior. Even then, he knew Kamau could lose his position as a kapteni for keeping this secret at all. "Thank you."

Kamau put a hand on his shoulder. "Gather your supplies quickly, and get going as soon as you can," he instructed. There was a fervor in the command. "Father Olufemi will probably need a few more days to organize the hunting party, and *you* need to stay ahead of us. Keep off the more obvious paths, but don't go completely off trail or you'll end up lost. Also, try not to leave tracks." He gave Ekon a meaningful look. "Or anything else that would allow you to be followed."

Ekon nodded. "I won't."

"Remember what you know from your training, be resourceful."

"I will."

Kamau nodded. "You also need to understand that, once you go, you'll be absent without leave, subject to punishment—"

"Father Olufemi won't punish me," said Ekon quickly. "Not when I bring him what he wants, that thing's head."

Kamau offered a half smile before his expression grew more solemn. "Promise me one thing, Ekkie." Abruptly his tone changed. "Promise me that, whatever you do, you won't let trying to find that thing be more important than your life. I can't . . ." He glanced at his feet. "I can't lose you too. You're all I've got left."

Ekon held his brother's gaze, ignoring the tightness in his chest. Never in his entire life had he lied to Kamau. He would have to now.

"I promise," he said. "I'll be back in a few weeks, maybe less."

Kamau nodded.

"I'm going to do it, Kam," said Ekon. "I'm going to find that monster, I'm going to kill it, and I'm going to avenge Baba." *And I will earn my place in the Sons of the Six,* he promised himself. *If it's the last thing I do.*

The Shetani had stolen his destiny. Now Ekon would steal it back.

CHAPTER 9

A TRUTH AND A LIE

Koffi caught a final glimpse of the city's bustling streets before Baaz tossed her into his mule-drawn wagon.

The scents in the air were familiar—hay and sweat and manure—but inside the wood-paneled confines, they were nauseating. For several minutes, the wagon jostled and swayed as Baaz drove, and she listened as the city's sounds grew faint. Eventually, it stopped, and she heard the distinct click of a key turning in its padlock. She tried to shield her eyes as sudden sunlight burst into the darkness, but she was yanked out before she could. She had to blink several times to clear her vision. When she did, her heart seized.

The lawns of the Night Zoo were in ruins, ripped apart and scorched black. Several cages had been toppled, their barred metal doors swinging in the morning breeze. In the midst of them, where the Hema had once stood, there was now little more than a graveyard of crimson scraps, burnt furniture, and a collection of structural rods bent at odd angles that bore an unsettling resemblance to a massive charred skeleton. Koffi stared in disbelief. She'd never really liked the old zoo, but it had been the only real home she'd ever known. It was surprisingly sad to see it this way.

"Koffi?"

She looked up sharply. The voice that had called her name wasn't low and gruff like Baaz's, but friendly and familiar. She turned, and her heart nearly leaped from her chest.

"Jabir?"

The young beastkeeper was sprinting toward her barefoot across the blackened grass, several wild dogs on his heels. It was a strange, almost-eerie refrain to the way he'd run to her just last night. When he reached her, there were no words. She threw her arms around him, squeezing until her ribs hurt. Jabir made a small sound of relief as he hugged her back. After a moment, she held him at arm's length to examine him. His gray tunic's hem was slightly singed, but overall, he appeared unharmed.

"I thought you were gone," she said.

"I made it out." Jabir's voice rasped like someone who'd inhaled smoke. "Just before the Hema came down, luckily. I looked for you and your mother, but it was dark, I couldn't find either of you . . ."

A mixture of both guilt and grief constricted the words in Koffi's throat. She tried to find the right words to tell Jabir what had happened, to explain everything. She had so many more questions too. One of the wild dogs near their feet yipped, and she looked down at it before meeting his gaze again.

"The pups are all okay?"

"For the most part." Jabir picked up one of the smaller ones and cradled it. "Teku's still a little shaken, but—"

"*Girl!*"

They both started. Baaz was still standing by the wagon, his arms crossed, mouth set in an uncompromising line. Koffi looked to him.

"Sir?"

"Come here. *Now.*"

Jabir's grip on her instantly tightened, but Koffi gently pried his fingers off her. If she was about to be punished for running away, she'd wouldn't drag Jabir down with her.

"It's okay," she murmured. "I'll find you in a bit."

Jabir hesitated before nodding and heading back toward the beastkeepers' huts with his pups. She made sure they were far enough away before facing Baaz again. He was still watching her, waiting. She braced herself, then returned to him, careful to stop just short of his reach. Now that she was closer and seeing him properly, she noticed there were bags under his eyes. Several of the fake jewels in his rings had come out, leaving sad empty pockets where they'd once been. Like the Night Zoo, he looked diminished. His gaze swept over her, full of disgust.

"I know it was you," he said without preamble. For a terrible moment, real fear shot through Koffi's body before he added, "None of this would have happened if you'd secured Diko's lead, if you hadn't shouted for everyone to leave the tent and started all the uproar."

Koffi bowed her head. She didn't want Baaz to see her relief. He blamed her—rightfully—for not securing Diko's lead and inciting panic in the Hema, but it seemed he didn't know about the candle. *Good.*

"What happened to Diko?" she asked quietly.

"Who knows?" Baaz threw his hands up. "Half my beasts are dead or gone, and my reputation is in shambles!" He stomped, and

Koffi had to use every ounce of self-control not to snort aloud. Nothing about this was funny, but trust Baaz Mtombé to be theatrical whenever opportunity presented itself.

"Word of this disaster will spread," he went on. "Show attendance will continue declining, and, with it, my profit margins. On top of that, the Kuhani and his committee of curmudgeons have denied my request for financial aid . . ." He seemed lost in thought for a moment before he refocused on her. "And it's *all—your—fault.*"

Koffi swallowed. Of course she'd suspected what was coming, but that made it no easier to contemplate. She imagined the whipping post on the other side of the grounds, no doubt the sole survivor in this wreckage. There would be pain, a lot of pain, but best to get it over with quickly. She regarded her master evenly.

"How many strikes?"

Baaz's eyes narrowed. "What?"

"How many?"

Baaz frowned. "What are you talking about, girl?"

A hint of unease flitted over Koffi. Baaz seemed to genuinely not know what she was talking about, which meant he'd either inhaled too much smoke last night or had far worse plans for her punishment. She wasn't optimistic that it was the first option.

"Aren't I . . . aren't I being sent to the post?"

At last, understanding dawned on Baaz's face, followed by something else. It took Koffi a moment to recognize that what she was seeing slowly spread across the man's face wasn't anger now, but amusement.

"No, Koffi." Baaz said her name quietly, studying her the way a cat might study a cornered mouse. "You're not going to the post. Not this time."

Koffi drew a sharp breath in. "Then . . . what are you going to do to me?"

"Oh, I won't be doing anything to you." Baaz leered. "You'll be doing something for *me*. You see, your little mistake with Diko cost me thousands in damages to this zoo that you cannot repay because you are already indebted to me." He steepled his fingers. "Thusly, I have decided that these new costs will be retroactively added to the current outstanding balance on your indenture contract."

Koffi swayed. "What's that mean?"

"It *means*," said Baaz, "that it will be added to your debts. By my own quick calculations, you should be able to pay it back in approximately thirty-five years, precluding interest."

Koffi felt her last bit of resolve abandon her in a rush, as though someone had wrenched it from her with a violence. The world around her spun, blurred, and she found she couldn't even speak as Baaz's words pierced her.

Thirty-five years. Thirty-five years. Not weeks, or months, but years.

In her mind, she caught snatched glimpses of old memories, the tattered edges of the life she'd had before this one. She remembered being small, sitting atop her father's shoulders one morning as he'd explained that they were going on an adventure. At the time, it had sounded fun, working in a zoo full of interesting animals. She'd been too young back then to truly appreciate the severity of things like terms and conditions, and only after Baba had died had the terrible reality shown its true face. Her father's remaining debt had become hers. For nearly a decade after, she and Mama had worked every single day to pay down those debts, and they'd come so close.

Thirty-five years. Years.

131

Now that debt would increase by thousands.

"That . . . that can't be right." Koffi swallowed the sour bile rising in her throat, tried to still her buckling knees. "You can't just do that. I'm not an adult, I didn't even sign my own indenture—"

"It's done, girl." Baaz's eyes were devoid of any compassion. "And the law is on my side. I will inform you of your new balance once my contractor completes his assessment of the damages and the cost of repairs. In the meantime, get to cleaning, before I change my mind about the post." He eyed the grounds around them, disgusted. "Filthy . . ."

Koffi watched him saunter away, feeling numb. She'd always known the punishment for what she'd done was going to be bad, but this was far worse than anything she could have fathomed. *Thirty-five years.* She was sixteen. Thirty-five years in this Night Zoo was more than a prison sentence; it was an entire life gone—*her* life. She felt as though she was sinking into something, a nightmare she couldn't wake from.

Her feet led her without direction, until she'd stopped before the smoldering remnants of the Hema. Up close, she took in its stink, the sharp smell of burnt things. Her eyes wandered over the blackened debris until they caught on something bright nearly lost among the ashes, something small and brilliant blue. Upon closer inspection, she recognized what it was, and her heart hitched. It was a piece of that turquoise peacock statue, maybe a fragment of its beak, or of its tiny head. She'd always hated the thing, considered it gaudy and ridiculous with its overlong neck and extravagant tail feathers. Now this was all that was left of it, a burnt piece of pale blue stone. Of course the bird had burned. Like everything else in this Night Zoo, it had been a fake, a delusion. *Real* turquoise would have been stronger, able to withstand the fire's heat. It had been a worthless thing all along. Still, as Koffi stared at the piece, a strange sort of grief undulated inside her. She wanted to put that stupid peacock back together again, to put the life she'd had before back together again and create a second chance. In that alternate life, she would never have forgotten to secure Diko's lead, and he would never have attacked the merchant's wife. Mama wouldn't have taken the blame for a mistake she hadn't made, and Koffi would never have done that strange thing with the candle. She wished with all her heart that she could take back every bit of it, trade the wrong choices for the right ones, have a second chance to—

Her breath caught in her chest suddenly. She was still staring at the Hema's remnants, still standing in its ashes, but a single word had ensnared itself in her mind.

Trade.

It happened slowly, pieces clicking together in her mind.

Trade.

She recalled a precise moment from last night in the Hema, a fragment of a conversation she remembered between two people: Baaz and Bwana Mutunga. They'd been discussing something, the Shetani.

That would be quite an addition to your show, would it not? The merchant had said those very words, joking.

Well, a man can dream, Baaz had answered. *But I think I'd have to barter my soul for such an acquisition.*

Trade. Barter. Koffi realized it then. That was the first time she'd heard that word, *barter*; not sitting with the old woman in the market this morning, but yesterday evening from her own master. *Trade. Barter.* The old woman had said something else to her a short while ago.

Anything can be bartered for, if you know its true value.

Anything could be bartered for. Anything.

Koffi's heart hammered in her chest as she spun around, eyes searching the grounds of the Night Zoo until she found who she was looking for. Baaz was several yards away, but certainly within earshot.

"Sir!" she practically shouted as she tore after him, ignoring the pain in her legs as she pushed herself to run faster. "Sir, wait!"

Baaz glanced over his shoulder, annoyed, then fully turned as he saw Koffi barreling toward him. She stopped before him and took a moment to steady her voice before speaking.

"Sir," she repeated. "I want . . . to propose a barter."

Baaz's brows had pinched together in confusion; now they shot up in surprise. "You want to propose a *what*?"

Koffi swallowed. She wasn't sure if the words were right, but she didn't care anymore. This was her last hope, and she had to try. "I said, I want to propose a barter," she repeated more firmly. "In exchange for my indenture contract."

Baaz stared at her blankly for a moment before his expression split between irritation and incredulity. "You can't *barter* with me."

Koffi held her ground. "Why not?"

Baaz narrowed his eyes. "Because you have nothing to barter. You are indebted, *penniless*. You own absolutely nothing."

That was true. All her life, Koffi had been poor, saddled with debts that didn't belong to her. Baaz was right in saying that she didn't *own* anything. But that didn't mean she had nothing.

"I do have something," she said quickly. "The thing you want most of all."

Baaz answered with a refreshed scowl. "And what would *that* be?"

"The Night Zoo's newest attraction, which *I* can procure for you." Koffi bowed her head, trying to look demure. For this to work, she would have to sound convincing, but natural.

"What are you talking about?" Baaz growled.

Koffi took a deep breath. "Last night, after I escaped the Night Zoo and went over the wall, I saw a creature in the lemongrass fields," she said.

Baaz's eyes narrowed. "What *kind* of creature?"

"A massive, terrible beast," she said ominously. "With night-black eyes and teeth longer than my fingers—"

"Your . . . your *fingers*?"

"It's true." Koffi held her master's gaze. If she'd learned one thing from watching him at the Night Zoo all these years, it was how to tell a story, how to capture an audience with embellished words and dramatic pauses. "And I know what it was: the Shetani."

The word's effect was instant; Baaz stiffened. "That's not possible."

"It *is*," Koffi contradicted. "I saw it myself. It came toward me."

"And yet, here you stand." Baaz crossed his thick arms. "*Unharmed.*"

"It didn't touch me," Koffi explained. "It ran away because . . ." She hesitated. *This* was the moment of truth, the tethering of a truth and a lie. "Because I commanded it to go, and it obeyed."

There was a pregnant pause, so long Koffi began to sweat. Baaz stared at her, stunned, then threw back his head with a laugh.

"You . . ." he said between wheezes. "You expect me to believe that you—a scrawny child—gave the Shetani of the Greater Jungle a command and it *obeyed*?"

"I wouldn't be standing here if I hadn't." Koffi kept her expression stoic. "And neither would the warrior who went over the wall and came after me. He was so scared he ended up letting me go."

Baaz stopped laughing at once. A shadow of something passed over his face as her words seemed to sink in, and with them a comprehension she didn't understand. Then she saw a new emotion. Fear.

"You . . . you really saw it in the flesh?" His eyes were round, horrified. "And you really commanded it to spare you?"

"I did."

"How?" Baaz whispered. "How did you do it?"

"Magic hasn't always been confined to the pages of stories." Koffi parroted back the very words the old woman had said to her in the market. "It's faded, but it still exists in Lkossa for a chosen few. *I'm* one of those few."

Baaz raised a finger at her. "What you're saying now is blasphemy," he warned. "I could report you—"

"You could," said Koffi quickly. "*Or* you could change your fortune, significantly."

Baaz stared. "What do you mean?"

"I sent the Shetani away last night," said Koffi. "But what if I could find it and bring it back to the Night Zoo? What if it became your newest attraction?"

"It would never work." Baaz swallowed. "People would never pay to see something so horrid—"

"I know one person who would," Koffi countered. "The Kuhani.

You heard what the merchant said last night. Traders won't come to the city anymore; people are afraid. How do you think the man who controls the deepest coffers in the region would express his gratitude to the person who takes care of his biggest problem?"

She watched as the fear in Baaz's face turned to hunger. She knew then, at that exact moment, that she had him. Her master was cruel, violent, and greedy, but above all else, he was a businessman.

Her performance was nearly done.

"You mentioned a barter," he said slowly, calculating. "What would you trade in exchange for the Shetani?"

"The permanent erasure of my family's debts to you so that I'm free to leave the Night Zoo forever," said Koffi immediately. "Jabir's debt too. And I'll have to go into the jungle to find the Shetani, so I'll also need a small stipend for food and supplies."

"Naturally." Baaz's answering smile was razor-sharp. He tilted his head as though seeing Koffi for the first time. "You know, this *does* put us at what some would consider a conflict of interest. Once I let you leave this place again, you're free to just run off again."

"I'll be back for Jabir," said Koffi. "I won't leave him."

Baaz shook his head. "You already abandoned him once. What's to stop you from doing it again?"

The words stung, and Koffi was suddenly glad Jabir wasn't nearby to hear this conversation. Of course, she hadn't *known* he was still alive and trapped here—she'd immediately assumed the worst—but that didn't change the truth. Baaz was right; she *had* abandoned him. His smirk deepened.

"I think what we need here are some stipulations," he said cheerfully. "To ensure you are truly invested."

Koffi swallowed. "What do you want?"

"Clearly set parameters," said Baaz. "Your little hunt will have a time limit. You have until the start of the monsoon season to find the Shetani and bring it back here. If you do not, I will add an inconvenience fee of seven hundred fedhas to your debts."

Koffi frowned. Monsoon season was almost here, so she only had a week or so at most. *"Fine."*

"If you return on time, but without the Shetani, there will also be an inconvenience fee."

"Got it."

"*Finally*, if you do not return to this zoo at all," Baaz continued, "the new debts you have incurred and the inconvenience fees will fall to Jabir . . . and to your mother."

Koffi froze.

"What?" She tried to disentangle the jumble of thoughts ricocheting through her all at once, demanding her attention.

Mama.

It was impossible, unless it wasn't. Baaz was lying, unless he was telling the truth. *Could* it be the truth? She gnashed her teeth, fighting pain, fighting hope.

Mama.

Violent images collided with beautiful ones in her mind. She saw her mother curled beside her in a hut, singing folk songs under her breath, and she saw the way Mama's eyes had rolled back in her head. She remembered Mama's face, touched by golden morning sunlight, and she remembered Mama's body in a pool of blood.

Mama was alive? How?

"I take it we have a deal?" Baaz offered a sinister smile.

"Where is she?" Koffi's lips were numb.

"Your mother was taken to the infirmary hut last night." He started walking again and looked over his shoulder. "I do hope you plan to keep your side of this barter, girl. The cost of failure is quite high . . ."

Koffi didn't hear the rest of his words. She'd already started to run.

The crooked collection of mud-brick huts in the beastkeepers' quarters seemed so much smaller in the daytime.

Koffi sprinted down the path, feet pounding in the red dirt with each step.

Mama. Mama was *alive*.

In her periphery, she felt people watching her—other beastkeepers who'd perhaps thought her either lost or dead—but she ignored them. Her eyes searched the huts until she noted one at the end of the path, small and unassuming. The infirmary hut. She ran to it and nearly ripped its door open.

An onslaught of smells assaulted her at once, a coppery tang thick in the air, but other smells too, ones she didn't like. She took in wafts of homemade salves, healing herbs, the distinct smell of bandaging linen and ointments. None of the scents were particularly bad, but they felt too familiar; they reminded her of Baba. Her eyes searched the few beds lined up side by side. There were beastkeepers in every single one. Some nursed gashes and cuts, while others were so badly burned she didn't recognize them. She flinched.

You did this, a voice said to her. *They're all hurt because of you, because of whatever you did with the candle . . .*

She tempered the voice as her eyes adjusted to the darkness and settled on a bed at the end of the line. Jabir was sitting beside it with his head bowed. Blood roared in Koffi's ears as she ran to it. Mama was lying on her back, eyes closed. A thin blanket had been pulled up to her bare shoulders, but it wasn't long enough to cover her entirely, and her feet stuck out from the other end. Koffi noted with a pang the bandage near the base of her head. It was stained a dark reddish brown.

"She comes in and out," Jabir explained. "But I think she'll be okay, eventually. I've been making sure someone changes her bandages."

She'll be okay. Those were the only words Koffi heard. *Okay. Mama would be okay.* Her words came out choked.

"Thank you, Jabir. For everything."

Neither of them spoke as they watched Mama's chest rise and fall for a while.

"I was worried for you, Kof," Jabir whispered to her. "I was worried that you . . . that you weren't going to come back."

Guilt pinched in Koffi's chest. The truth was, she *hadn't* planned to come back, but not for the reasons Jabir would have thought. She'd thought there was nothing left for her here, nothing to fight for. Now everything had changed. Not only did she have Mama and Jabir to fight for, but she had a chance to take back something she thought she'd never have again—freedom.

"Jabir," she said quietly. "I'm not staying."

"What?" There was a hardness in Jabir's voice, but beneath it she heard the hurt. "Koffi, you can't run away again. If Baaz catches you a second time—"

"I'm not running away. Baaz knows I'm going," said Koffi in a lower voice. She leaned in. "I've made a deal with him."

A momentary surprise flitted across Jabir's face. He looked like he wanted to ask a thousand questions all at once. Instead, he nodded for her to go on, and Koffi did. She told him everything that had happened, from the fateful moment with the candle to what she'd seen on the other side of the Night Zoo's wall. She told him about the old woman she'd met, and what she'd learned about magic in Lkossa. Finally, she told him about the deal.

"And I told him I wanted your debts cleared too," she finished in a rush. "So we can all leave together—you, me, and Mama."

Jabir didn't say anything, but dropped his gaze.

Koffi paused. "What?"

"It's just . . ." Jabir sighed. "I wish you'd talked to me first, before making that kind of deal."

Koffi opened her mouth to answer, then didn't. She'd thought including Jabir's debt in her barter was the right thing to do, but . . . maybe it wasn't. She hadn't stopped to consider the implications of doing so, it had just felt right, and she hadn't questioned it. At once, Mama's words came back to her:

Sometimes, though, you can't lead with your heart. You have to think with your head.

"I'm sorry," she said in earnest. "I really am. But . . . I didn't want you to feel forgotten. You're as much my family as Mama."

Jabir looked away from her a moment, blinking hard. "You're my family too, Kof." He seemed to gather his resolve. "You know, the Shetani's never been found before, so if you're going to find it, you're going to need help."

Koffi stiffened. "Jabir, you can't come with—"

141

"I'm not talking about *me*." He shook his head. "I mean you'll need some sort of guide to the Greater Jungle, a map."

"Right." Koffi nodded. In truth, she hadn't even begun to think about what she might need for this mission, but a map seemed most obvious. "Any idea where I might find one?"

"None that comes to mind." Jabir massaged his temples. "Didn't you say you were in the market earlier this morning?"

"Yeah."

"Well, you should try there first," he suggested. "There are merchants there selling almost anything you could—"

"Wait a minute." Koffi stopped, eyes going wide. "That's it."

"What's it?" asked Jabir.

"The merchant," Koffi repeated. "Last night, do you remember what Bwana Mutunga told Baaz he traded in?"

"Actually . . . no."

Koffi's heart began to race. "He said his specialty was in *administrative supplies*, specifically for the temple. Papyrus, quills, and Baridian ink for books and—"

"Maps." Jabir's eyes widened with understanding. "There are *maps* in the Temple of Lkossa!"

"Which means that's where I have to go," Koffi determined. "*That's* where I'll find my map to the Greater Jungle." She met his gaze, hopeful. "Think you can help me get in?"

Jabir rubbed his chin a moment, thoughtful. "It wouldn't be easy, but . . . I think I know a way in."

"Thank you." She gave Jabir's hand another squeeze before turning back to Mama's sleeping form. For several seconds, neither of them said anything at all.

"I'm going to hunt it down, Jabir." She didn't know if the words were for him or for herself, but they felt good to say aloud nonetheless. "I'm going to find the Shetani and bring it back, and then I'm taking back our freedom." She didn't say the last words of her promise aloud:

Or I will die trying.

PART TWO

EVEN THE ELEPHANT IS ENTANGLED IN A SPIDER'S WEB.

A TRUE VESSEL

ADIAH

"Adiah!"

I pull my eyes from the glaring sun overhead and snap back to attention. A few feet away on the temple's sparring lawns, Brother Lekan is glowering at me. Not a single one of his gray dreadlocks is out of place, and his mouth is pulled into a stern wrinkly frown. He looks sweaty, uncomfortable—I can't imagine the heavy blue robes masters and brothers of the temple are required to wear are comfortable during the Zamani Region's hot season—but I don't dare to ask. He's carrying his khaya wood staff in hand; my backside has had many unfortunate encounters with that stick, and I'd rather not get reacquainted with it today.

"If you'd prefer to dawdle and daydream . . ." The old master's voice croaks like an old bullfrog. "I can have someone else lead the demonstration—"

"No!" At once, I stand straighter, shoulders back and feet firmly planted as I've been taught—the very picture of a well-trained daraja. "No, teacher, I am prepared."

Brother Lekan's shrewd eyes study me a second longer before, begrudgingly, he gestures for me to step forward. The sparring lawns are usually filled with visiting patrons—some coming to the temple to pray, others coming to watch us train—but today they're closed to the public so that we can practice in privacy. It's a shame, really. I love an audience.

"No showing off." Brother Lekan hands me a short wooden shaft that, to the untrained eye, might look like a sword hilt missing its blade. "Demonstrate the assigned exercise, and *only* the assigned exercise, Adiah."

I nod, needing no further prompting as Brother Lekan steps away and the other watching darajas give me space. This is my favorite part of the day, practical drills, getting to actually work with the splendor. I'm useless in the temple's library, memorizing passage upon passage of boring scripture, but out here on these lawns, I come alive. My grip on the bladeless hilt tightens, and I summon the splendor from the earth. It comes to me as always, more than willing. I feel it hum through my fingers, snaking up my arms and into my hands until it reaches that wooden hilt. I focus my mind, envision what I want to happen, and then it does. Where a blade should be on the sword, an outpouring of iridescent light appears instead, shimmering. It starts out small and thin, like a rapier's blade, but I push more of the splendor into it, until I'm holding what looks like a massive broadsword. Far away—too far away for me to care—someone tuts with disapproval, but I ignore it as the splendor builds in my core. I swing the illuminated blade and hear it sing. I know what I'm supposed to do next—I'm supposed to release the splendor back into the earth—but I can't resist the temptation to hold on to it just a little longer. This energy, this power, feels good, like nothing else I've ever felt before. I will just a little more of it from the earth, and the light-sword starts to change form, the blade growing longer and longer. People gasp, but I'm amazed by it, curious. I wonder how far it will—

"Adiah Bolaji!"

The shout interrupts my concentration, and I falter. At once, I release the splendor as it erupts, thundering loudly before it separates from me and my blade to seep back into the earth. Slowly, I turn and find that the rest of my classmates are standing much farther back than they were before. Brother Lekan is charging toward me, looking apoplectic.

Uh-oh.

"Give me that!" He snatches the wooden sword hilt from my hand without ceremony.

"Hey!" I say before I can stop myself. "What was that for?"

"Undisciplined!" Brother Lekan jabs a finger inches from my nose. "Reckless! Irresponsible! What on earth were you thinking?"

Now it's *my* temper rising. "I was fine." I'm so annoyed, I forget to use the proper honorific when addressing a teacher. "I was in complete control."

"You *thought* you were in complete control." Brother Lekan shakes his head. "If I've told you once, I've told you three hundred thousand, four hundred and twelve times, girl: you *must* stop keeping the splendor within you for so long!"

"It was only for a few minutes—"

"It doesn't matter!" He speaks over me. "The splendor is a powerful force of nature. It is not meant to stay inside a mortal body, even a daraja's. It is meant to flow through you, *in and out.*"

"But I—"

"Enough. I will have a more suitable daraja demonstrate." Brother Lekan dismisses me with a wave of his hand, looking to someone else. "Lesedi, front and center. I'd like you to show the class instead." His eyes cut to me. "Pay attention to her form, Adiah. Watch her *control.*"

My face burns as Lesedi—a short, compact girl with pretty pink beads at the ends of her braids—steps forward. She gives me an apologetic look before taking the wooden hilt from Brother Lekan and moving into the center of the sparring lawns. I go stand among the other darajas to give her space. In truth, I don't want to watch when she closes her eyes and summons a small shot of the splendor from the ground just as I did, but I find it impossible to look away. The blade Lesedi summons is thinner than mine, but looks sharper and more defined. With practiced steps, she twirls the sword through the air in graceful arcs, thrusting and parrying against an invisible foe. Her moves are elegant, choreographed, enviable. I see exactly what Brother Lekan means about her form. Lesedi truly lets the splendor move through her, in and out, like he said; she is a true vessel. It's an admirable display, graceful. It's also weak. I can tell, even from afar, that she's not using the full extent of the splendor; she's not allowing herself to take in as much I did. When she finishes her demonstration, she offers a neat bow, and several of the other darajas around me clap. Notably, none of them clapped for me.

"Well done, Lesedi."

Jealousy pricks at my skin as Brother Lekan takes the wooden hilt—now devoid of light—from Lesedi and offers an approving nod. He saves his scowl for me. "You see, Adiah? *That* is how it's done."

⚜

"The old cow!"

Brother Lekan's words have been echoing inside me all day, still taunting me hours later. I know I shouldn't let them, but I do.

"Did you know that bovines have a typical gestation period of approximately two hundred and eighty-three days?" As usual, Tao, my best friend, is sitting on a bench with his nose in a book. He has a soft, chestnut-colored face and huge umber eyes that still hold an innocence even though we're both fifteen. When I groan and make a face at him, he looks up, combing a hand through his short black dreadlocks.

"What?"

"You know, they're going to make you cut those off soon." I nod to his hair. "Only masters and brothers of the temple are allowed to grow locks."

"Call it aspirational," says Tao, going back to his book, which looks to be about beetles. "Someday, I'm going to be a famous scholar of the temple."

"I don't doubt it."

It's just the two of us here, hiding in our secret spot. Very *technically* speaking, this garden at the top of Lkossa is probably prohibited to us, but not a single one of the masters of the temple has the agility to shimmy up the trapdoor that leads to it, so it is our domain. This high up, songbirds glide through the breeze in blurs of red, chirping and trilling as they pass. Sometimes I sing back to them; today, I'm too annoyed.

"They never let me do anything."

"Who?" Tao asks.

"Brother Lekan, Brother Isoke, Father Masego, all of them." I pace, trying to temper the old frustration. "They never let me really *try*. They're always holding me back."

"*Or* they're trying to teach you," Tao suggests, pinching a hole in his threadbare tunic.

"Hey, whose side are you on?"

"Yours." Finally, Tao closes his book, his expression softer. "I'm always on your side, Adiah."

It's true. Tao has been my best friend since we were ten, and a loyal one at that. Five years later, he's probably my *only* real friend.

"I know." I stop my pacing and sit beside him, resting a head on his shoulder. He smells like ink and leather. "I just don't understand."

I feel Tao stiffen against me for a moment, his heart pattering against my ear before he relaxes again. When he speaks, he sounds unusually nervous. "Uh, understand what?"

"How can I be taught to use the splendor *well* if no one wants me to ever use the full extent of it, to explore its true potential?"

"Maybe that's the point." Tao's voice has changed, but I can't put my finger on why. My head is still on his shoulder, so I can't see his expression either. "Maybe you're not supposed to know the full extent of the splendor. It could be dangerous."

"Yeah," I murmur against his tunic. The cotton is soft against my cheek, warm. "You're probably right."

"You'll master all of this eventually, Adi." Tao props his head against mine, sighing. "You just have to keep working at it, keep practicing. I believe in you."

I offer a nod so he knows I've heard him, but I don't say anything else. Tao has been my friend and confidant for so many years, but . . . he isn't a daraja. It's just one more thing that differentiates us. Tao is a boy, I am a girl. Tao is an orphan, I am not. Every year as we grow older, we grow a tiny bit further apart, the differences becoming more noticeable. When we were ten, I felt like there was nothing I could tell Tao that he wouldn't understand. Five years later, there are lots of things about me that I don't think my friend understands. Tao thinks my biggest fear is that I won't master my power with the splendor, but in truth, that is not what I fear most.

My fear is that I'll never get to use it.

CHAPTER 10

On the Subject of Monsters

Perhaps more than in any other place, Ekon found his home in books.

He inhaled, taking in the familiar smell of old books all around him, listening to the faint creak of his chair as he shifted in it. Around him, the leather-bound tomes of the Temple of Lkossa's library seemed to reach into the heavens, stacked so high that some shelves required ladders to reach. In the time he'd been there, he'd counted one thousand nine hundred and eighty-six volumes. He knew there were thousands more, but he stopped there—best to leave things on a dividend of three.

He closed his eyes and listened. Distantly, he imagined he could hear the low hums of the temple's brothers in the adjacent wing's worship hall, the scuffle and slide of their sandals as they prepared for the day's visiting patrons. It wouldn't stay quiet much longer; eventually, he'd be called away. He opened his eyes again and sighed.

The table he was sitting at was surrounded by books of every size, color, and genre. There were yellow-paged dissertations like

154

Master Kenyatta's *In Defense of East Eshōzan Dendrology*, thicker-bound treatises like Master Azikiwe's *A Chronicle of Curious Creatures*, even a somewhat-concerning old pamphlet on the varying benefits of carnivorous plant life written by a scholar simply called Nyerere. The published works around him were considered priceless treasures, the very history of his region and his home carefully recorded and preserved.

And yet, *none* of them were helpful.

Ekon inhaled again, but this time the exhale was more frustrated. He liked books, generally speaking, because they could be trusted to be consistent. A book could be read a thousand different times, a thousand different ways, but the words on the page would never change. *Unlike* people, books couldn't be disappointed in you. They couldn't abandon you; they couldn't fail you.

Well, until now.

One-two-three.

He watched his fingers find that easy rhythm, a beat that felt steady.

One-two-three.

Three. Three was a good number.

He shifted one of the stacks on the table just slightly so that they were even, arranged from thickest and largest to smallest and thinnest. He didn't need to do that quite as much as he needed to count, but the exercise still brought him some comfort.

He'd been there for hours searching through books. The sun seemed to be mocking him, deliberately growing brighter to remind him of the time. A piece of his brother's words echoed in his mind.

A hunting party is being assembled.

Kamau had said it would happen over the next few days, but he hadn't said exactly *when* the warriors would then head into the Greater Jungle. That bought Ekon some time, but not much—he had to figure out a plan to hunt down the Shetani before then.

He had to beat them there.

He screwed his eyes shut, recalling the moment he'd last seen the Shetani. He remembered its teeth and eyes well enough, but the most vivid part of the memory was the fear. It had gripped him, then consumed him like a living thing, and it wasn't the first time. He'd now seen the Shetani twice and lived to tell the tale; both times, he had been completely useless when it came time to face it. He hated himself for feeling that way, but it couldn't be helped.

He needed a way to *defeat* that fear.

Behind closed lids, he reimagined the entire scene outside the Night Zoo's walls. He saw the creature stalking forward, then stopping short as something distracted it. The girl. The thought of her still plagued his mind almost as much as the monster, but for an entirely different reason. That girl had single-handedly faced down the Shetani; more than that, she'd commanded it.

Go.

He heard her voice, the calm in it. She hadn't even had to yell. She'd given the monster a simple order, and it had obeyed, returning to the jungle without a second glance. He gnashed his teeth. What he would give for that kind of ability, for that *lack* of fear. The girl's face swam in his mind, and he groaned. It had been foolish to let her go. No doubt she'd left Lkossa entirely by now.

His eyes flitted to one book sitting on the very edge of the table, small and opened up so that its pages seemed to soak in the morning sunlight. He'd cast that particular book aside early in his browsing, but he picked it up again. It was brown, the binding was unraveling slightly, and its etched title was barely visible. *Myths and Fables of the Eshōzan Continent*. He turned to its index until he found the reference he needed—page 394. He flipped to it and let his eyes skim until he found what he was looking for, a single stanza, written in tight elegant calligraphy:

On the subject of monsters, those mundane and those divine, none is so wretched and feared as the Shetani. It is a vicious thing, and a cursed thing, surely to be cast away by gods and men alike. We the scholars of the Temple of Lkossa's Great Library thusly deem that no literature about it shall be recorded or preserved, except for a simple record of those whose lives it takes.

He groaned. Useless. The words were useless. He already knew the Shetani was *a vicious thing*, knew that it had killed plenty of innocent people. What he needed was a book that gave him information about its origins, its diet, its weaknesses. He stared down at his baba's hanjari, still looped into his belt. Could he kill the thing with a simple dagger? He thought of how big the creature had seemed and shook his head.

No, better to go with a longspear, or two—

"Okojo!"

Ekon jumped. He'd been so lost in his thoughts that he hadn't even heard Brother Apunda enter the chamber. The old man had a stooped back, a sagging belly, and a concerning amount of white hair peeking out of his ears. He was regarding Ekon much the way one might regard a spider in their morning tea.

157

"Sir." Ekon stood to attention at once. Brother Apunda's eyes narrowed.

"You're supposed to be shelving the medical journals for Brother Ifechi," he croaked, voice full of disapproval. He pointed to the other side of the room, where the aforementioned journals were still stacked, notably untouched. "What *are* you doing in here?"

"Uh—uh—" Ekon stammered. "Well, I was . . ."

"Never mind." Brother Apunda waved a dismissive hand. "You're needed elsewhere. I'm afraid Brother Dansabe's gout has gotten him again, so in his stead you're going to supervise the apprentices while they muck out the stable this morning."

"I—" Ekon barely hid his disbelief. He wanted to spend this morning in the library, not in the stable. "But, sir—"

"That is . . ." Brother Apunda raised one bushy gray eyebrow. "Unless *you'd* like to do the mucking yourself? It needs to be done quickly, as the temple will be opening to patrons in an hour."

Ekon shut his mouth quickly. Two days ago, he'd lost a lifelong dream, his chance to prove his manhood, and his opportunity to fulfill a family tradition. He wasn't interested in adding his personal dignity to this week's losses.

"Sir." He bowed his head and kept his voice level. "I'll go immediately."

If Ekon loved the Temple of Lkossa's library, then he hated its stable.

He scrunched his nose on principle as he descended the last set of stairs and headed down the hall that opened up to it. Down here, in the temple's literal bowels, there was no faint smell of ink and parchment, only the clashing smells of old wood, sweet hay, and mucked dung. It was a place of unending noise, of constant movement. There was no order here, no calm—it was just the opposite of a library.

He stepped onto the straw-swept floor and frowned. Wooden stalls contained under a thatched roof stretched for several yards in every direction, full of the temple's varying livestock. There was no one else in here that he could see, and he noted that the broad shovels and pitchforks typically used for mucking were still propped against a wall to his right, untouched. It took exactly one more minute before he heard the distinct groan of a cow in distress on the other side of the stable. His eyes narrowed. By the time he turned a corner and found the three apprentice boys crowded around the poor creature's udders and snickering as they sprayed each other with milk, he was in a foul mood.

"What are you three doing?" He almost winced at the sound of his own voice. He may not have been an anointed Son of the Six, but he could certainly talk like one. At once, all three boys whirled around. In different circumstances, the looks of terror on their faces might have almost been funny.

"Sir!" One of them, a scrawny boy no older than thirteen, spoke up first. His eyes stayed downcast. "We were . . . uh, just waiting on Brother Dansabe—"

"Brother Dansabe is indisposed today." Ekon shook his head and crossed his arms. "So *I'll* be supervising you this morning. First services of the day begin in less than an hour; is there a reason you haven't started your work?"

"Uh . . ."

"What? Think you're too good to do what every man in this temple has once done?"

All three of them bowed their heads, chastened. One at a time, they mumbled quiet apologies.

"Get to work, then, starting with the pigsty first." He paused, then added: "And don't touch the cow's udders anymore. It's immature and probably blasphemous."

Ekon watched with a small pang as they bowed in respect, then scampered off without another word. In a sad way, he felt for those boys. Years and years ago, this had been one of his and Kamau's jobs as temple apprentices. Technically, apprentices were supposed to start their work at age twelve and gradually matriculate into higher roles, but Kamau—ever charming, ever likable—had appealed to Father Olufemi. With the help of Brother Ugo, who'd unofficially taken them on as wards, they'd become two of the youngest apprentices in the temple's history. Ekon sighed. Even from boyhood, Kamau had been saving him. He hadn't appreciated at the age of seven how bad it was to have no parents, to be an orphan in a place like Lkossa. In any other circumstance, he and Kamau would have been sent to one of the city's orphanages, and perhaps they would have been separated, but his brother hadn't let that happen. From the time they'd been little, Kamau had protected him from the worst things this world had to offer. He'd always tried to find a way for him. Yesterday, he'd done it again.

Promise me that, whatever you do, you won't let trying to find that thing be more important than your life, he'd said yesterday. *I can't lose you too. You're all I've got left.*

You're all I've got left.

Ekon sighed. By not telling Father Olufemi about his plans,

Kamau was helping him, but also giving up the one thing he had fought so hard to hold on to—his younger brother. He was making a sacrifice, letting go of the one thing he had left.

Ekon couldn't waste that kind of sacrifice.

With the apprentices off doing their work, he was alone, but that didn't make him feel better. He didn't want to be there; he wanted to be in the armory gathering weapons, in the kitchen grabbing food, and in the library collecting information. He thought of that stack of books he'd left. None of them had had what he'd needed, so he'd have to go back to the shelves as soon as possible. He'd mostly looked at academic papers, but maybe there were more encyclopedias behind the medical journals Brother Ifechi had asked him to shelve . . .

He stopped midthought, stunned. Journals. *Journals*. Of course.

There was a book that would have information on the Shetani, information about the Greater Jungle and everything he needed. Of course, why hadn't he thought of it sooner? It had been obvious.

Master Nkrumah's journal.

He'd only seen it once, many years ago, when Brother Ugo had shown it to him in passing, but he still remembered it vividly. A green hardback book with golden lettering on the cover and deckle-edge pages. He remembered the book because he thought it had looked beautiful, magical, like something cast from another world entirely. Goose bumps covered his arms the longer he thought about it. Yes, a journal like that of Satao Nkrumah— a famous scholar of Zamani natural history—would surely include vital information on the Shetani. After all, the man had probably been around when the Shetani's attacks had first started all those years ago.

Yes.

His heart began to race. Where would a journal like that be kept? The temple's library was plausible, but unlikely. Master Nkrumah's journal would be considered invaluable because of its age, almost sacred. He suddenly recalled something Brother Ugo had said to him just yesterday.

I believe Father Olufemi has several of his works in his study; he keeps the oldest volumes there.

Of course, Father Olufemi kept the temple's most treasured books in his study, which meant if he wanted Nkrumah's journal, he'd have to find a way to—

His thoughts were interrupted by a whisper.

"This is as far as I can take you."

Ekon stilled, not daring to move an inch. From his place leaning against one of the stable's walls, he was partially obscured in shadow. He squinted between the partition's wooden panels, curious, and noted that two people had just stopped mere feet away on its opposite side, a boy and a girl. He could see them, but they couldn't see him. Both were wearing identical gray tunics that had seen better days. The boy was facing him and looked a few years his junior. He was the one who'd spoken before. He cleared his throat, then went on.

"You're on your own from here." His whisper sounded raspy, like someone getting over a sore throat. "You sure you want to do this? The penalty for trespassing in the temple—"

"I have to," the girl replied quickly. Her back was turned away so that Ekon couldn't see her face, but he was surprised to find her voice almost sounded familiar, like the tune of a song he'd heard before but couldn't place. He leaned in slightly, trying to hear more without being noticed.

"Then, good luck," said the boy. "I love you. We both do."

Ekon tensed, and for a moment all thoughts of the Shetani and finding Nkrumah's journal were abandoned. He didn't fully understand what he was overhearing, but he didn't like the sound of it at all.

There was a pause, and then the girl spoke again. "I love you too."

Ekon watched the boy and girl hug, then pull apart. The boy offered a final nod before turning on his heel and heading toward the stable's exit. The girl faced the opposite direction. She was eyeing the entryway that led into the temple, the very entry Ekon had come through just minutes before. He could still only make out a sliver of her profile, but yet again something plucked within him. A second passed in which the girl squared her shoulders, as if bracing herself. She cocked her head left and right, searching a moment, before she started for the entry. She didn't run, but her steps were quick, lithe, and silent like a stalking cat's. Ekon couldn't believe what he was seeing. An intruder was trespassing in the temple before his own eyes. He watched the girl cast one final wary look over her shoulder as she reached the doorway; then she disappeared into the building's shadows.

He waited a beat, then followed.

CHAPTER 11

A FAIR TRADE

Lkossa had been beautiful once.

Of course, Koffi had been born long after that golden age, but she still tried to imagine it as she traversed the city's ancient streets. It didn't help much, anxiety and nerves still clung to her insides like maize porridge, but she forced herself to appear relaxed as she walked, trying to remember to swing her arms with each step so she didn't look stiff.

"We're almost there."

Beside her, Jabir's face was a picture of calm. He pressed closer to her so that their shoulders were nearly brushing. "You ready?"

Koffi nodded but didn't trust herself to speak. She'd been up since dawn, going over every detail of the plan in her head. With each step, her grip on the strap of her burlap shoulder bag reflexively tightened. There wasn't much in it—two apples, a dented water gourd, and the small purse of copper shabas Baaz had begrudgingly given as a "stipend" for her venture—but she pulled the bag closer. That meager allowance was the most she'd ever had to call her own. Each clink of the coins at her side was a metallic reminder, a goading force driving her forward. She *would* succeed in this, she had to—the price of failure was too high.

She swallowed hard and tried not to even think about that possibility.

Her toe stubbed on a loose rock in the street, and she felt a jolt of pain. For one hopeful moment, she thought it might be that strange tingle she'd sensed in her feet before, but all too soon it subsided, utterly ordinary. She picked at her fingernails as she thought of yet another thing to add to her list of worries. Her magic. It still felt strange to acknowledge it, like answering to a name that didn't belong or slipping into clothes that weren't quite the right size, but she made herself say it in her head. Magic, she had some kind of magic in her body. She thought of the old woman at the market, of the things she'd said; then she thought of her mother. For whatever reason, Mama had chosen not to tell her about magic, but Koffi couldn't dwell on that now. There was no time to think about where her magic came from; she needed to know what she could do with it. Could she find the Shetani with it, and if she did, could she order it to obey her again? The question went unanswered within the walls of her mind.

They turned onto a new road, and Koffi eyed the massive golden gates at its end, heralded by two Sons of the Six. Well-dressed people in flowing dashikis and wax-print dresses were passing through with no trouble . . . She resisted the urge to look down at her own clothes. She'd washed again before she left the Night Zoo, but that hadn't drastically improved the state of her old beastkeeper tunic.

Nothing to see, she willed as they neared the gates. *Just let us pass.*

She dropped her gaze, listening to the easy rhythm of Jabir's breathing. Her teeth ground together as she felt one of the warriors' eyes on her, but just as quickly, he looked away. The corners of Jabir's mouth quirked just slightly as they passed under the arch.

"Told you we'd be fine," he murmured. "They recognize me."

Koffi said nothing, but her shoulders relaxed just slightly. Phase one of the plan had been a success. Beside them, there was a loud, woeful bleating that made them both jump, and Koffi looked down at the goat staring indignantly back up at them with large brown eyes. Tied around its neck was a rope, which Jabir was holding on to. As though delighted to have their attention, the goat bleated again. In answer, Koffi frowned. It was best not to dwell on the fact that this entire plan hinged on the silly creature.

One of Jabir's odd jobs at the Night Zoo was to deliver a Zamani goat to the temple every week for ritual sacrifice. Normal, common goats were easy enough to procure, but Baaz had convinced the Kuhani some time ago that purebred Zamani goats were better, thus creating a standing agreement and the perfect excuse for two beastkeepers to enter a temple they normally would never be permitted in. Not the most sophisticated plan ever contrived, but the only one they had.

The din of the city's markets and vendors faded as they made their way up a well-manicured red dirt path lined with blue Zamani tulips and Lkossan fire roses. In the distance, the imposing grandeur of the temple came into view. Koffi gnawed her lip. From the vantage point of the Night Zoo, she'd only ever seen the barest glimpses of Lkossa's namesake temple; up close, it seemed more than a little daunting. It was a complicated structure, all doors and windows and pillars and wings added on over the years, and also

166

far too bright. Even in the pale early-morning sunlight, the white alabaster of its front gleamed painfully in her eyes. She squinted and just made out clusters of well-dressed people congregating on its beautiful front lawns. Some were gathered at the top of the stairs.

"They're waiting for the morning shukrani service," Jabir explained. "The stable is around back. This way."

They continued around the temple's main entrance until they'd reached the large stable. It had been built from wood and iron, and was by far the most beautiful and well-kept stable she'd ever seen, certainly far nicer than anything in the Night Zoo.

"Why does a temple even *have* a stable?" she muttered.

Jabir's eyes cut to her, amused. "They sell 'anointed' goods— milk, eggs, wool. They keep their own animals so the products are 'authentically' from the temple. What's a theocracy if not occasionally profitable?"

"Corrupt."

"Isn't that what I said?"

Koffi rolled her eyes, then almost immediately tensed. A young man was standing at the opening to the stable, staring straight at them with arms crossed. She didn't think he was a Son of the Six—he wasn't wearing the distinguishing sky-blue kaftan, and he didn't look quite old enough to be a warrior—but seeing him still didn't put her at ease.

"State your business here." His voice wasn't deep, and he wasn't much taller than Koffi, but he made a point of looking down his nose at them as they stopped before him.

"Good morning, sir." Jabir bowed his head, keeping as much of his Gede inflection from his words as he could. It was almost startling. "We have brought this week's Zamani goat for the temple's ritual sacrifice."

"I'll take it from here." The young man advanced, but Jabir raised a hand in warning. Had Koffi not known him better, she'd have actually believed the concern on his face was genuine. He was an exceedingly good actor.

"Sir, with all due respect, I think it best if we take this one into the stable ourselves," he said, voice solemn. "Shida can be . . . temperamental. She's been giving us trouble all morning—lots of kicking."

The young man's scowl deepened as he looked between the two of them and then at the goat. "Give her here, now."

Koffi stiffened, but Jabir seemed to be expecting this. He shrugged, offering up the rope.

"As you wish," he said. "But I should also warn you . . . Shida has a problem with her, um . . . well, with her poops."

It was so subtle, Koffi might have missed it if she'd blinked. Jabir's fingers twitched, the subtlest of hand commands. The watching goat obeyed, moving into a distinct squatting position as though it were about to . . .

"All right!" The young man stepped back, face twisting with disgust. Apparently, while a kicking goat was permissible, a pooping one was a problem. "Take her to stall three, then see yourselves out." He looked over his shoulder at two other similarly dressed boys. They were gesturing to him. He gave Koffi and Jabir one final glance before running off to join them. Once he was gone, Jabir turned to Koffi.

"Follow me."

They ducked into the stable and made an immediate right. They passed several pigsties, mules nibbling quietly on bits of hay, even some guinea fowl. When they reached an empty stall with a hand-painted 3 over its entrance, Jabir stopped.

"Sorry, my friend," he said, looking to Shida. In answer, the Zamani goat bleated back at him. He stooped down and gave the goat a light pat on its head; it was a surprisingly sad gesture. He straightened, then lowered his voice. "I've got to head back to the Night Zoo. That door"—he pointed to a large entryway on the other side of the stable—"leads into the actual temple. I've never been inside that part, but I know this is the bottom floor. Find stairs and go up. Any maps would be kept on higher floors. This is as far as I can take you. You're on your own from here." He paused. "You sure you want to do this? The penalty for trespassing in the temple—"

Koffi swallowed. The truth was, she *didn't* want to do this; she was terrified. She made sure her voice was even when she answered: "I have to."

Jabir held her gaze a second longer. "Then, good luck." He paused. "I love you. We both do."

It was almost too much. Koffi choked on the words. "I love you too."

He pulled her into a hug, and she let him, hoping he couldn't feel her trembling from head to foot.

When they broke apart, he gave her a nod, then without another word, he headed toward the stable's exit. She wanted to watch him go, to make sure he got back to the Night Zoo safely, but there was no time. She looked to the entryway Jabir had indicated, braced herself, and started in that direction. More than anything she wanted to run, but she forced herself not to. The hallway leading into the temple seemed to grow larger as she neared it, and she had to temper the distinct feeling that it was going to swallow her. In one moment, she was before it; in the next, she'd plunged into darkness, alone.

The air seemed to cool with every step, gray stone walls all around her pressing in. Instinctively, she reached into her shoulder bag, fingers wrapping around the neck of the old water gourd. It wasn't much of a weapon at all, but worst-case scenario, it would have to do. Gedes weren't allowed in the Temple of Lkossa under any circumstances; to be caught here would not only ruin her mission, but it would also almost assuredly land her in serious trouble with the Sons of the Six. There were rumors the city's worst criminals were kept in another part of the temple, in a cellar perhaps even lower than this. She shuddered at the thought of being thrown into one of those cells.

She turned a corner, letting her free hand trace along the walls to gain a sense of place. Despite the many windows she'd seen from the outside as she and Jabir approached, this part of the temple appeared to have none at all; save for the occasional sconces mounted on the walls, there was little light. Slowly, she made her way up the halls. It seemed this was a place where odds and ends were kept too; every few feet, her toe stubbed against an old broom or mop, a broken chair long since forgotten. A dull ache spiked up her foot when she stubbed it yet again, but this time, she actually stopped. In the flickering light it was difficult to make out the old statue propped against the wall, but she still recognized its likeness: Badwa, goddess of the jungle.

It was said that each of the six gods had been born from the universe's own teardrop, three drops each from two eyes to create six immortal beings. Mama had taught her about them through stories. Koffi knew all their names and realms, but it was still strange to see the great goddess's likeness before her, so large, so grand. Badwa's face was rounded, her cheeks full, as though she were on the verge of smiling. Black and green mold had begun to cover one side of her face—no doubt the reason this statue had been relegated here—but the goddess didn't seem to mind. Koffi was still studying her, eyes dropping to the large stone snake carved at her feet, when she heard it.

"Hello?"

Her blood ran cold. She barely had time to dart behind the statue before she heard footsteps. They weren't loud or confident like the march of a Son of the Six; these were softer, more hesitant. She crouched behind the statue, willing herself to keep still even as the footsteps drew closer.

"Hello?" A voice rang out again in the darkness, distinctly low and male. The accent definitely belonged to a Yaba. "Who's there?"

Koffi's grip on her gourd tightened. She had two options, and she was going to have to decide on one fast. If the owner of that voice stayed where he was, there was a chance he wouldn't see her and would eventually go away. But if he got much closer, he *would* see her—and then she'd have to act. She tried to recall anything she'd learned at the Night Zoo that could help her, and drew a blank. Beasts were predictable; humans were not.

Her breath grew shorter as the footsteps drew nearer, louder. Sweat slicked her palm as, slowly, she shrugged her bag off and eased it onto the ground. Better to have the full range of her arm.

Fight, then flight, she silently instructed, bracing herself. *On the count of one, two, three . . .*

She leaped from behind the statue with a cry, the arm holding her gourd high, but stopped short.

The young man standing before her was tall, lean in build. He wore a plain white kaftan with light blue embroidery around the neckline and hem. His dark curly hair was cut into a precise top fade, prominent against his brown skin. A leather-hilted hanjari was sheathed into a belt on his hip, but that wasn't what numbed her.

It was that she *recognized* him.

She'd seen him in the Night Zoo, coming after her and Mama. The memory returned to her, vivid. She remembered the way the boy had looked at her, the scary focus she'd seen in his gaze as he and another boy ran across the zoo's grounds. That fierceness was gone now, and he seemed younger, maybe not much older than her.

"You." He spoke first, his eyes going wider still as he seemed to come to the same conclusion. "You're . . . you're her."

No, no, no. Koffi nearly swore. This was even worse than she could have imagined. She raised the gourd threateningly. It looked even less intimidating taken out of her bag, but she still held it firm.

"Get back." She said the words through her teeth and hoped they sounded more intimidating than she felt. "I—I mean it."

The boy looked from her to the gourd in her hand. To her dismay, his expression went from alarmed to distinctly confused. "Wait, were you going to hit me with that?"

172

Were. He was speaking in the past tense even though she was still holding the gourd. He was speaking as though he'd already decided she wasn't a threat to him at all. For some inexplicable reason, that didn't scare her, it annoyed her. She took a step closer, clutching the gourd so hard she heard two of her knuckles crack.

"I still will, if you don't get out of my way."

"Your grip is wrong."

"What?"

"I mean . . ." Now there was no mistaking it; the boy looked . . . embarrassed. One of his hands dropped to his side, drumming against his side impossibly fast. He looked lost for a moment before speaking again.

"I saw you come in through the stable," he said with more authority. "You're trespassing, and you have exactly one minute to explain why."

Koffi stepped back. This wasn't part of the plan. She tried to think of what her friend would have done in a situation like this, but she and Jabir weren't alike. Jabir was sweet-faced, and clever, and quick-thinking. He knew how to be charming, how to make people like him. Koffi didn't know how to make people like her, but she did know how to lie.

"Money." The word escaped Koffi before she could stop to consider it. "I'm here for . . . money."

"Money?" The young man was still standing several feet away from her; now one of his eyebrows rose. "You came to the Temple of Lkossa for *money*?"

"That's right."

The young man shook his head. "There are literally a thousand other places in the city where it's easier to get money."

173

Not enough for what I need. She met his gaze and hoped she looked earnest. "Why pay for milk when I could steal the cow?"

"I don't believe you." He was still staring at her, and it was hard to read the look on his face. "I remember you. I let you go, just outside the Night Zoo." His face grew stormy. "Why are you *here*?"

He doesn't know. It registered in Koffi's mind instantly. The last time this young man had seen her outside the Night Zoo's walls, she'd been a runaway. He had no idea about Baaz or the deal she'd struck. She could play this to her advantage. She jutted her chin, hoping she looked defiant.

"Like I said, I need money."

She didn't like the way he was regarding her. Gone was any sense of hostility or wariness as he studied her.

"How did you do it?" he asked after a moment.

The question perplexed Koffi. That certainly wasn't what she'd been expecting. "Do . . . what?"

"That thing with the Shetani," said the young man. "You sent it away. You made it listen to you."

At once, Koffi stiffened. Even as he said the words, memories of the night before last had already started to return to her. They were hazy recollections, but certain parts stayed fixed in her mind. She remembered an open field of lemongrass, a starry night sky, and a beast, larger and more terrible than any creature she'd looked after in the Night Zoo. There'd been no explanation for what she'd done when she'd seen it; her hand had reached out of its own accord as though pulled by a puppet master's string. She had felt, in the space of that brief moment, strangely drawn to the beast. That wouldn't bode well for her, especially if this boy took her to the Kuhani.

"I didn't do anything." She was still trying to sound confident, but her voice was failing her. The memory was still too real, too close. "I swear."

"I know what I saw." The young man stepped forward, and she instinctively mirrored the gesture by moving back. For a moment he looked undecided; then he raised his hands. "And I don't think you're here for money."

Koffi cursed. There was no use denying it. She was caught. "Fine. I'm here because I'm . . . looking for a map," she said as evenly as she could manage.

"A map?" This seemed to catch the young man off guard; his expression changed entirely. "A map of what?"

"The Greater Jungle."

The boy's eyebrows shot up. "Why?"

"So that I can hunt down the Shetani." Koffi felt the power of the words as they bounced off the hallway's stone walls. She watched a momentary shock pass over the young man's face, a look she didn't fully understand, but she kept on. "I want to find it again."

The young man cocked his head. "There are plenty of maps here in the temple," he said slowly. "But you won't be able to read any of them."

Koffi stiffened. "What are you talking about?" This was a trick; he was clearly trying to throw her off. She wouldn't let him.

The young man's expression didn't change. "The masters of the Temple of Lkossa read and write in the traditional language of academia, Old Zamani," he explained. "It's nothing like normal Zamani. It takes years of study to learn; even then, not everyone can pick it up."

Koffi felt something inside her deflate. Mama had made sure she could read and write in Zamani—even if her penmanship was barely legible—but she couldn't speak any other languages. If what the boy was saying was true, her plan was ruined before it had even begun.

"Unless . . ."

Koffi's head snapped up. She'd almost forgotten the boy was there. He was eyeing her, tentative, uncertain.

"Unless?"

"Unless . . . you had someone who could read Old Zamani," he said. "Someone like me."

Koffi stopped short, bewildered. She'd been anticipating several different reactions, but that hadn't been one of them. Her eyes narrowed as she studied the boy.

"Someone like *you*?"

"Sure." The boy shrugged. "I was raised here in the temple. I could help you get the map, and I could translate it for you."

It sounded too good to be true. Koffi shook her head. "I don't have money or any other way to pay you."

He raised his hands. "I wouldn't charge anything," he said quickly.

Even more suspicious. "Then what do you want?"

"I want in."

"In?"

"On the hunt," he said quickly. "I want to go with you, and I want to help you kill it." He gave her a once-over. "That *is* what you're planning, isn't it?"

"I . . ." Koffi paused. In truth, that wasn't what she'd been planning at all. Her plan depended on her bringing the Shetani back to Baaz very much alive. She thought again of the bargain she and

Baaz had just struck, the time she had left to complete her mission. Monsoon season would be here soon, and going with this boy who also wanted the Shetani could improve her chances of finding the beast and bringing it back. Abruptly, Mama's voice came to mind.

Sometimes, though, you can't lead with your heart. You have to think with your head.

In her heart, she didn't trust the boy. He was a Yaba, probably well-off, her opposite in every possible way. The offer he was making sounded impossible, even more dangerous than her original plan, but . . .

But you don't need to trust *him,* that same voice murmured. *You just need to use him.*

She had the power to make the Shetani obey her; she'd done it once before. Once she found it again, she could command it to do whatever she wanted. She only needed a guide, and this boy could be one to her.

It could work.

For several seconds, she said nothing, then: "Fine. You have a deal. You help me read the map that leads to the Shetani, I help you take it down."

"A fair trade." The young man nodded. He seemed to be considering something a moment. "You know," he said tentatively, "if we're going to be working together, it'd be helpful if I knew your name."

"It's Koffi."

"I'm Ekon."

Ekon, a distinctly Yaba name. She tried not to make a face. "First things first. Where's the map?"

Ekon paused. "There are several in the Temple of Lkossa's library, but the one I'm thinking of in particular is inside a journal, and it's special."

"Why?"

"It's the only complete map of the entire Greater Jungle, charted almost a century ago by a scholar named—"

"I don't actually need the history lesson."

He frowned, looking almost offended. "It's kept in the Kuhani's private study, for safekeeping."

"Right." She nodded. "Then that's where we're going."

CHAPTER 12

THE MAMBA AND THE MONGOOSE

Generally speaking, Ekon preferred not to meet the eyes of gods.

He moved through the worship hall's crowds slowly, as quietly as he could, while other patrons milled about, chatting animatedly or otherwise waiting for the service to begin. Every few seconds, pressed between expensive fabrics and glittering jewels, he could pretend that he was lost among them, invisible in his simpler kaftan. It never lasted, though. Every time he started to get comfortable, he felt the glare of the six statues arranged at the other end of the room. Each of their stone-carved gazes was all too shrewd, as though they *knew* he was about to steal from them.

"Remind me why all of this is necessary."

He started, and beside him Koffi's eyes cut to him. She was wearing a pale blue dress, a gossamer veil, and a scowl, gesturing at herself. "It's very uncomfortable."

Ekon resisted rolling his eyes. "I told you before," he said as they continued weaving through people. "Guests are required to cover themselves when visiting the—"

"*You're* not covered up."

"Men aren't required to."

Koffi made a rude sound before tripping on the hem of her dress. Ekon steadied her, but she still swore under her breath. Several nearby patrons looked around, visibly scandalized. Ekon stepped even closer to her so that their arms brushed.

"You have *got* to stop swearing."

In answer, Koffi looked up at him. It was an uncanny recall back to the night they'd met. "Are you bothered?"

"In case you forgot, we are in a temple, not a tavern," he said through his teeth. "Therefore, swearing is frowned upon. Besides, if you're not careful, someone will hear you—and *you* have a Gede accent."

Koffi's scowl deepened further still. "I do *not*."

"You also argue a lot," Ekon muttered.

"No, I *don't*."

Ekon said nothing else as they neared the front of the worship hall. He'd thought finding appropriate clothes for Koffi would be the hardest part of their plan, but he'd been mistaken. As it happened, there was very little she did without some sort of commentary. He caught the way she was looking around at the temple and its gods with a shrewdness.

"What?"

"I don't get it," she said with a frown.

"Get *what*?"

"This." She gestured widely. "The point of all . . . this."

"The shukrani service is a daily ritual," Ekon explained. "Each morning, Father Olufemi visits the worship hall to receive prayers and offerings from the temple's patrons."

Koffi rolled her eyes. "Sounds pretentious."

For a moment, Ekon was mildly offended, but then curiosity got the best of him. "Don't *your* people worship the same gods?"

"Of course we do," she said brusquely. "We just do it with less pomp and circumstance."

It was Ekon's turn to frown. "If you don't give your prayers and offerings to the Kuhani, then how do the gods receive them?"

A smile tugged at the corners of Koffi's lips, wry but not unkind. "We pray to their familiars." She pointed to the base of each god's statue. Ekon knew what he would see, but looked anyway. Near the feet of each god or goddess was an animal meant to represent them—a heron, a crocodile, a jackal, a serpent, a dove, and a hippo.

"We send our prayers off in the night, and the familiars carry them on our behalf straight to the gods' ears."

"Interesting . . ."

She gave him a look. "Haven't you ever heard expressions like 'From the hippo's tongue,' or 'By the heron's beak'?"

"No."

"Well, they come from that tradition. We revere the gods' familiars," she said. "I mean, it's not like we're allowed to come *here* to pray." There was a touch of sadness in her voice. "The old faith was denied to us, so we found another way to be devout."

Ekon shifted uncomfortably. In truth, despite spending most of his life in the Temple of Lkossa, he'd never really thought about the fact that Gedes weren't allowed to worship there. Now that he did, it didn't feel right, but he didn't know what to say. He cleared his throat, changing the subject.

"Okay, so you remember the plan?"

Koffi nodded.

"Time is limited," he murmured. They were mere yards from the front of the worship hall, the statues of the Six rising to meet them. "Father Olufemi will make some opening remarks before he begins the shukrani service, and then everyone will be trying to get to him. So right before that is your best chance to—"

"I know." Koffi didn't bother keeping her voice low. "You've said it three times."

Ekon went on as though he hadn't heard her. In honesty, he would have preferred to go into Father Olufemi's study himself to get the journal, but some quick deliberating had put an end to that idea. He was big where Koffi was small, noticeable where she was not. Strategically, it was better for her to do this, but he still didn't like it.

"I'll be waiting here in the worship hall," he said. "As soon as you've got the map, we'll head down to the stable and leave through its exit." He gave the stairs to their left a cursory glance. "You remember how to get to the—"

"Up those stairs, down the hall, third door on the right."

"If the door's locked, the spare key—"

"Is under the hallway rug," Koffi finished for him with narrowed eyes. "How do you even know that?"

Ekon kept his expression inscrutable. "I grew up in the temple. My mentor, Brother Ugo, used to have me read—"

"Sounds boring."

Ekon opened his mouth to argue, but his words were cut off by a long, sonorous toll. At once, they both straightened, and all around them the patrons looked up.

"That's your cue." Ekon didn't look at her as he murmured the words. "You should go."

"Right," said Koffi brusquely. She drew her veil closer so that more of her face was obscured, then lost herself in the crowd. Ekon swallowed, tapping his fingers at his side and reviewing their plan in his head.

She'll be fine, he reassured himself. His eyes cut back to the front of the temple, where others were looking and waiting. Father Olufemi hadn't come yet, but their race against time had begun.

Twenty minutes.

Twenty. Not a great number, but that was how long Koffi had to get to the study and back again. *She can do it,* he reasoned. *She'll be back in no time.*

Or she won't, a shrewder voice in his head suggested. *Maybe she'll just take the journal and make a run for it.*

No, you have a deal. She needs you to translate it, he argued back with himself, but within the words there was a hint of uncertainty. He remembered the way she'd looked at him down in the temple's basements—untrusting, skeptical. He'd watched the way she assessed the terms of their deal, probably finding a dozen loopholes to get herself out of it if things went wrong. It was a gamble, but he'd have to take it.

"We will begin the shukrani service momentarily," one of the brothers of the temple called out. "Please have your offerings ready so that as many prayer requests can be received as possible!"

Ekon jumped slightly as people around him began digging in their bags and peering over each other's heads while they waited for Father Olufemi to emerge and lead the worship ceremony. Despite himself, despite everything coursing through his mind at the moment, he felt another pang of guilt. He was standing in the Temple of Lkossa, the oldest and most hallowed place in all the city. As a boy, he'd regarded this place as the physical representation of everything he held dear, everything he valued. Now he was plotting to steal from it, to *desecrate* it.

Again, his eyes were drawn to the gods and goddesses, arranged in birth order. It was said they were brethren and sistren, each tasked to watch over a particular piece of the world—the skies, seas, jungles, deserts, mountains, and realm of the dead. Gods and goddesses could not be bothered with hearing prayers from mortals; that was why Father Olufemi held shukrani services to receive and relay prayers on the people's behalf. It was, technically speaking, against decorum to address one of the Six directly. Ekon found himself doing it anyway.

Please, he prayed to each one. *Please let this plan work.*

"Hey, Okojo! That you?"

Ekon turned, and at once his shoulders tensed. Shomari and Fahim were making their way toward him through the worship hall's crowd, the blue of their brand-new kaftans painfully bright even in the temple's shadowed light. Seeing them hurt Ekon more than he'd expected.

"Hey." He nodded as they stopped before him. "How are you?"

"It's good to see you, Ekon." Fahim was beaming. "We didn't think you'd be around for a while!"

Ekon kept his tone even. "And why would that be?"

Fahim paused. When he spoke again, his words were more careful. "Well, it's just that . . . we didn't think . . ."

"He's not going to say it, so I will." The new haughtiness in Shomari's stance was insufferable. "We didn't think you'd dare show your face around here after that *embarrassment* at the Night

Zoo." He said the words loudly so that people in the vicinity would certainly hear them. Fahim looked away and Ekon shifted his weight from foot to foot. More than ever before, he wanted to disappear, to sink through the temple's ancient stone floors and never be seen again. He had to work to keep his expression smooth.

"All Yabas are free to request blessings at a shukrani service," said Ekon lightly. "Surely, holy warriors wouldn't deny me that right?"

"It's not a right." Shomari's voice lowered to a growl, his expression holding nothing but disgust. "Not for Gede sympathizers like you, Okojo."

"As a matter of fact, it *is*." Ekon pretended to inspect his fingernails.

"I could have you dragged out of here," Shomari said, eyes growing dark. "I could do it myself."

"I'd like to see you try."

It happened without warning.

There was a guttural roar as Shomari lunged. Ekon stepped back, avoiding him by only inches. Several people in the crowd gasped as he spun on his heel and faced Ekon with a snarl.

Fahim's brows rose in horror. "Shomari, *what are you*—?"

Ekon didn't wait. Shomari was already barreling toward him again, nostrils flaring. Ekon feinted left, then turned on his heel. This time, Shomari nearly crashed to the floor before catching himself. Several patrons screamed and got out of the way.

"Coward!" Shomari yelled. "*Fight* me!"

Ekon steadied himself, bracing. His mind detached from his body as instinct took over, as a memory kicked in. Then he wasn't in the temple anymore. His mind was back in the borderlands, remembering a night many years ago with Brother Ugo, walking side by side.

"Look, Ekon."

It'd taken Ekon a moment to understand what he was seeing, a scuffle in the red dirt. His eyes had gone wide as the dust settled and he made out two figures in it: a long brown snake and a small, furry tan creature. Their eyes were locked on each other, completely still, oblivious to their audience.

"We are fortunate to witness one of nature's oldest curiosities," Brother Ugo had said. "Have you ever watched the dance of the mamba and the mongoose?"

"Dance?" Ekon asked incredulously. "Brother, they're not dancing, they're *fighting*."

"Ah." Brother Ugo's eyes crinkled merrily. "But what is any fight if not simply a form of art in motion?" He gestured toward the black mamba and the mongoose again, and as if cued, the mongoose hissed, baring small, pointed teeth as its amber eyes flashed. "It is a peculiar thing," Brother Ugo whispered. "More often than not, people assume that the mamba always will win—he is, after all, large, venomous, and quick."

The mongoose swiped a paw through the air and the mamba lunged, striking at its paw with terrifying accuracy. The mongoose let out a small yelp of pain. Ekon winced on its behalf.

"What most people do not understand," Brother Ugo continued, "is that the mongoose is far wiser than she looks. She is resilient, immune to the mamba's venom, and . . ." He nodded one more time. "She is *quicker*."

It happened fast, so impossibly fast that Ekon would have missed it if he'd blinked. The black mamba slithered forward, advancing on its prey. It struck a second time but never found its target. Instead, the mongoose snatched the snake from the air and sank its teeth into the serpent's spine with a short, brutal crunch. The snake fell limp, blood pooling in the dirt. It was still alive but paralyzed, sentenced to a slow death. Ekon hadn't realized he was holding his breath until Brother Ugo placed a hand on his shoulder.

"You do not have to be the largest or most dangerous fighter, Ekon," he said quietly. "So long as you are *fastest*."

So long as you are fastest.

Shomari was larger, probably a better fighter, but Ekon was quicker. The next time Shomari charged, Ekon was ready. His feet seemed to move of their own accord, pivoting him left as Shomari barreled forward and missed him like a charging bull. The momentum propelled the larger boy onward and he stumbled. Fahim grabbed him before he could stand again.

"You coward!" Shomari yelled. "You arrogant, smug piece of—"

"Warrior Mensah!"

All three of them looked up, as did several other watching patrons. Brother Ugo was weaving through the crowd calmly, but his face was stern. He looked among them all. "What is the meaning of this?"

At once, Shomari stopped struggling and stood at attention, grumbling something unintelligible.

"I am *quite* sure the Kuhani would not condone such conduct here," said Brother Ugo. "You'll come with me. As I understand it, you've been given certain new responsibilities from Father Olufemi, is that right?"

"Yes, Brother," Shomari muttered.

"Then we best get you to see him. Honestly, acting that way in a place of the gods . . ."

Ekon and Fahim watched as he escorted Shomari away. Once he was out of sight, Fahim's expression grew serious. "How are you, Ekon?"

Ekon's heart hitched. There was such genuine concern in Fahim's voice that it hurt. A bit too curtly, he said:

"I'm fine."

Fahim met his gaze and held it a moment. When he spoke again, his voice was lower. "You didn't deserve what happened to you."

A hard lump rose in Ekon's throat, making it hard to speak. "It's okay, Fahim. I—"

"It's *not* okay," said Fahim. "It was one mistake. You worked harder than all of us; even Shomari knows that. You deserved warriorship most."

The lump in Ekon's throat was becoming unbearably tight, and his eyes were beginning to sting. He blinked hard until that feeling went away. He'd suffered more than enough embarrassment without crying like a little girl in front of Fahim. Quickly, he changed the subject.

"How have things been for *you*?" he asked. "How's life as an official Yaba warrior?"

He hadn't expected the shadow that suddenly fell over Fahim's face. It was as though an invisible veil had been lifted, and beneath it a different truth flickered in his friend's eyes. It had only been a day since they'd last seen each other, but Fahim looked strangely older, or perhaps just more fatigued. The skin under his eyes was puffy, and Ekon noticed that Fahim's usually neat topknot of dreadlocks looked frizzy and slightly unkempt.

"It's been . . . difficult." Fahim massaged his closed eyelids. "Father Olufemi isn't happy about the Shetani's most recent killings." He lowered his voice. "Between us, the public's losing confidence. To reassure them, he's increased patrolling in all the districts and the borderlands. The problem is, there aren't enough of us. Since Shomari and I are the rookies, we get the worst shifts. Everyone's exhausted. That's probably why he was being . . ."

"More obnoxious than usual?"

"Yeah."

Ekon was careful to keep his tone casual. "So, is there any new information? Any new sightings?"

"No." Fahim frowned. "We think it's gone back into the jungle, at least for the time being. Actually . . ." He paused. "There's something you should probably know, Ekon. I'm not supposed to say, but you're my friend and—"

Ekon worked to keep his face impassive. "I know about the hunting party."

Relief flooded Fahim's face for only a moment before his expression grew taut. "Father Olufemi's asked me to join it. Shomari too."

A distinct stab of jealousy pricked against Ekon's skin. He couldn't help but wonder if—in a different world—he would have been chosen for such an honor too. Surely he was just as qualified as Shomari and Fahim? He tried to keep the tension from his voice when he answered.

"Do you know when you're going?"

"Not yet." Fahim shook his head. "But I think it'll be soon, probably in the next few days."

Days. Ekon tried to calculate that in his mind. How much of a head start could he and Koffi get if they left tomorrow, or even tonight? If they kept an aggressive pace, how long would it take the Sons of the Six to catch up with them . . . ?

"In the meantime," Fahim continued, "our patrol shifts are doubled, and every morning, one of us has to go to Father Olufemi's study and give a status report." He looked over his shoulder. "Shomari is supposed to be doing that right now."

"Wait." A bolt of panic lurched through Ekon as Fahim's words sank in. "I thought Father Olufemi was leading the shukrani service this morning?"

"Usually he would be." Fahim yawned. "But in light of these new attacks, he's allocating more time to his direct duties with the Sons of the Six. Brother Lekan has been appointed to lead the service in Father Olufemi's stead." He gestured to one of the brothers emerging from the corridor. At once, people began pushing to get to him, and Ekon pressed his lips together. Fahim said something else, but he didn't hear it. A dull roar filled his ears. His and Koffi's plan had been predicated on the assured fact that Father Olufemi was *not* going to be in his study during the shukrani service. He'd told her it was safe, and she was on her way there at this moment or even already inside. If she was caught . . . how long would it take for her to name him? Panic lanced through him.

"Uh, good to see you, Fahim." He glanced over his shoulder. "I'm going to . . . get some water." Too quickly, he sidestepped a confused-looking Fahim and made his way to the back of the worship hall and the halls that led into the rest of the temple. He waited just until he was hidden within their shadows before breaking into an all-out run.

He had to find Koffi, fast.

CHAPTER 13

LEATHER AND CEDARWOOD

Koffi had never been more uncomfortable in her life, which was saying something.

As a beastkeeper, she'd been in all sorts of less-than-desirable situations over the last eleven years. She'd once used her bare hands to help Mama turn a baby kondoo's head while it was still inside its mother during a difficult pregnancy. Another time, when Baaz had been in a foul mood, she'd been ordered to spend hours mucking hay and giraffe poop from the paddocks. She'd had plenty of uncomfortable experiences, but this particular kind of discomfort was new.

For what felt like the hundredth time, she tripped on the hem of her dress. Silently she swore, then glowered at the material. It wasn't that the dress was ugly—in fact, the beautiful wax-print pattern was easily the nicest thing she'd ever worn—but her legs felt trapped beneath the rippling fabric. The beaded blue sandals Ekon had found for her were slightly too small, and her heels hung off the backs, slapping the soles of her feet with every step. She felt unusually clumsy, and missed the old shin-length tunic stashed in her bag.

Carefully she maneuvered between the clusters of well-dressed people, trying hard not to catch attention. It wasn't easy; as Ekon had predicted, everyone was pushing forward. According to him, once the Kuhani entered the hall, patrons would be busy making offerings and asking him to relay their specific prayer requests. She looked to the far left side of the room. The stairs leading to Father Olufemi's office were down a corridor only a few yards away; she just had to find a way to get to them unseen. She inched slightly closer, then quietly swore again. Several people looked her way again, and she had to duck her head.

Whoops. Maybe Ekon had a point about the swearing.

A Son of the Six was standing a few feet from the corridor she needed to go down with his hands behind his back. He was tall, commanding in stature, but upon looking closer, Koffi noted that his eyes were drooping with fatigue. If she could just get past him or distract him . . .

"Patrons!" One of the blue-robed brothers of the temple cupped a hand around his mouth to make his voice carry to the other side of the temple. Everyone looked in his direction. "We will begin the shukrani service momentarily. Please have your offerings ready so that as many prayers can be received as possible!"

At once, people dug in their purses. Like everyone else, Koffi withdrew one of the coins from her purse. She watched a corpulent man beside her pull out a gold coin from a purse on his hip that looked to be near bursting. A smirk touched her lips. She had an idea.

Carelessly, she let her shaba fall, satisfied to hear it clink loudly against the temple's polished stone floor with each bounce. The old man beside her looked up, surprised, and she offered an apologetic look.

"Sorry," she said quietly. "My mama says I'm careless."

The old man offered a simpering smile. "Quite all right, child, quite all right. The Six are merciful." He stooped down to retrieve the shaba, and she took her chance. With a quick tug, the purse on the man's hip ripped, and a stream of golden coins poured from the sack.

"Oh!" Koffi stepped back, feigning horror. "I'm so sorry, I—"

But the old man wasn't listening. Dhabus were rolling in every direction, gleaming pieces of gold rolling between patrons' feet. Several people around them tried to help, but every time the old man moved, more coins fell from his purse.

"Sorry!" Koffi stooped to help, but the old man held up a hand, wary.

"That's all right," he said, more curtly this time. He looked over his shoulder at the guard standing by the corridor. "Young man, if you could assist us . . . ?"

It was just what Koffi had been hoping for. The guard moved among the other patrons and bent to help them pick up the coins, and Koffi took her chance. Making sure he was distracted, she crept around him and bolted down the corridor and up the stairs as fast as she could. Her heart was still racing when she reached the top of the landing, but it slowly calmed as the crowds' buzzing below faded and she took in the much quieter hallway before her.

Step one, done.

Ekon had told her the hall would be long and dark, but that seemed an understatement now. An old embroidered blue rug covered in geometrical white shapes wound down its length, and the razor-thin windows lining both its sides offered only strips of Lkossa's pale morning light. She started down the hall without hesitation.

Door on the right, it's the third door on the right.

She came upon it faster than she'd anticipated. It was a surprisingly new-looking door, modern and ill-fitting in a place that otherwise seemed so historic. Her hand trembled as her fingers wrapped around the polished door handle and twisted. It gave with a low creak, then cracked open slightly. As soon as Koffi wriggled inside, she closed it behind her.

A new smell filled her lungs instantly, one she didn't immediately recognize. As her eyes surveyed the Kuhani's study, she identified it. Not one smell, but two—leather and cedarwood.

That's sort of what Ekon smells like, she realized. *Leather and cedarwood.* She didn't have time to dwell on that.

The study was longer than she'd expected, a rectangular room bathed in the flickering golden light of several fat waxy candles. A large wooden desk was arranged in the center of the room, and two of its walls were covered from floor to ceiling with bookshelves. Other things occupied the room—towering stacks of crates presumably filled with more books, several neatly pressed robes placed delicately on a chaise in the corner—but Koffi's eyes settled on something toward the back of the room behind the desk: a smaller bookcase with glass doors.

That had to be it. Ekon had told her about that bookcase earlier.

Apparently, it was where the Kuhani kept historic documents and books for his special collection. If Nkrumah's journal was in this study, that was where it would most likely be.

She started for it, balancing on the balls of her feet as she crossed the room with caution. It felt silly, tiptoeing in a visibly empty room, but she still felt the need to be quiet there. Slowly, she pulled open the glass door of the bookcase and let her eyes wander over the spines of each book. Ekon had mentioned that Nkrumah's journal was dark green, but there were several green books here. He'd said she'd know it when she saw it, but . . .

A flash of something else on one of the shelves caught her eye, and she stopped. There was a small assortment of trinkets on the shelf, wooden figurines of animals, quills that looked expensive, but what she was looking at was easily most impressive. It was a tiny dagger, no longer than her hand. She picked it up to examine it, then nearly dropped it.

It's made from bone, she realized, running a thumb carefully along its pale white edge. Three dark red jewels were embedded into its hilt, ruby if she had to guess. She was immediately enamored by it, fascinated, but there wasn't time for further investigation here, so that would have to wait until later. Quickly, she stowed it in her bag and looked back to the bookcase. Its first and second shelves were filled with tomes, scrolls, and other unremarkable documents, but she stopped when she reached the bottom one. Her heart caught as her eyes found a notably large green book, thicker than any other she'd seen thus far. She pulled it from the shelf, noting the dark gold lettering on its cover that Ekon had also described. A good sign. She opened it and paused.

Inside the book's front cover was one of the most beautiful

maps she'd ever seen. It was clearly hand drawn, embroidered by a lush border filled with any number of creatures within the leaves. She saw meticulously scrawled text, intricate labels, and a compass shaped like a lion's head. This was home, the entire Eshōzan continent, represented fully. Ekon had been correct, she couldn't read the language the words were written in, but she recognized that this book was special. She turned the next page and saw a second map, this one similar in style, but the focus was different. She saw leaves, winding paths between roughly sketched trees. *This* had to be a map of the Greater Jungle. It had its own labels, just as indecipherable to her as the ones on the first map, but as her eyes roved over it, she felt a distinct sense of something like hope. The map and information in this journal could be invaluable, even crucial to helping her find the Shetani and bring it back to Baaz. Her grip on it tightened. Without another moment's pause she tucked it into her bag, relishing its new weight. She was grateful finding the journal had been easier than she'd expected. Now all she had to do was get back to Ekon so they could get out of here.

She started around the desk, eyeing the contents spread across it. There was an assortment of papers and books there, but also, to her surprise, a pipe. It was fashioned from beautifully carved wood, lying on its side near the edge of Father Olufemi's desk. Something was inside its chamber, packed in too deep to see. She was leaning in, trying to get a better look, when—

There was an audible *click*.

Koffi dove behind a stack of book crates beside the desk at the very moment the doorknob turned. To her horror, a man's voice filled the room.

". . . just as you directed, Father."

Koffi's heart began to drum fast and hard in her chest, and she silently swore as two men entered the study. They were opposites. One was young, tall, and muscled and wore the bright blue kaftan of a Yaba warrior; the other was significantly older and wore a cerulean robe.

No. Koffi's mouth went dry. The older man was Father Olufemi; she knew it without a doubt. She'd never seen the man before, but everything in his countenance confirmed it. He walked with the slow, deliberate gait of someone who rushed for no one, with the confidence of a man who ruled the city. Fear and confusion spiked through her body. *How?* He wasn't supposed to be here—he was supposed to be downstairs leading the shukrani service. Had she miscalculated her time, or . . . she had a darker thought.

Had Ekon lied to her?

"Good."

She retreated farther into the shadows as Father Olufemi neared her, then stopped, hands clasped behind his back. "And the remaining cremations are complete?"

"There's still one more, Father," answered the second man. "But it's planned for this afternoon, if your schedule allows."

The Kuhani nodded. "I will be in attendance."

"Other orders, Father?"

"None presently," said the Kuhani. "You and Warrior Adebayo may have the duration of the day to rest. You will resume your next patrol shifts this evening."

The young warrior bowed. "Thank you, Father."

"That will be all, Shomari."

The warrior gave another deep bow and a salute before leaving the room, but the old man stayed standing in its center. Koffi didn't dare move so much as an inch. How long would he stay here? There was only one door to this study, no other way out. If she wasn't back downstairs to meet Ekon in the next ten minutes . . .

It seemed to take years, but eventually Father Olufemi looked up. Koffi lowered herself just slightly as he surveyed the room. Her heart sank as she saw his eyes stop and fix on something: the bookcase behind the desk. It looked as it had when Koffi had walked in, as old and elegant as ever, but she swallowed hard when she realized her mistake.

One of the glass doors was slightly ajar.

Her mouth went dry as Father Olufemi, now frowning, moved closer to both her and the bookcase. He moved behind the desk and quickly closed it with narrowed eyes. He seemed distracted, but what if he noticed Nkrumah's journal and the dagger were missing? To Koffi's surprise, he turned away from it abruptly. He gave the room one final, satisfactory sweep before lifting the hem of his agbada and making his way out of the study, a low hum on his lips. Koffi waited several seconds, then pressed her palms to her eyes, relieved.

That had been entirely too close.

She pricked her ears, trying to listen for sounds from the worship hall below. Someone was still speaking in long, dramatic tones to the temple patrons—assumedly the person who'd replaced the Kuhani for the shukrani service. There was still time to get back downstairs, to get out of this wretched place.

She rose carefully, adjusting the now much heavier bag on her shoulder. Soundlessly, she padded across the room and unlocked the study's door. Relief flooded her as she stepped into the dark hallway and found it still shadowed, but empty.

Thank the Six.

She'd just started toward the stairs when a hand latched on to her wrist.

And Father Olufemi's gaze met hers.

CHAPTER 14

The Heart of the Jungle

Ekon was running.

The hallways and doors of the temple went by him in a blur as he tried to lay out a blueprint in his head. He'd spent the last ten years of his life here, this temple was like a home, but that only made it slightly easier to maneuver through in a crisis. There were an infinite number of halls and rooms and stairways, and he needed to find the one that would get him to Koffi fastest—*without* being caught.

Koffi wasn't in the corridor that led to the Kuhani's study; he'd checked. A new wave of anxiety racked his body as he thundered back down the stairs and ran down a new hallway. This temple was huge, a maze of chambers and halls and atriums. Where could she be?

He turned a corner sharply and nearly collided with two men clad in blue. His heart leaped from his chest. They were both Sons of the Six, senior warriors.

"Okojo?" One of them, a short man named Zahur, frowned at him. "What are you doing?"

Ekon swallowed, his fingers tapping along at his side. He made his answer sound as calm as he could. "I . . . I heard there might be trouble?" he said. 'Thought I could help.'

"There *is* trouble." The second warrior, a man called Daudi, was scowling. "We've just received word that there is an intruder in the temple, a thief!"

Ekon had to work to keep his expression neutral. "Really? What did they steal?"

"We're not sure yet," said Daudi. "Father Olufemi is going to have to do an inventory of his study after he . . . recovers."

"*Recovers*?" Ekon repeated. This time, his surprise was genuine.

The warriors exchanged an uncomfortable look before Zahur lowered his voice. "Ahem, it seems the assailant assaulted the Kuhani before making her escape."

"*Her?*" Ekon chose to focus on that instead of on what troubling things Koffi might have done to Father Olufemi to constitute "assault." "Did you say *her*?"

"Yes." Daudi nodded. "A young Yaba woman, well-dressed."

Ekon sighed with slight relief. At the very least, they hadn't figured out that Koffi was Gede.

"We're going to do a full sweep of the temple's east wing. Father Olufemi thought he saw her go in that direction," said Zahur. "Where are *you* headed?"

Ekon started to say something, then froze. His eyes had just fixed on a large tapestry hanging on the wall behind the two warriors. A pair of small brown feet were sticking out from the bottom of it, wearing *very* familiar-looking sandals.

"Uh . . ." He stalled, hoping the panic wasn't audible in his voice. "I'm going to check the . . . dormitories."

The warriors looked confused a moment, then nodded.

"As you were, then," said Daudi. "Report back to us if you see anything irregular."

Ekon looked again to the feet sticking out from the tapestry. "I will . . . absolutely do that."

They nodded, continuing past him down the hall. Ekon waited until they were gone before moving to stand beside the tapestry. After a moment, he cleared his throat.

"My mentor told me a joke once," he murmured. "What did the rug say to the floor?"

Koffi stuck her head out from behind the tapestry, glaring at him.

Ekon smirked. "It said, I've got you *covered—ow*!" He jumped back, rubbing his arm. "What was that for?"

"A terrible joke, first of all," said Koffi, emerging fully from behind the tapestry. Her veil was gone, and she looked distinctly rumpled. She was clutching her burlap sack to her chest, and her mouth was set in a severe line. "*Second* of all, because I just barely escaped the Kuhani."

"I'm sorry," Ekon said quickly. "I didn't know he wouldn't be leading the shukrani service today, honestly. I was trying to find you."

Koffi threw him a withering look. "You're a little late."

Ekon looked over his shoulder, then gestured for her to follow. "Come on, those warriors just said they were going to the east wing first. We can still get to the stable before they do and get out of here. Follow me!"

Koffi looked like she wanted to argue, but thought better of it as they started to run west. The temple's halls were quiet, but Ekon still felt on edge.

"Did you get the map?" he asked. He pointed toward a set of stairs and gestured for Koffi to go first.

"I did," she whispered. "But Father Olufemi caught me on my way out. I had to use an . . . evasive maneuver."

Ekon followed her down the steps. "Did you really assault him?"

"*Assault* is a strong word," Koffi said, shrugging. "I just gave him a good kick right between the—"

"Down there!" someone yelled behind them. "I just saw someone go down the stairs!"

They met each other's gaze for only a second before breaking into a sprint, skipping stairs two at a time. Ekon thought he knew where these led—to the other end of the temple's ground floor, not far from the stable. He was relieved when they reached the last stair and he saw he'd been right: They were back in the lower-level hall where they'd been earlier that morning.

"That way," he said to Koffi, pointing up ahead. They had started toward the double doors that led outside, when—

"Hey! Check downstairs!"

Fear shot through Ekon's body. Without thinking, he grabbed Koffi by the waist and hauled her into one of the hall's alcoves just as footsteps sounded at the other end. He peeked and, to his horror, recognized who'd just entered. Fahim and Shomari.

"Was someone already here?" There was wariness in Fahim's voice.

"Not sure, but it's better we confirm." Shomari sounded much more confident.

Ekon froze as torchlight neared their hiding spot. The alcove wasn't deep enough to hide them completely; any minute now they'd be exposed. He felt Koffi's back pressed hard against his chest, her body shuddering against his as she tried not to make a sound. Shomari and Fahim had looked over the other side of the room, but they were getting closer, dangerously close—

"Mensah! Adebayo!"

Ekon nearly jumped out of his skin as yet another voice echoed from down the hall. He would know that voice anywhere, and his heart seized. It was Kamau. His mouth went dry as his brother came running into the room, looking between Fahim and Shomari. "Let's go! Father Olufemi thinks the intruder went into the kitchens!"

The three turned on their heels without another word and raced up the stairs. Ekon didn't relax until the hallway was silent again. Koffi's breathing was still shallow, and he found his own heartbeat had synchronized with hers. Slowly, their bodies relaxed, but they still didn't move. Warmth flooded his face when he realized his hands were on her waist. He moved them immediately.

"Now what?" Koffi whispered.

"The other door," said Ekon. He moved from behind her, inching toward the door to the stable. The hallway was still silent, but he kept his ears pricked for noise nonetheless. His fingers wrapped around the old brass doorknob and pulled. Bright sunlight poured into the hall, and in that moment it was the most glorious thing Ekon had ever seen. Without another word, they both slipped through the door and into the blazing sunlight.

There was no mercy in an afternoon Lkossan sun.

But Ekon was grateful for it; he relished its burn on his bare arms and face as he and Koffi wove through the lunch crowds of

205

the city's central market. He kept waiting for them to be stopped, to be caught. He hadn't gotten permission to leave the temple, so this was probably going to ruin the second chance Kamau had given him. Even now, he fought to keep his breathing slow and even. His fingers tapped at his sides.

One-two-three. One-two-three. One-two-three.

They'd found separate places to change clothes in the stable before heading into the market, and now he was wearing a plain brown kaftan instead of the white one befitting a servant of the temple. It wouldn't prevent someone from recognizing him if they saw his face, but at least it would garner less attention. He glanced at Koffi.

"We need to look at the journal," he said in a voice only she could hear as they walked side by side.

"Where?"

Ekon looked around, frowning. After a moment, an idea came to him, and he nodded. "I know a place," he said. "Follow me."

They said nothing as they cut through streets and alleys, Ekon leading the way until they reached another district of the city. His lungs burned as a stench like earth and fire filled them, and a metallic clanging assaulted his eardrums in a steady, repetitive rhythm he could appreciate. Billows of black smoke thickened the air, nearly obscuring them in darkness, and by the time the first of the blacksmiths' tents came into view, he was relieved to find his instinct about this place was right. He gestured toward a spot behind one of the many working tents, and Koffi obliged.

"The Sons of the Six don't linger in the Kughushi District." He had to lean in to be heard amid the constant hammering of the anvils. "No one really does unless they have to."

"I can see why." Koffi was holding both hands over her ears, grimacing. "I can barely hear myself think."

"Let me see the journal."

Koffi shrugged her bag off her shoulder and started to withdraw it, but Ekon's eyes caught the white glint of something else. He squinted. With a distinctly guilty look, Koffi tried to shove whatever it was back into her bag, but he caught her wrist.

"What is *that*?"

"If you must know." Koffi gave the journal a final tug to get it out of the bag before shooting Ekon a daring look. "It is a dagger."

"From *where*, exactly?"

Koffi fidgeted. "I *may* have procured it while I was in the Kuhani's study."

"You weren't supposed to take anything else from the study—"

"Yeah, well, it's too late now, isn't it?" She rapped him on the arm with the book, and he scowled. "You want to look at this thing or not?"

Ekon started to say more, then thought better of it. He nodded and carefully took the book from her. He sighed as he read the foiled lettering on the cover:

SATAO NKRUMAH

SCHOLAR OF THE ESHŌZAN CONTINENT IN GENERAL

AND THE ZAMANI REGION IN PARTICULAR

"Wow."

"You can read that?" Koffi asked.

"I can." He felt Koffi's eyes on him as opened the front cover. The first page featured a map of the entire continent of Eshōza; the next page featured a map of the Greater Jungle. He studied each in turn. The journal's pages were made from old papyrus, soft to the touch. Perhaps it was the sunlight filtering in, but there was a strange beauty captured in them, a special care. He flipped back to the first map. It stretched like an intricate web, a thousand lines and shapes spidering out in all directions from the map's very center to the farthest corners of the paper. He took in the Zamani Region's most famous features—the treacherous bay known as the Tusks for its jagged shape, the Eastern Ndefu River that Brother Ugo had told him stories about—but there were places new to him too. He saw the Ngazi Ranges of the north, the Nyingi Isles of the south, even the legendary Katili Desert in the west. It was the entire continent of Eshōza, laid bare. Some parts of the ink still held their original black; others had faded to gray translucence. He couldn't believe a single person had created a thing so detailed.

Koffi ran a finger over one point on it before looking up at him. "What's that?"

"The Kidogo River, northwest of here."

"And here?" She pointed to another spot, bordered by a large cluster of trees.

"*That* is Lkossa," he said. "There are other small townships in the Zamani Region, of course, that aren't on here, but Lkossa's the largest. This big cluster is the Greater Jungle, and the one below it is called the Lesser Jungle."

Koffi leaned in, then pointed to something small at the bottom of the map. "What's that?"

Ekon followed her finger again and squinted. It was a word he didn't recognize.

"It says . . . *sanda*," he read with a frown.

"What's that mean?"

"Don't know." Ekon shrugged. "Could be a reference note. The old masters used all sorts of specific codes to make their maps." He flipped over to the map of the Greater Jungle again and took a second look. This map was clearly drawn by the same hand, but it still felt different. The quill strokes seemed slightly less precise, the labels messier. This map looked more like a first sketch. He noticed something on it and paused. "Huh, *that's* interesting."

"What?"

"This section." Ekon nodded. "It's called 'the Heart of the Jungle.'"

Koffi raised an eyebrow. "Is that important?"

"It *could* be." Ekon raked his fingers through his hair. "My guess is that it's probably considered the center of the jungle, or maybe the oldest part of it."

Koffi stared at the map a second longer, then: "I think that's where the Shetani lives."

Ekon frowned. "That wouldn't make sense. Look at where that is." He pointed again. "That's at least a few days' walk—"

"For something with *two* legs."

He stared at her. "You really think it could go back and forth that quickly?"

Koffi pressed her lips together, thoughtful. "What do we *know* about the Shetani?"

"Well, people say—"

"Not speculation," said Koffi. "What do we know to be fact?"

Ekon hesitated, thoughtful. That kind of question reminded him of the way Brother Ugo had quizzed him as a boy. *Answer the question I ask, and answer the entire question*. He paused.

"We know the Shetani has been alive for nearly a century, at least," he said. "Possibly longer."

"What else?"

"We know the Shetani attacks at night."

"Always?"

"Always." Ekon nodded. "There's a pattern. People go missing after sundown, then their bodies turn up the next morning at the jungle's edge. The timing is always the same."

"Which means this thing is nocturnal and deliberate. It hunts like a classic predator, with a practiced method. Find the prey—"

"Kill the prey."

"Then hide."

"The most recent killing happened three days ago," said Ekon.

"So it would be hiding now," said Koffi. "Waiting until everyone's guards are down again. Which means . . . it would be somewhere no one would go. No one's ventured that far into the Greater Jungle before and returned. It would think of that place as a safe haven."

Ekon looked at the map, walking his fingers back and forth between the Heart and Lkossa. "It would take us three to four days to get there, if we don't . . ." He hesitated. "If we don't run into trouble." He traced along the edge of the jungle. "This small space that separates Lkossa from the jungle is called the borderlands. That would be the most direct path into it. It's also part of the Sons of the Six's patrol route."

"Is there a way to get past them?"

Ekon paused. "There is, but it's a slim chance."

"Then it's the one we have to take," said Koffi. She massaged her temples. "Thank the gods it's just us going after this thing," she muttered. "I don't know what I'd do if this were any more complicated."

Ekon swallowed the words in his throat. He'd just been about to inform Koffi of the hunting party, but something stopped him. What if, after he told her, she reneged on their deal? What if that one extra detail ruined the whole thing? No, he decided it then. He wouldn't tell her about the hunting party, at least not yet.

Koffi looked from the map to him. "When can we go?"

"Tonight." Ekon looked to her. "If you're ready."

Koffi nodded. "I am."

"We'll buy supplies," said Ekon. "Then lie low near the borderlands until dusk so that we can go in without being seen. If we keep to that schedule, we'll be in the jungle before nightfall." He didn't say his last words aloud.

And then, the hunt begins.

INVISIBLE STRING

ADIAH

In and out.

I blink hard to keep the tears in my eyes from falling, but I taste their salt anyway.

In and out.

I can't find Tao, so today I don't go up to our secret place to hide. Instead, I sit at my parents' house, in my tiny bedroom, dreading when they'll be home from work. I know by then they'll have gotten the report from the temple, so they'll know about what happened today. I can already imagine their disappointment, the shame. This time I deserve both.

This time, I really messed up.

Even now, the memory of Azaan's face makes me nauseous, a stain on my conscience like spilled palm wine on linen. I remember every detail, the full lips and straight nose, the squarish shape of his jaw. I remember the way his features pinched when the pain hit him, the sound he made.

I remember all the things I don't want to.

My memories pull me back to an earlier part of the day, to the before. Azaan and I are standing in the midst of the temple's sparring lawns, inside a large circle made from fist-sized stones. To our right, Brother Dwanh presides.

"We will follow the standard rules of sparring conduct." He eyes us both, explaining the rules in his reed-thin voice. "The match is over when one of the participants steps outside of the outlined parameters. Remember, this is strictly a *hand-to-hand* combat. Do not summon the splendor."

"Ready." Azaan, standing several inches taller than me, offers a cocky smile. "Don't worry, Adi. This will be quick."

I keep my expression neutral, impassive. "That's just what I was thinking."

"Very well." Brother Dwanh nods and steps back. *"Begin."*

We take our stances at opposite sides of the circle, feet apart and arms spread wide. I know Azaan well enough to know how this is going to go. He's a Combatant, built tall and lean like a scarecrow, probably best in our class after me. He tends to strike to debilitate, light rapid hits that take an opponent down before they even know what's hit them. He's fast.

I'm faster.

He winks at me, kicking his foot in the ground to create a cloud of dirt that's meant to distract. I don't fall for it, and brace myself as he lunges for me and tries to kick me out from under my feet.

I jump just in time.

I've barely landed before Azaan switches tactics, using the advantage of his height to drive me back in an onslaught of quick punches I have to duck from. In other cultures, people don't believe that men and women should fight each other this way, but Azaan and I are equals. I know he won't hold back because I'm a girl.

One of his punches finally connects, a blow to the shoulder that tears a cry from me. The sound of his triumphant laugh is infuriating, and carelessly, I go for an undercut that he immediately blocks. I don't have to look over my shoulder to know that we are nearing the edge of the circle's border; a few more steps and I will lose this.

That can't happen. I *can't* lose today.

I feint right, and just as I was expecting, he takes the bait, following my body. Instead of throwing a punch or kick, I shove him square in the chest to give myself space, then leap into the air. As though time has slowed, I bring my knees up to my chest and open my hands, drawing the splendor to me like an instinct. It rises from the earth, answering my call as it courses through my veins in a sudden rush. When I come back to earth, my palms slap against the ground, a tremendous boom shaking everything around me. I watch with a thrill as the splendor leaves my hands and moves in unnatural ripples toward Azaan.

I know as soon as it reaches him that I've made a mistake.

The earth shudders a second time as the force of my power sends Azaan flying high, as though he's been pulled backward by an invisible string. There's a terrible pause while his body arcs, suspended, and then he comes crashing down. I hear the clean snap of his bones as they break on impact, watch blood seep into the dirt around him. One of his legs is bent at an odd angle. He doesn't move as the other darajas run toward him. I know I should too, but I can't.

"It was an accident." My words are barely audible, but I need to say them, I need someone to *understand*. "I didn't mean to. I—"

"*Adiah.*" Brother Dwanh's eyes cut to me, wary. He doesn't sound angry; he sounds afraid. "It's . . . probably best you go."

I want to say more, but I don't. I just turn and run. I'm fast, but I'm not fast enough to outrun the whispers I imagine chasing at my heels.

Dangerous, those whispers say. *Volatile. Unstable.*

Later, I learn that Azaan was taken to the temple's infirmary with several injuries, but thankfully none that are life-threatening. His broken bones will mend, and the open wounds on his body will heal.

My reputation will not.

Dangerous. I hear my classmates now, the things they're probably saying about me back at the temple. *Volatile. Unstable.*

I start to wonder if they're right, to wonder if there's something wrong with me.

In and out.

I have to learn how to control myself.

In and out.

I have to learn how to control this power.

In and out.

Before it controls *me*.

CHAPTER 15

The OLD DARKNESS

Ekon felt the jungle's presence long before he saw it.

When he was honest with himself, he supposed he always felt it in a way, lurking in the back of his mind, waiting for the quiet moments. They were still a little under a half mile from the borderlands, but already he could see the tops of the Greater Jungle's oldest and tallest pines peeking above rooftops. With each step, the old voice in his head grew louder. He'd expected it, of course, but that made it no easier to hear.

Ekon. Baba's voice was faint this time, wavering, the sound of a man truly suffering. *My son, please . . .*

Ekon screwed his eyes shut as the usual images flooded him: thorned vines as thick as his arm, the roots of black trees rising from the soil like coiled serpents determined to entrap him. Suddenly, he was a little boy again, alone. He heard a low snarl, met the gaze of an ancient creature with cold, empty eyes. He'd been so small in comparison, and its teeth had been so *large*. His skin turned clammy at the memory, lips going numb as a familiar darkness began to seep into the corners of his vision. It was getting harder to breathe by the second; his mouth was far too dry.

Not now. His lungs protested as he forced a sharp breath in through the nose and out through the mouth, as Brother Ugo had once taught him. At his side, Ekon's fingers began to tap. With their steady rhythm, he found comfort.

One-two-three. One-two-three. One-two-three.

This was no time to fall apart, and he wouldn't allow it. In his imagination, he pictured a wall being erected, a barrier between himself and the nightmares. Those walls would keep the worst things out and safeguard his secrets within.

Please come back for me. Baba was weeping, an eerie, unnatural sound. *Please don't leave me alone here.*

I can't help you, Baba. The words tore at something in Ekon's very being. He imagined the bricks of his wall coming together, forcing out that horrible voice. *I'm sorry, but I can't help you. I can't help you, I can't—*

"Hey, are you okay?"

Ekon jumped. He hadn't realized that he'd stopped walking. Koffi was staring at him with an inscrutable expression. This moment was an echo of the one he'd had just days ago walking with Kamau. He needed to be better about that, about letting the nightmares debilitate him.

"Yeah," he said brusquely. "I'm fine."

Koffi looked at him a second longer, as though she wanted to say something else, then seemed to think better of it and kept walking. Ekon followed. They were nearing the edge of Lkossa, a grittier part of the city littered with old crates, debris, and other filth. Ekon thought about the last time he'd been there, about the old woman he'd encountered. She clearly wasn't there, but he almost felt her presence in some strange way. He glanced over his shoulder, wary.

"We need to walk faster."

Koffi raised an eyebrow. "Why?"

"We're . . . behind schedule."

Koffi stared. "Huh?"

"The *schedule*," Ekon repeated, picking up his own pace. "Sons of the Six do a patrol along the edge of the Greater Jungle every half hour, every thirty minutes. We need to time it so that we get to the borderlands right after they've just passed through, which means we're two minutes and thirty-nine seconds behind schedule."

Koffi rolled her eyes. "Of *course* you've managed to calculate that."

Ekon paused, momentarily uncomfortable. He couldn't help the way numbers came together in his mind, automatic and sure. Lots of times, that ability to compute and calculate information rapidly was helpful, like when he was reading about complex mathematical theories. But sometimes, it made him feel . . . strange, different. He thought of the disapproving way Kamau sometimes stared at his fingers, the way other boys at the temple had laughed at him for using bigger words as a child. Most of his memories of growing up at the Temple of Lkossa were good, but that didn't mean it had been perfect.

"Well, at least *one* of us is good with numbers," Koffi added, eyes staying ahead. "That could be useful once we're in the jungle. No doubt you'll know how to divide and ration food properly or something."

It was a brief, offhand comment, but something about it made

Ekon feel just a little bit better. Koffi didn't find his counting strange, it seemed; she thought it could be useful. He stood a little taller, keeping in step with her as they continued through the outskirts' winding streets. Above, the sky was darkening fast, melting into a fluid watercolor blend of deep blues, oranges, and pinks fractured by the telltale lines left from the Rupture.

"How long do you think it'll take us?" Again, Koffi pulled him from his thoughts. "To find the Shetani once we're in the jungle?"

"I'm . . . not sure," said Ekon in earnest. "According to the map, the Heart of the Jungle is northeast of Lkossa, about a three-day walk from here if we enter from—"

"Didn't you say four-day earlier?"

"Three," he corrected. "I . . . like three better."

Koffi stared at him a second longer, before tightening her grip on her shoulder bag. Ekon had a matching one of his own, purchased from the market hours before. They'd spent most of the afternoon gathering supplies for the hunt—water, dried foods, whetting stones for their weapons. The sum of it had almost entirely depleted the modest savings Ekon had accrued from his time at the temple, not that Koffi needed to know that, or anything else about his financial situation.

They turned a corner together, crossing onto a slightly wider street, and Ekon tensed. A throng of people was crowded at its end, stopped by something he couldn't see. The sight immediately put him on edge.

"What's going on?" Koffi craned her neck, trying to see over people's heads as more came from behind them and blocked them in. "What is it?"

"Ugh. Looks like a checkpoint."

Koffi looked up at him, confused. "A what?"

Ekon stopped walking and gestured for Koffi to do the same while others passed them by. While she wasn't quite tall enough, he could see slightly farther. A few yards away, at the end of the road, several Sons of the Six had cordoned off the area and stood lined up to keep anyone from advancing. He leaned toward Koffi and tried to keep his voice low.

"Sometimes, when there's a major crime and the culprit hasn't been apprehended, the Kuhani will order an impromptu checkpoint to be set up. There are warriors ahead, and they'll be searching the bags of every person on this street to make sure no one has anything they shouldn't."

At this, Koffi stiffened. "I don't suppose they'll be happy about that old book in your sack, then, or the dagger in mine."

"Decidedly not." Ekon swallowed. "That's probably the reason it was set up in the first place." He looked around, trying to stay calm. They were still too far away to discern which Sons of the Six were manning the checkpoint, but it didn't matter. Any one of them would recognize him immediately, and after what had happened at the Night Zoo, he knew not one of them would hesitate to arrest and turn him in if he was found with stolen goods. He thought of Father Olufemi's eyes, cold and disapproving, then Kamau's, full of disappointment and shame. He couldn't let that happen; he couldn't let this mission end before it had even started. Without thinking, he took Koffi's hand. She gawked, but he held on to it.

"Follow my lead," he murmured, nudging her slightly to the right. There was a narrow side street just a few yards away from them. If they could get to it unnoticed, there was a chance they could escape. Catching on, Koffi followed his example, keeping her gaze straight ahead as, slowly, she inched in that direction. The crowd around them thickened, bottlenecking the road as more people pushed forward. Strategically, that was good—more people provided better cover—but it still made Ekon nervous. Slowly, he watched the distance between themselves and that side street close, getting nearer by the minute.

Thirty yards, twenty-seven yards, twenty-four—

"Attention!"

Ekon nearly knocked Koffi over as she stopped short at the command. A male voice from somewhere behind them had called out, entirely too close for comfort. He glanced over his shoulder, and his stomach swooped. More Sons of the Six were coming in from the other end of the road to close the crowd in. He immediately recognized the warrior at the front.

Shomari.

"Listen up!" There was an annoying ring of authority in Shomari's voice as he yelled at the top of his lungs. "Every single person on this street is subject to a mandatory search, by high order of the Kuhani. Failure to comply may result in fines and imprisonment. Make a neat and orderly line."

Sweat gathered on Ekon's forehead. His gaze met Koffi's, and he saw she was deliberating. Her eyes cut to the side street.

"We have to run."

"Bad idea." Ekon shook his head. "That'll make us look guilty."

"And being caught with stolen temple artifacts won't?"

"There are hundreds of people in here." Ekon said the words just as much for himself as for her. "They won't have the time or patience to check every single person thoroughly. All we have to

221

do is open the flaps of our bags, give them a quick peek, and they'll pass us through."

Koffi pursed her lips. "I don't like it."

"Just *stay calm*."

They continued being pressed into the crowd as the warriors from the back herded them forward, and continued moving carefully toward the side street. Ekon looked up again. It was hard to tell exactly how many people were ahead of them with all the movement, but he counted nineteen, a bad number. He watched as one harried-looking woman with two small children stepped up to the checkpoint.

"Empty the contents of your bags, please," one of the warriors ordered.

"Here." The woman, half-distracted by her children, opened the flap of her bag to show what was clearly a sack full of fruits and produce. "Can I go?"

"Afraid not, Bi." The warrior shook his head. "We're checking the contents of all bags. You'll need to take everything out and put it on this table . . ."

Beside him, Ekon heard Koffi swear. Her eyes had begun to dart back and forth between the checkpoint ahead of them and that side street to their right.

"Koffi," he said between his teeth. "Listen to me, just stay—"

There was no warning. She bolted.

"Hey!"

No. "*Koffi!*" Ekon tried not to yell as she jostled through disgruntled people. "Koffi, wait—!"

"You two, stop!"

Ekon ignored the command and broke into a run, trying to keep his eyes on Koffi's retreating back. She glanced over his shoulder, and their gazes met.

"Run!"

It seemed Koffi needed no further prompt as she tore down the road. Ekon followed, right on her heels. From somewhere behind them, he heard a shout, then pounding footsteps.

No, no, no.

Koffi ducked into the side street, disappearing into its shadows. It reminded Ekon uncannily of him and Kamau chasing the little girl through these very streets mere days ago. It was a strange sort of refrain.

From cat to mouse, from the hunter to the hunted.

Up ahead, at the end of the street, he made out a stretch of red dirt. They were approaching the borderlands.

"Koffi." Ekon couldn't keep up with her strides and yell at the same time. "Koffi, we have to—"

If she heard him, she gave no indication of it. Behind them, Ekon heard more footsteps, whooping.

"Stop!" someone called. "By order of the Sons of the Six!"

Ekon didn't obey. They emerged from the alley and sprinted into bloodred sunlight, the last of the setting sun's rays. In his peripheral vision, he watched the edges of the city fall away as the Greater Jungle rose to meet them. Koffi glanced back at him but kept running toward it. With every step, Ekon felt it—the distinct sensation of releasing a life raft and casting himself into unknown waters. There'd be no turning back from this. He prayed he wouldn't drown.

He bucked against the sudden cold that touched his skin as the first shadows of the trees reached him. It felt wrong, preternatural; it shouldn't have gotten so cold so quickly. It was like being plunged into an ice bath, a thousand small knives pricking at his skin. Leaves and vines brushed against him, and he imagined they were fingers. Hands. Claws. All reaching for him.

At last. Baba's voice was wretched with glee, eerie. *My son returns to me, returns to his father.*

Ekon was still running, still moving between the tree trunks, but it was too dark, too loud. Only a few brave shafts of light could pierce the jungle's canopy here, and new sounds filled the space around him. He heard his baba's voice, but other things too: a bullfrog's croak, the buzz of a thousand cicadas, creatures he couldn't name. There were low hums and high-pitched shrieks, roars, and the occasional click of something above him. For a moment, he was entirely lost in its cacophony.

"Hey! Over here!"

Ekon's eyes adjusted to the darkness enough to make out a small silhouette just a few feet away from him. Koffi. In spite of himself, he felt an undeniable sense of relief as she slowly made her way to him, stepping over brambles and tree roots. To his utter bewilderment, she looked distinctly pleased.

"Well, that wasn't exactly the way I thought we'd enter the jungle," she said with a grin. "But hey, it got the job done. For a second there, I thought we were—"

"What—was—*that*?"

Ekon heard himself, the anger in his own voice, but he couldn't quell it. He watched Koffi's smile flicker for a moment, showing real confusion, before her expression hardened.

"*What?*"

"You—you—" Ekon spluttered. He could barely get the words out. "You just—you just took off, without even warning me! We had a *plan*—"

"That was about to get us caught and arrested," Koffi snapped back. "So we had to adjust, which was what I did."

More anger rose in Ekon, but so did something else he couldn't explain. In the back of his head, he knew that his reaction was irrational, unjustified, but . . . but he couldn't explain to Koffi the way he felt—unmoored, off-kilter, unsettled. They'd had a plan for entering the Greater Jungle, a plan he'd been relying on. Now that was dismantled, and with it so was his peace. Anxiety rolled over him as he thought about the Sons of the Six they'd run from. What if one of them had recognized him? What if they were assembling at this very moment? He felt the mental wall he'd erected to keep the nightmares at bay slowly crumble to dust, so that nothing would stop them from advancing. Images of blood-soaked leaves and horrid bodies filled his imagination, and he tried to shake them from his mind.

Focus, he told himself. *Don't think about the jungle, just focus.*

But it was harder now. The jungle was no longer something he could just distance himself from—he was within it, entirely consumed. He closed his eyes and rubbed his temples, willing his father's voice to go away, willing the wretched memories to go away.

"Ekon." Koffi's voice broke through. When he looked up, her face had softened. "Are you all right?"

The truth was, he wasn't all right, not in the slightest, but Ekon had no desire to tell Koffi that. Too roughly, he nodded.

"It's fine, I just have . . . a headache," he grumbled. "I need to sit down for a moment, and we need to take a look at the journal to figure out where exactly we are. If we came in from farther east than expected, we'll need to compensate by moving slightly northwest . . ."

"I don't think we should stop here," said Koffi.

"*I* do," said Ekon, not looking up from the journal. "We could already be off course. The last thing we need to do is go charging aimlessly into this jungle. It's huge. Once we confirm our direction—"

"We're sitting here like guinea fowl," said Koffi. "What we *need* to do is keep moving."

"Koff—"

"Look, I know you had some sophisticated plan!" She threw up her hands, exasperated. "But I don't feel good about sitting here. Something . . . something doesn't feel right."

As soon as she said, Ekon felt it too, a wrongness. He didn't know how to tell Koffi that that sensation wasn't unique, that it belonged distinctly to the Greater Jungle. There was a reason it was one of the few things Yabas and Gedes could agree on: This jungle was no place for mortal beings. A shiver passed over him as he saw the end of a long yellow snake disappear into the branches of a tree a few yards away from them. He tucked the journal back into his bag and nodded.

"We'll head north for a few miles," he determined. "But after that, we need to stop and reevaluate our plan."

Koffi nodded. "Fine."

The jungle grew impossibly darker as they trekked into its depths. Around them, its noises settled into something quieter, as though it had grown used to their presence, but that didn't help Ekon's nerves. He'd been much smaller the last time he'd been here, but that didn't change the way this place made him feel. Every footstep seemed to pull him deeper down into the caverns of his memories. He tapped his fingers against his side.

One-two-three. One-two-three. One—

My son.

Ekon stumbled, caught off guard by the suddenness of his father's voice. Here in the jungle, among the old trees, it seemed louder, colder.

After all this time, you have returned . . .

A hard lump rose in the back of Ekon's throat. He focused on the steps before him, trying to count them in his head instead of listening to that voice.

It's all in your head, he reminded himself. *There's nothing actually in your throat. You know how to breathe. Just take it slow and keep walking, one step right after the other.*

It was no use. His fingers were clumsy, unable to find their rhythm, and he faltered in his steps.

"Koffi." His voice echoed strangely in the darkness. "Koffi, I think we should think about . . ." He stopped, blinking hard. Koffi had been only a few feet in front of him, just seconds ago; now he couldn't see her.

"Koffi? Koffi, where are—?"

Ekon.

The voice stopped him dead in his tracks, raising the hair on the back of his neck. He suddenly realized the jungle had gone quiet. There was no trill of cicadas or chattering apes in the trees, just a low creaking in the breeze, a whisper.

My son, help me.

Something brushed the back of his neck like the stroke of a finger. He whirled to face it, but there was nothing there, nothing but the trees. Somehow, that was worse.

Ekon, Baba's voice moaned into the darkness. *Please make it stop. Make the pain stop . . .*

Where is Koffi? Ekon looked in both directions, working to keep himself calm. He didn't trust his mind anymore, didn't know if what he was seeing before him was real or the stuff of nightmares. The trees were pressing in, tendrils of white mist curling at their roots and rising. He backed away, but there was no escaping it; it was all around him, tickling his ankles.

"Koffi." Saying her name seemed to cost him something. He looked down and saw the mist was now at his knees. Where it touched his skin, it was cold, strangely numbing. He felt his eyelids growing heavier, the old darkness creeping in from the corners of his vision. Somewhere distant, he heard Brother Ugo's words.

Nightmares hunt like beasts of prey . . .

He shivered, felt the world tilt slightly as he swayed. All around him the world was getting cooler, fuzzier. It was getting harder to breathe, as though someone had thrown a cotton blanket over his head. He wanted to lie down, just for a moment . . .

"Ekon!" Suddenly someone was calling his name, the sound oddly distant. "Ekon, where are you?"

Ekon sank to his knees, relishing the warmth that flooded his body. Yes, he need only rest for a moment, just a moment . . .

"Ekon! Where are you?"

Somewhere in the back of his mind, he knew he recognized that voice, but he couldn't answer it, not now. A numbness was creeping up his body, pulling him down into the earth. It was a surprisingly nice feeling.

And then he felt nothing at all.

CHAPTER 16

The FOLLOW-THROUGH

The moment Koffi opened her eyes, she knew something was wrong.

That understanding, the fear that came with it, seeped into her body slowly, like cold water poured over her head on a scorching day back at the Night Zoo. She had no sense of where she was or how she'd gotten there, but she *did* know two things.

She was outside, and she was on her back.

Slowly, she sat up. The world was a verdant blur of color all around her—hues of deep green colliding with browns and blacks, and the occasional pink or yellow. Overhead, the sky was a bright morning blue, interrupted by vines and leaves . . .

Without warning, it all came back to her.

She was in a jungle; specifically, the *Greater* Jungle.

With the realization, she jumped to her feet and at once regretted it. The world spun for a moment as she recalibrated, trying to get a sense of place. All around her, filtered sunlight pushed through the trees, casting touches of gold on random spots. Her eyes caught one of those spots a few yards away from her, and she went cold.

Ekon was lying on his back in the grass. He wasn't moving.

"Ekon!" She crossed the space between them in a matter of strides to kneel beside him. Her hands shook as she first pressed a flat palm to his chest to feel for a pulse, then held up his wrist to check again. She felt nothing.

No. Not another body, not another one. Ekon's face was too smooth. It reminded her of Sahel's, of Baba's. Instinctively, she looked around. They were alone here; no one else was coming to help.

This wasn't good.

For a brief moment, she thought of the old woman from the marketplace, what she'd said about magic. Darajas, those with the ability to use it, had once healed the sick and injured. Koffi stared at her own hands. She hadn't felt even a trace of magic since the night of the fire, she didn't trust herself to figure out anything here. She pushed the old woman from her mind and instead tried to think of what Mama would do in this situation. Mama was calm, steady, ideal in a crisis. Koffi closed her eyes and searched until she found a memory, a lesson Mama had taught her once at the Night Zoo. They'd been trying to help a baby kondoo calf that had stopped breathing, its heart hadn't been strong.

Lift the chin like this, Mama had indicated. *Then place your palms at the center of the torso . . .*

Koffi imitated the gesture as well as she could remember, placing her overlapping hands in the center of Ekon's chest. With as much strength as she could manage, she began pressing down on it in a steady counting rhythm.

One . . . two . . . one . . . two . . .

He didn't move.

231

Come on, come on, don't be dead.

An idea flitted in the back of her mind like a small bird, hopeful. She stared at her hands, then at Ekon's body.

There was one other trick she knew, another thing Mama had taught her. Koffi hesitated. She really wasn't sure about *this* one, but . . .

It could save him. It could bring him back.

She didn't stop to think about it any more as she bent over Ekon to pinch his nose with one hand and tilt his chin upward with the other. Every muscle in her body tensed as she leaned down, closer to his *face* this time. *She just had to . . .*

Her nose was less than an inch from his when he opened his eyes.

"AH!" Koffi jumped back so suddenly, she actually landed on her backside. It hurt, but that was nothing compared to the absolute horror she felt coursing through her. Ekon was sitting up and staring at her, his eyes wide.

"Um . . . hello. What were you doing?"

"I—" Embarrassment flooded her cheeks. What *had* she been doing? Suddenly, the idea of trying to resuscitate Ekon the same way Mama had taught her to resuscitate a kondoo calf seemed more than a little foolish. And what if Ekon hadn't opened his eyes in time, what if she'd . . . She shook her head before she could think about it.

"You were unconscious," she said, deliberately changing the subject. "I was too, a few minutes ago. I only just woke up."

Ekon searched the trees all around him for a moment before his eyes dropped to the jungle floor. Then he looked up at Koffi, alarmed.

"Where are our bags?"

"Our—" A terrible dread rose in Koffi. *Their bags.* She'd been so distracted by Ekon that she hadn't noticed the strange lightness on her back, the absence of something crucial. Instinctively, her hands flew to her hip. The dagger she'd taken from the temple was still there, at least, but that brought her little comfort. Their bags had everything they needed—food, water, supplies, the *journal.* She looked all around them, retracing her steps as best as she could; it didn't matter. "I . . . don't know where they are," she finally said.

At this, Ekon jumped to his feet. "How did this happen?"

Koffi frowned. Her recollection of the previous night wasn't good, it felt more like a fever dream in hindsight, but there was one thing . . .

"I remember a mist," she said. "It came out of nowhere, and then . . ."

As though her words jogged something, Ekon looked up. "I . . . I remember it too," he said. "I heard your voice, but I couldn't find you. It made me sleepy."

The longer she thought of it, the more vividly Koffi recalled it. She remembered wispy white tendrils gathering around her ankles, numbing her feet. She'd been looking for Ekon, calling out to him, but he didn't answer. She'd thought she was alone.

"It did something to us," she said quietly. "It's like it . . . *sedated* us. How is that possible?"

Ekon gave her a skeptical look. "You *do* know where we are, right?"

Koffi didn't answer but kept looking around them. There was nothing on the jungle floor save for bits of moss and bramble.

"Whatever happened to our bags, it happened when we were knocked out."

"Which wouldn't have happened if you'd listened to me . . . ," Ekon muttered.

"What?" Koffi felt something rise in her that took a second to identify. After a moment, she realized what it was: anger. *"What* did you just say to me?"

Ekon narrowed his eyes. "After we ran into the jungle, I told you we needed to stop, to reevaluate our plan." He pointed. "You wanted to keep going, you didn't—"

"Wait a minute." Koffi's eyes were still searching the jungle floor when she noticed something. "Look at this."

Ekon was at her side in a few steps. It took seconds for him to find what she already had. "Are those . . . ?"

"Footprints." Koffi nodded. "Human footprints." As soon as she said it, she knew she was right. Years at the Night Zoo had inadvertently made her something of an expert on the matter. She could tell the difference between a zebra's hoof and an antelope's, or the pawprint of a lion versus a hyena's. These tracks were distinct, narrow and rounded, with deeper indents in the dirt near the heel and toe. She followed their path until they were lost in the jungle's foliage. They were too large to be hers, and too small to be Ekon's. She pointed. "Look where they start." Carefully, she stepped around them and indicated. It was difficult to make them out in places, but there was definitely a trail leading deeper into the jungle.

"I thought no humans came into the Greater Jungle."

"I did too." Koffi's mind was racing, but she tried to keep her voice even and calm.

Ekon studied the trail a moment. "The tracks lead east."

Koffi stared at him. "How do you know that?"

He took a few steps and pointed to one of the trees. It was thicker than his entire body, and one side of it was covered in a thick blanket of moss. "Moss grows on the north side of the tree. Once you find north, everything else is relative to that."

A useful fact, Koffi noted to herself. After a moment, she nodded. "Whoever those footprints belong to was here recently. They would have seen us lying here unconscious. I think we should follow them."

"What?" Ekon looked up. "Why?"

Koffi gave him a pointed look, as though he was missing something obvious. "Let's see, we wake up in the middle of a magical jungle with all of our valuables taken. Just a few feet away, there's a set of footprints that belong to someone who isn't here anymore. I think whoever these footprints belong to took our stuff, and I want it back."

Ekon shook his head. "We're here for the Shetani, not a random chase through the jungle."

Koffi rolled her eyes. "Everything we had, everything we *needed*, was in those bags. We're not getting to the Heart of the Jungle or finding the Shetani until we get that stuff back."

Ekon hesitated. She could see the calculations happening in his mind. Another second passed before he sighed.

"Right." He nodded. "Let's go."

Under the thick canopy of trees, it was difficult for true sunlight to find its way through, but that didn't stop the heat from rising as the hours passed. Koffi had worked in the Night Zoo for eleven years—looking after its beasts in every condition, from torrid rainfall to scorching sunshine—but she'd never felt a heat quite like *this*. It was oppressive, domineering, and deliberate. She huffed, pinching bits of her dampened tunic away from her skin. She felt like an intruder in the Greater Jungle, a thing that didn't belong. It was as though the jungle was feverish, trying to sweat them out of its depths like a sickness. She didn't want to be there, and like an ungracious host, it wanted her out. Absently, and perhaps for some comfort, she let her fingers brush the hilt of the dagger on her hip. Whoever had taken the rest of their things had let her keep it, and she didn't know whether that was an oversight or a small mercy. Not that she'd know what to do with the thing if something attacked her. She felt Ekon's gaze on her and looked up.

"You know, that's a pretty rare weapon these days," he said, nodding to the dagger.

"Is it?" Koffi deliberately tried to sound offhand. In truth, from the moment she'd picked up the small white blade, she'd sensed that something about it was special. It held a sense of agelessness, like it was a piece of something born in another time.

Ekon nodded. "They don't really make jino blades in the Zamani Region, not anymore."

Jino blade. *Tooth* blade. At once, Koffi felt a bit silly. She hadn't known the knife's proper name. She looked up again.

"How are they made?"

"From the teeth of large animals," said Ekon. "Elephants, lions, anything big enough, I suppose."

Koffi didn't know whether to be impressed or horrified. She

236

thought then of the beasts of the Night Zoo. There'd been the ones that were obviously dangerous—like Diko—but there'd been others too, ones that only *looked* dangerous. She thought of Kubwa, the warhyppo, with his long white tusks. He was partial to corn. She remembered Mkaida, the three-horned ram, with silver horns longer than her arms. The idea of someone hurting them, taking pieces of them away, disturbed her. It left her to wonder what beast this weapon had been born from. Had it come from a vicious beast, hunted down by warriors, or had it belonged to something innocent and afraid? She'd never know.

"Do you know how to use a dagger?" Ekon asked, still watching her.

Heat crept into Koffi's cheeks. She'd had very little in life that she could call her own, least of all any kind of weapon. She covered up the embarrassment quickly.

"I'm perfectly capable of defending myself." She wriggled her foot for emphasis. "Remember?"

Ekon rolled his eyes. "That doesn't count."

Koffi cocked an eyebrow. "I think Father Olufemi disagrees."

In response, Ekon cringed. "That tactic is . . . somewhat effective, but you should always have a variety of moves in your repertoire. When you only have one, you become predictable and easy to defeat."

Koffi frowned. A part of her was annoyed to realize he was probably right, but another part was genuinely curious; after a few seconds, the latter won out. "Did you have some other move in mind?"

Ekon studied her a moment before seeming to come to an idea.

"There's one dagger technique I think I could teach you pretty easily. Let's see . . ." He looked around them, evaluating, then to her. "Step back, please."

"Ooh." Koffi almost laughed at the politeness of the request, but complied.

Ekon withdrew his own hanjari from the sheath on his belt. It didn't look quite as old as the jino blade, but it was obvious that it wasn't new. Someone had taken good care of it over the years, and Koffi wondered if it'd been him. The wooden hilt was clean and polished, its silvery metal blade sharpened to a lethal point.

"There are all sorts of weapons." Ekon rotated the blade in his hand, letting it catch in the late-morning sunlight. "But personally, short blades are my favorite. The combat is intimate; you have to get close to fight properly. There's no room for hesitation when you use one."

Without warning, he spun on his heel, stabbing the dagger through the air in a perfect ring. The movement was so fluid, so agile, that the air actually whistled. Koffi tensed. In that fleeting moment, Ekon had looked like someone else entirely; his face had been razor-sharp with focus, discipline.

"That move is called the duara." He said the word carefully. "It means 'circle.' "

Koffi held up the jino blade. "Teach me."

A small smile tugged at the corner of Ekon's mouth, and he went back to looking more like himself. "Daggerwork is part skill, part instinct. What's important is that, whatever move you try, you move with confidence—"

"Like *this*?" Koffi cut the air from left to right as fast as she could. The air didn't whistle, but it felt good to have something to protect herself with for a change. "How was that?"

Ekon looked mortified. "What . . . was *that*?"

"The same thing you just did."

"That's definitely *not* what I just did."

"Sure it is." Koffi tried again, turning on her heel. It wasn't as graceful, true, but she thought she'd mastered the general idea. "Just swing and . . ."

This time, Ekon cringed.

"Your feet aren't anchored," he said, shaking his head. "And your grip is . . ." He stopped himself, fingers tapping against his side in a rhythm. When he noticed Koffi was watching them, he made himself stop, looking distinctly embarrassed.

"Sorry."

Koffi frowned. "Why?"

"My fingers." Ekon looked down at them, almost condemning. "Sometimes they move when I—"

"I don't care what your fingers do," Koffi said quickly. "Are you going to show me this circle thingy or not?"

A curious expression passed over Ekon's face before he refocused. "Right." She wasn't expecting him to close the gap between them in two strides. At once, the air around her filled with that same smell, leather and cedarwood. It was a strange blend, sharp and faint all at once. He put his hand over hers, and began adjusting her fingers on the jino blade's hilt.

". . . grip is *horrendous*," he grumbled to himself, manipulating her hand. "Keep these four fingers over the hilt, and your thumb flat. Both your elbows should be tucked in, legs apart . . ."

He circled her, gently pulling her shoulders back and nodding for her to move her feet.

"To keep your stance grounded," he explained, still moving around her.

Koffi followed the instructions and tried not to think about how close Ekon was. At the Night Zoo, there had been other beast-keepers—*boy* beastkeepers, like Jabir—but he'd always been like a little brother to her. This particular closeness felt different. She found she almost didn't mind that leather and cedarwood smell . . . Ekon stepped back.

"Okay." He nodded. "I want you to try again. This time, keep your feet apart and throw your weight to the right. Let the force of it pull you around to complete the circle. It's all about the follow-through."

Koffi raised the blade, tentative. Her fingers felt stiff and awkward the way Ekon had arranged them, but he was looking at her expectantly. After a pause, she threw her arm back and spun in a circle with the blade in hand. At once, she felt the difference. Ekon had only changed her grip slightly, but the result was profound. The blade sliced through the air, impossibly fast. Ekon nodded in approval.

"Not perfect," he said with a smirk. "But . . . not terrible."

Koffi felt an undeniable surge of pride. "Could I win a fight with that move?"

"With some practice, sure." Ekon paused, thoughtful. "You know, another name for that move is actually called the pie, because you move in a circle like a—"

"Are you joking?"

He kept his face stoic. "I *never* joke about pie."

They stared at each other a moment, neither one of them

moving, before they both burst out laughing. It felt strangely good, and Koffi realized it was the first time in a long time that she'd really laughed.

Eventually, they continued on, tracking the odd footprints into the noon hour. Koffi followed the path as it wound, but it was becoming increasingly harder, and not just because of the heat. The back of her neck ached from keeping her head bent, and occasionally her eyes blurred between the dirt and leaves she had to search through to keep focused. It was clear from the way the footprints were imprinted in the dirt that they were fresh, but they were also . . . strange. She'd never seen tracks like them before. Sometimes, they were normal, a pair of feet walking in a single direction; other times, one foot turned the wrong way, or seemed to walk over the same piece of earth more than once. She couldn't make sense of it, and she didn't like it.

"I see why the Shetani would want to live here," she said aloud. "Everything about this place creeps me out, even in the daytime."

"Yeah." Beside her, Ekon was staring up at the canopy of trees, now allowing filtered light to shine through. "Me too." His eyes shot to Koffi, as though thinking of something. "Speaking of the Shetani, I've actually been meaning to ask you something."

"What?"

"You said before that you didn't know how you made the Shetani leave when you told it to," he said. "But I was wondering if you had any . . . hypotheses."

"Hippo what?"

Ekon sighed. "I was wondering if you had any guesses."

"Oh." Koffi shrugged. "The truth is, I really don't know exactly how I did it. Something about it just felt like the right thing to say." She considered a moment before continuing. "A little while ago, I met an old woman while I was in Lkossa's markets. She told me that there had once been magic in Lkossa years ago. I don't exactly know how I came by it, but I think I have that same magic."

Ekon's brows drew together, as though he were trying to figure out a particularly difficult math equation. It was almost endearing. "I've never read about that in any books," he said after a moment. His frown deepened.

"Not everything is written in books." She gestured at the sky. "I mean, how much do we know about what actually caused the Rupture?"

Ekon relaxed slightly. "Well, actually, there's been a respectable amount of academic study done on it. Most scholars agree that while it's visible from anywhere on the continent, it's most prominent in the Zamani Region. Other posit that it's the result of a barometric—"

"I'm not talking about what scholars write in books." Koffi interrupted him with a wave of her hand as they continued on. Her eyes cast over the streaks of black in the sky. They seemed less prominent here, but she couldn't tell if that was because of the changing season or the jungle canopy. "I'm talking about what really happened to cause it. Haven't you ever wondered?"

"Not really." Ekon shrugged. "I mean, the sky's always been that way. It's not like we can change—" Suddenly he stopped short, his eyes fixing on something in the trees and growing wide. "Koffi, *look*."

Koffi followed his gaze, then froze. How she'd missed the hundreds of silver-white strands hanging from overhead like silk, she wasn't sure, but she certainly saw them now. They came together and fell apart, connecting and disconnecting to form an infinite number of shapes. In the sparse sunlight filtering through the treetops, they glistened eerily.

Ekon shivered. "Is that a . . . ?"

"Yeah." There was no hiding it. Real terror gripped Koffi's voice as she stared upward too, her mouth barely moving. "It's a . . . *web*."

CHAPTER 17

TRICKS ᴀɴᴅ TRUTHS

Ekon had known what he was seeing from the moment he'd looked up, but somehow hearing it confirmed aloud made it worse.

Never in his life had he seen a spiderweb so big, and he didn't want to know what sort of creature—or creatures—had made it.

"I think we should turn around."

"For once, we are in complete agreement," said Koffi. She started walking backward, as though afraid to turn away from the eerie web. Ekon felt the same way. The air around them seemed to be cooling, *thinning*. It wasn't right for it to be this temperature, not when it had just been sweltering only minutes ago. Ekon had turned to run when a voice sounded from above.

"Children shouldn't wander in the jungle."

Koffi yelped, and instinctively, Ekon tensed, bracing himself for an attack. His stomach swooped as he noticed one strand of the giant web vibrate like a plucked string, and then something large skittered down a tree to his immediate right. A scream rose in his throat.

The creature eyeing them had the face and torso of an old,

bare-chested man, complete with thinning gray hair and wrinkles etched deep into his features. Two blank white eyes stared back at them like cold milk, unblinking and unmoving. But that wasn't what frightened Èkon; it was what followed after the creature's torso. Where two human legs should have been, instead there were eight long, stilt-like legs that weren't human at all. Each one was bent at the knee and ended in a bare brown human foot. Ekon fought a shiver. The odd tracks suddenly made sense, and he understood why they'd gone in strange directions. The creature leered, as though it could hear his thoughts.

"Humans." Its whisper was like a snake slithering over dead leaves. "It has been many years since Anatsou has seen humans, and now they come to see *him*. Anatsou is delighted."

Ekon stepped back. "What are you?"

The creature threw his head back in a laugh then, letting his airy cackles echo off the trees around them. Ekon shuddered when he saw his yellowed teeth were pointed, like fangs. "Anatsou is a maker of mischief and magic, a trader of tricks and truths. Humans will never know what Anatsou is."

"We're sorry to disturb you." Koffi's voice shook with every word. "We aren't looking for any trouble. We'll leave—"

"Ah, but they *are* looking for something." Anatsou stopped laughing as his head turned to Koffi at an unnatural angle. "The human girl is looking for her bag of treasures. Anatsou has *two* bags of treasure that he found this morning, all by himself."

Ekon shivered. This creature, this *thing*, had come while they were unconscious. Knowing that disturbed him, and he felt . . . violated.

"Those are our bags," Koffi said carefully. "They belong to—"

"Anatsou *knows* who the treasure bags belong to," the creature said. "Anatsou wanted to play a little game. He wanted to know if the humans would follow his funny trail to come find their lost treasures. Did the humans *like* Anatsou's game?"

Ekon frowned. He wanted to tell this creepy thing exactly what he thought of its "game," but before he could, Koffi stepped forward.

"Yes." She said the word with a notable touch of respect. "It was a very, *very* clever game. We found it quite difficult. It took us hours to find you."

As though this was just what Anatsou had hoped to hear, his face split into a wicked grin. "Ah, excellent. Anatsou finds the humans so entertaining, even if he also finds them simple."

"Since we won your . . . uh, game, do you think we could have our things back?" Ekon was surprised to see Koffi's expression turn almost scolding as she added, "That's only fair."

"Fair," Anatsou repeated. "Anatsou prefers his tricks, but . . . but he supposes the human girl's logic is sound. She has won Anatsou's game, and so . . ." Without warning, he skittered back up the giant web and tugged one of its strings. A large ball of white that reminded Ekon of yarn came rolling across it and dropped to the ground. Anatsou tapped it with a foot, and at once their bags fell out of it and into the dirt. Instinctively, Ekon reached for his own, but to his alarm Anatsou moved to block his path. His whitish eyes were gleaming.

"There is something else the humans want." Anatsou looked between Ekon and Koffi, addressing them. "Something else they are searching for."

"What do you mean?" Ekon asked.

Anatsou's toothy smile widened. "Humans come into Anatsou's jungle looking for his friend: the Shetani."

Koffi actually stepped forward, wide-eyed. "You know where it is?"

Anatsou bowed his head. "Anatsou will show the humans the meadow where it lives, if they would like. It is just up ahead."

Something struck hard in Ekon's chest, coursing through him like an invisible current of energy as the words sank in. This creature could *take* them to the Shetani. They could capture it and leave the jungle, well before Father Olufemi's hunting party came. He started forward, but a hand caught his arm, stopping him.

"Ekon."

He turned. Koffi was at his side, much closer than she'd been before. Her expression held uncharacteristic caution. "I don't think we should go."

As she said the words, a part of him knew she was right, that this was dangerous. Yet something else pulled, a tug low in his stomach as he looked over Anatsou's shoulder and down the crooked path to which he was gesturing. The Shetani could be waiting at the end of the path. It could be over as quickly as that. He looked back at Koffi, trying to sound reassuring.

"I think we should at least check," he said so only she could hear. "And if we don't see the Shetani, we can turn back."

Koffi shook her head. "I don't like it."

"You didn't like my idea to stop and reevaluate our plan last night either," said Ekon. It was a low blow, and he knew it. "So can we try *my* way now?"

Koffi's eyes flashed. She seemed to be weighing the options, considering. After a moment, she bit into her cheek and nodded. *"If we don't see the Shetani immediately, we leave."*

Ekon didn't wait for her to say anything else before turning back to face Anatsou. "Show us."

Anatsou skittered forward and gestured for them to follow. Koffi took steadied herself, then fell into step beside Ekon as they grabbed their sacks and headed down the path beneath the stretching web. With every step, the air seemed to chill. Ekon drummed his fingers against his side. He heard Koffi's tentative steps beside him, felt the unease lapping at him, but he still couldn't ignore that tug, the irresistible pull leading him on. The Shetani was close, he was sure of it. He'd catch it, *kill* it, and then this would all be over.

They reached a set of trees grown close together like friends sharing a secret. Anatsou stopped.

"The meadow is beyond those trees." Anatsou bowed his head again. "Find what you are searching for there."

"Thanks." Ekon needed no further prompting as he and Koffi stepped around Anatsou and between the trees. Instinctively, he gripped the hilt of his hanjari, and a long beat passed before he braced himself to step through the trees. He stopped short.

The meadow he'd entered was too vivid. Vines covered most of the tree trunks, but their colors were oversaturated, almost lurid in their brightness. Slowly, something familiar tickled in the back of his mind. He realized it—he'd been here before.

"No! NO!"

A shock ran through Ekon's body as he turned in the direction of the noise, and his heart stopped. Koffi had dropped to the ground, her body curling into a ball as she writhed. Her eyes were screwed shut in horrible pain, and her hands were pressed hard against her ears.

"No!" she screamed. "Run! Mama, Jabir, run!"

Ekon's heart lurched. He stared up at the black-trunked trees around them, and the hairs on his arms stood on end. There weren't trees staring back at him anymore.

There were faces.

He watched the black bark of the tree nearest him twist, re-shaping itself into something else: the face of a woman. Her mouth hung slack, viscous sap the color of molten gold glistening on her lips. The voice that rose from within, however, did not belong to her.

Please.

Ekon bit down on his tongue hard as his Baba's voice filled the meadow, echoing from every direction. Another tree to his left contorted its shape, this time into the face of a child. Hollowed cavities took the place where its eyes should have been.

Ekon, Baba's voice moaned. *Please.*

Around him, more of the trees changed. Koffi was still at his side, still crying, but he couldn't move. A stench had filled the air, like old moss and rotted oak; it was the smell of something dying.

My son, please . . .

"No!" Ekon closed his eyes and covered his ears, desperate to block out the words. "It isn't real! *You're* not real!"

He let his fingers tap against his head as he covered his ears, trying to find a count.

One-two-three. One-two-three. One-two-three.

He's not real, Ekon reminded himself as the numbers filled his mind. *It's all in your head, it's not real. He's not real.*

He opened his eyes again, but the trees with faces were still there, still glaring. He blinked again, but they remained fixed, no longer the dregs of his imagination.

No.

What he was seeing now wasn't in his head at all. To his horror, he found that, in fact, the trees were moving, slow and menacing as they began to sway in place. He watched as some unfurled their branches while others curled theirs into huge wooden knots—fists.

One-two-three. Five-eight-ten. Six-two-one . . .

His numbers abandoned him.

"You're not real!" Ekon sank to the ground, repeating the words as though saying them aloud could make them true. He felt Koffi's body shaking beside his own, racked by sobs, but he couldn't comfort her. He couldn't even comfort himself. The world was beginning to grow dark again. "You're not real," he repeated softly. "None of you are, you can't—"

"Ekon."

Ekon's eyes flew open. He recognized one of the faces in the trees, a first. It was sculpted around the bark of the trunk, but unmistakable. He took in the face of a man with high cheekbones like his, a full beard, round eyes that—had they not been empty—would have reminded him of Kamau's. The name escaped his lips before he could stop himself.

"Baba."

The face in the tree blinked. "Hello, Ekon."

Seconds passed, seconds when Ekon knew his heart should have been beating in his chest. But he couldn't make it restart again, his body wouldn't obey. His baba had been dead for ten years; now he was staring at him.

"How are you here?"

Baba's lips, formed from the tree trunk's bark, were pressed tight, his ligneous face full of a quiet sadness. "Why have you returned to the jungle?"

Any number of answers filled Ekon's mind. He'd come here to gain respect, approval—forgiveness. "I'm here to kill the beast that took your life, Baba," he said aloud. "Once I do, I'll be given my manhood, and my honor."

The emotion in Baba's face was inscrutable, but his words were soft. "No one can *give* you manhood or honor, Ekon. You must earn those for yourself."

"But how?" Ekon heard the crack in his own voice, but he couldn't stop it. "How else do I earn it, Baba?"

Baba's mouth opened, as though he meant to say something, but then he stopped. His expression turned panicked. "You must leave this place," he said in an entirely different voice. "Leave, and take the girl with you. Go!"

Ekon started. He looked between his father and Koffi, who was still lying on the ground. "Baba," he asked, "what's going—?"

Fear lanced through him as his father's face began to transfigure. He looked as though he were trying to speak but couldn't. He sounded as though he was gagging, choking.

"Baba!" Ekon jumped to his feet. *"No—"*

It happened without warning.

A horde of black spiders erupted from the tree, covering the place where Baba's face had been. Ekon screamed. He knew he should have grabbed Koffi, should have run, but his feet were rooted to the ground. He couldn't move. The spiders seemed to multiply like magic, growing and pulsating into an intangible mass. He stepped back, and the movement caught the spiders' attention; at once, he felt an infinite number of tiny black eyes turn his way.

No.

He turned to retreat but wasn't fast enough. Like a terrible sea, the spiders came for him in a rush, pinching and biting his legs and feet. He ran, trying to smack them off with each step, but it was no use. The horde surrounded him on all sides, millions of creatures. They covered the trees, filled the webs above him, and rained down on his shoulders and neck. A tree root caught at his ankle, and the world came crashing toward him as he fell. The spiders seized their chance. They crept and scuttled all across his body, between his fingers, into his ears; they covered every inch of him. Fangs pierced his flesh over and over, relentless bites in his skin. Slowly, his vision grew cloudy and black around the edges as a numbness grew.

"Ekon!"

He wondered if that was Baba screaming his name or someone else. He was dying—of that, he was certain—but he wondered how long it would take for his body to really sever from this world. He would not be cremated, so his soul would not be freed. Perhaps he would spend the rest of eternity here, among the spiders.

"Ekon!"

The voice that cried his name was much closer and louder

now, not a delusion. Something smacked across his legs, his back, his arms, over and over. It took him a moment to understand. Someone was *hitting* him, trying to get the spiders off his body. He blinked hard, forcing himself to look up.

"Koffi?"

She wasn't on the ground anymore, and Ekon didn't understand the tears in her eyes as she looked down at him. Spiders continued to fall around them both as her eyes roved over his body in fear, then snapped back to meet his gaze. "You have to get up!" she shouted. "Please get up! We have to get out of here! They're coming from above, from the web!"

Get out. Ekon focused on the two words, on the urgency and fear in Koffi's voice. *Get out. Get out. We have to get out.* She tugged harder on his arm, pulling him back to his feet. Hundreds of spiders fell from his body. *Get out.* That was the new focus. *Get out.*

Koffi pulled her jino blade out and held it tight, and that was the thing that finally brought Ekon back.

"Run!" he shouted. "Go!"

Koffi didn't need to be told twice. She raced down a path between the trees. "Come on!" she said over her shoulder. "I know the way out!" She darted between another set of trees, Ekon on her heels. He heard the menacing clicks of thousands of pincers around him, the rustling of the spiders as they scuttled across the underbrush, but he didn't dare look back. Up ahead, barely in view, there was a bright spot of blue—the sky, uninterrupted by the web's milky strands. They were almost there; they could make it out.

Koffi hurled herself over a log, and Ekon followed. She ducked beneath a long curtain of vines and disappeared. Just as Ekon reached them too, the vines gave a terrible shudder. He stepped back as they turned to blackish brown, as each one of them seemed to fill with spiders. They formed a barrier, an uninterrupted wall of tiny bodies.

"Ekon!" He could hear Koffi's voice on the other side of the vine-spider wall, frantic. "Please, come on!"

He couldn't do it. In the second it took him to try and fail to count the legion of spiders surrounding him, he knew it was true. He wasn't strong like Kamau or Baba, and he wasn't strong enough for this. His fingers, despite their bites, still tried to add a rhythm to his fear.

One-two-three. Can't do this. One-two-three. Just give up.

Abruptly he heard a new voice in his head. Not Koffi's or his father's but Brother Ugo's. *You do not have to be the largest or most dangerous fighter, Ekon,* the old man had once said to him. *So long as you are* fastest.

Fast. He didn't have to be strong to get out of here, he just needed to be fast. He clung to that word with a viselike grip, bracing himself. Fast, he just had to be fast. He took a deep breath and charged forward, eyes shut tight as he passed through the mass. His skin erupted, stinging as the spiders bit into his flesh. When he opened his eyes, the spiders were gone.

The jungle around him was warm again, the sun beating down in generous shafts of light as he found Koffi's wide eyes. Their chests rose and fell hard, and her expression asked a thousand questions he didn't want to answer.

So he ran.

CHAPTER 18

SCARS

Koffi and Ekon ran through the jungle's underbrush, the crunch of their footsteps the only thing filling the silence.

In the privacy of her mind, Koffi faintly wondered where they were heading, whether their new direction would get them any closer to finding the Shetani or send them back to where they'd started. In all honesty, she didn't particularly care at the moment. She and Ekon hadn't spoken in the hours since they'd escaped Anatsou's web, but there seemed to be a tacit understanding between them that, for now, the priority had changed. It was essential that they got as far from those wretched spiders and their wretched webs as possible.

The jungle grew cooler as midday gave way to dusk, drawing from its depths a different kind of sound and life. Cicadas trilled through the humid air; overhead, the rustling leaves made their own kind of serenade, a sign that, perhaps here, things were safe. Warily, Koffi slowed, and she was relieved to see Ekon do the same. Adrenaline had numbed her body for hours, abating all the usual signs of fatigue, but suddenly everything returned in a rush. The soles of her feet ached mercilessly, and her lungs felt tight with each breath. She was hungry, thirsty, and exhausted, but she couldn't quite relax, not yet. Her nerves were still as frayed as old rope; every sudden skitter and crunch of leaf underfoot rattled her insides. Her eyes dragged across the trees and fixed on a large snake wrapped around one of its branches. The thing's body had to be thicker than her arm, rings of black covering its golden scales. It stared at her a moment longer with deep emerald-green eyes before slithering farther up the tree's trunk and out of sight. She shivered. That serpent's gaze, cool and piercing, felt unnatural, like everything else in this jungle. She thought of Anatsou and his milk-white gaze. Even now, she recalled the thin, mocking quality of the creature's voice, the cool prickle of his laughter.

He can't hurt us, a voice of reason assured her as she and Ekon kept walking through the trees. *He's gone. He can't get us.*

She believed it was the truth, but she couldn't help remembering. The nightmarish images in the meadow were still vivid in her mind's eye. She saw her mother, lying in a pool of blood, Jabir in an identical one beside her. Over and over they had called her name; over and over they had died. It had been something born straight from her worst nightmares, horrid.

Ekon cleared his throat, and she slowly realized he'd been looking at her, waiting for her to speak. Guilt racked her. If Anatsou and his spiders had been scary for *her,* she could only imagine what they'd been like for Ekon. She still remembered the way he'd looked in that thicket, covered in spiders and curled into a fetal position like a child. His face had been contorted in what looked like unimaginable pain. What had he seen? What had put him in so much pain?

"Ekon," she began tentatively. "I—"

"We're losing light." Ekon's words were clipped. "No use going farther. We might as well stop here and make some sort of camp."

Koffi clamped her mouth shut again. Was that unusual curtness directed at her, or was it something else? Unsure, she nodded in agreement and shrugged off her bag.

Ekon didn't give her another chance to speak before he turned and headed behind a cluster of trees. He was gone just long enough for Koffi to begin feeling panicked, but then she heard his returning footsteps. When he came into view again, he was carrying an armful of twigs.

"We've still got some dried food in our bags," he muttered. "It's not a Kuhani's feast, but it'll do."

"Right." She watched him kneel before the twig pile and grab two to rub together for a fire. He knew what he was doing—that was obvious to Koffi from the methodical way he worked—but every time wisps of smoke started to rise from the sticks he was holding, he'd flinch in pain and have to start over. After the third failed attempt within the hour, Koffi spoke up.

"Let me try something."

"It's all right, I've got—"

She snatched the sticks away, then stooped beside him. Almost everything about the jungle felt new and foreign, but doing this felt like home; Mama had taught her years ago how to start a fire. She relished the familiar feeling of the sticks rolling faster and faster between her palms, the smell of smoke and then the gradual warmth.

She threw it in with the kindling, and fifteen minutes later, they had a fire. Ekon huffed.

"Thanks."

Koffi looked to him, about to make a joke, when she noticed something.

"Ekon, you're covered in bites!" Closer to him, she could clearly discern them, countless red pinprick wounds freckled all over his arms, neck, and face. She resisted the urge to shudder.

"Yeah." Ekon stared into the fire. "It's fine, though, none of them really hurt. They'll heal on their own, hopefully."

It took everything in Koffi not to roll her eyes. She sighed before she spoke again, in a tone she hoped sounded reasonable.

"They could get *infected*."

To her frustration, Ekon merely shrugged. Koffi looked to the sky. It was nearly nightfall, the trees' shadows growing longer in the absence of the sun. She looked around until her eyes fixed on something a few feet away, then abruptly stood.

"Where are you going?"

Koffi didn't answer but walked over to the familiar yellow-leaf plant she'd just noticed. It was covered in tiny pea-shaped seeds the color of a peanut. She picked as many off the bush as she could before returning to Ekon's side to drop them before her. She didn't have the mortar and pestle Mama would have used in this situation back at the Night Zoo, but she improvised, using a rock to grind the seeds against a large leaf. Something prickled in her eyes as she took in their earthy smell and thought of Mama, but she worked until she'd created a lumpy paste. When she looked up, Ekon was watching her intently.

"What is that?"

"You taught me how to do that duara thing earlier," she said calmly. "Now I'm going to teach *you* something. This is called ponya seed, and when you mash it into a paste, it's a great treatment for wounds." She began to dot the paste onto each spider bite with her index finger. The moment she touched him, Ekon hissed in pain, but she used her other hand to hold him steady. "Don't move," she instructed. "It'll smear."

"It's . . . *tingling*," he said through his teeth.

Koffi nodded. "Ponya seeds are anti-inflammatory, disinfecting, and, incidentally, an excellent source of protein. Here." She held the paste-covered leaf up to Ekon's nose and let him take a long whiff. He frowned a moment before surprise passed over his face.

"It . . . smells good, kind of sweet," he said.

Koffi kept dabbing at Ekon's arms, legs, even his face. It was strange being so close to him twice in the same day. He sat perfectly still as she thumbed his neck, the line of his jaw, and a spot next to his mouth. She studied his lips, a second too long for her own liking. At once, she backed away.

"Um . . . does that help?"

Ekon looked down at his body. When he looked back up again, there was a softness in his eyes that made him seem younger, like a curious boy who'd discovered something new and intriguing.

"Yeah, it does," he said. "This stuff's amazing."

Koffi nodded. "When I was little, my mama used to call me her ponya seed. They're small, but strong, and no matter where they're planted, they always thrive."

Ekon's eyes were careful. "Is your mother still at the Night Zoo?"

Koffi stiffened. She didn't want to acknowledge the truth because then it couldn't be avoided, but the words escaped her anyway. "Yeah. She and my friend Jabir."

"Jabir," Ekon repeated. "Is . . . a boy?"

"Yeah," said Koffi with a shrug. "He's like a little brother to me."

She didn't understand the look on his face just then—a mix of curiosity and relief. After a moment, he spoke again. "I heard you call out to them, in the meadow." His voice was surprisingly soft.

Koffi swallowed a tightness in her throat. "They're my family," she said quietly. "They're all I have left."

Ekon said nothing but continued staring at her. He still had that analytical look in his eyes, but it was touched by something else. Abruptly he spoke again.

"How did you end up in the Night Zoo?"

"Bad luck," said Koffi bitterly. "Years ago, my parents and I lived in Lkossa proper, selling produce. It was a good life, but . . . my baba made some bad investments. We ran out of money and had to take out loans, then *more* loans to cover the old ones. Things just got worse and worse." She looked to Ekon. "Then one day, my baba met Baaz Mtombé. He offered to pay our debts if we signed indentured servitude contracts and agreed to work for him to pay off the debts. A few years after we moved to the Night Zoo, a sweating fever went around. My baba got sick, and then he didn't get better. When he died, the city's inheritance laws were applied."

"Inheritance laws?"

"I am my father's only child," she explained. "So his debts were transferred to my mother and me. We've been paying them off ever since."

"I'm sorry, Koffi." Ekon's words were quiet but sounded genuine.

Koffi didn't answer. She didn't know what to say to that; she never had. For several minutes, they were both content to sit in silence while they nibbled on their dried fruit and meat. Eventually, she broke the silence again.

"What did *you* see?" she asked. "In the meadow."

Ekon visibly stiffened. "Nothing. I didn't see anything."

It was a lie, and a bad one. Koffi persisted. "You know, you don't have to be embarrassed—"

"I *said*, I didn't see anything. Drop it, okay?"

Koffi tried not to recoil. In that moment, anger had flashed in Ekon's eyes, but so had something else. Pain. It reminded her of another lesson Mama had given her at the Night Zoo. Often, the beasts that lashed out the worst were also the ones hurting the worst. Maybe it was the same with Ekon. Maybe something was hurting him far more than she could ever hope to understand.

"I'm sorry," she said quietly. "For prying."

Ekon paused, then exhaled hard. "You're not the one who should be apologizing," he said. "I shouldn't have snapped at you. It was undisciplined. I should have kept myself in check."

Koffi couldn't help herself. "You don't have to be in check all the time, you know."

Ekon frowned. "That's not the way I was raised."

Koffi understood then that whatever was buried in Ekon was buried deep. If he wanted to dig it out, he'd have to do that himself.

No one else could make him, and certainly not her. She decided to change the subject, pointing up to the sky overhead.

"I've never seen those before," she said with a nod to the wisps of silver-white spilled over the blackness above.

"I've read about them," said Ekon, following her gaze. Koffi watched the scowl slip from his face gradually, watched his expression soften to something like wonder. "They're small clusters of stars, gathered by Atuno the sky god himself."

Koffi hugged her knees to her chest. "You know, when the sky's like this, I forget about what the Rupture did to it," she noted. "I forget it's broken at all."

"It's still damaged," said Ekon. He said the words with a particular kind of scorn, and Koffi had the sense that, perhaps, he wasn't just talking about the sky anymore. "Even if you can't see it now, it'll never be right again. It'll always be scarred, flawed."

Koffi paused before speaking, choosing her words with care. "Maybe there's a beauty in the scars," she said. "Because they're a reminder of what's been faced, and what's been survived."

Ekon said nothing in answer, but Koffi snuck a glance at him and thought she saw his muscles relax, saw the slightest shift in his stiffened posture. Tonight, that was enough.

They sat like that, in perfect silence, until whatever magic had filled the air seemed to dissipate and the dying fire turned to glowing orange embers in the dirt. Eventually, Koffi found a place amid the dirt and leaves, and curled on her side. She noted Ekon had taken his bag and propped it underneath him to use as a pillow, and she did the same. After all that had happened today, she thought she'd never be able to fall asleep in this jungle again, but now she found that her eyes were growing heavier and heavier with fatigue, that sleep was beckoning fast. Her mind floated lazily between reality and sleep, taking in the intermingling smells of smoke, ponya seed paste, and the surrounding trees as they creaked and rustled in the darkness.

CHAPTER 19

A BEAUTIFUL VIOLENCE

When Ekon woke in the morning's faint hours, the leaves around him were slicked shiny and wet; the dirt was soft and damp.

Carefully, he rose, surveying the world warily. His gaze narrowed as it dragged over tree trunks and up to the lush green canopy where sunlight filtered through. *It's changed here,* he mused. *Something's different.*

Only hours had passed since Koffi's brave little fire had succumbed to the darkness, but in that brief expanse of time, everything seemed to have grown greener, lusher; even the smell that suffused the air felt fresh in his lungs. It took him a moment to name that change, to understand—it had rained. Instinctively, he touched his clothes and found—to his surprise—that they were perfectly dry, and that, in fact, the place where he'd slept had remained entirely dry thanks to the leaf overhead. It was a colossal plant, with leaves easily the size of a small mule cart.

"Huh." Ekon stared at it a second longer. "Go figure."

As quietly as he could, he dug in his bag and pulled out Nkrumah's journal. By either luck or a miracle, it seemed the old book had survived its most recent adventure. Ekon found a nearby tree to sit against and held it balanced on his lap. Mornings were his favorite part of the day, a perfect time for reading. He flipped through its pages, trying to find where he'd left off. There was plenty of vegetation all over the jungle, and he had his hanjari if he wanted to hunt—maybe the journal could offer some guidance on what was edible here and what was not. Slowly, he skimmed its botanical section.

It still amazed him how extensive the old naturalist's notes had been, how accurate they were even nearly a century after he'd disappeared. Ekon's thumb stopped on an illustration of a silvery leaf. It certainly *looked* interesting. His eyes dropped to the caption beneath it.

SPECIMEN 98A

NAME: HASIRA LEAF

PRONUNCIATION: *hus-EER-ah*

INFORMAL NAME: ANGRY LEAF, SOOTHING LEAF

HABITAT: *The Greater Jungle, Zamani Region (Old East)*

DESCRIPTION: *Green leaves, silver-veined*

LIFE EXPECTANCY: *Unknown*

ADDITIONAL NOTES: *This plant, indigenous to the Zamani Region, grows in abundance in the Greater and Lesser Jungles alike near the roots of old trees, or trees who have been personally offended. Dried and burned, hasira leaves may become a dangerous and addictive hallucinogen, causing those affected by it to exhibit unusual mood swings, hyper-aggression, and memory loss.*

Ekon shuddered. Since entering the Greater Jungle, he hadn't seen a hasira leaf, but it certainly didn't sound like a plant he wanted anything to do with. Suddenly he was grateful to have this journal as a guide.

"You're up early."

Ekon jumped. He'd been so immersed in his reading that he hadn't heard Koffi stir. She was now wide awake, sitting up, and staring right at him. He couldn't quite figure out her expression or the cause of the sudden uneven pattering in his chest. He nodded.

"Uh, I guess I am."

She blinked. "How are you feeling?"

"I—" It took Ekon a moment for the details of the previous evening to return to him. He looked down at his arms and legs. The ponya seed paste must have dissolved in the night, because it was gone, leaving his skin only faintly touched with its scent. Notably, the bite marks were almost entirely gone too. He met Koffi's gaze again. "I feel . . . better."

"Good." She paused for a moment, then frowned. "Do you always wake up early?"

"Of course." Ekon frowned. "I like to."

Koffi wrinkled her nose. *"Why?"*

"My mentor, Brother Ugo, taught me at a young age that mornings are the best time of the day to exercise the mind," he said. "You should try it some—"

"No, thank you."

Ekon shook his head, hiding a small smile. "I also thought it'd be good to take a look at the map before we get going," he added. "We've got a long day ahead of us. That . . . detour with Anatsou put us off course, so we'll need to pick up the pace today to get us to the Heart in a reasonable amount of—"

"Actually . . ." Koffi cleared her throat, and Ekon saw hesitation in her expression. "I wanted to talk about that."

"About what?"

"Our course." Koffi wrapped one of her twists around her finger. "I was thinking . . . what if the Shetani *isn't* at the Heart of the Jungle?"

"What?" Ekon frowned. "What do you mean? Where else would it be?"

"I don't know," said Koffi. "It's just . . . when I think about it, don't you think that a place like the Heart of the Jungle, the very center of this entire place, seems a bit . . . obvious?"

Ekon didn't like the direction of this conversation. He'd woken up this morning revitalized, determined to see their mission through. He'd had a very precise, clear-cut plan; now, as usual, Koffi was dismantling it. "If the Shetani isn't in the Heart of the Jungle, where else could it be?"

Koffi pursed her lips. "I don't know why, but I have this feeling we should head northwest today."

"Northwest?" Ekon repeated. "As in, the exact *opposite* direction of the Heart?"

Koffi twisted the hair around her finger faster. "I know it sounds weird, but—"

"You want us to change our entire plan, because you had a *feeling*?"

At once, Koffi's eyebrows rose. "Didn't *you* have a feeling yesterday, when you led us into a lair full of spiders?"

267

The accusation was offhand, but it still stung. Ekon's voice came out harsher than he intended when he answered. "The whole reason we ended up anywhere near there was because *you* led us into a magical fog that knocked us unconscious, which caused a giant spider thing to *rob* us—"

Koffi rolled her eyes. "Gods-smite, you might be the most dramatic boy I've ever—"

"Stop swearing!"

"Point proven."

Against his will, Ekon's voice rose. "Do you ever act your age, or are you always this immature?"

Koffi scowled. "Do what you want. I'm going northwest. Have fun with your little picture book."

"It's *not* a picture book!" Ekon held Nkrumah's journal against his chest protectively. "It's a historic journal of *illuminated natural—*"

A long shriek made them both go stock-still at the same time Ekon felt a tremor in the dirt. His blood ran cold, and he watched Koffi's expression change from one of defiance to utter horror. The wet growl that tore through the quiet was unlike any other sound he'd heard in all his life. Slowly, he turned and felt his skin prickle.

Never had he seen such a creature like the one before them.

His first instinct was to call it a snake, a name largely attributed to its thick serpentine body and dark brown scales. But no, as soon as Ekon thought the word in his mind, he knew that was woefully wrong. This creature stood ten feet high; it was no mere snake. His throat tightened in horror as his eyes traveled up its limbless body to its head and found that where he'd expected a reptilian skull was something else. He saw large brown eyes, leathery gray ears that looked familiar but wrong, a trunk, and sharp ivory tusks longer than his arms. An elephant—this beast had the body of a snake and the head of an *elephant*. It seemed to look between Ekon and Koffi, musing, and as its gaze landed on Ekon, its proper name rose to the forefront of his mind, pulled from the pages of Nkrumah's journal.

Grootslang.

"Koffi." Ekon kept his eyes on the beast, willing it to stare back at him as he spoke. He kept his voice low and didn't turn to look back at her. "Move away. Slowly."

He waited for the crunch of retreating footsteps but heard none. The grootslang let another wet snarl escape its horrid gray mouth, and Ekon couldn't stop himself from trembling. He'd trained all his life to take down men; none of that training had prepared him for this.

Without warning, the grootslang shot forward, too fast and lithe for a creature so large. Ekon dodged just in time, rolling away over leaves as it struck at a nearby tree and splintered the wood. The world spun as he righted himself and leaped away before the grootslang could strike again. He looked over his shoulder just in time to see Koffi jolt, as though waking from a stupor. The grootslang turned her way, and his heart sank.

"No!"

He ran but wasn't fast enough. The grootslang reached Koffi first. It opened its gaping mouth as it loomed over her, but just as it neared, there was a flash of white. Ekon ran along the other side, surprised to hear the beast hiss in pain as it recoiled. Koffi still had her jino knife in hand and was swinging and stabbing at the air.

She was keeping the creature at bay, but she'd tire out eventually.

Think. He racked his brain for ideas, frantic. *What do you know about grootslangs?* He'd just read about them, but his mind was scattered. He tried to remember the finer points of the scholar's notes. Grootslangs usually dwelled in caves, pits, and other dark places, but could occasionally be drawn out by . . .

An idea came to him.

"Koffi!" He shouted her name as the creature bellowed again. "Throw the dagger at it!"

"What?" Koffi didn't take her eyes off the beast, but her voice held nothing but disbelief. "Why?"

"Just do it!" Ekon crept to the right, trying to keep out of the monster's peripheral vision. The idea was a slim shot, but just maybe . . .

"This is the only weapon I have!" Koffi spared him a second's glance as she continued retreating slowly. "If I throw it, I won't have anything to—"

"You have to trust me!" Ekon yelled. "Please, Koffi!"

She shot him one more look before steeling herself and planting her feet in the dirt. In response, the grootslang drew itself up to its full height, blotting out what little light filtered through the trees. Koffi raised her arm high, then hurled the dagger as hard as she could at the beast's middle. The tooth blade gracefully twirled through the air before bouncing uselessly off the grootslang's armored scales and landing in the dirt. The beast hissed with new rage.

No.

Ekon didn't know what came over him, just that—before he could stop to think about it—he was running. He closed the gap between himself and Koffi, flung his arms out, and barreled into her so that he was draped over her as they both toppled to the ground. Underneath him, she curled her body into a ball, and he used his arms and chest to cover as much of her as he could. Ultimately, he knew the gesture wouldn't do much against the grootslang's wrath, but maybe while the thing was busy eating him, Koffi could run. He caught a glimpse of her beneath him; her eyes were screwed shut, waiting for pain. A part of him wanted to close his eyes too, but he found he couldn't do it. He turned his head to face the grootslang again. It was still eyeing them with malice. The leaves rustled as it slithered toward them, closing the distance as its massive gray ears flapped eerily in the wind. It was getting closer and closer, and any second now, one of its tusks would gore them. Ekon held his breath, braced for it, when—

The grootslang stopped short.

Ekon's heart thundered in his chest like a war drum as he watched the monster turn its head slowly to the right. He followed its gaze to the thing that had given it pause. A single shaft of golden sunshine was piercing the jungle's canopy, shining light directly on the jeweled hilt of Koffi's jino blade. In the luminance, the deep red of the rubies embedded in the carved ivory glittered like blood, a beautiful violence. The beast flicked its forked tongue as it used its trunk to pick up the blade and examine it, two beady black eyes narrowing with scrutiny. Ekon didn't move a muscle as it completed its appraisal. A second that felt like a century passed before it wrapped its trunk around the rest of the blade and turned away from them. As quickly as it'd come, it slithered into the jungle's depths, consumed in the darkness. Still, Ekon didn't move.

"Did it leave?" Koffi's voice was muffled against his chest, and immediately, he rolled off her and helped her up. She stared in the direction the grootslang had gone, looking visibly shaken.

"Yeah." Ekon looked over his shoulder, trying to make his heart-beat steady again. "I think so."

Koffi looked from the trees back to him, bewildered. "How did you do that?"

"Do what?"

"How did you know it would go away?"

Ekon nodded to their sacks, still sitting just a few yards away. "I've read about them before," he said. "Grootslangs are classified as hoarders."

Koffi frowned. "What's that mean?"

"They're like magpies, they like to collect things," he explained. "Especially things of value. Your jino blade had those rubies on the hilt, so I figured that might be enough to distract it." Suddenly he felt guilty. "Sorry about losing it, by the way."

"Meh, I'll find another. Besides, I still prefer kicking," she said. "I'm just glad it worked. For a minute there, I thought we were done for."

Ekon chuckled. "Nah, it would have eaten me first, promise."

Koffi's expression abruptly changed, as though something had just dawned on her. "You—you covered me." She spoke as though the words were from a foreign language, one she barely under-stood. "Why?"

Ekon stopped. The truth was, he hadn't known why he'd done it, he just had. "I . . ." He faltered. "I was just returning the favor. You helped me with the spiders yesterday. Figured this round was on me."

"Thank you." Koffi's voice was earnest, perhaps the most earnest he'd ever heard it.

"Uh . . ." Ekon massaged the back of his neck, suddenly feeling warm. "Don't mention it. You hungry?"

Koffi grinned. "I'm starving."

They continued north together, side by side. Though, technically speaking, Ekon noted that they still hadn't determined their exact plan or path yet, he found he didn't mind. He inhaled and took in the smell of moss and rich dirt, which he'd never smelled before. The air was still warm, but not oppressively so, almost pleasant.

"Ah." Koffi stopped walking. She lifted her eyes and pointed at one of the trees up ahead. "Look."

Ekon's gaze found the tree Koffi was pointing at. It was easily the largest he'd ever seen. Its wood was a deep, rich brown, with bulbous bumps on its trunk that reminded him of warts. Leaves of deepest green clung to its branches, which were weighed down by large red fruits Ekon had never seen before. They were like pomegranates, but bigger.

"She looks like the mother of the jungle." There was a touch of admiration in Koffi's voice as they drew closer.

"I was going to say *grand*mother."

They stopped just before the tree, the tops of their heads not even reaching a third of the way up its trunk. In the afternoon light, the fruit weighing down its boughs seemed to glisten. Just the sight of them made Ekon's mouth water.

"I think we've just found lunch," said Koffi, triumphant. "And possibly dinner for the next few days."

"Wait a minute." Ekon withdrew Nkrumah's journal from his bag and began flipping through its pages, trying to find the chapter he'd been reading earlier. "Just give me a second . . ." He felt Koffi's gaze on him as he continued searching.

"Well?"

Ekon frowned. It seemed he'd reached the end of the journal's botanical section, but he hadn't seen any notes or illustrations to match the tree before them. "I'm not finding anything on it yet, but that doesn't mean—"

"Look, you said yourself that this Nkrumah guy was the expert on this jungle," said Koffi, crossing her arms. "Which means, if this tree isn't noted in there as dangerous, it's fine."

"I still think we should check to make sure—"

Without warning, she leaped, fingers wrapping around the lowest bough so that she swung from it with surprising grace. Ekon watched, somewhat horrified and somewhat impressed, as she pushed herself up and reached for the next highest bough, climbing higher and higher until she was several feet above him.

"Koffi, be careful—*ow*!"

"Watch your head!" Koffi gave him an impish grin as she shook one of the boughs and sent more of the tree's fruit to the ground. They came off with surprising ease, showering the space around him. Ekon frowned when a few more hit him on their way down, but found he couldn't stay mad. After a few minutes, Koffi glanced down at him again. From the tops of the branches she looked like an ancient queen of the jungle, presiding over her domain.

"Right." She tested one foot on the branch below her, and it wobbled. Her eyes dropped to the ground below, where Ekon was standing, then widened. "Um . . ."

"Seriously?" Ekon fought to keep exasperation from his voice. "You know how to climb *up* trees but not down?"

Koffi's eyes narrowed. "It's not like I had to learn. We had ladders at the Night Zoo."

Ekon rubbed the bridge of his nose before looking around. "Jump. I'll catch you."

"Jump?"

Ekon's frown deepened. "Unless you'd like to stay up there all night?"

There was a pause before Koffi rolled her eyes. "Fine." She lowered and let her legs dangle over the branch, swinging them back and forth. "I'll push off."

"On my count," said Ekon. "One . . . two . . ."

"Three!"

Ekon's heart leaped to his throat as Koffi came flying down at him in a rush. His arms barely shot out in time to catch her. Their bodies collided, his back slamming against the tree's trunk to take the worst of the impact. When he opened his eyes, Koffi was still in his arms, and scowling.

"You *closed your eyes*?"

"Not on purpose," said Ekon defensively. His heart was thundering in his chest. He suddenly realized his hands were still on Koffi's waist, and they were still *very* close together. For exactly three seconds, he was keenly aware of their chests rising and falling against each other. "I mean, I still caught you."

Koffi stepped back from him and started gathering the fruit she'd shaken off the tree. "We should have enough here to make a decent meal." She looked at him. "I know you're good with a dagger, but . . . how are your mincing skills?"

275

A few minutes later, with the help of Ekon's hanjari, they had a small feast before them. The tree's massive roots were large enough to use like a makeshift table, and some of the larger leaves served as plates. Koffi sat on one side of it, he took the other. Admittedly, Ekon wondered if, along with the fruit, he'd have to eat his cautionary words about them. They'd looked delicious hanging from the tree's branches, but cut up into pieces, they emitted an aroma unlike anything he'd ever smelled before—the scent was intensely sweet, almost sugaring the very air around it. As if reading his mind, Koffi smirked.

"See?" She picked up a piece of the fruit and popped it into her mouth. "A perfectly good lunch, despite your bossiness."

Ekon noted that the fruit had stained her lips dark red; he was still staring at them when her words really hit him. "Wait." He put down the piece of fruit he'd been about to eat, frowning. "I'm not . . . *bossy*?"

Koffi raised an eyebrow.

"I'm not!"

"You really are."

Ekon sat back, thoughtful. "I'm just cautious," he said after a moment. "I mean, this jungle's dangerous, and I don't like to see people I care about hurt. It—" He caught himself. "Uh, sorry, that was a weird thing to say."

"No." Koffi's expression had changed; gone was her smirk, and in its place was something he didn't recognize. "It wasn't."

Neither of them spoke for a moment. In that quiet, something hummed near Ekon's navel. He didn't know how to describe that feeling, what to do with it. Quickly, he changed the subject.

"That monster was called a grootslang," he volunteered.

Koffi stared at him a moment, then seemed to come back to herself. "Oh."

"There's a legend that when the six gods created the world, many of the animals we know today were different. Over time, the gods split some of them into two separate animals to make them less dangerous," he explained. "Grootslangs are said to be the origin of both elephants and all snakes, incredibly powerful."

"It was impressive, the way you used your book smarts to get rid of it." Koffi popped another piece of the fruit into her mouth. "Pretty spectacular, actually."

Something inside Ekon swelled with pride. He didn't receive praise often, especially when Kamau was around. The compliment felt good. "Well, you weren't so bad yourself," he said, smiling. "I mean, you completely ignored my tutorial with the dagger, but—"

"I prefer a freestyle method." Koffi stuck out her tongue, bright red from the fruit.

"You've got good form, I'll give you that." Ekon chuckled, putting the fruit down. "I've never seen a girl move the way you do." The minute the words left his mouth, he hesitated. "Uh, sorry, I—"

"You should meet more girls." Koffi's voice was soft. "But that's nice of you to say." Something in her eyes had changed. Ekon couldn't put his finger on it, but it was there. His gaze dropped to her mouth again—*why couldn't he stop looking at it?* He felt that hum again, stronger. Something was building, an urge to say something, to *do* something. He kept waiting for his fingers to start their tapping, to find their rhythm, but to his surprise, they didn't. He found that, in this moment, he much preferred to be still. He didn't want to count things; he didn't need to.

"Koffi." His voice was lower, quieter. Somewhere distant, there was a faint crackling sound, but he barely heard it over the roaring in his ears. Suddenly, he was all too aware of how little space there actually was between the two of them, only an arm's length. She stared at him a second longer, and then, almost imperceptibly, she leaned forward slightly. It was the smallest movement, but it was enough. There was a quiet permission given with that fractional gesture, a permission he hadn't realized he wanted until he had it.

"Ekon." Koffi's voice was barely audible, a whisper. She closed her eyes, and her lips parted. Ekon swallowed. They were impossibly close now. He could see the individual eyelashes fanned across her cheeks, could smell the red fruit on her breath. It was sweet, and he wondered vaguely if *she* would taste sweet . . .

"Ekon." She said his name again, this time more quietly, with an urgency. Her eyes shot open and met his own, and then Ekon drew in a sharp breath. Something was wrong. The eyes that met his were glassy, vacant. A sheen of sweat had formed along her hairline, and her breaths were growing shallow, raspy. Ekon froze.

"Koffi?"

Another sound filled the space around them, more crackling. Ekon turned to find its source and felt the blood drain from his face. The trunk of the tree they were sitting beside had changed. No longer was its bark a rich brown, but gray, flaky. Above them, more of its fruit was falling, but it wasn't red anymore. A chill shivered up his spine when he saw the flesh of the fruits was black, shriveled, almost like . . .

"Ekon . . ."

Ekon turned, but not fast enough. With horror he watched as Koffi stared at him, her body rocking from side to side where she sat.

Then she collapsed.

PART THREE

WAKE NOT A SLEEPING HYENA.

THE BOY FROM THE WEST

ADIAH

"His family's from Asali in the west, *that's* why he's so handsome."

I roll my eyes for the thousandth time as Nuru and Penda, two of my classmates, burst into yet another fit of giggles a few feet away from me. They don't know that they aren't alone in this corridor, that I've been crouched hiding behind an old statue of Fedu for nearly fifteen minutes. I don't intend to enlighten them.

"I heard he's already been picked for an apprenticeship." I recognize the more smug voice—Penda—when she speaks. As another daraja, she and I have practically grown up together in this temple over the last seven years, but we're decidedly not friends. I can imagine her painted face and annoyingly perfect Bantu knots even without seeing them. Absently, I touch my own hair. Almost a week ago, Mama put it into two practical plaits down my back, but they're getting frizzy at the edges. It's probably time for a washday. Ugh, I *hate* washdays. Maybe I can get away with a co-wash . . .

"He's working down in the Kughushi District, under Bwana

283

Martinique," Penda continues, her tone full of knowing. "I'm going to see if I can find an excuse to stop by the shop tomorrow. Maybe I'll ask to have something made."

"Ooh." The higher-pitched voice, the one who'd spoken before, belongs to Nuru. I can practically imagine her huge doll-like eyes widening, the way they always do when she's excited. We're not really friends either, but she's certainly nicer than Penda. "Can I come with you? I'd *love* to meet him!"

They giggle again, and I suppress a groan. After all, I'm not supposed to be here.

My original plan had been a simple one—I'd hide behind this statue until afternoon classes had started, then make my way to the sky garden to meet up with Tao. No doubt my best friend is already there waiting, doing what he always does in his spare time—reading—but just about anything sounds better than yet another afternoon spent in a stifling temple classroom with old Master Lumumba. He's my literature and linguistics teacher, and he's currently trying to teach me how to conjugate basic Kushoto verbs. I'd thought nothing could be worse than listening to him drone about the proper inflections of my vowels; now I'm starting to wonder if I was mistaken.

"He's just so gorgeous," Nuru continues, sounding breathless. "Those eyes and those shoulders, and have you seen his *hands*? They're huge—"

"You know what they say about big hands . . ."

"Penda!"

They start snickering again, and I eye a nearby window, seriously considering a leap. It isn't that I mind talking about boys— gods know there are more than a few very handsome ones in my daraja cohort—but all anyone has been talking about for the last week has been *this* boy. I don't even know his name, and at this point I don't care. Every single person in Lkossa remotely close to my age seems to be obsessed with him. Girls think he's cute, and even some of the guys seem preoccupied. I think it's all ridiculous. You'd think no one in this city had ever seen someone new.

"What are you going to say to him," Nuru asks Penda, "if you see him tomorrow?"

I peek around the statue just long enough to catch Penda's sly smile. "He's new to the city, and no doubt in need of a guide. I'm going to offer to give him a tour of the temple, maybe the western gardens."

"Oh," says Nuru. "Did they finally finish the repairs?"

"Yes, earlier this week actually. Adiah really did a number on the hedges."

Even though I know they can't see me, I shrink farther into the statue's shadow at the mention of my name. Embarrassed heat flushes my skin.

"I can't believe she took out that beautiful statue," says Nuru. "I don't think Brother Yazeed has gotten over it yet."

I grit my teeth, annoyed. Brother Yazeed is being completely unreasonable. After all, I didn't *mean* for the splendor I was using to hit the statue of Amokoya; it was an accident. Besides, *I* think the goddess of water looks better without that ridiculous tiara. Art is subjective.

"Honestly," says Penda, "that girl's a menace."

I feel anger building inside me.

"She can be nice," Nuru says gently. "It's just that sometimes, she's . . . too much."

Those words cut worse than Penda's. I take back what I thought about Nuru being the nicer one of the two. *Too much.* I've certainly heard words like that before. *Too loud. Too strong. Too everything.* I know I'm too much, but I don't know how to be less.

"Let's go pick out something to wear for tomorrow," I hear Nuru suggest, renewed excitement in her voice. "Penda, can I pretty please borrow your ankara dress? The green one from—"

"You mean, the one you spilled ogbono soup on last week?"

Their voices fade as they finally get up and make their way down the hall. I've been waiting for them to move for the better part of a half hour, but I don't immediately get up. The girls' words are still in my head.

That girl's a menace.

Sometimes, she's . . . too much.

They're both right. I *am* a menace, too much. I don't want to be. I want to be like the other girls in my year who know how to do their own hair and make clever conversation. I want to learn the beauty of being poised. The problem is, I'm not poised at all.

I'm not that kind of beautiful.

Not for the first time, I think back to that afternoon in Father Masego's office when I was twelve, the day he told me I was extra-ordinary. It's been a year since he died, since a new Kuhani took his place. Father Masego told me once that he thought I would do remarkable things. I'm less and less sure of that every day.

Slowly, I emerge from behind the statue. In this rendition, the god of death is sculpted to look like a cunning old man, his hippo familiar by his side. The statue unsettles me the longer I stare at it, and I waste no more time leaving the corridor to head to the sky garden. My detour, thanks to Penda and Nuru, has taken up valuable time, but with any luck, I can still meet up with Tao before—

I nearly crash into a person rounding the corner. They're carrying a large crate, and when we collide, it nearly lands on me. I act without thinking, the splendor comes to me as always, and I use a small bit of it to push the sliding crate back into the carrier's arms. Their face is still obscured, but I see the top of a head nod.

"Sorry about that," says a low male voice.

"It's fine," I say quickly, trying to step around him.

"This is my first delivery job to the temple." The carrier shifts to the right at the same time I do, inadvertently blocking my path. "Guess I made a wrong turn. I'm still trying to learn all the ins and outs—"

"*Tuh*, good luck." I step left, and this time find a space to squeeze around. "I've been training here for almost seven years, and even I still don't . . ."

The words die in my throat as the carrier puts down the crate, and for the first time I see his face. The person staring back at me isn't some crusty old master of the temple, but a boy with light brown skin and black hair. I know at once who he is: the one they've all been talking about. This is the boy from the west.

And begrudgingly, I have to admit—he's decidedly *not* unattractive.

"Hello," he says, offering a smile as he puts a hand to his heart. I recognize that gesture; it's a common greeting in the Dhahabu Region of the west. He seems to realize what he's said, and his expression turns slightly sheepish. "Uh, sorry," he says in accented Zamani. "I'm still . . . getting used to the customs and languages of the east."

"It's all right," I say before I can stop myself. "I know a little

Kushoto." As soon as the words leave me, I want to smack myself. Why did I just say that? I don't speak Kushoto, I can barely conjugate a verb correctly. Suddenly, I regret not paying more attention to Master Lumumba's lessons . . .

"Really?" His face lights up, hopeful. "That's really impressive."

Impressive. The compliment feels strange to me. There are lots of words—some of them choice—that people generally use to describe me. *Impressive* doesn't usually make the list. After a moment, the young man extends a hand.

"My name is Dakari," he says with a bigger smile. "I'm new here."

I take his hand and shake it. It's warm to the touch and almost entirely envelops mine. So he *does* have big hands . . .

"I'm Adiah," I offer.

"Adiah." He repeats my name and it sounds different on his tongue, like a song. "That's lovely."

"Thank you."

He's still watching me, studying me the way I've seen some of the masters study artwork. I'm not used to anyone looking at me for this long without looking away. It almost feels strange.

"Are you one of the . . . darajas?" he asks after a moment. "One of the students that train here?"

"I am." At once, I stand taller, unable to resist a bit of pride. To my pleasure, he looks appropriately admiring.

"That's amazing. There aren't many darajas in Asali anymore, where my family's from."

So Penda and Nuru were right about that too.

"Darajas have been training at the Temple of Lkossa for years," I explain. "It's an ancient tradition."

"Fascinating," he says, and he actually looks like he means it.

288

Something passes over his face, a hesitance, before he asks, "Could you . . . maybe you could show me around here sometime? If it wouldn't disrupt your training?"

Something strange flutters in my stomach. He's still staring at me so intently. It takes an effort to make myself sound offhand. "Sure." I shrug. "I could probably find some time."

"Tomorrow?"

"I guess."

"Very well, Adiah." The second time he says my name is different; there's a hint of something else in the tone that I can't name but don't mind. "I look forward to seeing you again tomorrow."

He bows his head then, a surprisingly regal motion for a boy who looks my age. I don't know what to do in return, so I offer a small nod before skirting around him and back down the hall. I think I feel his eyes on me as I go, and so I wait until I round a corner to smile.

I realize that maybe, for the first time in a long time, I have a new friend.

CHAPTER 20

THE LESSER SON

"Koffi!"

Ekon felt something inside him plummet as Koffi's eyes rolled back into her head, exposing the whites. He moved to kneel beside her, shaking her gently by her shoulders. She didn't respond, but shivered against him. He pressed the back of his hand to her forehead. It was hot—*alarmingly* hot—to the touch. He looked around, frantic.

How? His eyes searched her face, then the trees. He laid her down again, then snatched Nkrumah's journal from his bag. This time, he nearly tore the pages flipping through them, trying to find some explanation. He stopped at one of them. The tree in this illustration, gray and flaky, looked like the one before him now.

No, he realized. *It's the same.*

And it was. There were lots of notes on this page, scrawled tightly as Nkrumah had tried to cram as much in as he could. Ekon's eyes stopped halfway down the page.

SPECIMEN 70R

NAME: UMDHLEBI TREE

PRONUNCIATION: *oom-LEH-bee*

INFORMAL NAME: DEAD-MAN'S TREE

HABITAT: *The Greater Jungle, Zamani Region (Old East)*

DESCRIPTION: *Green leaves, red or black fruit, wood color may vary from brown to gray*

LIFE EXPECTANCY: *Unknown*

ADDITIONAL NOTES: *The umdhlebi tree may in fact be one of the oldest trees to inhabit the Greater Jungle; attempts to ascertain its exact age have been unsuccessful, but it is believed to be more than five hundred years old. Its informal name, dead-man's tree, is owed to its extreme toxicity; nearly every part of the umdhlebi tree is poisonous. Unlike most trees, it finds nutrients by killing those that feed on its fruit and by using the bodies of its victims to fertilize the soil around it. Victims may experience a variety of symptoms, including fever coupled with delirium, swelling of the intestines, and severe headaches. Once consumed, the fruit's poison's metabolizes instantly. Vomiting is ineffective, and death is imminent.*

Ekon kept reading, eyes flying across the page furiously. Koffi had only eaten one, maybe two small pieces of the umdhlebi tree's fruit; he'd watched her. He skimmed over the other passages, looking for some information about an antidote to treat the poison. He found none. The last line of Nkrumah's note repeated itself in his mind.

Death is imminent. Not probably, not likely—assured.

"Ek..."

He jumped. Koffi's mouth was open, trying to form words. She was sweating through her clothes, spots in the front of her kaftan rapidly dampening. He gritted his teeth.

Stupid, stupid, how could I have been so stupid?

Koffi's chest was rising and falling more rapidly, and her lips were darkening.

"Hey, stay with me." Ekon's own voice cracked. He slapped his hand against her cheek over and over, trying to keep her awake. "Koffi, *stay with me.*"

"It ... hurts ..." Koffi mumbled the words, her hand shifting to her stomach. A groan escaped her lips. Ekon remembered another part of Nkrumah's note.

Victims may experience a variety of symptoms ... swelling of the intestines ...

"Come on, come on ..." Ekon slipped one of his arms around Koffi's middle to keep her upright, then used his other arm to grab their bags. It was beginning to dawn on him how truly alone they were here. He racked his mind, trying to think of a plan.

Leave her.

The voice in his head reminded him uncannily of Kamau— blunt, straight to the point. He flinched. That voice was practical, and served as yet another reminder. The Sons of the Six could be in this jungle, hunting. He remembered what Kamau had once said to him about trails, about the warriors' ability to find and follow them.

Leave her, the Kamau voice repeated. *You have a purpose here, a job, and your time is running out. Take the journal and leave her here.*

Her fate's sealed, but yours isn't. Find the Shetani, find your destiny. This is your last chance . . .

The more strategic thing for Ekon to do now was leave Koffi to die, he knew that, but . . . no, he couldn't do it. Koffi had had the same chance to abandon him in Anatsou's meadow; he wouldn't abandon her. He looked down at the journal's map again before coming to a decision.

He might not be able to save Koffi like she'd saved him, but he had to try.

The rest of the afternoon passed like a year, growing more and more humid even as the sun set. Ekon's feet had begun aching hours ago, but he didn't stop, and now he felt that pain throbbing through his body with every step. He thought he could see opaque tendrils of steam rolling off the very trees in wispy sighs, slicking their arms, legs, and foreheads in a sheen of sticky sweat. He licked his cracked lips involuntarily at the same time Koffi's stomach audibly rumbled. Since leaving the grove, her condition hadn't worsened, but it hadn't improved either. Sometimes, she'd have fits of consciousness and try to walk beside him at a slow limp, but it never lasted long. More times than not, he carried her on his back. He tried to quell a rising dread. If they didn't find help soon . . . He didn't want to think about what would happen.

Night fell faster than he expected, sudden and consuming. After propping Koffi against a tree, Ekon made something of a camp, then evaluated their food options. Her rations were—as he'd expected—not much better than his, but he pooled them together to make a sort of meal. After this there'd be no more left, but he couldn't think of that now. He filled their gourds with water from inside a tree Nkrumah's journal said was potable, and tipped Koffi's to her lips to encourage her to drink. She cracked open an eye, the smallest of smiles light on her lips.

"Guess we're not even anymore," she murmured. "But I don't think I'll be able to repay you for this."

Ekon shook his head, refusing to let himself think about how very small Koffi suddenly looked. "You don't have to repay me, Koffi."

"I'm tired."

"You *have* to stay awake." He hated how harsh the words sounded, but he couldn't help himself. He'd trained with Kamau and Brother Ugo on how to be a proper warrior, how to clean wounds earned from combat, but he had no other medical experience. He didn't know how to treat this kind of ailment. "Do you understand me? I'm not letting someone else die in this godsforsaken jungle. It can't happen again." The words slipped from him before he could stop them, then hung heavy in the air.

"Again?" Koffi repeated the word, her voice faint.

"Never mind," said Ekon brusquely. "I don't want to talk about it."

"Fine . . ." Koffi closed her eyes, letting her head tilt back against the tree trunk.

"Hey, keep your eyes open!"

"How about a barter?" Koffi said, smiling even as her eyes stayed closed. "You tell me what you were talking about, and I'll stay awake."

Ekon hesitated. He'd never talked about this before, not even with Kamau or Brother Ugo. But Koffi's eyes were still closed, and he didn't like it. Even with her dark skin, he could see the blood

294

was draining from her face, and she looked weaker and weaker by the second. If this was the only way to keep her awake . . .

"Fine. You asked me what I saw back when we were in Anatsou's meadow," he said quietly. At once, Koffi's eyes opened. "I didn't want to tell you because . . . I've never told anyone before. I—" He hesitated. Once again, he felt like he was on the precipice of something, about to leap into an unknown. His fingers drummed against his knee, moving faster and faster.

One-two-three. One-two-three. One-two-three. One-two—

"Ekon."

He started. Koffi had sat up and taken his free hand, the one that wasn't counting. She met his gaze and held it. "I was just joking about the barter. You don't have to talk about this if you don't want to, but if you do . . . I'll listen."

Ekon let a shudder pass through him. He felt the secret building up inside him, a living thing rattling around his rib cage. He sensed that, once he let it out, he'd never be able to keep it locked up again, and that frightened him to his core. He stared at his fingers, still drumming a rhythm against his leg.

One-two-three. One-two-three. One-two-three.

He looked at his other hand, the one Koffi still held in her own. The pad of her thumb was moving back and forth against his skin in circles, slow, deliberate. It wasn't like counting, but something about watching those circles calmed him down; they made him feel better. He took another breath, then stared at his feet.

"When I was in the meadow, I heard the voice of my father."

Koffi's brows rose, but she said nothing, and Ekon went on.

"When we were little, my brother and I liked to give each other dares," he said. "Most of them were jokes, harmless stuff, but one day, my brother gave me a very specific dare. He bet me five shabas that I wouldn't go into the Greater Jungle. At first, I told him I wouldn't do it, but I changed my mind. I didn't tell him, but the next morning, while he was still asleep, I got up and went in by myself. My plan was to find a rock or flower to prove myself, but I got lost."

He'd known the images would return, braced himself for them, but that didn't make it any easier when they did. Physically, he was still sitting with Koffi, but in his mind, he was small again, one tiny body set against a massive jungle. He still remembered the unnatural chill he'd felt taking his first steps into it, the strange hush that'd filled the air as he trekked into its depths, then the gradual helplessness he'd felt as he realized he didn't know the way back.

"I thought I was going to die here," he said. "And then . . ."

"And then?" Koffi prodded.

"And then my father came," Ekon whispered. "I don't know how he figured out where I'd gone, how he found me in the middle of the jungle. I just remember his voice, the way he said my name."

Ekon, please.

Ekon shook his head. "He told me we needed to leave the Greater Jungle, that it wasn't safe for us to be there, and then . . . then, we saw it."

"It?"

"The Shetani." Ekon nearly spat the word. He wanted to be angry at the memory of the creature, enraged, but the truth was that even now, thinking of that moment drove a spike of raw fear into his bones. He remembered two black eyes, a low growl interrupting the stillness of the jungle. He recalled the way his father had tensed, hand flying to the hilt of his hanjari. The beast had fixed its eyes on him.

"What happened?" Koffi asked.

"I . . ." A wave of nausea rose from the pit of Ekon's stomach. The next words he had to say were the hardest, the ones he didn't want to say. His skin grew clammy as his lips tried to form them, and yet again he watched Koffi's circling thumb. He made himself focus on that motion instead of on the way he felt. "I . . . *ran.*"

It physically hurt him to say it, the pain worse than he'd imagined. Tears of shame pricked behind his eyes, and his throat tightened until he could barely breathe. He tried to speak again but found he couldn't. His skin felt as though it'd been set on fire; everything inside him burned. And he deserved it. He *deserved* to suffer for what he'd done. He screwed his eyes shut as Baba's voice filled his mind, no longer slurred and pained, but cold and razor-thin.

You left me, the new voice said. *You left me to die.*

Ekon winced. He *had.* He'd been a coward. Baba had come to save him, and in return he'd abandoned his father. He'd let that creature—that *monster*—tear his father to shreds. He'd let him die alone in this jungle.

Coward, his father said, his voice full of derision. *You are a coward. Kamau would never have left me, my better son would have stayed . . .*

It was true. Kamau *was* better—stronger, smarter, braver. His brother had always been the better son, and he'd always been the lesser son.

"Ekon."

Something cool tapped his chin, lifting his gaze from the jungle floor. Koffi was staring at him, eyes intent. "Tell me the rest," she said quietly. "Please."

"There's isn't much else." Ekon kicked at the dirt. "I made it back, and my father didn't. The next morning, they found his body at the jungle's edge. Apparently, he'd tried to get home, but . . . he didn't make it. He was later honored as a hero for trying to single-handedly kill the Shetani. No one ever found out the *real* reason he died—because of me."

"Ekon . . . ," said Koffi softly. "You were just a kid."

He shook his head. "My father was killed trying to save me," he said harshly. "The Shetani destroyed his body, but I'm the one that took his life." He gestured up at the trees. "Even this jungle knows it."

Koffi's brow furrowed. "What do you mean?"

"I . . ." He paused. This was another thing he'd never told anyone before. He thought of the old woman he'd seen not so long ago, the way she'd seemed to know the jungle called to him. He swallowed. "Sometimes, when I'm near the jungle, I can hear my father's voice. It's like a ghost calling to me, *blaming* me . . . I've heard it for the last ten years."

"Ekon." Koffi seemed to be choosing her words carefully. "What I'm going to say might sound a little strange, but hear me out, okay?"

Ekon nodded.

"I haven't read many books in my life," she said tentatively. "I'm not like that Nkrumah guy, or any of those other old men with lots of important things to say. But in the time since we came into this jungle, I've noticed something." She lifted her gaze to stare at the trees around them. "This place, the Greater Jungle, is *alive*. Maybe not in a way we can really understand, but I think . . . I think it has a personality, even a mind of its own when it wants to."

Ekon frowned. "So?"

"So," she pressed, "I think that, in a way, it gives back what you give to it. Think about it." She kept on before Ekon could interrupt. "When we ran into Anatsou, we were scared, and what happened?"

"The spiders," said Ekon.

Koffi nodded. "And remember the grootslang? It only showed up *after* we started arguing about which way to go."

Ekon said nothing.

"It makes me wonder," she pondered aloud. "If something bad happened here when you were a little kid, if the emotions you have when you think about the jungle are always bad, maybe *that's* what the jungle will always give back to you. And the only way to make that stop is to face that bad thing head-on."

Ekon considered the words. They reminded him of something Brother Ugo had once said to him:

Nightmares hunt like beasts of prey, vanquished in the light of day.

The light of day. Brother Ugo had told him that the only way to make problems go away was to face them, but . . .

"How?" His throat was dry, his voice hoarse. He barely heard it himself.

"Face it," Koffi said firmly. "Don't run from it anymore." She squeezed his hand. "And you don't have to do it alone. I'm here with you."

"I don't know how to face it."

"Acknowledge what happened," she murmured. "What *really* happened. And then forgive yourself for it."

Ekon closed his eyes and clasped his hands together. The images came unbidden; he expected them to, but he tried not to look away from them. He saw the jungle, the blood on the leaves, the eyes of a monster coming toward him. He remembered the fear, a preternatural chill, the way his heart had pounded in his chest.

Ekon.

Baba had been beside him, not lying in a pool of blood, just standing next to him. He remembered meeting his father's gaze.

Ekon, Baba had said. *Go home.*

No. Ekon hadn't wanted to leave his father. *But, Baba—*

Ekon, please. There'd been an edge in Baba's voice, but not from fear. The Shetani was still a few feet away, watching them, no doubt choosing which one of them to go after first. His father had looked from it to Ekon slowly. *It's all right. I'll distract it,* he'd said. *Count your footsteps until you get home. Moss always grows on the north side of the tree, so move in the opposite direction of the moss. Head south until you're home. I'll catch up. I'll be all right.*

Baba. Ekon had felt hot tears on his face. *I don't want to leave you.*

I'm right behind you. Baba's voice was warm. He was lying, but Ekon hadn't known that. *Please, son, go.*

And so Ekon had run. The trees had risen to meet him as he darted back the way his father had directed. He remembered trying to find the moss, trying to count his footsteps, but he'd kept losing track of his numbers in his head.

One . . . two . . . five . . . seven . . .

He couldn't count that high without getting disoriented. He'd tried again. *One . . . two . . . three. Three.* He could count to three without getting overwhelmed. He focused on those numbers, making his steps match their cadence.

One-two-three. One-two-three. One-two-three.

His fingers had begun to tap at the air, helping him along. He'd found a rhythm, and then the running had gotten easier.

One-two-three. One-two-three. One-two-three.

Three: He'd decided then that *three* was a good number. Three would always be a good number.

Ekon. He heard his baba's voice, no longer angry or suffering; there was another emotion in its place.

Ekon, please.

His father hadn't begged him to stay—he'd begged him to go. He hadn't thought he was the lesser son.

He'd loved him.

"Ekon."

Ekon opened his eyes, feeling as though he'd just emerged from deep water. He could breathe again, and the voices were gone. Koffi offered him a small smile.

"How do you feel?"

"Better," said Ekon quietly. "I feel . . . *better*."

Ekon was up before the sun, cleaning their rudimentary campsite and reviewing the map. It seemed strange that this was only his third night in the jungle; so much had happened in such little time. He pulled Nkrumah's journal from his bag again to review the map.

They still weren't close to any sort of civilization, let alone a physician. He glanced at Koffi. She was sleeping—he'd relented eventually—but still shivered with fever. He swallowed. According to Nkrumah's journal, she should have died by now. The fact that she hadn't was a small miracle, but he knew she wouldn't make it much longer without treatment, and they were out of supplies.

As carefully as he could, he lifted Koffi to her feet. He crouched to let her climb onto his back, then looped his arms under her knees to hold her in place. It wasn't the most comfortable way to walk—while Koffi wasn't particularly heavy, she *was* tall—but Ekon didn't mind it. Two different emotions were warring inside him, vying for his attention. There was fear there—he was still very worried about Koffi—but there was also undeniable joy, a profound relief. What Koffi had said to him last night, what she'd helped him realize, had been life-changing; he literally felt lighter.

Baba loved you.

All this time, he'd thought Baba hated him. He supposed it made sense in hindsight that a nightmare had impersonated the truth, then settled in his mind. But now he had the real truth. It was still painful to realize his baba had died for him, but it made him feel better to know that it had been his father's choice; that made all the difference.

Morning became midday more quickly than he would have liked. Ekon stared at the sky overhead. Evening would be upon them in a handful of hours, and they didn't have another night's rations. They were running out of time and running out of options. He was still considering that when he heard the snap of a twig and a sharp breath in, a gasp.

As quickly as he could with Koffi still on his back, Ekon swiveled, fist wrapped around the hilt of his hanjari. Koffi groaned at the sudden movement, and Ekon felt her heart pattering hard against his back. His own heartbeat quickened too. He realized they'd been lucky not to have encountered any more wildlife since the grootslang, and now he suspected that luck had run out. He had a choice to make. He'd fight better without Koffi on his back. He could defend them, but that would mean putting Koffi on the ground, leaving her vulnerable. He tensed as a second twig snapped, this time behind him, and then he heard a distinct sound, a hissing. His blood ran cold. If it was another grootslang or something like it, they had no chance at all.

"Koffi." Ekon kept his voice as low as he could while his eyes searched the trees. "Listen to me. I know you're tired, but you're going to have to run. I can't fight and carry you, you'll have to—"

Ekon stopped so suddenly that Koffi nearly slid off his back. He'd been staring straight ahead and into the trees, but the jungle was playing tricks on him now. From the shadows, two women emerged, like none Ekon had ever seen before. Their skin was dark brown like his, but transparent, and their curly dreadlocks were the color of a pale silver-white moon. Like the trees they'd emerged from, they looked ageless, and Ekon didn't know whether to find that fascinating or frightening. One of them lifted a longspear high, and he froze. She stared at him a second longer before inclining her head, gaze full of question.

"We don't mean harm." He couldn't lift his hands to show good intent without causing Koffi to slide off his back, but he let go of his hanjari slowly and deliberately. "We just need help, please."

"I speak not well the human languages." The shorter of the two women looked to her companion and frowned before looking back to Ekon. "Do you?"

Ekon's heart sank as the second woman shook her head. The first one raised her spear higher yet, and he flinched. She was close enough to impale them both with an easy throw.

"Please." Ekon repeated that single word, then tried nodding over his shoulder to indicate Koffi. She hadn't spoken or moved since the two women had appeared, and that scared him. "Please, my friend will die—"

"Yes, she will."

Ekon jumped, searching for the new voice before looking back to the two white-haired women. To his surprise, both had lowered their weapons and bowed their heads at something behind him. Ekon turned and saw what they had.

A third old woman, smaller than the other two, was ambling toward them through the trees with unnerving quiet. It took Ekon a moment to understand the cause of the unease running down his length, but then he pinpointed it. There was something in the way the old woman carried herself, strong despite her feeble body, unbothered by the jungle's danger. Her black tunic was simple but clean, and she wore a large head wrap that covered any hair she might have. Wooden hoops dangled from her ears, and when she waved a hand, the thick bangles on her wrist clacked against each other noisily.

"Your friend has eaten fruit from the umdhlebi tree." There was a surprising touch of sympathy in her voice that contradicted her stern, dark eyes and hard-set mouth.

Ekon nodded. "We didn't know it was bad."

The old woman shook her head, and Ekon thought he saw a twinkle of something else in her gaze. "Not bad, merely misunderstood. The umdhlebi tree is very old, very wise, and rather temperamental when offended." One eyebrow rose. "Though I expect Satao did not capture as much in his notes."

"Satao?" Ekon started. "You . . . you know Satao Nkrumah?"

The old woman's eyes turned distinctly sad. "I did, once."

"But how—?"

She held up one of her hands, cutting off the rest of his question. "The umdhlebi's fruit can be eaten and consumed, but not without the tree's consent; otherwise it becomes poisonous. It is meant to be a lesson. Man is not always entitled to take what does not belong to it." She looked from Koffi to Ekon. "How long ago did she consume the fruit?"

"Yesterday afternoon." He hesitated, then added, "She has . . . abilities. She can—"

"I'm aware of what she is." The old woman tsked, shaking her head. "But it matters not when it comes to things like the umdhlebi tree, which cares not who it poisons. It's a wonder this girl is not already dead, though she will be within the next few hours."

Ekon tensed. "Is there no way to stop it?"

The woman pursed her lips, thoughtful. "There may be one, but it is not guaranteed."

"Please." Ekon found he could barely form words. Koffi couldn't die here in this jungle, not like Baba. He couldn't let that happen. "Please, can you try?"

A beat passed before the woman nodded, then met Ekon's gaze. "Come with me."

CHAPTER 21

BLOOD, BONE, AND SOUL

Koffi didn't open her eyes until she heard the rattling.

At first, she thought the sound was part of a dream, another small illogical part of the strange stupor she was in. But no, the longer she listened, the surer she was. That rattling—and whatever was causing it—did *not* come from her imagination. She pushed herself up to her elbows and at once regretted it.

Acute pain filled her stomach the moment she moved, as unforgiving as a hanjari dagger impaled deep in her entrails. Something a few feet away from her moved, and a whimper of pain escaped her lips. She started. She wasn't alone.

"Here."

Never before had she seen the old woman hobbling over to her from across the hut. She wore a modest black tunic and a head wrap to match. Without preamble, she pressed a large gourd into Koffi's hands.

"Drink."

It didn't occur to Koffi to disobey. In fact, the minute her hands wrapped around the gourd's hard shell and she heard that delicious slosh within, her mouth had turned as dry as paper. She'd never been thirstier in her life. The pain in her stomach subdued as she brought the gourd to her lips, even more so once she'd swallowed several mouthfuls of water. She sighed, relieved.

"Thank you," she said. "I appreciate it."

The old woman's back was turned to her, but Koffi still heard the tension in her voice. "Don't thank me yet, child. We must act quickly if you're going to survive."

Huh? The words didn't make sense to Koffi. For good measure, she took another long swig of water. "What do you mean?" she asked tentatively. "I'm feeling better already. This water—"

"Is nothing more than a temporary balm." The old woman was still not looking at her, and finally Koffi saw where the rattling had come from. She was shaking a small burlap purse clutched in her fist as hard as she could. "Your friend was right to bring you here, but as I told him just before, you are very ill. That water will not cure the true sickness."

The true . . . ? Then, as though the words had conjured something, Koffi felt it. Her head began to pound mercilessly. It made that sharp pain in her stomach seem a trifle in comparison. The gourd slipped from her hands as she started to double over, but with surprising speed, the old woman was at her side again, holding her upright. Her eyes were pleading.

"Hold on, child," she murmured. "Hold on just a little longer. They are coming."

They? Even in her pain, Koffi found the words odd. The woman held her upright a second longer before turning back to the bag, and in her absence, Koffi looked around for the first time. The hut they occupied was larger and far grander than any at the Night

307

Zoo. Every mud brick was precisely cut, and they were almost flawlessly masoned together around her, and the black, white, and green mudcloth rug beneath her was of a finer design than even the ones Baaz had back at the Night Zoo. It was an unquestionably beautiful place, but . . . She reflected on the old woman's words.

They are coming.

"*Who's* . . . coming?" Koffi's words came out more slurred than she intended as her vision began to tilt and spin. A black fuzziness was growing in the corners of her eyes, making it harder and harder to see anything. As though looking through a tunnel, she watched as the old woman ambled back over to sit cross-legged directly opposite her again, this time holding a large black bowl between her knees. Curious, Koffi leaned forward slightly to see what was inside it, and what she saw made the hair on her arms stand on end.

"Are those—?"

"Your forearm." The woman did not even give the collection of bones a cursory glance. Her eyes were locked on Koffi. "*Now.*"

Instinctively, Koffi recoiled, but the movement was too fast. The dizziness amplified tenfold as she clutched her left forearm—the one with her birthcut on it—protectively against her chest. "Why?"

The touch of impatience that crossed the old woman's features was unmistakable this time. "If you wish to live," she said forebodingly, "you will do it."

If you wish to live. Simple words, but they recalled something old in Koffi's memory. In the moment it took her to take another labored breath, she fell backward in time and remembered another day, another hut. The one she was thinking of was nothing like this one; it had been small, and dark, and dirty. No rattling had filled

308

its mud-brick walls; instead, it had been filled with the sounds of people coughing, and spewing, and moaning in pain. The Night Zoo's infirmary hut, the place Baaz sent sick and injured beast-keepers. Koffi remembered the crude beds of old hay, crammed together to fit as many people as possible inside, all suffering from the same mosquito virus. She remembered Baba lying on his own, withered, forehead shiny with sweat as fever ravaged what was left of him. Mama hadn't cried the day Baba had died, but Koffi still remembered the fleeting look that'd crossed her face. It had been a look nothing short of agony, a look of unfathomable pain. That look had frightened her as a little girl, *haunted* her, and she'd never wanted to see it again. A kind of resolve suddenly built in her chest.

If you wish to live.

She would not be the reason Mama felt that kind of pain ever again. She had to survive this, she had to go home to her mother and Jabir, and she'd do whatever it took to make sure of it. She waited a beat before meeting the old woman's gaze again.

"All right. Fine." She started to extend her arm but wasn't quick enough. Like a striking snake, the woman snatched her arm with both gnarled hands, and Koffi didn't see the blade until it was too late. She cried out as a stinging pain erupted in a spot just above her birthcut, and nausea crept up her throat when the old woman rotated her arm and held it directly above the bowl of bones. They watched together as one, two, three droplets of dark crimson splattered against them. The moment red touched white, the bones began to tremble.

"What—?" Koffi scrambled away from the bowl in horror, not caring as more blood dripped down her arm to stain the beautiful rug. "Wh-what's happening?"

The old woman hadn't moved from her spot, but laid the bloodied knife at her side. She held the bowl perfectly still in her lap as the bones within it trembled more and more violently. When she closed her eyes, her words were soft.

"It is in their hands now," she murmured. "*They* will decide."

Koffi had just opened her mouth to ask, for the second time, who *they* were, but no sooner had the words formed on her lips than she saw it: sparkling particles of light. At first, she thought it was a trick of her imagination, a by-product of the pain still throbbing in her head, but . . . no, this light was *real*. The particles floated in the air before her, glittering and twirling as though dancing to a song of their own. She didn't just see them, she *felt* them, felt a kinship with them. Without warning, they grew larger, and an echoing *boom* reverberated through the air. There was a flash of white light, so bright Koffi had to shield her eyes. When she opened them again, she started. She was still sitting in the hut, and the old woman was still sitting a few feet away with her bowl of bloodied bones in her lap.

But the two of them were no longer alone.

Dark-skinned women sat around her on all sides, each clad in gleaming white linen. Some wore gold-beaded wraps atop their heads; others had hair coiffed into short Afros, Bantu knots, twists, and dreadlocks. It was unnerving; Koffi hadn't heard their entrance, the hut's flap certainly hadn't opened, but here they were, at least twenty of them. They varied in age—several of the women had cottony white hair, while others looked to be no older than her mother—but all of them shared a sameness she couldn't place. It wasn't because of the way they looked or because their white clothes were the same; there was something else. Finally, Koffi realized what it was. Each of the women was staring at her with an identical kind of wonder, as though they were just as amazed to see her as she was to see them.

"She's gotten so big," one of the younger-looking women whispered to her neighbor. "Goodness, they grow fast."

Koffi's mouth fell open. The younger woman had not only spoken in Zamani, but in her own dialect; she was a Gede like her. She stared around the circle, marveling. Were they *all* Gede? She hoped so. Never in her life had she seen even one of her own people with visible wealth, let alone several. These women carried themselves like queens, chins jutted out defiantly and eyes blazing with confidence, with *power*. She'd never seen anything like them before.

"Who are—?"

Abruptly, one of the women stood, and Koffi shut her mouth. There was no explicable way she knew it, but she sensed this woman was the leader of this peculiar group, its matriarch. All other eyes went to her, and the other women stilled. Strings of cowrie shells were tied to the wooden staff she held in her varicose-veined hands, and she leaned on it with each step as she approached. A few feet before Koffi, she stopped to stand over her. Unlike the others, her hair was shorn clean from her head, her dress long and flowing like a river's waves. When she spoke, her voice was impossibly sonorous.

"*This one* has given blood on the old bones." The bald woman's words seemed to hum through the tent. "She has called to us, and she is in need of our assistance."

Koffi didn't understand what she meant, but it seemed the women around her did. They began to murmur among themselves, casting curious eyes her way and whispering behind their hands.

"We will help her." The bald woman made the declaration with a tone of finality. *"Rise."*

It was one simple word, spoken softly, but at once every woman in the circle obeyed, getting to their feet. For her part, Koffi stayed seated. She wasn't sure why, but something kept her rooted to the floor as the white-clad women towered over her, watching.

Then, they began to sing.

It started low and wavering, like a fula flute's careful notes, before it grew. Like the particles of light Koffi had seen before, she felt the nameless song's movement in the air, notes of a song she could not name but knew. She held her breath as its octaves rose, the tune climbing higher and higher until it reached an impossible crescendo. Something powerful moved through her body, and suddenly the pain that had resided in it vanished. She felt a peculiar sensation on her face, and it wasn't until she touched her own cheeks that she realized they were wet with tears. The white-clad women finished their song, and the bald woman knelt so that her gaze was level with Koffi's.

"Shed no tears, child," she murmured. "We are with you, *always.*"

There was another flash of light then, so luminous Koffi turned away. When it faded, the bald old woman who'd been there was gone, as were the others from the circle. The hut felt oddly empty in their sudden absence. An immeasurable collection of seconds passed before Koffi spoke, awed.

"They . . . *healed* me."

"Of course they did. I expected nothing less."

Koffi looked up. She'd entirely forgotten about the first old woman. In her black attire, she was a stark contrast to the white-clad ones who'd just been there, but a smile touched her withered face. Koffi thought, in some strange way, she even looked younger.

"Where did they go?" Koffi stood, actually looking around the hut. "And why did they help me?"

The old woman did not rise. "It is not my place to answer your first question," she said sadly. "As to the matter of why your fore-mothers healed you? Darajas look after their own, even when they have passed on. Their connection to you is born from an old, al-most forgotten magic, but not one that is entirely lost."

The words settled on Koffi like dust, each layering its own kind of understanding.

"You knew," she whispered. "You *knew* that I had magic?"

"From the moment I saw your handsome friend carrying you." The old woman smiled. "When you have lived for as long as I have, you learn what to look for."

Koffi was massaging her temples, still trying to make sense of the words, when abruptly, she noticed something. The cut that had been sliced across her forearm was . . . *gone*. The skin had stitched back together, as seamlessly as though there'd never been a cut there at all. She looked up, confused.

"I don't understand."

The old woman folded her hands. "You ate of the umdhlebi tree without its consent," she explained gently. "The poison in its fruit is not like others of this jungle. It takes a tremendous power to expel something like that from a mortal body. What I just did is called a summoning, a ritual that allows those still tethered to this mortal world to call on those who are free from it." She gave Koffi a meaningful look. "You gave blood, and so you summoned those who *share* that blood. You called on your foremothers, and they answered."

"My . . . foremothers," Koffi repeated the word slowly. "As in, my *ancestors*? Those women were . . . *related* to me?"

"Some more directly than others, but yes." The old woman nodded in confirmation. "The specific connection that summons them is ethereal, a bond of blood, bone, and soul."

Koffi stared at her, letting the gravity of the revelation sink in. "The power that my foremothers used to heal me," she asked, "I have that same power too now, don't I?"

The old woman smiled. "You've always had that power, child. If your foremothers have done anything, they've merely further awakened it."

"I *feel* it." Koffi stared at her arms and legs. They looked the same as they always had, but warmth was traveling to them. It stretched into the tips of her fingers and all the way to her toes until it felt as though she'd been sitting in the sun for hours. It was marvelous but terrifying. "I've felt it for a little while in fleeting moments, but . . . it's like it's moving through me all the time, constantly."

"As it should," said the old woman. "As it *always* should, for a true daraja."

Daraja. Koffi recognized that word. The first time she'd heard it, she'd been in the marketplace. It had been the first time she'd learned that magic was real, that it was something she had and something that could change her life. She hadn't asked that old lady in Lkossa's marketplace—a *different* old woman from the one before her—for help or more information, but she wouldn't make that mistake twice.

"I want to learn," she said in earnest. "I want to learn how to use my power properly." She swallowed. "Can you teach me?"

The old woman regarded her for several seconds, as though evaluating her, before nodding in acquiescence. "Yes, child," she whispered. "I believe fate has deemed that I am meant to do so, and so I will." She stood and reached behind her head to begin untying her black head wrap. Koffi rose too.

"Really?" She almost couldn't believe it. "You mean, you'll teach me everything? About magic, and how to use it?"

"Yes, child." The old woman threw her a look touched by a hint of amusement. "I will teach you what I can. But the first thing to know is that your ancestors never called what you can do *magic*."

Koffi frowned. "They didn't?"

"No." The old woman finished untying her head wrap and let it fall to the ground. Koffi stilled, and the old woman smiled.

"They called it . . . *the splendor*."

CHAPTER 22

MYTHS AND FOLKTALES

Ekon paced between the trees, hands clasped tight behind his back.

Above him, the sky was changing. It had been an ominous gray when he'd first brought Koffi to this clearing, but now the sun seemed to be making its final appearance for the day, stretching long and bright over the sky in ribbons of orange, pink, and gold, only interrupted by the Rupture's cracks. It was a cruel sort of mockery. The prettier the sky looked, the worse he felt.

For what seemed like the thousandth time, he took in his surroundings. After he'd agreed to follow the old woman, she'd led him to a break in the trees where, to his surprise, he'd found a campsite bustling with people.

Well, he wasn't quite sure *people* was the right word.

Like the two women he'd encountered before, most wore plain brown tunics, and some had even accentuated their attire with brightly colored leaves woven into their kinky white hair. The old woman had paid them no mind as she took Koffi from him and

316

carried her to a large hut in the clearing's center with surprising ease. It had been at least an hour since she and Koffi had disappeared into it.

Every so often, he felt the strange people's eyes on him, wide and curious, but he didn't engage. They gave off an aura similar to the old woman's, a certain oneness with the jungle that he didn't understand. Sometimes he saw the people walk between trees and disappear among them. Other times he saw their children playing, with silhouettes oddly blurred in some places.

No, definitely *not* normal people.

"Ekon!"

Ekon did a double take. A dark-haired girl had just emerged from the hut. Koffi. She looked . . . radiant. Heat crept up Ekon's neck as he realized it, but it was impossible to ignore. Where Koffi had been clammy-looking before, now everything about her seemed to glow. Her smile was bright, her dark brown skin was luminescent, and even her twisted hair seemed to hold a slight, nearly imperceptible hint of gold in its depths. She stopped a few feet away from him, then paused.

"I . . . feel better."

Relief surged through Ekon like a tide. He wanted to say the right thing, but he didn't know what. *I was scared. I was worried. I'm happy.* Instead, he just nodded. "Good." He leaned in and lowered his voice. "Um, I think we should probably get going. Those white-haired people have been eyeing me since I got here and a few of them have weapons."

Koffi's smile held a touch of amusement. "They won't hurt us."

Ekon frowned. "And you know that because . . . ?"

317

"Because they're *yumboes*." She glanced over her shoulder fondly. As if recognizing their own name, some of the white-haired people looked up, waving. "They're the caretakers of the jungle."

Ekon's squinted. "How do you know that?"

Koffi's eyes lifted, taking in the forest around them. "My mama used to tell me stories about them," she said softly. "All this time, I thought they were just made up from myths and folktales, but . . . I was wrong."

Ekon's frown deepened further. As a rule, he didn't trust myths and folktales; they lacked accreditation. His eyes went to his bag perched against a tree. "Strange, Nkrumah doesn't mention yumboes in his journal—"

A rustling interrupted him mid-sentence, and Ekon's words died in his throat as his eyes dropped to the jungle floor. He froze. A massive golden snake was slithering toward him and Koffi, its jewel-like green eyes fixed on them both. At first, he was sure he'd never seen a snake so large and long—from here, he couldn't even see the end of its tail, and its body was thicker than his own waist—but then he realized that wasn't true. He had seen this snake once before, when he'd first entered the jungle with Koffi, before they'd wandered into the fog. Back then, he'd thought it was a hallucination, another one of the jungle's illusions, but he saw clearly now. This creature was no illusion. Instinct urged him to pull out his hanjari, but he found he couldn't move. He could only stare at the serpent as it got closer and closer. Every muscle in his body seized as it reached them, and he was so occupied by the very presence of it that he didn't even notice Koffi hadn't said a word. The giant snake lifted its head slightly and opened its mouth, exposing two long white fangs a moment as it hissed. Then, just as abruptly, it lowered and slithered past him into the jungle's bramble. Ekon watched it go, stunned.

"It . . ." He couldn't believe it. "It left us alone."

"Because *I* instructed him to."

He turned in the direction of the low voice that'd clapped across the clearing like thunder. Simultaneously, every single one of the white-haired people stopped what they were doing and fixed their strange pale eyes on the hut's door flap. Someone—the *owner* of the booming voice—was emerging from the tent, and Ekon went rigid when he saw who it was. The old woman he'd entrusted Koffi to a short while ago was still wearing the modest black tunic she'd had on before, but she was no longer old. She was traipsing toward them with the grace of a dancer, the wrinkles once covering her face vanished. Tangerine-colored sunlight cast itself over her body as she approached, and by that time she was close enough for Ekon to see her face—to *really* see what he had not recognized before. Slowly the pieces came together in his mind, the giant golden snake that had just passed, the countenance he had seen carved in stone a thousand times inside the Temple of Lkossa. He knew who this woman was, and what she was not.

"You're not . . . you can't be . . ." Words failed him.

The goddess met his gaze directly, eyes piercing. "Be at peace, child," Badwa commanded. "All is well here." She turned to Koffi, and Ekon thought he saw a knowing look pass between them. "I would speak with the two of you together, while the yumboes prepare food and drink. We will dine after."

After. The words were like disconnected threads in Ekon's mind that he couldn't tie together. *After.* What came *after* a goddess—a real goddess in the flesh—looked you in the eye? What happened *after* she spoke to you? It hurt to even look at her too long, like staring directly into the sun, or trying to see the entire ocean all at once but never being able to stand back quite far enough to take it all in. What if he said something wrong, somehow offended the goddess? Would she turn him into a bug, strike him down with lightning? He jolted in surprise when a soft hand touched his arm, tearing him away from his thoughts.

"It's okay, Ekon." Koffi held his gaze as she murmured the words. "I promise."

Ekon didn't know what it was about the tone of her voice that slowly doused his anxiety, only that it did so instantly. Her fingertips on his skin held the warmth of a clay pot left out in the sun. He focused on that warmth.

"All right. Let's go."

The horned goddess gestured for them to follow her into a clearing several yards away from the hut and the yumboes. Once the three of them were seated, she clasped her hands.

"This place and its inhabitants fall under my domain," she began. "I see every living thing and creature within it, and every one of them answers to me. Thusly, I want the two of you to know that I have watched you from the moment you came into my jungle."

In spite of himself, Ekon felt a fleeting annoyance. If what this goddess was saying was true, it meant she'd been watching them struggle through this jungle for a while. She'd seen them encounter mists, spiders, and a grootslang, and had done nothing at all to help until now. He tried to smooth his frown quickly, but Badwa caught it before he could. As though reading his mind, she smiled.

"I do not expect you to understand," she said softly, "the responsibilities I carry as the ruler of this realm. I am aware that several of my subjects have been less than hospitable since your arrival."

A polite way of putting it, Ekon thought, recalling Anatsou specifically.

"But I cannot and *will not* punish the creatures of this jungle for being true to their own nature." Badwa's voice took on a more stoic tone. "To do so would defy my obligation to them as their guardian."

Ekon chose not to respond aloud. He'd grown up inside the walls of the Temple of Lkossa, memorizing scriptures about reverence to gods and goddesses, and he was fairly certain that nothing he had to say at the moment would be considered "reverent." Beside him, he noted Koffi hadn't moved, that she was still watching Badwa with perfect awe.

"What I *can* do, however," Badwa continued, "is provide you with answers to some of the questions you have entered this jungle seeking answers to. I can give you truth."

At once, Ekon sat up again, excited. This goddess had answers? Good, he already had a question. "If everything in this jungle is within your domain," he said, "then you can help us find what we're looking for, you can tell us where the Shetani is, and we can finish our hunt, right?"

He knew at once that he'd said the wrong thing. Badwa's face darkened, like a gathering of clouds before a monsoon. Her expression turned stony and the lines pulling between her brows and at the corners of her mouth seemed to harden. When she regarded Ekon, she looked distinctly cool.

"You speak a false name."

Ekon exchanged a glance with Koffi, who seemed just as nervous as he was, before addressing the goddess again.

"Uh . . . pardon?"

"You called her a shetani, a demon," said Badwa. "*That* is a false name."

Ekon had opened his mouth to say more but stopped suddenly. Something the goddess had just said repeated in his mind.

"Her?" he said again. "Did you just call the Sh—um, the *creature*—a *her*?"

Slowly, Badwa nodded, and it was a sad gesture. "The being your people have hunted for the better part of a century, the one they've named a monster, was not always so." She looked between him and Koffi. "*She* was once human, like you."

Ekon did not instantly comprehend her words. He didn't know how much time passed before they truly sank in.

"*What?*" He felt numb, detached. He didn't look at Koffi, but beside him, he imagined shock rocking through her too as she stared in disbelief. "How . . . how can that be?"

Badwa folded her hands in her lap and sighed. "It begins and ends, as everything does, with the splendor."

Ekon frowned. "The what?"

"A power known by many names," Badwa went on. "But best known by what it was called in the old tongues."

"But what does it—?"

"*Shh!*" Koffi pressed a finger to her lips, silencing Ekon with a sharp look, then gestured for Badwa to continue. The goddess looked between them and spoke again.

"The splendor is an ancient, primordial energy," she explained.

"It is a raw, natural power. My brethren, sistren, and I were born of it, and we Six used it to build the temporal world as you know it to be now. When our work was complete, and the realms of the world were partitioned, we locked the great majority of the splendor away, deep in the heart of the earth itself. We made only one exception to this: The mortal beings we deemed worthy to wield small amounts of that power. We called those mortals *darajas*. Eventually, when those mortals died, they passed their abilities on to their descendants and created a subset of the human race. We gods, content with what we had created, then decided to take our rest." A shadow passed over Badwa's face. "All of us, except for one—our youngest brother."

"Fedu." Ekon said the name before he could help himself. "The god of . . . death."

Badwa nodded. "As the earth aged, my brother began to see its flaws, its worst attributes. Over time, he came to believe that only darajas were fit to exist in the world we gods had created. He planned to use the splendor we'd locked away to start the world anew, but he could not do it on his own. So he sought out a daraja powerful enough to help him realize his vision, to be his *tool*. Eventually, he found one—a young girl born of the same region the two of you are from. Her name was Adiah. He pursued her."

Ekon started to ask a question, then thought better of it. Badwa seemed to appreciate this, because she went on.

"My brother understood that, during specific times, the splendor locked in the earth's core becomes more powerful, more easily accessed and channeled. Such an opportunity only happens once a century, regarded as a holy day—"

"Wait." Ekon sat up, unable to keep from interrupting. "Are you talking about something like . . . like the *Bonding*?"

"The very same," said Badwa. "You mortals observe it as a day of annual reverence and respect to us, but we gods have always known it to have a centennial significance as well. Using deception, Fedu tried to convince Adiah to help him unleash the splendor, but when she realized his true intentions, she thwarted him, at great personal cost."

"What happened to her?" Koffi's voice was soft; she almost sounded frightened. The foreboding in her expression was so strong that Ekon felt it emanate in the air. He looked to Badwa, and she bowed her head.

"Adiah did do a part of my brother's bidding mistakenly," she murmured. "She released some of the splendor from the earth and used it to wreak havoc on Lkossa. The marks of that destruction are still infamous today."

"The Rupture," Koffi whispered. "It wasn't an earthquake. *She* caused it."

"A mistake she lives with each day, I am sure." Badwa blinked, eyes glistening for a moment. "When Adiah realized what she'd done, she took back the splendor Fedu had convinced her to misuse and held it within her to prevent him from inflicting further harm on the rest of the continent. When my brother threatened her, I offered her refuge in a place where he could not follow. No god can enter the realm of another god without consent. And so she has remained here ever since." She looked to Koffi. "Except for briefly one night, when she felt the call of another daraja."

"But there's something I still don't understand." Ekon spoke slowly, trying to bring the many pieces of the puzzle together in his mind. "If Adiah has been here all this time, in refuge, how did she become"—he hesitated—"the *Shetani*?"

Badwa's face grew drawn. "The amount of the splendor that Adiah absorbed at my brother's behest was unnatural; no god should have been able to absorb it, let alone a mortal being. The power has preserved Adiah, allowing her to live well past a human's normal years," she said. "But she paid a price for it, and a terrible one at that."

Koffi stiffened, and the hair on the back of Ekon's neck stood on end.

"The splendor feeds off her body," Badwa explained. "It has distorted her appearance savagely. Her mind remains human and intact, but her body is that of a beast and will remain so until the splendor is extracted from her."

"She's been sacrificing herself." Koffi's voice was hollow, her expression full of horror. "For all these years. Lkossans have called her a monster when . . . when actually she's been *protecting* us, all of us."

"Yeah." Ekon frowned. "When she's not slaughtering people in droves."

Badwa's eyes cut to him. "Adiah has dwelled in my realm for ninety-nine of your mortal years," she said sharply. "Not *once* has she killed a human being."

Ekon shook his head before he could stop himself. "That's not possible. The Shetani has single-handedly been killing Lkossans for years. There are record books of its death—"

Badwa's chin lifted. "You question the word of a goddess?"

Like that, Ekon remembered himself. He didn't want to contradict a goddess—it seemed like an exceptionally *bad* idea at every angle—but in this, he couldn't think of another possibility. He knew what he had seen with his own eyes all his life, the mutilated bodies and pools of blood at the Greater Jungle's border. Something twisted inside him when he thought of his father. Baba, who had died in this very jungle . . . *Baba*, who had died so violently . . .

"I don't want to question you," he said to the goddess slowly. "But that doesn't match up. I *know* what I've seen with my own eyes, there are lists of the Shetani's victims—"

"Unless . . ." Koffi was staring ahead, doing her own kind of silent figuring. "Unless those people *weren't* the Shetani's victims."

"What are you—?"

"Bear with me for a second." Koffi's eyes were narrowing. "What do we know to be fact now?"

Ekon paused. "We know that people in Lkossa have been getting brutally killed for decades in the same location, in generally the same manner every time."

"Right," said Koffi. "And until today, we thought the culprit of those killings was the Shetani, but . . . *now* we know that's not possible." She looked up. "Think about it, Ekon. Why would Adiah bother to hold all the splendor inside of her body to protect Lkossa's people, if she was just going to go around killing its citizens anyway?"

"Because she's been turned into a monster with an insatiable bloodlust?"

"*Or*"—Koffi folded her hands—"because she hasn't been the one killing people—something else has."

At the words, Ekon felt a chill. "Something *else*?"

"Something methodical," Koffi continued. "Something that wants the blame for the killings to go to Adiah."

They came to the conclusion together. "Fedu."

"He's been behind the killings," said Koffi. "He's been using something to kill Lkossans and blame Adiah for it."

"Because if everyone thinks Adiah did it, she's hated," said Ekon. "It would make people want to find her and hunt her down for him, like people have been trying to do for a century."

"Like *we've* been trying to do," Koffi murmured.

Ekon sat back for a moment, stunned. It was as though his entire world had been suddenly and violently uprooted, shaken to its very core. For as long as he could remember, he'd both feared and hated the Shetani. He'd blamed it for most of the bad parts of his childhood, for the death of his own father. That constant anger at it had been like an energy of its own, *fueling* him. It felt strange to know that anger had been misplaced all along, that it belonged somewhere else.

"We need to find the thing that's been really killing people." Ekon grimaced, an entirely new resolve rising in him. "We need to find whatever Fedu's been using to hurt Lkossans and put a stop to it."

"No." Koffi shook her head, frowning. "What we need to do is find Adiah, and *help* her."

"There may be a way," Badwa said quietly, "for you to do both."

They looked up, but it was Ekon who spoke first. "What do you mean?"

"My brother is many things," said the goddess. "Cunning, ambitious, and calculating, but above all else, he is *deliberate*. He has been facilitating the vicious killings in Lkossa all this time, but with purpose, with a constant goal in mind."

"To try to get Adiah," said Koffi.

"Because, with the splendor still inside her body, she is *useful* to him," Badwa went on. "But if Adiah no longer had what my brother wanted . . ."

"Then she *wouldn't* be useful to him," Ekon finished.

"And he'd have no reason to kill people anymore," said Koffi. "The murders would stop."

Badwa said nothing, but her eyes twinkled. Ekon addressed her again directly. "How do we help Adiah get rid of the splendor in her body?"

The goddess steepled her fingers a moment, thoughtful. "Adiah was able to take that volume of splendor into her body nearly a hundred years ago, during the Bonding, when it rose to the earth's surface in a greater magnitude than usual," she said. "In order to put it back, she would need to do the opposite."

"Could she release it in small quantities?" Ekon asked.

Badwa gave him a considering look. "Imagine you have held a heavy basin of water for a century," she said. "Now imagine trying to pour that basin out slowly, drip by drip. It could be done, but it would require a great deal of control, an amount I don't know that Adiah has anymore." She sat back, thoughtful. "What she needs is another opportunity to get rid of it safely all at once, something like—"

"Another Bonding," Koffi interjected. "That would allow her to deposit the splendor back into the earth safely, without another Rupture."

"The next Bonding is in two months," said Ekon. He actually

stood and started to pace. "We'd have to find her before it starts, then get her to a place where it's safe for her to deposit the splendor without hurting anyone. It would have to be remote, away from people . . ."

"The Kusonga Plains!" Koffi jumped to her feet too. "You said it yourself once, there's nothing out there but open grassland. It would be a safe place for Adiah to get rid of the splendor still inside her."

"According to the map in Nkrumah's journal, the Kusonga Plains aren't close," said Ekon. "It would take weeks to get there on foot, more time if we had Adiah with us and had to keep her hidden from Fedu."

"So we have to find her," said Koffi. "Sooner rather than later."

"And if Fedu figures out what we're doing?" Ekon asked. "If he comes after her?" In the back of his head, another thought crossed his mind. Fedu wasn't the only one who still wanted to find Adiah. He swallowed. The Kuhani's hunting party was likely somewhere in this jungle by now, hunting and searching; perhaps they weren't far off even at this moment . . .

"She won't be alone." Koffi's eyes suddenly hardened. "*I'm* a da-raja too. I can help protect her." She faced Badwa. "You said you'd teach me how to use the splendor," she said. "When do we start?"

The goddess of the jungle turned her gaze to the trees, and suddenly Ekon had the sense that the goddess was seeing far more than they ever would.

"Tomorrow," she said after a moment. "Your first lesson begins at sunrise."

CHAPTER 23

THE SPLENDOR

Koffi was awake by dawn.

She'd done her best to do as Badwa said, to eat dinner, then get as much rest as she could, but it was impossible. Her dreams had been brimful with all the things she'd learned the day before—Adiah, the Shetani, the splendor, the truth about the Rupture. When she woke up and remembered everything all over again, a fresh jolt passed through her being.

She rose from her bedroll as the first rays of dawn touched the still-dark sky. It was a modest thing, lent to her by the yumboes, but certainly more comfortable than anything she'd ever slept on before. Her eyes roamed around the makeshift campsite, looking for her courteous hosts, and she was surprised to find the grounds were empty except for herself, Ekon, who was still asleep a few feet away, and the hut where Badwa assumedly was. There was no sign of the yumboes. She quirked an eyebrow, curious. Did yumboes even *need* sleep? Where did spectral caretakers of a magical jungle go? What did they *do*? She realized she didn't really know.

In silence, she crept away from the campsite and into the looming trees. At this hour of the day, the jungle was not yet awake, and she was more than happy to keep it that way. She stopped when she found the small pond Badwa had referenced the night before, and knelt down to look into its uninterrupted surface. She paused. It was the first time in gods-knew-when that she'd actually looked at herself. She didn't know what to feel when she saw her reflection in the faint morning light. The girl staring back at her was barely recognizable; somehow she looked older. Her dark twists had unraveled partially into delicate spirals that stuck out in all directions. She looked the same but different. It took her a moment to pinpoint why.

You're not alone, you're not the only one.

When she'd made that candle burst in the Hema another lifetime ago, she'd thought she was alone. When the old woman in the market had told her about magic in Lkossa, she'd felt *less* alone, but now . . . now there was another person like her, a girl she had something in common with, maybe even a friend.

Not a friend, she reminded herself. *A prodigy.*

If what Badwa had told them the day before was true, Adiah wasn't going to be a friend; she was a *master* of the splendor, with more skill than Koffi could ever hope to have. She thought again of the promise she'd made to both Badwa and Ekon yesterday; she'd said that she would protect Adiah if she had to, but the longer she considered the words, the more foolish they sounded in her head. She'd barely been able to protect herself in this jungle. With a stab she thought of her deal with Baaz, the implications of what this change in plans would mean for her bargain with him. If Adiah was really the Shetani, it meant she couldn't be taken back to the Night Zoo, and she certainly couldn't be turned over to Father Olufemi. A faint panic crept in the longer she thought about Jabir still trapped in the Night Zoo, about Mama still lying in that infirmary bed—

"Hey, you okay?"

Koffi jumped. Ekon was standing a few feet away, between two trees, looking guilty. Heat rose in her cheeks when she realized how alarmed she must have looked. Gods, he was good at not being heard.

"Sorry." Ekon raised his hands. "I saw you get up, and I—"

"Thought something might try to eat me?"

"More or less." He offered a stiff nod before dropping his gaze and letting his fingers tap against his side. Ekon looked strangely nervous. "I'm glad you're okay."

Koffi swallowed. "Thanks for checking."

"Right." Finally Ekon looked up, clasping his hands behind his back. "Well, in that case, I'll head back to camp—"

"I wanted to thank you for saving my life too." Koffi stood. "A lot of what happened before is still blurry, but . . . I know I wouldn't be here without you."

Ekon offered a small smile before shaking his head. "Don't thank me, it's what any decent person would have done." As though he'd just thought of something, his expression changed. "You said a lot of what happened before is still blurry. So, you probably don't remember . . ."

"I remember the story you told me," said Koffi quickly. For some inexplicable reason, it felt important to reassure him of that. "I wouldn't forget that, Ekon."

Ekon looked relieved, but only partially. "And, um, after you ate the umdhlebi tree's fruit? Do you remember anything else from then?"

Koffi dropped her gaze. The truth was, those moments after she'd eaten the strange fruit were blurriest of all, sort of like a dream, but . . . there was *one* thing . . . Her cheeks burned. A piece of a memory had just returned to her. She remembered sitting beneath a tree and feeling Ekon's eyes on her. She remembered the way he'd looked at her, the way he'd leaned in slightly at the same moment she had. The way she'd wanted to—

"Good morning, child."

She and Ekon looked up abruptly. The sun had finally appeared over the jungle's treetops, and with it so had the jungle's goddess. Badwa, weaving quietly between the trees, as serene and powerful as she had been the day before. Koffi marveled at the sight of her.

"Good morning . . ." Koffi paused. "I'm not actually sure what to call you."

"My name will do." Badwa's eyes twinkled. "Are you ready to begin your lessons?" She looked from Koffi to Ekon, a bit of knowing touching her features. "Or, if I have interrupted you, I can wait . . . ?"

"No need!" Ekon's voice was at least one octave too high as he turned on his heels to make his way back to the camp. Maybe *he'd* seen that knowing in Badwa's eyes too. "Please don't let me delay you."

He disappeared into the trees, leaving Koffi and Badwa alone. Koffi felt a distinct pluck of sadness in his absence, but when the goddess cleared her throat, she refocused. "Are you going to teach me how to use the splendor?" she asked.

The goddess gave her an unmistakably wry look. "Not just yet.

There are a few practical lessons to be learned, the first of which is that the splendor is not a thing to be *used*, but rather an energy to be *borrowed*, transferred from one vessel to another, and then properly released. Think of water." She gestured to the pond before them. "It is fluid, ever changing. A single drop of rain is inconsequential, but one million drops of rain creates . . ."

"A monsoon," Koffi finished.

"Precisely," said Badwa. "It is also important that you understand the relationship between the splendor and the darajas. I told you yesterday that the first darajas were handpicked by my brothers, sisters, and I, but do you know what the word *daraja* means?"

Koffi shook her head.

"Like the word *splendor*, it comes from the old tongues we gods gave to mankind. Its meaning is simple: *bridge*."

"Bridge," Koffi repeated. "As in, something you cross?"

"As in, something that *connects*," said Badwa. "The splendor is a spiritual energy similar to the air you breathe—it is constant, pervasive, vital to all living things. As a daraja, your body is uniquely equipped to draw it from the earth itself and redirect it. In doing so, you act as a physical conduit between the mundane and the divine."

"So, what can I do?"

Badwa shook her head, but her expression wasn't unkind. "The splendor manifests for each daraja slightly differently. To discover how it manifests within you is one of our objectives today. Typically, you will feel it most noticeably in extremities like your hands and feet, so . . ." She sat down and patted a spot of dirt opposite her. "Please sit and press your hands to the earth. We are going to test the strength of your connection to the splendor."

Koffi stiffened but obeyed nonetheless. Once she was seated with both palms flat against the ground, Badwa clasped her hands.

"Close your eyes."

Koffi did, feeling foolish. She waited, each passing second like a century. When she finally cracked one eye open, she found the goddess was staring at her, visibly perplexed.

"You felt nothing at all just then?"

Embarrassment flooded Koffi's cheeks. It felt as though she'd just failed a test she didn't know she was taking, but she didn't dare lie. She shook her head.

"Strange," Badwa mused.

"Actually . . ." Koffi fidgeted. "I've been meaning to ask you about something you said yesterday."

"Go on."

"You said the first darajas passed their abilities on to their children," she said. "So, does that mean it's a, um, family thing?"

Badwa's eyebrows arched. "It *is* an ability passed through families by blood, though not always consistently in each generation. Why do you ask?"

Koffi looked down at her hands. "It's just that neither of my parents were darajas—at least, I'm pretty sure of it."

"And *their* parents?"

"They all died before I was born, except for my mother's mother," said Koffi. "But then *she* died when I was really small. She lived with us for a little while I think, but I can't remember her."

Badwa's expression turned thoughtful. "Well, you are certainly a daraja. I sense it within you. Have you ever deliberately tried channeling the splendor?"

Koffi didn't meet the goddess's eyes. "Not . . . on purpose," she whispered. "But a little while ago, I got upset when someone threatened my mom and . . . I'm not sure if I consciously meant to do what I did, but it wasn't good."

"I see."

There was new understanding in Badwa's eyes. The goddess folded her hands before speaking again. "As I said, the splendor is a spiritual energy. When you draw it from the earth and channel it, it should move through your body like a river, but it can only do so if your mind and body are both at peace. If they are not"—she gave Koffi a meaningful look—"there can be complications."

"Complications?"

"If your mind and body are not at peace when the splendor is moving through you, it can create an obstruction that keeps it inside of you," Badwa explained. "It can build like a toxin, and if it remains, it can wreak havoc on the physical body. You now know what's happened to Adiah, but in the worst scenario, keeping too much of the splendor within you could cost your very life."

Koffi swallowed, remembering the Night Zoo. She remembered taking that breath and holding it in, feeling heady, before feeling a release. It scared her to think of some dangerous thing building inside her, something that could kill her. "How do I stop that from happening?"

"Before you try to draw and channel the splendor, you must relax your mind and body entirely. You must find inner peace," said Badwa. "I want you to close your eyes again. This time, take slow, even breaths. Count each one as a beat, like a rhythm."

336

Koffi did as she was told, closing her eyes to the world around her. In the darkness, she listened to the sound of her own breathing. It felt silly. She imagined what she must've looked like sitting there, hands in the dirt like a child.

It's not going to work, said a ridiculing voice in her head. *Not for someone like you. Your mind is never at peace.*

She tried to imagine a fortress like the Night Zoo, high mud-brick walls all around her mind. The voice of doubt lapped against her, persistent and unabating, but she built her fortress up higher. Tentatively, she reached for that light she'd felt inside Badwa's tent. Like an answering call, it came, warming her fingertips for the briefest of moments. Just as quickly, it vanished. Koffi opened her eyes.

"It comes, but it won't stay."

Badwa's eyes were measured. "Your mind isn't at peace."

Koffi looked around. "Sure it is. I haven't been this well rested in . . . well, ever."

"Being well rested isn't the same thing as being truly at peace," said Badwa. "There is something inside you preventing the splendor from flowing properly, something you haven't acknowl-edged. You have suppressed it, and so suppressed your channel."

Koffi's eyebrow rose. "I don't feel . . . suppressed." She paused, thoughtful. "If anything, I get myself in trouble for not suppressing things enough."

Badwa steepled her fingers. "Think back to a time in your life when you were truly upset about something, the last time you cried. How did you handle it?"

Koffi didn't have to think far back to find a memory. "I don't cry, really." She realized as soon as she said the words how silly they sounded. "Well, I mean, I *do* cry, but not often. When I thought something had happened to my family, I sort of wanted to, but . . . I also didn't."

"Has your family ever upset you?" asked Badwa.

"No." Koffi's answer was immediate. "My mama is . . . well, she's just *good*. She's always sacrificing for me and putting me before herself. And technically Jabir isn't related to me, but he's as good as family too. All he wants to do is make people smile and—"

"What about your father?" Badwa's voice was its softest yet. "Has he ever upset you?"

Koffi stiffened. "My baba is dead."

"That is not what I asked."

A beat passed between them before Koffi tried again. "It . . . wouldn't be fair to be upset at my baba anymore. He's gone."

Badwa readjusted in the dirt. "Just because a person dies doesn't mean their impact does. How do you feel when you think of him?"

"Bad." Koffi wanted to close her eyes, but found she couldn't. "He was . . . a kind man. He made my mama laugh, and he made us feel loved. I—we both miss him all the time."

"But?"

Something tightened in Koffi's chest. She forced herself to speak the words anyway.

"He didn't always make good decisions," she whispered. "He was irresponsible sometimes, and Mama and I paid for it."

"He disappointed you."

Koffi flinched against the accusation. It was too severe, too harsh for someone as kind as Baba. Yet, as soon as Badwa spoke the words, she knew. Some inkling of truth touched her. Her nod was quick, almost imperceptible.

"You must acknowledge your emotions, child." Badwa's expression was firm but not unkind. "Acknowledge them, acknowledge their origins, and then let them leave your body naturally. Breathe in, and then release. It might also be wise to unclench your fists."

Koffi looked down at her lap. She hadn't even realized she'd balled her fists. When she opened her palms, her skin was marked with angry red crescents from her fingernails.

"I want you to try channeling the splendor again," said Badwa. "But this time, when it comes to you, I want you to relax your entire mind. You cannot put up walls. Let whatever feelings that arise enter your body. Acknowledge them, then let them leave."

"What if it still doesn't work?" asked Koffi.

Badwa said nothing.

Koffi took a deep breath as she pressed her hands to the dirt again. Her eyes automatically closed, and behind her eyelids she stared into a red-black nothingness. She waited, hoping, praying. And then she felt it: a quiet twinge. It was timid, like a lute's first notes, and then it grew stronger, warmer. Heat flooded her fingertips, but this time it did not fade. It reached for her too, like an old friend. It made its way up her knees, her hips, and when it reached her chest, she stiffened.

"Acknowledge it." Badwa's gentle voice sounded so far away in this nothingness. "Acknowledge it, and then let it go."

Koffi's muscles tensed as something formed in the nothingness. A figure materialized, sitting opposite her where Badwa should have been. It was a man.

His burlap tunic was shabby but familiar, and faint stubble dusted his jaw. Koffi met his kind brown eyes and, with a pang, saw her own reflected in them. This man had gray in his kinky hair;

her father didn't look the way he had when she'd been small. This felt like a figment of her mind, the man she'd imagined her father would have become if he'd lived longer. He offered her a small, sad smile.

Kof. His voice echoed in the chambers of her mind. *My girl, beautiful inside and out.*

A lump rose in Koffi's throat that she couldn't swallow. "Thank you, Baba."

You left the Night Zoo. Baba's eyes were alight, filled with that same boyish sense of adventure. *I knew you would. Ah, my girl, we always understood each other. We were always the same, free spirits.*

"I am *not* free, Baba." Koffi tried to keep the trembling from her voice. "And neither is Mama."

Baba's smile faltered. *You're . . . you're not upset with me, are you? Look at what you have accomplished because you* dared. *You were bold, you took risks, and they've paid—*

"*You* took risks, Baba." Anger churned in Koffi's chest. "And then you died and left Mama and me to pay for it, literally. All my life, I've been paying for your risks, *and* your mistakes."

The smile completely vanished from Baba's face, replaced with something else. Guilt. *Kof, I didn't mean to—*

"But you did. And I'm . . . I'm *mad* at you. I needed you, and you let me down. You let us both down."

At her words, Baba hung his head. Long beats passed before he spoke again, his voice only a whisper.

I'm so sorry, Koffi.

And then they came, the tears. They were instant, and consuming. Koffi's stomach twisted as sobs racked her body, and she felt something release in her core. It was painful at first, and then it wasn't. Warmth flooded through her entire body, washing over her in a wave. When she looked up again, she found her father's eyes were wet too.

You are better than I deserve. He took her hand in his and squeezed. *One day, I hope you can forgive me.*

Koffi squeezed back. "I already do, Baba."

No sooner had she spoken the words than the darkness began to dissipate. The splendor's energy moved down her limbs, then left her. Something else left too. When she opened her eyes, she was back in the Greater Jungle and sitting across from Badwa. The goddess was smiling.

"*Look*, child."

Koffi dropped her gaze. Her palm was open, and there, resting inches above it, was a small cluster of particles. Her mouth fell open as she stared at it, and then, just as quickly, the particles vanished. "Yes!" She jumped to her feet. "I did it! I channeled the splendor on my own!"

Badwa's smile was wry. "So you did," she said. "*This* time."

"What?" Koffi's eyes shot back to her. "What do you mean?"

Instead of answering, Badwa patted the dirt and gestured for Koffi to sit back down. "I am very happy you were able to successfully channel the splendor, Koffi; it is no small feat. But your work is far from done."

"Well, that's okay," said Koffi. "You'll be able to teach me—"

"No." Badwa shook her head. "I won't. You do not have time."

"Oh." The reality of the situation came crashing back to her without warning. Of course they didn't have time, as the Bonding was fast approaching. They still had to find Adiah and get her to the Kusonga Plains. She recuperated quickly. "I *do* believe this will work." She tried to say the words as confidently as possible. "I'm going to try my hardest."

She'd hoped saying so might make the goddess smile; instead, the look on Badwa's face turned sadder still. There was a decidedly somber touch to it.

"You must do more than try, Koffi," she said quietly. "You must *succeed.*"

Koffi faltered. "What do you mean?"

The goddess's eyes were steely. "What my brother tricked Adiah into doing to Lkossa nearly a hundred years ago was . . . cataclysmic, an unprecedented violence against the innocent." She grimaced. "But it will pale in comparison to what Fedu will do if he finds Adiah again. Make no mistake, child, he believes his cause just, and he will pursue it until he has destroyed any semblance of the earth you know. He seeks to introduce a new world order, the manifestation of his arrogance, and he will stop at nothing to see that endeavor through."

"But what about the other gods?" Koffi asked. "Atuno and Amakoya, Itaashe and Tyembu." She paused. It felt strange to speak of beings she'd worshipped all her life this way. "Can't they do anything to help, to stop him?"

Badwa's expression hardened into something inscrutable. "My brethren and sistren are more, shall we say, *detached* from this world, more detached than I choose to be," she said in a neutral voice. Koffi thought she heard a touch of emotion beneath it. "In a way, I cannot blame them—like me, they have existed for thousands of years—but I fear they will not understand the threat my brother poses until it is too late. For all intents and purposes, we must assume they will not interfere."

342

Koffi stiffened. She was far from home, Lkossa and the Night Zoo were distant, but she still remembered the things she'd heard as a child, the stories elderly beastkeepers had recalled. They'd only talked about it when they were drunk and numbed, but that hadn't stopped the terror from seeping into their voices. The cracks in the earth, the death, the terrible heat that had driven droves to madness . . . Koffi imagined all of it happening tenfold, not just to a single city, but to an entire continent, to millions of people.

"Ekon and I won't let that happen," she said, her voice full of resolve. "We'll find Adiah and get her to the Kusonga Plains. Fedu doesn't know what we are planning, so we still have an advantage. It can work."

The goddess met her gaze in earnest before taking Koffi's hand and squeezing gently. "But if it does not . . . I must ask you to make me a promise."

At once, Koffi nodded. "Of course. Anything."

"You must promise me," said Badwa, "that you will do anything in your ability to prevent my brother from using Adiah's power to exact his plans." Her eyes turned meaningful. *"Anything."*

Koffi paused. She didn't know exactly how to interpret Badwa's words and chose her own carefully.

"I understand."

Badwa offered a small smile, and reluctantly Koffi returned it, trying simultaneously to ignore the unease settling inside her. The first time she'd seen Badwa for what she truly was inside the hut, she'd thought her glorious, the most beautiful being she'd ever seen. In a way, she still was, but behind that veneer, Koffi caught a glimpse of something else, something older and far cooler. She said the only words she could say.

"I . . . I promise . . . ," she said. "That I will do what I need to."

It seemed to be enough for the goddess. Satisfied, she leaned back and folded her hands. "You will need to continue the kind of exercises we have done today, drawing small amounts of the splendor in and through your body," said Badwa. "To do it well will also require you to practice *emotional intelligence*. You must learn to rule your heart, and to be constantly aware of what you are feeling, and why you are feeling that way."

Rule your heart. Koffi considered the words. They bore a distinct similarity to the ones Mama had said to her at the Night Zoo.

Sometimes, though, you can't lead with your heart. You have to think with your head.

Mama hadn't told her the whole truth about what she was, but she'd given her that small token of truth as a guide. All this time, she'd thought the last thing Mama had given her was that second chance at life on the Night Zoo's wall, but maybe her mother had given something else.

Badwa cleared her throat. "I would like you to try once more," she said. "Are you ready?"

Koffi nodded.

"Good." Badwa pressed Koffi's hands to the dirt. "Now, *again*."

Koffi practiced channeling the splendor with Badwa for the rest of the day, *and* the two days after.

The lessons on splendor theory were long, the physical exercises intense. After the first day, Koffi had stopped waking up early. Every muscle in her body ached, even parts she hadn't known existed. She didn't think she could retain one more concept, directive,

344

or lecture about the history of the splendor's use. It was grueling, but Badwa didn't let up. According to the goddess, in older times darajas had begun their formal training with the splendor around age ten, and spent an additional decade learning its nuances under the tutelage of several masters. Koffi didn't have several masters, or a decade of time to play catch-up, so *she* was getting the expedited experience. Gradually, her command of the splendor improved.

Each time she closed her eyes and reached, it seemed to come more and more willingly. By the second day, she found that she could not only summon particles of the splendor but could send it in certain directions when she focused hard enough. It was a curious, fascinating phenomenon. Sometimes, the energy hummed through her, gentle and warm; other times, it was scalding, like swallowing a mouthful of too-hot tea. When she held it in too long, she felt light-headed. When that happened, Badwa grew stern.

"Resist that urge," she said. "You *must* train yourself not to keep the splendor inside of your body for too long. It's dangerous."

"But that's how it gets stronger," Koffi argued. "When I hold on to it, I can feel it building—"

"You *must* let it go." Badwa's voice was insistent. "The splendor will make you feel powerful in the moment, yes, but even as a daraja, your body is not equipped to hold on to it. You are only meant to channel it and then move it from one place to another. *Never* forget that."

It felt strange when, on the third day, Badwa told them their lessons were concluded. On the one hand, Koffi was grateful for the respite; the splendor had a distinctly fatiguing effect after a while. But on the other hand, stopping made her anxious, even afraid. Badwa wasn't going to be around much longer. Badwa wouldn't be there to encourage her when she failed, or chastise her when she overextended herself. The reality of the situation pressed in. Soon, she and Ekon were going to have to leave this place and find Adiah. Not only would they have to convince her to come with them, but they'd have to travel miles west to get her to the Kusonga Plains in time for the Bonding, all while avoiding detection. Doubt wriggled through Koffi's insides like an invasive worm. What if they couldn't find Adiah? Worse, what if they did find the other daraja but couldn't convince her to join them? The ideas wreaked havoc in her imagination.

She found Ekon back at the campsite, sitting among a huddle of what looked like yumbo children. Whatever misgivings he'd previously had about them seemed to have been abandoned, because he was fastidiously studying Nkrumah's journal while two little girls decorated his curly hair with flowers. When he noticed Koffi, he looked up.

"They . . . wanted to do my hair."

Koffi barely managed to look serious. "The pink and green *does* bring out your eyes."

A smile broke out over Ekon's face, and involuntarily she found herself smiling back. Koffi did her best to stay out of the yumbo girls' way as she settled beside him and nibbled on a fresh pawpaw from her bag. She was all too aware of how close they were, and of how little she minded that closeness.

"So, what are you up to?"

"Just some reading," said Ekon absently. With a book in his lap and sitting in sunlight, he looked perfectly peaceful. "The usual light stuff—variances of photosynthesis in carnivorous plant life, the migration patterns of plain tiger butterflies, to keep things poetic. I've had my eye on a chapter about rhinoceros beetles . . ."

Koffi smiled. "The usual."

"I've also been mulling over a plan," said Ekon, a bit more seriously. "I know training with Badwa is important, but . . . I was thinking we should probably leave soon."

Koffi nodded. "I agree."

Ekon flipped to the front of Nkrumah's journal to study its map.

"The Heart of the Jungle is still slightly north of here, a day's walking if we—"

"Hold on." Koffi's eyes had wandered south of Ekon's finger, back to the bottom corner of the map. Ekon tried to follow her gaze, confused.

"What?"

"That word." She pointed to it. She still couldn't read Old Zamani, and the characters looked unfamiliar to her, but she'd just remembered something. "Before we left Lkossa, you told me what it was."

"Yeah, I remember that." Ekon squinted. "It just says 'sanda,' but that's not a word in Old Zamani, or new Zamani, for that matter."

Koffi didn't answer. She was still staring at the foreign word, trying to picture it mentally in a language she knew. *Sanda*. Master Nkrumah, the author of the journal, had written it with beautiful penmanship, notably making the first and last letters of the word slightly larger. She stared at it a moment longer before it dawned on her.

"Not sanda," she whispered.

"Huh?"

"*Not* sanda," she repeated. She pressed a thumb over half of the word for a second, then switched to the other side. "They're two letters: *S* and *A*. Together, they look like *sanda*."

"The *S* could be for *Satao*, that was Master Nkrumah's first name," said Ekon. "But I don't know who the *A* is."

"*Adiah*."

They both looked up. Badwa was standing across the campsite, watching them. "The *A* stands for Adiah."

Ekon started. "Master Nkrumah and Adiah were alive at the same time?" he asked. "They knew each other?"

"I believe it was a bit more than that," said Badwa as she approached. "As I understand it, they were once very good friends."

Koffi looked between the goddess and the journal. "He wrote their initials here, together."

"After Adiah fled into the jungle, he searched for her," she said quietly. "The desperation to find her affected his mind as he got older, and I believe it stayed with him until the very end."

"The stories," said Ekon. "People said he started calling the Greater Jungle *her*, but—"

"But he wasn't talking about the jungle," said Koffi sadly. "He was talking about Adiah. He was looking for *her*."

Badwa sat down before them. "I could not tell Satao where Adiah was," she said calmly, though Koffi thought there was regret in her voice. "Keeping her safe meant keeping her hidden, even from the ones who loved her. But times have changed."

Koffi sat up. "You mean, you can tell us where she is?"

The corners of the goddess's mouth tugged into a small smile. "As I said before, this is my realm. I know everything that happens within it."

"Then you know where Adiah is," said Ekon.

Badwa nodded. "She is north of here, a day's walk from this camp. Leave tomorrow at first light and walk in that direction. Stay true to the path, and you will find her." The goddess's expression changed. "I'm afraid that, after tonight, we must part ways, children."

"We understand," said Koffi. "Thank you." She waited until the goddess left them again before looking at Ekon, the smallest smirk touching her lips.

"See? All we have to do it head north from here, no problem at all."

Ekon's eyebrow quirked. "Is it just me, or does that *almost* sound too easy?"

Koffi grinned in spite of herself. "Only one way to find out."

A COMPLETE BETRAYAL

ADIAH

"I don't care!"

In seven years, I've never seen Tao this angry.

I stand across the room from him, watching as he hacks into carrots that are supposed to be minced. The soup he's making smells delicious, a blend with onions, tomatoes, and spices. In better circumstances, I would ask him if I could try some, but not this time.

My best friend is livid.

"*Tao.*" I fight to keep the annoyance from my voice. This conversation hasn't gone the way I imagined it would, but I'm doing my best to salvage what's left of it. "Come on," I say gently. "It's really not as big a deal as you're making it—"

"*Not a big deal?*" Tao practically throws the ill-fortuned carrots into the pot, ignoring the hot water that splashes when he does. He regards me with something that borders on disgust. "It was a violation, a complete betrayal of trust."

I barely resist rolling my eyes. He's making it sound like I stabbed him in the back or pushed him off a cliff. "I really didn't think you'd care this much," I say placatingly. "If I had, I'd—"

"The sky garden has always been our place." There's still a bite in Tao's voice, but beneath it, he sounds injured. "It was *our* secret, something that belonged to no one else. You didn't have to show it to him. We've been going up there since the day we first set foot in this temple."

"Exactly," I say with exasperation. "Since we were little kids. It was silly."

"Not to me," Tao murmurs.

I pretend I don't hear him. "Don't you think it's time for us to change things a bit, to be more . . . adult?"

"Adult." Tao's eyes narrow as he repeats me. "Where'd you get that one from, your new boyfriend?"

My face goes hot, and it has nothing to do with the stifling kitchen. "Dakari isn't my boyfriend."

"He might as well be," says Tao, scowling. "The way he's always around you, always all over you like a jungle leech."

I look away, grateful my dark skin hides my blush. It's true Dakari and I have been spending more time together recently, but . . .

"We're just friends," I say defensively. "He's still new to Lkossa, still getting to know people."

"Tuh." Tao jumps down from his stool and grabs several spices from a nearby cupboard. "I think he's gotten to know *plenty* of girls."

I'm offended on Dakari's behalf. "What's your problem with him?" I ask, my voice angrier than I mean it to be. "Dakari is perfectly—"

"That's exactly it!" Tao throws up his hands. "He's *perfect*.

351

Perfect face, perfect demeanor, perfect everything. I don't trust it."

"You don't trust anything that doesn't come from a book," I mutter.

"*I* trust myself not to be fooled by a deep voice and some shallow compliments," Tao says scathingly. "I used to think you were smart enough not to be either."

The insult stings like a slap to the face; Tao has never spoken to me that way.

"Tao," I say quietly. "I really care about him."

It's hard to read the expression on my friend's face as he stops short. The pain there doesn't make sense to me. Just as quickly, it's gone. "Then there's nothing left to say," he murmurs, picking up the pot. "I'll see you around, Adiah."

He doesn't say another word as he leaves me in the kitchens, alone.

CHAPTER 24

SILVER BELLS

Ekon didn't sleep well their last night at Badwa's camp.

It wasn't for lack of trying or want; above him the sky was stunning, a smattering of silver-white stars more vivid than he'd ever seen in Lkossa. He crossed his arms behind his head and stared up at it. A few feet away, snuggled into her bedroll, Koffi slept, and the sounds of the jungle formed a melody he almost liked. Tomorrow, bright and early, they would leave and start their new search for Adiah. They'd been in this jungle for seven days and eight nights; finally, they were going to find the thing they'd entered it for. They were going to find Adiah, help her get rid of the splendor poisoning her body, and possibly stop the killing that had plagued Lkossa for almost a century. Those were *good* things, things that *should* have made him happy. But something else was on his mind.

The hunting party.

By no means was it the first time he'd reflected on it; thoughts of the Sons of the Six had invaded his mind intermittently since he and Koffi had set foot in the jungle. He had been actively avoiding those thoughts recently, but they'd finally caught up with him.

Tomorrow marked eight days. Eight, a *bad* number.

He thought about his conversation with Fahim in the temple, the last time he'd seen his friend.

Do you know when you're going?

Not yet. But I think it'll be soon, probably in the next few days.

Even if he was being generous, the *few* had likely meant three or four days at most. By now, the Sons of the Six were likely in the jungle too, trying to find what they thought was the Shetani and kill it. He remembered Kamau's words next, the warning his brother had given him.

You won't just be contending with what's already in there. The Sons of the Six will be hunting too, the Yabahari way.

Ekon could already see them in his mind. Father Olufemi would have picked the strongest, fastest, and keenest warriors for such a mission, and they'd prove their worth once in the jungle. What would happen if they found him here? What would happen if they found Koffi here? He cringed at that thought.

I don't know what I'd do if this were any more complicated.

Koffi had said those words back at the Kughushi District while they'd been looking at the maps. And in that memory, he recalled the moment he'd decided not tell her the whole truth, the moment he'd decided to lie. He hadn't planned to keep the information about the hunting party from her forever, just until they were far enough into the Greater Jungle to make it a moot point. Now guilt twisted his insides.

You have to tell Koffi, said a voice in his head. *You have to tell her the truth.*

And admit that you've been lying to her from the start? another argued right back. *No. Come up with some kind of a strategy first. Figure out the optimal time, then tell her.* Ekon liked that plan better. His entire life had been the summation of carefully tailored strategies, ideas, and objectives that could be planned, perfected, and executed. This was the kind of problem that needed the best strategy. He found comfort in that as his eyelids grew heavy.

I'll tell her the truth, he promised the stars overhead. *I'll tell her—when the time is right.*

Dawn came all too soon.

They packed their few possessions without speaking, and for that Ekon was grateful. Anxiety still churned in his stomach every time he looked at Koffi, every time he remembered his thoughts from the night before, but that didn't change his resolve. Badwa had kept true to her word; she and the yumboes were gone by the time they rose. He'd expected it, but that didn't make their absence feel any better. Once again, the jungle felt massive, dense, and even sentient. Something pulled within him when he saw their bags had been left fully stocked with rations and their water gourds full. He and Koffi gave the now-abandoned campground a final once-over, then set off into the jungle yet again.

"So, this trail will take us north?" Koffi was marching ahead, as usual.

"That's what Badwa said." Ekon nodded at her back even though she couldn't see it. "If we stay on it, we should find Adiah within the next day."

"Great."

They kept on, largely in silence, for the next few hours. For Ekon, it was the perfect time to think through his strategy. He could tell Koffi the truth about the hunting party if they found Adiah, *when* they found her, *after* they found her . . .

"Ekon?"

He jolted. Koffi was staring at him, appraising. "Sorry, what?"

Koffi's expression didn't change. "I was just asking if you wanted to stop for a minute to eat and maybe look at the map to check our progress? It's nearly midday."

"Oh." He'd been so lost in his own thoughts, he'd barely thought about food. "Yeah, that's fine by me."

They found a spot on the jungle floor and spread out their assortment of fruits from the yumboes. The trees in this area were thinner and richer in color, their roots carpeted with the delicate pink petals of flowers that looked to have finished their bloom a day or so before. Ekon's stomach growled audibly as he bit into one of his apples. He'd been hungrier than he thought.

"So . . . ," Ekon said between bites. "You've been quiet today."

Koffi took longer than strictly necessary to peel her orange. She chewed and swallowed slowly before answering. "So have you."

"Anything on your mind?"

At first, Koffi clamped her mouth firmly shut, as though she planned on saying nothing at all. Then words seemed to tumble from her unbidden.

"We came into this jungle looking for a monster," she said, poking holes into the dirt. "Now we're trying to find a one-hundred-year-old daraja so we can save her life and our home from the god of death." She looked up from the dirt. "That's . . . sort of weird, isn't it?"

Ekon laughed in spite of himself. "Yeah, it's a little weird."

Koffi's expression turned hesitant but intent. "Do you really think we can do this?"

Ekon swallowed. There was more than one question in that look, and he hoped he'd get the answer right. "Yeah, I do."

Her eyes brightened. "Thanks for saying it out loud. I guess I just needed to hear it."

There was a gentleness in her voice, a vulnerability Ekon had never heard before. Something about it made his chest tight. *She trusts you,* he realized. That understanding also made guilt coil in his stomach. She was being honest with him, but he was not being honest with *her.*

Tell her. Tell her the truth.

"I'm scared." Koffi spoke so softly Ekon barely heard her. "I haven't said it aloud, but . . . I'm scared."

Ekon was taken aback. "Really?"

"That surprises you?"

"Sure," he said with a shrug. "You're probably the most fearless person I know."

She smiled, but it didn't reach her eyes. "My mama says I lead with my heart, but . . . that I have to learn how to think with my head. I'm still working on it."

Ekon didn't miss a beat. "Why can't you do both?"

At this, Koffi's pretend smile fell. *"Both?"*

"Sure." He shrugged. "I mean, if leading with your heart and thinking with your head are both a part of who you are, why not use both?"

The question was simple, but Koffi stared at him as though he'd spoken a foreign language. He had trouble reading the expression on her face. Was it anger, confusion, or . . . something else? She opened her mouth to answer, and then her head snapped to the right.

"What?" Ekon straightened. "What's wrong?"

"*Shh.*" Koffi held a finger to her lips. "Do you hear that?"

Ekon's frown matched hers. Badwa had said Adiah was a day's walk north of her camp, but they'd only been walking for a few hours. His ears pricked as he looked around, nervous. Had some new unfriendly inhabitant of this jungle come to pay them a visit, or was it something worse, like the hunting party? The air around them was filled with its usual low buzz, but nothing seemed out of the ordinary at first. Then he heard what Koffi must have.

A sweet, metallic ringing.

"What is that?" Ekon asked in a whisper. Koffi didn't answer. Already, she was on her feet, fists clenched. Ekon rose more slowly and looked around again before zeroing in. The sound was coming from their right, and it wasn't far away. Instinctively, he reached for his hanjari.

"It's . . . strange," said Koffi. "It sounds like—"

"Bells." And as soon as Ekon said the word, he knew it was true. "Those are *bells.*"

"Why would there be *bells* in the middle of a jungle?" Koffi had already started toward the sound. Ekon followed.

"I don't know," he answered, staying on her heels. "But honestly . . . I'm not optimistic."

"Have you read about anything like that in the journal?"

Ekon paused. Some distant memory from the first night he'd

had the journal was curled up at the back of his mind, but he couldn't recall it. "No," he said. "Nothing I remember."

"Then we need to be cautious." She looked over her shoulder, visibly conflicted, before she spoke again. "And . . . *you* should probably be in front."

"Me?"

"You've got the weapon," said Koffi. "And I still don't know how reliable the splendor is when I channel it."

Ekon nodded. It felt strange to take the lead for the first time since they'd entered the jungle, but he did it nonetheless. With each step, the years of training took over. He changed his gait so that he walked on the balls of his feet, muscles tensed and dagger at the ready. The tinkling sound was getting louder, more prominent. *Definitely bells,* he concluded, *but for* what? A large oak tree stood up ahead. Whatever was making that sound seemed to be behind it. His gripped his dagger tighter, then signaled for Koffi to take the other side of the tree. As soon as Koffi moved forward, he rounded his side of the trunk, dagger raised—but someone screamed, stopping him short. It took him a moment to understand what he was seeing.

"What the—?"

A little girl was sitting near the tree's roots, knees hugged to her chest while she sniffled. Her tunic was overlarge, torn at the hem, and her eyes were bloodshot. Bramble and bits of leaf were tangled in her hair, and . . . two tiny silver bells looped on ribbon were tied around each ankle.

"Please," she said in a wispy voice, looking between them. Her hands flew to cover her face. "Please don't hurt me."

Ekon let the hand he was holding the dagger with fall to his side. Whatever he'd been expecting, it hadn't been this. For several seconds, he could do nothing but stare. Seeing a perfectly normal child here in the middle of the Greater Jungle was such an odd contrast that he wasn't even sure what to say. Koffi gave him an exasperated look before crouching down to meet the little girl's eyes.

"It's all right," she said gently. "We aren't going to hurt you."

The girl peeked between her fingers. "You're not?"

"No."

"Okay." The girl wrapped her arms around her knees, and her bells jingled again. "Then, who are you?"

"Our names are Koffi and Ekon." Koffi kept her voice at a murmur and spoke slowly. "What's your name?"

"Hila," the little girl answered. She was still looking between the two of them, wary. "Why are you here?" She directed the question at Ekon.

"Uh, well, we're—"

"Looking for *butterflies*." Koffi's eyes cut to Ekon in a very deliberate way. "Isn't that right, Ekon?"

"I—" Ekon clamped his mouth shut. "Yes," he muttered. "*Butterflies.*"

"Oh, I like butterflies! They're so pretty." Hila seemed to perk up at that. Her eyes widened a bit as she stared at Koffi. "*You're* very pretty."

"Oh." A smile touched Koffi's face. "Thank you."

Hila turned to Ekon. "Do *you* think Koffi is very pretty?"

Ekon made a sound like a cross between a cough and a hiccup. "I—"

"We have a camp nearby." Koffi was careful not to meet Ekon's eyes. "Are you hungry?"

"Mhm." Hila nodded enthusiastically while Ekon found his words again. Gently, Koffi lifted Hila to her feet and walked with her back to the spot where they'd left their bags. The bells rang merrily as she took the last few steps at a run and plopped down on the ground. She helped herself to one of the oranges in their food pile and nibbled at it. Koffi settled beside her; then Ekon followed suit.

"So, Hila," said Koffi. "Where are you from? And how did you end up here in the jungle by yourself?"

Hila popped another piece of orange into her mouth before answering. "I'm from one of the border villages," she murmured. "I don't come in the jungle often, but . . . well, I was trying to find kola nuts."

"*Kola* nuts?" Koffi repeated. "Those are common. You didn't have to go into the Greater Jungle to find them."

"Not the large ones," said Hila immediately, knowingly. "I've found some here that were bigger than my fist, and Baba can sell those for more at market." Her shoulders hunched. "It's just him and me. My mama died when I was small."

Ekon was caught off guard by the pang of pity he felt for the girl.

"Baba sent me into the jungle a few days ago," Hila went on. "But . . . something came after me."

Ekon straightened. "What was it?"

"Something scary," said Hila. "I don't know what it was, but it looked strange. It had a slithery body like a snake, and a head like an—"

"*Elephant.*" Ekon looked to Koffi. "That sounds like the grootslang we saw."

"Or one of its friends," said Koffi, pursing her lips.

"I ran away from it," Hila murmured. "But then I got lost. Baba tied these bells around my ankles so he could find me if that ever happened, but . . ." She looked down at them. "I don't think they work anymore."

Ekon swallowed. Try as he might, it was impossible not to draw the obvious comparison. *He'd* once been a child lost in this jungle; she was too. She was alone and scared; he knew what that had felt like. The little girl's eyes locked on his, and he came to a decision.

"We'll get you back to your family," he said. "Don't worry."

Koffi gave him a strange look before clearing her throat. "Actually, Hila," she said in a voice slightly too high, "Ekon and I are just going to step over here for a moment. Please enjoy your food. We'll be right back." She nodded curtly to a spot several feet away and gestured for Ekon to come with her. Once they were standing out of Hila's earshot with their backs turned, she scowled. "*What* are you doing?"

Ekon looked over his shoulder. "She needs our help, Koffi. We can't just leave her here alone."

"Are you forgetting about our *plan*?" Koffi's mouth formed a hard-set line. "We're supposed to be finding Adiah, not doing search-and-rescue missions. She's a distraction."

"She's a *child*," Ekon corrected. "What else would we do?"

Koffi crossed her arms. "If we showed her the map and the trails, maybe we could—"

"You're *very* pretty."

They both jumped. Hila had gotten up, as silent as a mouse, and was standing before them, a curious smile playing on her lips. She looked, if it was possible, even smaller and younger than she had before. She shifted her weight from foot to foot, and her ankle bells jingled merrily.

362

"Thank you." This time, Koffi's eyes were wary. "Look, Hila, we want to help you, but we need some more information about—"

"I like the way you wear your hair." Hila was still dancing in place when she pointed to Koffi. "My mama always tries to get hers to do that, but it never looks as good."

A quick throb shot through Ekon's temple, sharp but fleeting. He closed his eyes and rubbed his eyelids. When he opened them again, Koffi had stiffened. She was looking down at Hila, and her expression had changed entirely.

"You told us a second ago that your mother *died*," she said slowly. "You said it was just you and your baba."

"Oh." Hila stopped dancing. Her eyes went wide. "I'm sorry, I must have—"

"Forgotten your mother was alive?" Koffi frowned. "That's a very strange thing to forget."

"Koffi." Ekon looked from her to Hila, confused. "What's going on? You think she—?"

"I think something about you isn't right at all." Koffi wasn't looking at Ekon. Her eyes were on the little girl, expression hard. "And I think you should probably find your own way home."

"No!" Hila's voice rose an octave as she moved to stand by Ekon, ankle bells jingling with each step. She took his hand in her small one and squeezed. "No, no, no, please don't send me away! Don't leave me alone again, there are monsters!"

Instinctively, Ekon moved to stand between Koffi and Hila. The raw fear in the little girl's voice plucked at something deep within him. It made it all too easy to remember how he'd felt many years ago. "Koffi," he said. "There's no reason we can't help—"

"Ekon, *something isn't right about her*." Koffi actually took a step

363

forward. "She was alone in the middle of the jungle wearing those bells, her story doesn't match up—"

"She's our *friend*." The words didn't feel right, but his lips formed them anyway. "We have to help her."

"Yes, that's right," a nasty voice croaked. "You have to *help* me."

Ekon nearly jumped out of own skin. Hila's voice had changed, no longer wispy and sweet. When Ekon looked down, he saw it was no longer a child holding his hand. Something with wet black eyes was leering up at him, not human at all. Its body was wrinkled and swollen, filling out a tunic that had been too large before. The skin of the thing that had once been a little girl took on a horrid grayish pallor. Ekon tried to pull out of its grasp, but the creature smiled, exposing a set of pointed white teeth. Somewhere in the back of his mind, a single word finally unfurled from Ekon's memories of Nkrumah's journal.

Eloko.

"My new friend will help me," said the eloko in a low, gravelly voice. "He will use his nice dagger to cut off the pretty girl's face so that I can have it for myself, just like the *last* pretty little girl I found all alone in this jungle." The creature clicked its heels together, and the silver ankle bells rang out impossibly loud. Involuntarily, Ekon reached for the dagger at his hip.

"Ekon!"

From far away, Ekon heard the rising panic in Koffi's voice, saw the terror in her dark eyes. He knew, in a detached way, that her terror should have had some effect on him, but a numbness was creeping over him. The only thing he heard were those little silver bells, and the only thing he wanted was to obey, to help Hila. His grip on the dagger tightened, and he took a step forward.

"Ekon, stop!" Koffi was retreating, her entire body shaking. Her ankle caught on a vine and sent her crashing to the ground in a heap. The eloko cackled and hopped in place when Ekon took another step.

Help Hila, a voice in his head urged. *You have to help Hila.*

"Please." Koffi scrambled back in the dirt. Her eyes stayed fixed on Ekon's as she snatched up their bags and held them against her like a shield. "Ekon, it's me."

Now, *those* words didn't sound right. The longer he stared at the girl moving away from him, the less familiar she became. What was her name? All he could hear were the bells.

"Help me, Ekon." Hila's voice was soft and sweet again. "Help me, my *friend.*"

Ekon raised his dagger. The strange girl had nowhere left to go, so she would be easy to kill. She closed her eyes and buried her feet in the dirt. Ekon advanced until he was standing over her. The girl didn't look afraid anymore, but strangely at peace. He grabbed her wrist and pulled up so that her eyes were level with his, pressed the dagger's blade to her jaw, and . . .

And then he felt it. A hand.

The girl's hand was on his cheek, soft and barely there. At her touch, he felt a prickle. Then the sound of the jingling bells began to grow faint. The numbness that had overwhelmed his body started to recede like a tide, and he had the strange sensation of emerging from something, of his head clearing. A single word floated back into his mind, and he remembered.

Koffi.

She was still staring at him, eyes determined and focused, with her feet buried in the dirt. Tiny fragments of light seemed to be gathering all around her, dancing up her length and out of her hands.

"No!"

Ekon jumped. The eloko was standing a few feet away, its wicked smile falling away. He looked back at Koffi just in time. She raised her own hand and pointed at the creature. To Ekon's surprise, the sparkling fragments left her body and floated around her as though waiting. Then, without warning, the mass of them soared toward the eloko. The moment they touched the creature's skin, it shrieked.

"No! *No!*"

"Ekon!" Koffi was still staring at him. *"Run!"*

Ekon needed no further prompting. He snatched his own bag from Koffi's arm and took off, matching her stride for stride. There was a rustle behind them, a horrible keening, and then:

"Nooo! No, my friends, come baaack!"

Ekon glanced over his shoulder. The eloko was running too, batting away Koffi's fireflies as it pursued them. Its distended arms were outstretched, and there was a wild hunger in its gaze.

"Keep going!" Koffi flicked a wrist over her shoulder as though she was throwing something. Another wave of fireflies rushed from her palms, but not nearly as many as before. Panic flashed across her face. "I can't calm my mind," she said. "I won't be able to—"

"Friends!" the eloko screamed. "Don't run away, my friends!" It was impossibly close. Ekon's grip on his dagger tightened, and he braced himself.

Without warning, there was a flash, an aura of light far bigger and brighter than what Koffi had produced before. Like a golden beam, it shot overhead. The moment it touched the eloko, the creature's skin began to sizzle. A foul stench filled the air.

"Nooo!" The eloko cradled its burned arms to its chest, screaming in pain. It turned and ran, as fast as it could, in the opposite direction. Ekon watched its retreat, awed, before turning back to Koffi.

"That was *amazing*," he said. "How'd you do that?"

Koffi wasn't looking at him, and she wasn't smiling. Her eyes were set on something else when she spoke.

"I . . . didn't do that."

Ekon's blood ran cold. Slowly, he followed her gaze, new fear rising within him like a tide. When he saw what she had seen, he went still.

Something massive was staring back at them from the shadows of the trees up ahead.

Its eyes were cold and black.

CHAPTER 25

The OTHER DARAJA

Koffi didn't move. She didn't dare even blink.

The creature standing feet away, obscured in the shadows, was large; she could tell that instantly. She'd seen it once before, in the dark, but that made it no less terrifying in the late-afternoon sunlight. She saw the same raw pink skin, muscles stretched lean over a bony frame. Its face was wrinkled, a composition made of a long snout, two black eyes, and a sliced mouth full of teeth. Its tongue lolled as it stared at her, the color of blood.

"Koffi."

Behind her, Ekon's voice barely carried above a whisper. She heard him move so that he was standing beside her, his dagger still in hand and ready. "Stand back."

Standing back *was* the smarter thing to do. After all, she had no weapon, no way to defend herself. But an indeterminable pull anchored her where she stood. They'd been standing there for a full minute, and the Shetani had not yet moved. Back at the Night Zoo, she'd seen a monster, a beast filled with rage, but she saw something very different now. Not a monster, not even a beast, but a living creature. Her eyes met its own, and where she'd thought she'd seen bloodlust, she saw something else—a dull kind of pain, old and ever-constant. She saw other things: grief, helplessness. And then she knew what needed to be done.

"Ekon, I think . . . you should go."

"What?" She didn't turn to see his expression, but she heard his disbelief. "You're not serious."

"I am."

"Where exactly do you want me to go?"

"Not far." Koffi was still watching the Shetani. It had cocked its head slightly. "Just . . . I think it's important that I do this part on my own."

She felt him shift beside her, could practically hear his hesitation.

"Koffi." Ekon lowered his voice to a whisper. "I don't want to leave you alone with . . . her."

"Please," she said. "Trust me."

There was a long pause, a sigh, and then something that sounded a lot like *Be careful* before she heard the sound of fading footsteps and knew she and the Shetani were alone. The entire time, it hadn't taken its eyes off hers. Koffi almost thought it looked distinctly curious.

"I know what you are." Koffi stepped into a ray of sunlight dappling through the jungle's canopy. The moment it touched her, she felt slightly stronger. "And I know *who* you are."

In answer, the Shetani snarled. Anxiety and fear rolled over Koffi's body in waves, but she held her ground.

"You don't know me." She kept her voice low. "But we've met before. Do you remember?"

The Shetani snarled again, but not as loudly. It hunched low, claws retracting from the dirt. Koffi tried not to tremble as she took yet another step forward.

"I'm like you," she said. "Probably in more ways than you'd believe. I . . . I know what it's like to be misunderstood, to want to run away from the things that scare you. Sometimes it's easier to run away, isn't it?"

The Shetani stared but didn't make a sound. It wasn't encouraging, but it wasn't discouraging either. Koffi took a step closer.

"I know you're in terrible pain," she whispered. "And I know why. But I think there might be a way for me to help you, if you'll let me. *Will* you let me?"

The Shetani stepped forward. They were less than two feet apart now, little more than an arm's length. In the space between them, Koffi smelled earthen things—moss, tree bark, flowers blooming. She inhaled that scent. The Shetani's pink nostrils flared.

"I'm going to try something," she said. "I've never done it before, but . . . it might work."

She closed the space between them in a single stride, her palm hovering inches from the Shetani's nose. Badwa had told her during their lessons that splendor was an energy that could be moved, given and taken. If the splendor inside Adiah was what had altered her appearance, then perhaps . . .

She touched the Shetani's snout, her palm cupping its nose. She closed her eyes and tried to remember Badwa's words.

Calm your mind.

She thought of Mama twisting her hair, of the sound of Jabir's laugh. She thought of Ekon and the way he smiled at her. This time, when she reached for the splendor, she didn't pull from the

370

ground beneath her; she pulled from the Shetani's own being. She felt it instantly in the place her skin made contact with it, buzzing and humming through her hand. The Shetani's eyes widened with shock, then understanding, and it pressed its head harder into her hand. A jolt of pain ricocheted through Koffi's body as a part of the splendor moved from host to another, sweat slicked her neck as it moved, but she remained still. This was the most splendor she'd ever allowed in her body, but she could tell there was more, *so* much more. She closed her eyes and tried to visualize it, a cup filling to the brim. A cup that wasn't allowed to spill so much as a drop. She couldn't take it all, but she could take this much, she could hold on to it for a little while, offer some reprieve. A breeze tickled her cheek, a sound that reminded her of a sigh. The air shifted, and when she opened her eyes, there was no Shetani before her.

There was a young woman, holding her hand.

Her hair was thick, curly, the color of a blackbird's wings. She was tall—even taller than Koffi—and had a deep umber face made up of soft, rounded features: apple cheeks, a mouth curved like a warrior's bow. She was stunning. Nothing about her face gave away her age except her eyes, which belonged to another time.

"How?" Adiah touched her throat with her free hand, apparently surprised by the sound of her own voice. It was low and raspy, as though it hadn't been used in years, and there was still a touch of a growl in it. "How . . . did you *do* that?"

Koffi nodded at their hands, still tightly interlaced. "I took part of the splendor from you." As though it had heard its own name, she felt that extra power twinge within her and winced. "It's only temporary."

The young woman was still staring, her expression inscrutable. "How did you learn to do it?"

"Badwa taught me."

The emotion on the young woman's face was clear, along with visible understanding. "You're the other daraja. I felt your power, your call, and I . . . I came to you."

Koffi nodded. "And you're Adiah."

Tears filled Adiah's eyes. "I haven't used that name in many years," she whispered. "I didn't know there were any of us left before I saw you. I thought . . . I thought I was the last."

"There might be more of us out there," said Koffi. "But none that live in the open, at least not in Lkossa. Things have changed since . . ." She faltered. "Since you left."

Adiah grimaced, visible pain pulling at the corners of her mouth. "I didn't know." Her words were quiet, pleading. "I didn't know what he was going to do, I swear it. He told me I could use the splendor to make Lkossa a better place, and I believed him. I was so young, so *foolish*. Had I been smarter—"

"It *wasn't* your fault," said Koffi. "You were a child."

Adiah scoffed. "I certainly didn't think of myself as one." She said the words bitterly, full of derision. "I was arrogant. I thought I was so much better than everyone else around me. Had I just listened to my teachers, to my friends . . ." A single tear slid down her cheek. "If I had listened to *Tao*, none of this would have ever happened."

"Fedu is a *god*," said Koffi firmly. "Which means he's had a long time to learn how to deceive people. You were just a girl—"

"Who did something terrible." Adiah shook her head. "The power I unleashed destroyed Lkossa, destroyed my home. It caused wars, ruptured the sky—"

372

"You can't change what's already happened," said Koffi quietly. "You can only change what *will* happen."

"And it still lives within me." Adiah continued like she hadn't heard Koffi. "I feel it all the time. You must feel it too if you are holding it within you now. It's a dangerous thing, and always will be."

In truth, Koffi *did* feel it. The splendor she had taken from Adiah was no longer a mere tingle beneath her skin; it was growing hotter, painful. As though she read Koffi's mind, Adiah started to pull away, but Koffi tightened her grip.

"There's a way you can get rid of it," she said. "A way you can return it to the earth, where it belongs."

Adiah shook her head. "That is not possible."

"It *is*." Koffi squeezed her hand for emphasis. "During the Bonding, the splendor in the earth rises to the surface, the same way it did a hundred years ago, when you took it. The next one is in two months, and you could put it back then."

"It's too dangerous," said Adiah. "To remove that kind of power—"

"You won't release it here," said Koffi quickly. "Ekon and I have come up with a plan. We're going to get you to the Kusonga Plains, where no one is around. You'll be able to release it there, safely." She watched Adiah process the words, weighing and considering them in her mind. When she spoke, she sounded every bit her age.

"The minute I step out of the jungle again, Fedu will catch me," she said. "He searches for me all the time, night and day."

"We'll hide you, and travel carefully."

"The Kusonga Plains are a considerable distance from here," she said. "I don't know if I could make it that far."

"You have to *try*," Koffi pressed. "Once the splendor leaves your body, you can come back home with us. You can tell everyone the truth, they won't fear you any—" She winced as fresh, new pain lanced through her, and Adiah's eyes grew wide.

"Return the splendor to me, child." Her voice was urgent. "Do it *now*."

"Not until you agree—" Something twisted in Koffi's stomach, another sharp pain. "Not until you agree to come with us."

"Very well," Adiah snapped. "I will go with you to the Kusonga Plains." She grabbed Koffi's forearm and pulled her close. "But know this, child. If your plan is unsuccessful, I cannot endure this pain for another century."

"You won't have to—"

"Hear me." Adiah's eyes were fierce. Koffi felt a tug, felt her taking back the splendor with a viselike grip. She watched the young woman's eyes grow colder as the power returned to its host. Her voice sounded more beast than woman when she spoke again. "I am not strong enough to fight Fedu if he captures me, do you understand?"

"I understand."

Those were the last words Koffi managed before Adiah pulled her hand away; this time, she let her. The moment they separated, Koffi felt a terrible vacuum, a void. Her vision grew spotty, her mouth went dry, but there was no stopping it. Her legs trembled violently, then gave out beneath her. She felt herself falling.

The last thing she heard was a roar.

"Koffi!"

Koffi opened her eyes. Her vision wasn't spotty anymore, and all around her she saw green. Green, and brown, and *Ekon*. He was staring down at her, worry etched into every muscle in his face.

"Are you okay?" His voice was tight. "Are you hurt?"

"No." Koffi sat up and looked around a moment. The Shetani—Adiah—was standing a few feet away from them, watching. She stared a second longer before bowing her head in an unmistakable nod; an agreement, a consent.

"I don't understand." Ekon was looking between her and Adiah, his voice full of confusion. "What's going on?"

Koffi smiled. "We're going to the Kusonga Plains."

CHAPTER 26

A STRONG LIKE

The air grew cooler as Koffi, Ekon, and Adiah made their way south.

With each step, Ekon sensed the world changing around him. The sky was still blue, but it was darkening; the air clear, but tinged just slightly with the scent of ozone. He recognized the signs of the Zamani Region's monsoon season fast approaching. In a matter of weeks—maybe less—most of the populace would be up to its ankles in puddles. Local merchants would change out their wares, offering inflated prices for more seasonally appropriate clothes that fared better in the constant torrents of rain; farmers would take short workdays and say more prayers for the welfare of their crops. As a boy, Ekon had liked this part of the year, when the world's problems seemed to wash away in a deluge so that things could start anew a few months later. This year would be different, though.

"Okay, so here's what I'm thinking..." He and Koffi had stopped again to consult with the map. It had been a few hours since Koffi had convinced Adiah to join them, and now they were less than a day away from the borderlands where they'd started. Carefully, he spread out the map between them in the dirt, tracing two connecting lines with his fingers.

"We're here," he said, pointing to their location. "As you can see, there are plenty of places for us to leave the Greater Jungle undetected; the border is massive, and there's no way the Sons of the Six can cover that much ground. It'll really just be about timing."

"When did you have in mind?" Koffi asked.

"First thing tomorrow morning," said Ekon. "Patrols are always heaviest at night, since that's when they think the Shetani is most likely to attack. In the morning, the night shift trades with the morning shift. It's a pretty well-executed hand-off, but if we go far enough south . . ."

"We could avoid them?"

"Right," said Ekon. "The other challenge we'll have is how to actually hide Adiah once we're out in the open. It's obviously easier here, but . . . the stretch between the Zamani Region and the Kusonga Plains is fairly flat, open land. We'll be at our most exposed there."

"We can hide in the lemongrass," said Koffi. "And move at night. Incoming traffic to Lkossa always lulls at the start of monsoon season—Baaz complains about it every year at the Night Zoo. As long as we keep a good pace, we could get to the Kusonga Plains in a few weeks on foot. Then all we have to do is lie low and wait for the day of the Bonding."

"Sounds like a plan." Ekon rolled up the map. "We leave tomorrow."

Their pace slowed as late afternoon turned to dusk; already, Ekon could tell it would be a cooler evening. Adiah trekked a few steps ahead of them, but Koffi walked in step with him. Abruptly, she cast an eye at the setting sun.

"We should stop here."

"What?" Ekon glanced at the sun too, wondering if he'd missed something. It was a deep golden-orange and would be setting soon but not yet. "We should keep going while we have light. The closer we get to Lkossa tonight, the less time we'll have to make up in the morning—"

"There's a pond." Koffi nodded a few yards to the right, to a small body of water glinting between the trees. Ekon looked from it to her, still confused.

"So?"

"So, we're about to completely change terrain," said Koffi. "For the next few weeks, we're going to be in open grassland with no guaranteed access to any substantial amount of water."

"So . . . ?"

"So, I'm taking a bath."

Ekon froze. It took him a moment to find his words. "You're taking . . . a what?"

"A *bath*," Koffi repeated slowly. "You know, the thing you do when you're dirty and would like to be clean? I won't be long, ten minutes at . . ."

Ekon didn't hear the rest of her words; he was trying to focus his mind. Bath. Koffi was going to be taking a *bath*. *Near him.* Without clothes. Thus far, they'd been good about giving each other privacy when they needed it, but *this* . . .

"Is there a problem?" Koffi's voice flooded back to him, all too sweet.

"Uh, *no.*" *Think of something else,* he pleaded with himself. *Think of something that's . . . not that. Think of the temple, the brothers of the temple. Gross Brother Apunda . . . anything . . .*

"Good." He jumped when Koffi patted him on the shoulder. He didn't like the glint in her eyes one bit. "You can get started on dinner, then. It'll just be us eating, I think. Adiah, are you okay to fend for yourself?"

In response, Adiah, who'd stopped a few feet ahead of them, blinked. Then she bowed her head in what looked like a nod, and stalked into the darkness. In different circumstances, Ekon would have been unnerved by how quietly she moved.

"What's *she* having for dinner?"

"It's probably best we don't know." Koffi grimaced.

"You know," said Ekon after a pause, "I almost feel bad for her."

Koffi looked his way again, visibly surprised. "Why? She isn't going to be like that much longer. Once we get her to the Kusonga Plains, she'll be human again, free from the splendor and the pain it causes her. She'll go back to the way she was."

"But her world won't," said Ekon. Koffi opened her mouth, but he went on. "She's more than a century old, nothing of the Lkossa she knew from before the Rupture would be there anymore, and none of the people she used to know would still be alive. Her friends, her family . . ."

"They'd be dead," said Koffi, her voice hollow.

"I don't know what that would feel like," said Ekon. "Returning to a home and a life you know is yours, but you don't recognize."

Koffi's expression was inscrutable a moment before she shrugged. The gesture was casual, but something about it felt slightly forced. "We can worry about helping Adiah acclimate after we've gotten her back to normal again." She nodded affirmatively before looking toward the pond again. "In the meantime, worry about our meal, I'll be back."

"Don't forget to check the water for snakes!" said Ekon to her retreating back. "And nkalas!"

Koffi didn't turn around, but he thought he heard her laugh. *Fine.* If she wanted to have her shadow eaten by a giant mythical crab-monster, that was *her* business, though in fairness his readings suggested those usually lived in larger bodies of water.

He turned to the matter at hand—dinner. The ingredients he had to work with were about as scant as his skill. Growing up in the Temple of Lkossa for the last ten years, the food hadn't been special, but it'd been all right, prepared by a cook. He stared for a moment at the piles of fruit, bread, and dried meats the yumboes had packed for him. And then the idea came to him.

"Okay, I'm done." Koffi announced.

By the time Ekon was putting the finishing touches on the meal and a small fire, Koffi had returned. Her clothes were slightly wet, but her face was scrubbed clean of the mud that had caked it before. Ekon glanced over his shoulder.

"Your hair looks different," he noted, careful not to look at her too long. He still didn't trust his mind. "Did you wash it?"

Koffi arched an eyebrow. "*That's* funny." She settled beside him on the ground, and a sweet smell filled the space between them.

"Did you find more ponya seed?"

"Nope." She unfolded her dirty tunic to reveal several light brown nuts tucked within its layers. They looked *similar* to ponya seeds, but bigger. She picked one up and held it to his nose. "These are shea nuts. You use them to make shea butter for your hair and skin."

"Shea . . ." Ekon leaned in instinctively. Without warning, something constricted in his chest. It took him a moment to figure out why.

"That . . . smells like my mom."

"Oh."

All this time, he'd known the scent, but he hadn't known where it came from. His eyes stung. His mother was gone, but this . . . this was like finding a whole new part of her, a part of her he'd thought was lost forever.

"You've never talked about your mother before," Koffi said quietly.

"Yeah . . ." Ekon scratched the back of his neck. "Well, that's because she left our family when I was little. I don't know where she went, haven't seen her in years."

"Oh." Koffi dropped her gaze, studying her fingernails. "I'm really sorry to hear that."

A long silence followed, too loud to be comfortable. Ekon was familiar with it. He didn't talk about his mother often, but when he did, the same things happened. Silence, and then the pity. Silence, and then the apologies, the platitudes. *Everything happens for a reason. Sorry for your loss,* as though her leaving their family was his fault, the consequence of *his* irresponsibility. He changed the subject.

"She used to make this dish," he said. "I think it was made up, but we had it for breakfast a lot. It was this fruit salad thing. This is my version of it."

Koffi looked at the pile of cut-up fruit, carefully arranged in a small ring. "You minced?"

"Twenty-seven delectable pieces."

"I'm impressed."

Ekon laid out two giant leaves with a flourish. "A feast fit for gods."

Koffi grabbed one of the makeshift leaf-plates and sectioned off part of the fruit pile for herself. Ekon didn't want to watch her eat necessarily—that would be strange—but he did want to know whether she liked the food. It was a silly thing, to care about what someone thought of a bunch of roughly chopped fruit, but for some reason, he did. He hoped Koffi liked it. He made himself look down at his own leaf-plate and count to eighteen before looking up again.

"So, how was it?"

Something in his chest plummeted when Koffi answered with a weak smile.

"That bad?"

"No!" She shook her head. "It's not that, it's just . . ." She looked down at several slices of fruit. "There are papayas in this."

"Yeah?"

"I sort of hate papayas."

Ekon blinked. "You . . . *hate* them?"

"Rather passionately."

"Of course." A real laugh rose from Ekon's stomach. He massaged the bridge of his nose, trying to keep it in. "Let me guess, you like some weird, suspicious fruit like . . . honeydew?"

Koffi frowned. "Honeydew *isn't* suspicious."

"I knew it."

She gave him a withering look before selectively pinching a

piece of banana from the fruit pile and popping it into her mouth. "I have a question for you."

Ekon tensed. "What sort of question?"

She set her leaf-plate down for a moment and grinned. "It's about Nkrumah's journal. You said he captured notes about all the creatures and plants that live in this jungle." She looked up. "But what does he say about stars?"

"Stars?" Ekon followed her finger. The sky above them was dappled with more stars than he could count, a thousand diamonds dropped into an inkpot. They were beautiful.

"Actually, there's not much about stars in the journal," he finally said. "Maybe because stars don't just belong to the Greater Jungle or the Zamani Region. We see them the same no matter where we are on this continent."

"That makes sense." Koffi was still staring up at them, but there was a touch of disappointment in her voice.

"But." Ekon scrambled, trying to think of something else to say. "I *do* know some stories about them, ones my brother taught me." He pointed. "See those two really bright ones, to your right?"

"No."

"They're just over—" He nearly jumped from his skin when Koffi scooted over to sit beside him, so close their shoulders brushed.

"Go on."

"Um, right, so the stars." Ekon's tongue felt clumsy in his mouth. "Those two are called Adongo and Wasswa; they're named after two brother giraffes," he explained. "The story goes that each brother wanted to be taller than the other, so they just kept stretching their necks to make them longer and longer until both their horns got tangled in the night sky and they turned into stars. Now they argue about which one of them shines brighter."

Koffi nodded. "Interesting."

"Sorry," said Ekon. "That . . . wasn't a good story."

"Yes it was." Koffi turned to him, and Ekon swallowed hard. He'd thought they were close before, but their faces were inches apart now. He could count the eyelashes framing her eyes.

"There's just one thing." As abruptly as she'd faced him, she looked at the sky again with a frown. "How did the giraffes actually *become* stars?"

Ekon started. "What do you mean?"

"Well, you said their horns got *stuck in the sky*, and they just turned into stars—but how?"

"I'm not sure." Ekon scratched his head. "But I don't think that's actually the point of the story. I think it's really just meant to be a lesson about jealousy—"

She turned to face him again, eyebrows knitted. "How can it be a lesson if it doesn't make sense?"

In answer, Ekon shook his head and chuckled. "You really do argue about everything."

Her frown deepened. "I do *not*."

"You *do*."

"I do n—"

He wasn't sure what made him do it, what made him obey the strange sudden impulse, but he closed the gap between them and kissed her.

He hadn't planned it, and he certainly hadn't prepared for it, but his lips found hers, and she didn't pull away. They were soft to the touch, warm. Her hand, feather-light, grazed his neck, and a pleasant shiver ran down his body. All at once he couldn't breathe, and he wasn't sure he wanted to. They came apart, chests heaving.

"Sorry." Ekon didn't recognize his own voice; it was lower, raspier. He couldn't stop looking at her mouth. "I meant to ask before I . . ."

Koffi pulled his mouth back down to hers, and something erupted in Ekon's brain. A roaring filled his ears, and every one of his senses went haywire. Suddenly Koffi was all he could see, smell, taste, and feel. It was consuming. After a moment, he pulled back again.

"Wait, is this okay with—?"

"You—are—*hopeless*." Koffi's voice was low too, barely a murmur. "Why do you think I moved to sit next to you?"

Ekon pulled back farther. "You—you *wanted* me to do that?"

"Of course I did." She dropped her gaze. "I like you."

And those simple words were enough—Ekon didn't need any more. The world around him tilted as they both sank to the ground, adjusted so that they were lying there side by side. He let his fingers trace along her outline, falling and rising again as they moved down her hips. A new heat pooled somewhere, low in his stomach. They pulled closer still, and suddenly he was keenly aware of all the places their bodies were touching, the places he *wished* were touching. All of these feelings, all of this want, was strange, like a thousand hummingbirds trapped between his ribs, but he liked it. He heard her words again in his head.

I like you.

He liked her too, a lot, and suddenly that seemed like the most obvious thing in the world. He liked the twists in Koffi's hair, the midnight color of her eyes. He liked the sound of her laugh, and the way she always argued with him. He liked everything about her. It wasn't love—he wasn't even sure he knew how to do that properly yet—but it was something *good*, something he wanted more of, *a strong like*.

Ekon kissed her again, and she made a small sound against his mouth. His eyes closed, and a thousand new questions came to mind. Was he supposed to do something else? Was *she*? What happened next? He opened his eyes slightly, curious to find out, and then he went rigid.

Koffi's eyes were still closed, a small smile on her lips, but his had caught something over her shoulder a few feet away from them—*movement*. It had been quick, almost imperceptible. He sat up abruptly.

"What's wrong?" Koffi sat up too, alarmed.

"Um, nothing." Ekon tried to keep the fear from his voice. "It's just . . ." He tried to find words. "I think we should . . ."

"Right." There was no mistaking the hurt in Koffi's voice. "Yeah, we . . . should probably stop that there."

No. It was the absolute last thing Ekon wanted, but at the same time his heart was beginning to pound in a new, unpleasant way. Again he glanced toward the trees, where he'd seen that brief flash of something. He didn't want to tell Koffi that he was almost certain someone else was there, watching them—especially when that someone was wearing a very specific shade of blue. He hoped he sounded calmer than he felt.

"It's just, we've got an early morning tomorrow," he said. "We could probably use the sleep."

Koffi didn't look at him. "Of course. Good night, then." She didn't say another word as she stood and brushed herself off before notably moving to the other side of the fire. She lay on her side, back turned away from him, and did not move again. Ekon waited until she was still before rising, quietly moving toward the two trees where he'd seen the movement. He'd only just stepped between them when a hand closed over his mouth.

"Don't. Move."

Both relief and anger doused the fear in Ekon's chest. He knew that voice. The hand clapped over his mouth withdrew. In the darkness, his older brother winked.

"Kam." Ekon tried to keep his voice low.

"In the flesh."

"How did you—?"

"Shh." Ekon ducked out of his brother's reach as they both watched a large silhouette emerge from the darkness directly across the campsite from them. Adiah. The great beast sniffed at the air a moment before circling a spot in the dirt and settling there. In seconds, she was curled into a ball, asleep.

"Incredible," Kamau said. His eyes were locked on Adiah as though she were a mountain of gold. "After all this time, I never thought I'd see it myself."

Ekon scowled. "Why didn't you announce yourself?"

"Didn't want to interrupt you." Kamau looked at him, waggling his brows suggestively. "You looked like you were having quite a good time with your friend." He turned back to Adiah. "That was clever of you, using the smell of your own food to lure that thing to your camp."

Ekon's head was beginning to hurt. This was too much; there

were too many emotions warring within him at once. He was angry and embarrassed, but above all things, he was uneasy.

"How did you find me?"

Kamau rolled his eyes. "You didn't exactly make it hard." Behind his charming façade, Ekon saw a trace of real concern. "I told you to cover your tracks, Ekon, gods. You couldn't have left a clearer trail for someone to follow."

Ekon tempered a wave of humiliation. He'd assured his brother that he knew what he doing, that he would conduct a competent hunt. Now he'd made a fool of himself. For the first time in days, his fingers itched to start up their old tapping. Deliberately, he changed the subject. "How long has the hunting party been here?" he asked.

"A few days," said Kamau.

"And you've . . . faired okay?"

In answer, a shadow passed over Kamau's expression, visible even in the faint light. "Not exactly," he said with foreboding. "We got caught up in a fog."

"Near the border." Ekon nodded. "We ended up in the same one."

"It took us a full day to get through it," Kamau went on. "By the time we did, two warriors were gone—Zahur and Daudi, I don't know if you'd remember them."

Ekon felt as though a stone had dropped in his stomach. He didn't tell Kamau that he remembered both of them, that he'd spoken to each of them just before he and Koffi had entered the jungle. It occurred to him now how lucky he and Koffi had been. When he looked up, his brother was still watching him in earnest. Apprehension filled him along with a strange kind of pity. He didn't know how he was going to explain everything he'd learned in the last few days in a matter of minutes, but in that moment he decided. He had to try.

"Kamau," he started. "I need to tell you something. A lot of it's going to sound unbelievable at first, but the Shetani is a—"

"That girl, by the fire. The one you were just kissing." Kamau's eyes flitted to Koffi, discerning. "Who is she?"

This time, Ekon winced. "Her name's Koffi," he said. "I met her in Lkossa, and—"

"Looks a little rough around the edges," said Kamau, craning his neck. He looked back just in time to see Ekon's deepening frown and raised his hands defensively. "Hey, no judgment. I just didn't think common Yaba girls were your type—"

"She's not *common*, whatever *that* means," said Ekon through his teeth. "And she's not Yaba. She's Gede."

Kamau's expression changed instantly. "What?"

"You heard me." He'd never spoken to his older brother this way. Kamau had always been bigger, so Ekon had never wanted to pick a fight with him. But the idea of him—or anyone—speaking ill of Koffi while she lay asleep just a few feet away was something he couldn't abide. He watched confusion spread across Kamau's face, then faint disgust.

"Ekkie, if you want something easy, there are other ways to get—"

Ekon's hand went to the hilt of his hanjari, a subtle movement that Kamau didn't miss. His brother shook his head.

"All that time teaching you about weapons, when I really should have been teaching you about *women*." He patted Ekon's cheek indulgently. "But don't worry. We can talk properly after we deliver that abomination to Father Olufemi."

"What?" Every muscle in Ekon's body grew taut. "What are you talking about?"

Like that, Kamau's smirk returned. "Come on, Ekon, I know you wanted to hunt it down yourself, but trust me, the fact that you went into the Greater Jungle and found the Shetani will be more than enough to qualify you for Yaba warriorship. Once we get it delivered to Father Olufemi, you'll be initiated in no time, maybe even made a kapteni."

Ekon spoke again before he could lose his nerve. "Kam, I *really* need you to listen to me. The Shetani isn't the monster we've thought it was, it's a human girl named—"

"Ekon." Kamau frowned. "You can't honestly be that foolish."

"I'm *not* foolish."

"No?" Kamau raised an eyebrow. There was a hard edge in his gaze as his eyes flitted from Ekon back to the campsite's fire. "Who told you the Shetani was a human, huh? The Gede girl? Let me guess, she told you that the monster was good and deserves to be free?"

"Kamau." A nerve in Ekon's temple was beginning to throb. "You haven't seen what I've seen in this jungle. And you don't know Koffi—"

"She's the same girl from the Night Zoo, isn't she?" A dangerous glint flashed in Kamau's eyes. "The one you let go?"

Ekon started. Why would Kamau bring up what had happened at the Night Zoo *now*? "Yes," he said quietly. "That's her."

Kamau leveled his gaze. "Strange, isn't it?" he asked. "How a girl who worked at the Night Zoo as a beastkeeper suddenly has an interest in helping you find the most dangerous beast in the entire region?"

The words stung more than Ekon cared to admit. "We had a deal," he said. "She agreed to help me track the Shetani down, and in exchange I agreed to—"

"To *pay* her?" Kamau's voice was full of derision. "You honestly think that would be enough to keep her loyalty if someone else offered so much as a shaba more?"

Ekon shook his head. "Koffi wouldn't do that. I mean, it started out like that, but she—"

"You don't know what she would or wouldn't do," said Kamau. "You don't know her. You've been in this jungle for a little over a week by my count, and that was all it took for you to believe her over your own people, over me?"

There was real hurt in his voice, a hurt Ekon had never heard before. "Kamau." When he spoke, his voice was barely a whisper. "I'm sorry, I didn't—"

"I don't need your apology." Kamau's voice was dangerously low. "But what I want is your word."

"My word?"

"The rest of the Kuhani's hunting party is on the way, they'll be here by morning. I want your word that you'll help us take it down tomorrow."

Betray Koffi. That was what his brother was really asking him to do. *Betray Adiah. Betray all your plans.*

"Kamau." He shook his head. "What you're asking, it's not that simple. I don't know if I can do that. I—"

"No, it's very simple, Ekon." His brother's eyes were hard. "Tomorrow, you choose. Stand with your people, or stand against us."

CHAPTER 27

FROM THE START

When Koffi woke, she was warm.

It had nothing to do with the splendor, though she did feel splendid, at least at first. The feeling started in her cheeks and prickled down her neck as she lay on the jungle floor, pretending to be asleep just a few minutes longer.

He kissed you.

She gnawed at her bottom lip as the words crossed her mind for the hundredth time, the thousandth. Ekon had kissed her, and she'd kissed him—several times. The memory of it had crept into her dreams like a vine, curling around her in vivid, oversaturated colors. She'd certainly liked some boys at the Night Zoo, but she'd never had one like her back. All of the tiny moments repeated themselves in her imagination. She thought of the way Ekon's lips had found hers, the suddenness of the gesture. He'd apologized for not asking—because of course he had—but then, when she'd told him it was okay, he'd kissed her again . . . and again . . . and *again*, and she'd wanted him to. She thought of his hands, the way they'd moved across her skin, that sound he'd made when they'd moved closer . . . she'd liked kissing Ekon, but the truth was there had been other moments too, before that kiss. She liked the way he sometimes saw the world in numbers, she liked the way he walked. And she liked the things he said.

Why not both?

Ekon was the first person in her life to suggest that she didn't have to choose between her heart and her mind; he was the first person to like both parts of her.

"Hey, are you awake?"

She shot up, ripped away from her reverie, and turned. Ekon was already on his feet, expression inscrutable. Their campsite was already packed up, including her things. A few feet away, Adiah was up too, stretching.

"Are we going now?" She looked around. The sky was still a deep blue, but the sun hadn't quite risen over the trees' peaks. It was the earliest they'd ever gotten up.

"The Sons of the Six will be doing their handoff soon," said Ekon. He wasn't looking at her. Instead his gaze was focused somewhere over her head. "We need to get going if we want to get to the border just after it."

"Oh." The handoff. In the wonder of last night, she'd nearly forgotten about everything—their plan, what they still had left to do. Life hadn't stopped.

"I just need to wash my face," she said. "Then I'll be ready."

She didn't give Ekon the chance to say anything else before jumping to her feet and heading to the pond she'd gone to before. It wasn't large, just a small interruption of water among the trees. Dawn's pale light now reflected on its smooth surface like glass, so perfectly still she almost felt bad for touching it. She cupped her hands around the water, relishing the cool on her face as she splashed herself with it.

You're imagining it, she told herself as the water dripped down her face. *I'm sure it's fine.*

She repeated the words to herself, but deep down, she knew. Something about Ekon had changed. She'd felt it the moment it had happened, the moment he'd stopped kissing her and grown stiff. Had he had second thoughts? Decided he didn't like her the way she liked him?

She heard a sound behind her, a quiet rustle, and turned. Adiah crept into view, a few yards behind her. She was a beast again, no longer the beautiful young woman she'd spoken to a day prior, but her dark eyes were uncannily expressive. She moved to stand next to Koffi at the pond's edge, nudging her shoulder. Koffi touched a hand to her nose.

"Thank you."

It was too dangerous to do what she'd done before, to take part of the splendor in Adiah's body away again so that she could be human; Koffi suddenly wished she could. Arguably, Adiah could understand her more than anyone else in the world. She wondered if—all those years ago—the other daraja had ever felt the way she did.

"Koffi." Behind her, Ekon's voice interrupted the silence. Koffi and Adiah both turned, nonplussed. Adiah then began to drink from the pond. For her part, Koffi stood and faced him.

"Yes?"

Ekon's hands were shoved into the pockets of his tunic. He looked visibly uncomfortable. "Before we head out, I think . . . we should talk—about last night."

It took every fiber of Koffi's being to keep her face impassive, to keep still. She didn't know whether to feel tentative or excited. Ekon wanted to talk about things. Maybe that meant things hadn't gone as badly as she'd thought. Surely, it wouldn't make sense to talk about something if it wasn't good? What if he was sorry about the way things had ended? What if he hadn't wanted them to end at all? She gave Adiah a pointed look and was grateful when the daraja subtly moved down the pond's edge to give them a bit of space. Then she nodded at Ekon.

"Okay, go ahead."

It seemed to take years for Ekon to speak. "Last night was . . . unexpected."

Unexpected. Koffi let the word marinate in her head. *Unexpected* wasn't an inherently *bad* way to describe kissing, but it didn't sound promising either.

"In fact," Ekon continued, "everything about this venture has been unexpected, from the moment we stepped into this jungle. I've tried to keep a strategy in mind, because that's the way I was taught to take on problems, but . . . but I've made a mistake. One I hope that, one day, you can forgive me for."

A *mistake*. That was the only word Koffi heard. *Mistake. Mistake.* Last night had been a mistake. Suddenly, the air was unbearably hot, and all she wanted to do was throw herself in the pond so she couldn't hear the rest of this.

"I feel . . . torn." Ekon was staring at his feet. "I thought I knew what I wanted, but lately things have gotten, um, complicated."

Complicated.

Like that, the hopeful flicker in Koffi's chest died.

"If you wish you hadn't kissed me, you can just say it." The words came out harsh, but she didn't take them back. "No need to beat around the bush."

"What?" Ekon looked up, eyes wide. "No, I—"

"It shouldn't have happened." Koffi forced the words, trying to ignore the growing sting behind her eyes. "And it won't happen again."

"Koffi." Ekon had gone stock-still. "Stop."

"No!" She blinked hard, tried to temper the growing heat in her stomach. Somewhere in the back of her mind, she heard Badwa's words about emotion, but they were drowned out by other words. Ekon's words.

Mistake. Complicated. Mistake. Complicated. Mistake.

You were a mistake, a new sinister voice hissed in her ear. *Of course he doesn't like you. Just look at you. You're a mess, you're complicated. You're too much.*

"Koffi!" Ekon took a step forward, but it was too late. A low growl had rumbled, and they both looked right to see that Adiah had risen to her feet. Her hackles were on end and her lips were pulled back in a snarl. Koffi went rigid.

"What's—?"

There was no warning as the spear cut through the air. It whistled over the pond, gliding like a hawk before its blade grazed Adiah's shoulder and landed in a nearby tree with a dull thud, splintering its wood. Her dark blood splattered, staining the dirt as she roared. At once, Koffi rose, but not fast enough.

She heard the whooping first, a terrifying sound echoing from all around her. Fear spiked through her body as, one by one, she saw figures begin to emerge from the jungle's darkness, all wearing a familiar shade of blue, a shade she recognized.

No.

It was impossible; her mind turned into a frantic hive of buzzing thoughts. Why were the Sons of the Six here? How had they known where to find them? Instinctively, she reached for the splendor, but it seemed to slip from her, like trying to grasp at water.

The warriors circled them like vultures. From their midst, one particularly handsome warrior emerged, and Koffi stiffened. There was an uncanny familiarity in the cut of his jaw, in the way he wore his dark, tapered hair, and in the narrow shape of his eyes. The only thing foreign about him was the triumphant smirk across his face that she'd never seen on Ekon's. She didn't understand the words that left the warrior's mouth, reverberating against the trees.

"Well done, Ekkie." His voice was rich and full of supreme triumph as he nodded. It took Koffi a second too long to realize he wasn't looking at her as he spoke. She followed his gaze and stared at Ekon. His expression was stony.

"Kamau—"

"Grab the rope!" The warrior Ekon had called Kamau beckoned several burly warriors forward. They were carrying rope as thick as Koffi's arms. Her heart sank.

"No." She didn't recognize the sound of her own voice. It was frail and soft, and it barely carried as the warriors' whooping grew. "No, you don't understand. You can't—"

It happened too fast. Adiah's eyes widened, full of fear. She had started to turn, to flee, when a giant noose snaked through the air, cast by one of the warriors. It landed around her neck and tightened. She tried to roar, but the sound was choked. The warriors jeered.

"How long do you think it takes to choke a demon?" One of them laughed.

"No!" The warrior who had spoken first raised a hand. "Do not harm it, and stick to the plan. Our orders are to take it to Father Olufemi, let him deal with this beast."

The words twisted like a knife in Koffi's side as she watched more ropes fly, watched Adiah struggle against them. *The plan. Father Olufemi. Our orders.* The Sons of the Six weren't here by accident, this had been coordinated, which meant—

"Ekon." A cold fear gripped her. "You *didn't*. Tell me you didn't—"

Ekon still wasn't looking at her; it was as though he couldn't hear her at all. He was staring at Adiah as she thrashed, eyes wide, but he didn't move. He didn't say a word.

"Stop!" Koffi ran to Adiah before they could grab her, tugging as hard as she could at the ropes. Real tears were blurring her vision, and it was impossible to see where one rope started and another ended amid the complicated array of knots and loops. A large hand grabbed her upper arm and dragged her back.

"Move!" The warrior who had snatched her looked down at her as though she were a bug. With his free hand, he jabbed his spear tip into Adiah's side. The daraja screamed.

"No!" Koffi struggled in the warrior's grasp, and a fresh wave of rage tore from her. She reached for the splendor again, fingers physically outstretched as though it were something she could grab. She wasn't at peace or calm, she was just angry, and she focused on that. This time it came greedily. It rose from the ground, traveling up her legs until she was filled to the brim with it.

Let it go, a small voice inside of her pleaded. *Let it go.*

She touched the warrior's bare arm, relishing as he screamed in pain. The distinct smell of burnt flesh filled the air. He let go of her and stepped back.

"She burned me!" he screamed. "She's a daraja!"

Fear collided with anger as her heartbeat quickened. She looked around, desperate for help from anywhere, anyone. Her eyes found Ekon's again.

"Help me!" she cried. "Ekon, please!"

But Ekon didn't move, and slowly she understood that he wasn't going to. As that realization doused the heat in her chest, she felt the splendor leave her and knew it wouldn't return. Instead, spots of black blurred her vision, as though the blood was rushing back to her head after being held upside down. Her fingertips and toes were losing their feeling, and she had the sense of falling into a deep, unending chasm. The world was getting farther and farther away.

"We should kill her," she heard someone say from that emptiness. "Before anyone else finds out."

"No." Another voice, the warrior who'd addressed Ekon. "Don't harm her either. Tie her up and take her with us. The Kuhani will . . ."

Koffi didn't hear the rest. Her mouth had filled with saliva, as though she was about to vomit, and her vision was fading fast. She could do nothing as hands found her wrists and bound them together with a rope that chafed against her skin. Someone grabbed her, dragging her across the dirt and bramble like a sack of yams.

"Ekon . . ." She could barely form his name on her lips. "Ekon, please . . ."

The last thing she saw, through her tunneled view, was Ekon's blurred silhouette as he marched away.

He did not look back.

PART FOUR

The CHEETAH DIES ONCE, the ANTELOPE a THOUSAND TIMES.

The Sky Garden

ADIAH

"Try again, Songbird."

The stars are bright tonight, a thousand sparkling jewels sewn into a dress only fit for a goddess. Their silver light is ethereal, impossibly beautiful as it spills over every rose and blooming gardenia in the temple's sky garden. I admire them, but I don't have time to appreciate them for long.

I hear a *whoosh*, feel the bite of the wind as it rushes toward me in a great gust. Instinctively, my hands fold like I'm praying, and then I extend my arms forward, cutting through the splendor as it diverts in either direction, barely avoiding me on either side. Across the garden, Dakari inclines his head. It's still strange to see him here, in this place that's been secret for so long. He knows all about the splendor now and loves watching me practice with it. The sight of him standing there, amid tangles of old flowers, is a peculiar juxtaposition. In a few strides, he closes the gap between us. His hands are warm as they rest on my shoulders.

403

"You're still holding back," he says gently. "I can tell."

It's true. I *am* holding back, but I don't want Dakari to know why. He is a clean slate, something new in my life. I don't want to scare him away, like I've scared almost everyone else away. A familiar guilt gnaws at my edges as I think about Tao, about the things he said to me in the temple's kitchens. That was weeks ago, and he and I haven't spoken since. It isn't for lack of want—I've tried several times to look for him—but it seems my best friend has turned into a shadow, impossible to find. He's avoiding me, presumably still angry at me for showing Dakari this garden. For the life of me, I don't understand it. The way he looked at me in the temple's kitchens still burns my conscience. I don't ever want Dakari to look at me that way. I want Dakari to like me. His hands are still on my shoulders.

"Sorry."

"*Don't* apologize." His words are firm but kind. He crooks a long finger under my chin, tilting my head up so that my eyes meet his, light brown flecked with gray. I have to work not to shiver at the touch; I have to work not to want more of it. His voice is deep, almost melodic.

"You should never apologize for being who you are," he murmurs. "Or make yourself small so that others feel big."

The words ignite something in me. No one has ever spoken to me like this before, with real *respect*. No one has ever encouraged me to push myself like this, to reach for *more*.

"Try again." Dakari steps back with a nod, and I already miss him. "This time, don't hold back. Give me everything."

I ignore the heat on the back of my neck, try not to think about the way those words feel layered. *Give me everything.* I *want* to kiss

404

Dakari, maybe more, but the Brothers of the Order say proper women should be chaste before marriage.

I grow tired of being proper.

Dakari swivels without warning, throwing three rocks into the air. I summon the splendor instantly. It crackles in the night, and I feel it moving through me in waves. This time, I let go of the inhibitions, the safeguards I've taught myself to always hold up. I push against it, imagine erecting a giant wall three times my own height. The rocks Dakari threw collide with it, then fall to the ground. I feel the power dissipate all around me, and then the earth settles. My skin tingles.

"I . . ." I'm not sure how to read the expression on his face. His eyes are wide. "I don't know how I did that. I've never—"

"That was . . . incredible."

And then I'm in Dakari's arms, spinning, and my world blurs. No boy has ever looked at me the way he is now. He sets me back on my feet and presses our foreheads together. My heart begins to race as his thumb traces along my jawline, as he leans closer to me.

"There's something I want to show you," he says with a small smile. "Tomorrow."

"Tomorrow?" For a moment, I'm pulled from the reverie of him, genuinely curious. "But the Bonding is tomorrow—"

His arms snake around my waist, pulling me closer. "It'll be worth it. I promise, Songbird."

Songbird. That's what Dakari calls me, a nod to the fact that I love to sing. He made up that name just for me. I like the way it sounds on his lips. I like that it's something private, something just for us.

"Okay, then." I nod. "Tomorrow."

Dakari's eyes dance. "Meet me at the jungle's edge just after midnight?"

"Yeah, I will."

I say the words like they're an oath; in some ways they are. A grin tugs at the corner of Dakari's mouth, and his lips brush mine. It's a fleeting gesture, so quick that it ends before I even realize what's happened. But it still sets my skin ablaze, it still makes me wish he'd do it again.

"It's going to be good, Songbird," Dakari whispers. "I promise."

My smile mirrors his own.

I trust Dakari. I think I love him. We haven't known each other long, but I feel like we have. I would do anything for him.

I would *die* for him.

CHAPTER 28

A SON OF THE SIX

Ekon watched the writhing bodies of six black mambas tangle in their basket, each one of their eyes locked on him in waiting.

He moved without warning, snatching his scrap of parchment from them so fast that he didn't have time to feel anything. They hissed but did not strike him.

Sweat slicked his palm as he unfurled his fist and handed that scrap to Father Olufemi without looking at it. He didn't need to, because he already knew what it said. The old man glanced down at the paper a moment, then nodded.

"Well done."

They were alone in the chamber, the same chamber he'd once stood in with his co-candidates. The quiet was unsettling, but Ekon didn't think about that either. He locked gazes with Father Olufemi for a moment, before the latter pointed to the ground.

"Kneel."

Ekon obeyed, ignoring the sudden cold of the room's stone tiles as he pressed one knee to them and bowed his head. It seemed to take years for the Kuhani to speak again.

"Ekon Asafa Okojo, son of Asafa Lethabo Okojo and Ayesha Ndidi Okojo."

Ekon looked up and found Father Olufemi staring down at him, eyes intent.

"You have demonstrated a true act of valor, and in doing so exhibited a righteousness, dedication, and loyalty far exceeding your years," he murmured. "You have honored your people, your family, and your gods."

Ekon bowed his head again. He still remembered the way Father Olufemi had looked at him inside the Night Zoo as he'd pronounced that Ekon would never be a Yaba warrior. So much had changed.

"Candidate Okojo."

Father Olufemi's words dragged Ekon back to the present as the holy man placed a hand on his shoulder. "Do you swear to uphold the tenets so bestowed upon the warriors of our people?"

Ekon nodded. "I do."

"Do you swear, for the rest of your days, to act with honor, courage, and integrity?"

"I do." In the back of his mind, he saw a girl's face, and his stomach twisted slightly.

"*Look at me*, Candidate Okojo."

Slowly, Ekon's eyes met Father Olufemi's. A small pang hit somewhere low in his gut as he reflected on how different those harsh eyes were from Brother Ugo's.

"Do you swear to always obey the Six and those through whom they speak, without hesitation?"

Ekon swallowed again before he answered, and prayed his voice was loud enough. "Yes, Father. I do."

"Then, in the name of the Six true gods, I anoint you."

At his side, Ekon's fingers tapped.

One-two-three. One-two-three. One-two-three.

"You are now a holy warrior, and a man of the Yabahari people," Father Olufemi declared. "Rise, warrior."

Ekon stood. He waited for the moment to hit him. He knew this was the moment he *should* have felt something. He'd dreamed of being a Yaba warrior since he was a child, for over a decade. This was the moment he should have felt the thrum of power coursing through him, the same thrum he'd felt the night he'd first attempted his final rite of passage. He should have been terrified, or excited, or both. Instead, he felt like he'd drunk bad well water.

Father Olufemi crossed the room to the door; the minute he did, a group of warriors rushed in. Sons of the Six were supposed to exhibit a constant decorum in the Temple of Lkossa, but they abandoned it as they swarmed him. The warriors roared their approval, stomping their feet and pounding the shafts of their longspears hard against the hallowed stone in triumph. Someone slapped him on the back, and another hand pressed something soft into his hands. When he looked down, Ekon saw that it was a sky-blue kaftan, embroidered in gold and folded into a neat square. He could tell, even at a touch, that this fabric was finely made, no doubt tailored by the city's best. No expense was spared for a Son of the Six. It was real now.

"Well, are you going to put it on?"

Ekon looked over the heads of the other warriors and found Kamau. In all his life, he'd never seen his brother look so proud. Kamau wasn't just smiling, he was beaming, a light all his own. A warmth emanated from him that Ekon swore he could almost feel, even feet away. *He's proud of you,* he slowly realized. *You've finally made him truly proud.* That epiphany should have flooded Ekon with happiness. He waited for that joy, for the relief. Neither came.

"You know . . ." A touch of merriment twinkled in Kamau's eyes. "If you don't want to wear it, I'll happily take—"

"Warrior Okojo, you will change into the attire befitting your new station," said Father Olufemi, nodding to Ekon. "When you are done, please make your way to the temple's worship hall."

Ekon nodded, grateful for an excuse to leave. He exhaled as soon as he left the room, as soon as he found a small room where he could change into his new clothes. He'd always admired the warrior blue on Kamau, even more so on Baba. As a boy, he'd imagined the day he'd wear it too.

He hadn't imagined it like *this.*

"Just nerves," he muttered to himself as he changed from his old kaftan to his new one. He cringed as the fabric slid over his head. This kaftan was sewn by the best tailors in Lkossa, made with the highest quality cotton, but . . . it felt wrong. It was slick against his skin like the scales of a snake, too cold. He swallowed, easing the nausea down his throat, and his fingers danced against his side.

It had been a full day since he and the other Yaba warriors had emerged from the Greater Jungle, covered in dirt and brambles and debris. The memories of that moment were like an unfinished quilt, patched together with careless thread and always threatening to unravel. He remembered the cheers of the Sons of the Six all around him, whooping and tossing their spears high as the first hints of true, unfiltered sunlight began to dapple the ground before them. There'd been a sudden onslaught of light, and then a roar had torn through the air. It had taken Ekon a moment to register that the sound was no animal, but *people*, hundreds of them, standing in the borderlands and cheering their approval.

Cheering for you, he'd gradually realized. *They're celebrating* you.

The rest of that day had been more difficult to remember. He knew—somehow—he'd gotten to the temple eventually. He'd bathed, changed into fresh clothes, and even shaved for good measure. By the time he'd gone outside again, the line of people waiting to see him stretched from the temple's front doors all the way down to the Takatifu District's golden-arched entrance. The Yaba warriors hadn't even been able to enforce the usual dress code; people from all over the city had gathered to lay eyes on him, to touch him. The elderly had bowed their heads in quiet respect; children had come bearing wreaths of laurels and flowers to lay at his feet. Vendors from all over the city had come offering pottery, and jewels, and food from their shops. They'd treated him like a god. Over and over, they'd said the same words.

Have made your family proud.

Just like his father . . .

A true hero.

It had been overwhelming, a dream come true. All Ekon had ever wanted was the respect and approval of his people; he'd gotten it tenfold. But the joy had been short-lived. It hadn't taken long for a nasty feeling to curdle in his belly, and a day later, it had continued to linger. He knew, somewhere in this temple, there was a beast locked away. The sickness inside him grew, and at once, a whole slew of thoughts he'd been repressing sprang free. He remembered the warriors circling them in the jungle, jeering and whooping. He remembered the ropes tangling around Adiah like hemp serpents, twisting and knotting until she'd been brought low. Worst of all,

411

he remembered the anger and shock on Koffi's face when she'd understood the totality of his betrayal. Her eyes staring into his with that confusion, that *hurt*, cut into him like a blade.

"Warrior Okojo?" Someone was knocking at the door. Ekon recognized Father Olufemi's voice. "Are you ready?"

Ekon jumped to attention. It still felt strange to hear that honorific. "Yes, Father." He opened the door and followed the holy man down the hall; notably, the other Sons of the Six were gone. Ekon had started to ask where they were when Father Olufemi opened a door and he was suddenly cast into a flood of golden light and noise. It was so bright, Ekon had to cover his eyes for a moment. When they settled, he saw the temple's worship hall had been transformed.

The usually conservative room was festooned with sashes and streamers of blue, green, and gold, and several tables were filled to the brim with food. It was a feast. Upon realizing the guest of honor had arrived, the waiting crowd cheered. It looked like every important Yaba family was here.

"What?" Ekon stopped short. "What's this?"

Father Olufemi was already stepping away, smiling, and in his place, several warriors came forward.

"A feast!" Fahim threw an arm around his neck and steered him into the room as more people cheered. "In celebration of the Shetani's capture!"

Ekon felt nauseated. This room was filled with Lkossa's elites, people dressed in their finest. They thought the thing that had menaced the city for years had been captured, that all would be well from hereon. He swallowed.

"This is too much," he said.

"Move." Shomari shoved past them none too gently, holding a goblet of wine. Judging by the way the wine sloshed, it wasn't his first. He passed without looking at them.

"What's *his* problem?" Ekon asked.

Fahim raised an eyebrow, incredulous. "He's jealous, Ekon. A lot of people are. What you just did . . . it'll probably never be topped."

Jealous. That word sounded strange. Not so long ago, Ekon had been jealous of Fahim and Shomari, wanted so badly to have what they did. Now things were reversed, another change.

"I don't want this," he said, shaking his head.

"Look, Ekon." Fahim's eyes weren't on him anymore, but instead focused on a group of well-dressed Yaba girls. They were staring back, giggling behind their hands. "I know you prefer books over a bottle of wine, but trust me, this is definitely a night to enjoy the finer things. And speaking of *finer things*." He gave the girls another meaningful look. "I think a few of our guests look lonely . . ."

Ekon watched Fahim cross the room to join the giggling young women. It was a cruel kind of contrast, seeing everyone so happy. All around him people were feasting and celebrating because they thought they were finally safe, but he knew better. His mind recounted the things he'd learned in the Greater Jungle. Adiah may have been captured, but she wasn't the one responsible for the attacks; something *else* was, something that was still out there, perhaps even at this moment.

Tell them, a voice in his mind implored. *Tell them the truth.*

He couldn't, not now, not after all of *this*. If these people learned that there was still another monster out there—something *worse* than the Shetani—he wouldn't just be expelled from the Sons of the Six, he'd be rejected by his people.

He couldn't stomach that.

Ekon's eyes shot across the worship hall and focused on two people huddled in one of its corners. Their heads were slightly bent as they whispered to each other; one was wearing a sky-blue kaftan, the other a deep blue agbada. Kamau and Father Olufemi. His mind was made up even before he reached them. He had to talk to one or both, and tell them that something else was out there. It wouldn't be the complete truth, but it would be something. By the time he'd reached them, they were already moving apart. Father Olufemi gave him a kind smile before turning on his heels to head up the stairs to his office. Kamau extended a hand.

"Congratulations, Warrior."

"Thank you . . . uh, Kapteni." It felt odd, using the formal term for his own brother. He cleared his throat. "I was actually wondering if you had a minute, to talk?"

"Ah . . ." Kamau's eyes were on the stairs, following Father Olufemi. "This isn't really the best time. I have some business to attend to."

A twinge of annoyance crept up Ekon's body when Kamau tried to move around him, but he mirrored his footsteps and blocked him. "Kam. It's important."

For the first time, Kamau met his gaze directly, and Ekon was surprised to see clear irritation in his brother's eyes. "What is it, then? What's wrong?"

Ekon faltered, hating himself for it. He and his older brother were the same height, equal matches by all societal standards now, but Kamau still had a way of looking at him that could make him feel so small. "I—I want to talk to you about Brother Ugo."

Kamau's brows rose. "What about him?"

414

Ekon gestured around the hall for emphasis. "I was wondering why he's not here. Surely, as a Brother of the Order, he'd attend a feast like this?"

Kamau frowned. "I told you yesterday that Brother Ugo has been in isolation, praying."

"Praying, at a time like this?" Ekon frowned.

"He's a reverent man."

"The Shetani, the creature our people have hunted for nearly a century, has been captured, and he goes to pray?" Ekon asked. "Doesn't that seem strange to—"

"Brother Ugo has been briefed on the matter of the Shetani." Kamau's voice was suddenly uncharacteristically crisp and official. "If he leaves his isolation, I will let you know, but until then, I have other matters to attend to." He gestured to the hall. "In the meantime, try to enjoy yourself, okay?"

Ekon didn't have a chance to say anything else. In a graceful swivel, Kamau moved around him and headed up the stairs. Ekon watched him go, perturbed, before he made the decision. What prompted it was inexplicable, but he followed. As he'd expected, the landing was pitch-black by the time he reached it, save for a single wedge of yellow light coming from the Kuhani's study. That light tugged at Ekon; it beckoned him. He didn't even realize he was holding his breath until his lungs began to ache in protest. He was within a foot of the slightly cracked door when the voices from within floated to him. He stilled.

"Father, *please*."

A chill brushed Ekon's skin, making the hairs on his arms stand on end. Never in all his life had he heard his brother like that. Kamau's voice, strong and confident moments ago, was now thin with fatigue, desperation, and . . . and there was something else, a hint of an emotion it took Ekon a moment to recognize. *Fear.* Through the crack in the door, Ekon discerned two profiles. Kamau and Father Olufemi. The former was on his knees; the latter was sitting on a beautiful chaise, his hands folded carefully in his lap.

"Speak plainly, Warrior Okojo." Father Olufemi's words were calm, as though they were discussing the weather. "What troubles you?"

"It's . . . it's my head, Father." Kamau looked up to meet Father Olufemi's gaze, and Ekon saw his lower lip was trembling. "I'm . . . I'm seeing things, getting confused. The nightmares . . ."

"Nightmares?" Father Olufemi's eyebrow rose, curious. "What kind of nightmares?"

Kamau dropped his gaze, fidgeting like a small child. "I don't understand them, Father. Sometimes they feel like dreams, but other times the people feel real, and . . . I hurt them. I see the blood and want to stop, but . . . I can't." Fat tears rolled down Kamau's face. "There are other Sons saying the same thing, Father. They're having the nightmares too. Father, we don't know what's happening to us—"

"Shh." Father Olufemi leaned forward, cupping Kamau's cheek like an indulgent father. At his touch, Kamau stilled. "Say no more, my child. Everything will be all right soon. Would you like some medicine?"

"I . . ." Kamau hesitated, drawing back from the Kuhani's hand. "I don't know if I should."

"Nonsense." There was a gentleness in Father Olufemi's tone. He turned slightly, and for the first time Ekon noticed the object sitting on the chaise beside him. It was a small, dark wooden pipe no larger than his hand. Though it was difficult to see from far away, he made out something glittering and silver packed into its small chamber, bits of what looked like crushed leaf. It took Ekon a moment to remember why that color seemed familiar. Then he remembered.

Hasira leaf.

Slowly, Father Olufemi lifted a lit candle from one of the tables beside him and held it to the pipe until it began to smoke. At once, a sickly sweet aroma tanged the air. Ekon tensed. He realized he recognized that scent. Father Olufemi handed the lit pipe to Kamau and nodded.

"Inhale."

Despite his previous protest, Kamau took the pipe from him eagerly, taking a long, practiced draw. Ekon stared, transfixed, as a violent shudder passed through his brother's muscled frame, and then he relaxed. When he looked up from the pipe, his eyes had gone glassy, pupils dilated. Father Olufemi touched his cheek again, and this time Kamau leaned into his palm like a lover.

"I know I have asked a great deal of you, Kamau," Father Olufemi murmured softly. "I know that, at times, my orders have been challenging. But it will all be over soon. Once the Shetani is dead, you and your brothers will not have to kill anyone else."

White-hot shock seared through Ekon's body. He waited for the vague, empty look to leave Kamau's face as Father Olufemi's words sank in. He waited for the disgust to show somewhere in his brother's eyes. It did not.

Father Olufemi touched the candle to the pipe again and nodded. "Have some more."

Kamau took the pipe again and inhaled, a small moan escaping him as another hit of the hallucinogenic leaf flooded through him. Father Olufemi looked on, amused.

"How do you feel?"

"I feel . . . good."

Father Olufemi nodded. "And you will continue to, so long as you remain obedient. Listen to me, boy." He crooked his finger under Kamau's chin, forcing their eyes to meet. "These are my orders: You will not speak of your nightmares to anyone else, and you will instruct your brothers to do the same. Do you understand?"

"I . . . understand." Kamau nodded, then gave Father Olufemi a sheepish look. "Father, can I . . . can I have more medicine?"

Father Olufemi's chuckle was mirthless as he lit the pipe a final time and handed it to Kamau. "Of course, my child. Of course."

Ekon didn't know when he'd stood and backed away from the door, his heart thundering in his chest. Father Olufemi's words reverberated against the walls of his mind.

You and your brothers will not have to kill anyone else.

Ribbons of memory returned to him, malformed. He remembered the last attack, the bodies that had littered the ground, and then . . . a conversation with Kamau.

I . . . asked where you were last night.

Father Olufemi had some work for me to do, confidential.

Ekon shuddered. There was no other monster, there never had been.

He moved away from the door slowly, praying Father Olufemi wouldn't look up. The last thing he saw as he retreated into the darkness was Kamau taking a final draw from the pipe, lost to a madness Ekon did not know.

CHAPTER 29

The TERRIBLE AFTER

Lkossa's stars twinkled like diamonds against its obsidian-black night sky. Through her barred window, Koffi could not see them.

It had taken her several minutes to understand where she was as pieces of consciousness seeped back into her, as her body self-assessed its damage. She was sore in places, cut, and never in her life had she felt so thoroughly drained. Slowly, she blinked away the grit in her eyes and tried to bring her unfamiliar setting into focus. She was on her back, staring up at the granite ceiling of a building she did not know, but the mildewy smell was vaguely familiar.

The hard surface beneath her was strangely cool and damp, and the air she breathed slightly dank. Something small and hairy skittered over her foot, and she shot straight up.

Alarm coursed through her as her head spun, sending her into absolute darkness for a moment, but her heartbeat steadied as her eyes adjusted. She was surrounded on three sides by walls of granite, perfect matches to the ceiling overhead. Before her, a set of thick blacksteel bars reached from ceiling to floor. She couldn't make out much beyond them, but somewhere down the hallway, a dull orange light flickered. She was in some kind of prison, she realized, but where? How? The questions came in a sudden onslaught; she had no answers for them.

Who had put her here, and why? Just like that, the sharp, horrible fragments of a memory returned to her like pieces of broken pottery. Each one hurt, and none of them made sense. The last thing she remembered was the Greater Jungle. She remembered a small pond, the sound of warriors whooping, and then a roar. She cringed. The memory was becoming clearer. There'd been an attack. Someone had—inconceivably—come after them in the jungle, someone had tried to take Adiah away, and . . .

Ekon.

It was the last piece of the broken pottery, and when Koffi placed it in her mind, fresh pain stabbed at her side as the rest of the memory came to her. It hadn't been just anyone who'd attacked them, and it hadn't been a surprise. They'd been ambushed, sabotaged, and Ekon had been behind it all. He'd betrayed their plans, betrayed Adiah, betrayed . . . *her*. A sour taste filled the back of her mouth that made her want to spit, but at the sound of approaching footsteps, she looked up.

"Ah." A gruff voice rang out from the darkness. "She's awake."

Koffi jumped to her feet as someone else snickered just out of sight. She ran to her cell's door and wrapped her fingers around the bars. They were cold to the touch, and stank of old metal, but she held on to them, looking up and down the corridor until the owners of the voices emerged from its shadows. One of them, a young man of stocky build, was carrying a small pot filled with a suspicious yellow-gray mush; the other boy was taller, with the saddest attempt at a beard Koffi had ever seen. He carried only a spear and a smirk.

"Dinnertime for the daraja rat," the first one said, holding out the bowl. "Here!" He stuck a hand through the bars and waited until Koffi reached to take the bowl from him before deliberately letting it slip from his fingers and shatter on the floor. At once, the slimy grayish goop—whatever it had been—splattered all over Koffi's legs, and a new foul smell soured the air. She stepped back from the bars, disgusted, and the warriors snickered again in earnest.

"Where am I?" Koffi tried to sound confident as she asked the question, but when she spoke, she found her voice was hoarse and scratchy, as though she hadn't spoken in days. Panic flitted through her. How long had she been here?

"Well, well, it speaks." Peach Fuzz cocked his head, amused. "You're exactly where you belong, Gede: in prison, which is where you'll stay until you face your punishment tomorrow."

Punishment. Another shiver of panic rattled through her body at the ominous words, and more questions darted through her mind. What "punishment" was this warrior talking about?

"What happened to A—um, the Shetani?" The question slipped from her mouth before she could stop herself, and at once she regretted asking it. The smiles fell from the warriors' faces instantly as their eyes hardened.

"That monster will be burned to a crisp," Peach Fuzz said in a dangerously low voice. "Right after we deal with *you.*"

They were words that should have scared Koffi, should have sent her into a deeper panic. Instead, she thought of Adiah. Her stomach roiled as she envisioned what the warrior had said. *That monster will be burned to a crisp.* With a terrible, twisting pang, she imagined Adiah being led to the city's square like a sacrificial cow. She saw the masses of jeering faces, spitting, hissing, and booing as she was tortured. The thought of it made her want to retch, but her body had nothing to give. She steadied herself and met Peach Fuzz's eyes again.

"Sir." She did her best to sound gracious. "Please, I need to speak to Father Olufemi. The Shetani isn't what people think it is at all. It—"

"*Shut up.*" Peach Fuzz's eyes flashed dangerously, and at once, Koffi clamped her mouth shut. There was an unspoken foreboding in the warrior's eyes as he leaned in as far the bars would let him. The other warrior watched, wary-eyed. "That abomination has killed people for *years*. Tomorrow, it will pay."

Koffi's heart sank, but she couldn't give up. "*Please.* Something else has been killing Lkossans, and it's still out there. It could be—"

"Enough!" Peach Fuzz's voice cleaved the air, cutting off the rest of her words. "It'll be killed tomorrow, right after your flogging. If I were you, I'd spend the rest of this night making your peace with the Six. You may not have another opportunity to do so."

Dread seeped into Koffi's bones. Her mouth went dry as she tried to summon more words, anything to make the Yaba warriors listen, but it was too late. As quickly as they'd come, they shot her final derisive looks before leaving her in darkness again. In their absence, it was painfully quiet, and the creeping thoughts that had waited in the back of her cell seemed to crawl forth to meet her.

You failed.

The two words latched on to her like talons, clawing at her and digging in no matter how hard she tried to shake them off. They hung stale in the fetid air, choking her, making her head pound each time they echoed in her mind. She tried to send them away with a hard swallow, but they stayed lodged obstinately in her throat.

You failed. You failed everyone.

There was no way around it, no way to avoid it. The truth of those words rolled over her in tides, each one crashing against her. She wasn't going to make good on her bargain. Mama and Jabir weren't going to be free. Adiah was going to die.

Her tailbone ached as she hugged her knees to her chest and rocked back and forth, considering plan after plan. Each one was like a bird, fluttering in and out of her mind too quickly to be logical, but she considered them just the same. She could beg the Kuhani for mercy, appeal for the clemency of the Six. But no, something told her that the old man would know. As soon as he laid eyes on her, saw the identical fear in her eyes, he'd recognize her from the temple. If her punishment was bad now, it would worsen tenfold when he pieced that together. There would be no mercy from him. Her eyes flitted again toward that tiny, barred cut-out window several feet above her. It wasn't within easy reach, but maybe . . . A third idea slithered into her mind like a poisonous asp.

You could run, it suggested. *Use the splendor and break out. Leave, and never look back.*

The thought curdled in Koffi's stomach, sickening, and she knew at once she couldn't do that either. She couldn't leave Mama and Jabir behind to suffer for her mistakes, or leave Adiah here to die after she'd promised to help her. She could neither help them nor leave them; she could do nothing. Slowly, she returned to the cell's stone floor again, letting that familiar cold seep back into her bones and, with it, resignation. She wasn't sure when she first heard the new set of footsteps, only that once she did, they echoed, hard and deliberate against the stone outside her cell. She sat up just as a figure appeared on the other side of the bars.

"Koffi?" The voice that said her name was familiar. "Are you in there?"

Her teeth gnashed together at the same time something jolted in her chest. It was a confusing feeling, happy and angry all at once. Ekon stepped forward, the hall's torchlight casting one side of his face in shadow. What little stubble he'd had the last time she'd seen him was gone; he was clean-shaven and wore a Son of the Six's telltale blue tunic. His expression was tentative.

"Koffi," he whispered in a voice only she could hear. "Koffi, I'm so sorry. I ..."

Something rose in Koffi just then, a heat. It wasn't pleasant or tingling, it wasn't like the way she'd felt when the splendor had coursed through her, and it wasn't anything like the joy she'd felt when Ekon's lips had found hers in the jungle. This time, the words came from her mouth unbidden.

"I *hate* you."

They sliced the air like a blade, and she watched as they found their mark on Ekon's face. He recoiled, eyes flashing a hurt that almost made her sorry. Almost. His gaze dropped from hers as he looked to his feet, mouth set in a tight line. "Look, Koffi. I know you're mad at me. You have every right to be. But I—"

"All those words ..." It took every bit of Koffi's willpower to keep her voice from trembling as she spoke. "None of them were true."

"They *were*." Ekon looked up, and though one side of his face was still obscured in shadow, the other side was pleading. "I wanted to say something, to stop them—"

"So why didn't you?"

Ekon stared at his hands, as though trying to find the words, before he spoke.

"For a long time, the only thing I wanted was to be a Son of the Six," he said quietly. "It was the only way I knew how to honor my family and my baba. Everything I did, every choice I made, was with that goal in mind. When I made my deal with you, it's what I had in mind. I didn't care about anything else. You were a means to an end."

Koffi flinched, surprised at how much the words stung. The deal they'd struck felt like something from another life, from a Before. That was how things felt now, two parts of a whole, cleaved into the time Before Ekon had betrayed her, and the terrible After.

"But once we got into the jungle," Ekon went on, "things started to change. What we saw while we were in there, what we did . . . I wasn't expecting it. And then, *I* started to change, started realizing that maybe I did still want to be a Son of the Six and make my family proud, but I wanted something else too, I wanted"—his gaze dropped—"I wanted *you*."

Koffi swallowed.

"Then my brother came to me," said Ekon. "And it was like being ripped from a dream. It was like I was being pulled into two directions, pulled between something old and something new." He looked up at her. "Haven't you ever felt that, that pull?"

Koffi didn't answer, she didn't want to. She *had* felt that pull, she *had* been pulled between things. For most of her life, she'd been pulled between following her heart and her mind. In the end, it had been Ekon who'd told her she didn't have to give in to that pull. *He'd* been the one to tell her she could follow both. She looked up and found Ekon's eyes had locked on hers. She couldn't read the expression on his face. Another minute passed before he spoke.

"Just so you know, I feel like dirt," he said quietly. "I've never felt so bad in my life, and I know that still isn't enough. I know I can't ask you to just forgive and forget what I did."

Koffi didn't know if she could forgive and forget it either.

"But I'm going to get you out of here," he said, voice strained. "I'm going to make this right."

"What about Adiah?"

Ekon tensed, looking away from Koffi and down the hallway before leaning in. "That's why I've come. I know what's really been killing Lkossans now."

Koffi straightened. "What?"

"It's been"—Ekon hesitated—"it's been the Sons of the Six."

Koffi stepped back. Cool dread coursed through her body as Ekon's impossible words sank in. No, it wasn't true, it *couldn't* be. The Sons of the Six could certainly be brutal, terrifyingly dedicated to their duty, but they weren't murderers. Their job was to *protect* the city's people. It didn't make sense.

"How?" Her voice was hollow. "How could they do such a thing?"

Ekon was shaking his head. "I'm not sure they fully understand what they're doing. They're being . . . drugged. When I was in the temple, I saw Father Olufemi with one of the warriors. The warrior could only kind of remember hurting people, but he described it like a dream, something he wasn't sure was real. Then

426

Father Olufemi gave him something to smoke, packed into one of his pipes."

Koffi swore, feeling the blood drain from her face. At Ekon's confused look, she met his gaze. "I saw that pipe when I was in the Kuhani's study looking for Nkrumah's journal. It was on his desk, but I couldn't see what was in it."

"It was hard for me to see too," said Ekon. "But it looked silver, like one of the plants I read about in Nkrumah's journal. I think it's called hasira, or—"

"*Angry* leaf." Koffi went still. "My mama and I use that stuff at the Night Zoo to sedate the bigger animals. It's incredibly dangerous. If a human ingested it—"

"The side effects are really bad," said Ekon. "It's a hallucinogen, and a highly addictive one at that. I think the Kuhani has been giving it to Sons of the Six, then ordering them to kill people."

Koffi shook her head, disturbed. She thought of the people, the countless people, who'd been killed; she thought of Sahel and the way his body had been found, lacerated. She shuddered.

"There's something I still don't understand," she said. "Why would Father Olufemi do this, Ekon? What does he have to—?"

They stilled, coming to the same understanding at once. They said the name at the same time.

"Fedu."

"Badwa said whatever was really killing Lkossans would come from him," said Ekon. "What if he's already here, controlling Father Olufemi?"

"But where would he be?"

"I don't know," he said. "But we need to find Adiah and get her out of here before he gets to her."

"Those other warriors." Koffi nodded in the direction the other two had gone. "They said they were going to kill her tomorrow afternoon, right after . . ." For the first time, she felt the cold touch of fear. "Right after I'm flogged."

Ekon's face hardened. "That's not happening. I won't let it. I'm going to get you out of here, Koffi, I promise, and then we'll get Adiah out too. We'll get to the Kusonga Plains and end this."

The words were noble, and Koffi found herself reminded of another time Ekon had said some noble-sounding words that had inspired her. She'd believed him then too, but . . .

"How? How are we going to do any of that?"

Ekon pressed his folded hands to his mouth, deep in thought for a second before he looked up again. "I have a plan, but I need you to trust me."

Koffi stiffened. She didn't trust Ekon at all. "What are you—?"

"Hey, Okojo!" A voice rang from down the hall. Peach Fuzz. "You still down there?"

Ekon looked down the hall, then back at Koffi. "Please."

The words tumbled from Koffi's mouth before she could stop them, and she prayed she wouldn't regret them.

"Let's go."

CHAPTER 30

A SMALL GRIEF

Sweat slicked Ekon's temple as he walked down the prison's dank hallway.

Beside him, he thought he heard Koffi's chattering teeth, but he didn't look at her. Her wrists were bound and his grip on her was tight—probably too tight—but he needed this to be convincing.

It *had* to be convincing.

They reached the end of the hall, where two Sons of the Six leaned against the wall. Ekon knew them, Chiteno and Fumbe, warriors from Kamau's initiation year. He didn't like either of them.

"I have to say"—Chiteno spoke first, looking down his nose as Ekon and Koffi approached—"I'm surprised to see you here, Warrior Okojo. Figured you'd be enjoying the party upstairs."

Ekon kept his face impassive. "I still have things to take care of."

Fumbe chuckled. "They're always overeager at first."

"Yeah." Something glinted in Chiteno's eyes. "It'll be a few months before the newness wears off, before you have to do the dirty work."

Dirty work. Ekon tried to ignore the chill on his skin. *You're murderers,* he thought as he watched them chortle. *One of you, maybe both of you. You're murderers.*

All his life, he'd wanted to be a part of this brotherhood, because he thought it would be the surest way to prove to himself and to his people that he was a man. He found he didn't want any of it anymore.

"What are you doing with the daraja rat?" Fumbe asked, nodding to Koffi. "We were told she was staying here until morning."

"There's been a change in plans." Ekon tried to sound as confident as he could. "Father Olufemi wants to see the daraja tonight. I have orders to escort her to his office, and to be discreet about it. He doesn't want anyone else to see her."

"Of course." A wicked smile slashed across Chiteno's face. "By all means, then, take her, maybe find a private corridor on your way there—she looks frigid."

Ekon's stomach twisted in disgust, but he kept his face impassive. "He told me to be quick about it, so I'll need to go now."

They nodded in acquiescence before letting Ekon frog-march Koffi past them. As soon as they were up the stairs and on the next landing, he let go of Koffi's arm and finally dared to meet her eyes. It was a strange recall. This was the hallway where they'd first met, albeit under very different circumstances. Her jaw was jutted out in defiance, but her eyes glistened as he cut through her ropes with his hanjari. When they fell to the ground, she nodded.

"Thanks."

"Did they hurt you, before I came?"

"No." In a way, Koffi's refusal to cry was worse than if she'd just done so outright. "I'm fine."

430

"Good." Ekon unshouldered his bag and pulled a blue cloak from it. "I brought you this," he said, wrapping it around her. Koffi pulled its billowing hood over her face, and her shoulders seemed to relax a bit.

"What do we do now?"

"Adiah's here, somewhere in this temple," he said. "My guess is that they're keeping her in the stable, but I'm not certain of it. Do you have any way to find her?"

Koffi frowned for a moment, thoughtful. Then: "The first time I met her, in the jungle, I was able to do something with the splendor in her body. I felt a connection to it as a daraja. There's a chance I could use the same connection to find her, but I don't know if it'll work."

"You have to try," said Ekon. "Do anything you have to do to find her." He pressed the hilt of his hanjari into her hands. *"Anything."*

"Ekon." Anxiety riddled Koffi's voice. "The splendor is affected by my emotions, I don't know how reliable—"

"We don't have many more options, Koffi," said Ekon. He tried to keep the panic out of his voice. "I just lied to those warriors, and eventually they'll figure that out. We need to find Adiah and leave Lkossa as quickly as possible."

Koffi seemed to come to some sort of reckoning. She swallowed. "What are you going to do while I'm looking for Adiah?"

"I . . ." Ekon faltered. This was the part of his plan he was least confident in, and also the part he knew Koffi would like least. "I'm going to be looking for someone too."

Koffi frowned. "Who?"

"My mentor," said Ekon. "His name's Brother Ugo."

"Wait, *brother*? As in a brother of the *temple*?" The incredulity in Koffi's whisper bordered on hysterical. "Ekon, are you out of your mind? We've just found out the Kuhani has been using the Sons of the Six to commit *murders*. For all we know, the whole temple is corrupted. Why would you be looking for someone within it now?"

"Because Brother Ugo is . . . different." Even to Ekon, the words sounded silly aloud, but he kept on. "He's been my mentor all my life, Koffi, and he's nothing like Father Olufemi. To be honest, I'm worried about him. No one's seen him since we got back from the jungle."

Koffi rolled her eyes, and Ekon was almost glad to see a hint of the girl he knew. "So you think *this* is the time to go looking for him?"

Ekon massaged his temples. "I can't explain it, but I have a bad feeling. I think something's happened to him. Brother Ugo would never stand for what Father Olufemi and the Sons of the Six are doing. If he found out the truth, and the Kuhani wanted to silence him—"

"Ekon." There was a touch of real sympathy in Koffi's voice. "If that's true, there's a good chance . . ." Her voice held a touch of apology. "There's a good chance they've already—"

"Please, Koffi." Ekon's words were a whisper. "Please. He might be dead, but he might also be alive, and if he's alive, he could help us."

Koffi's lips pressed into a hard-set line. "If you can't find him—"

"Twenty minutes," said Ekon. "I promise if I can't find him by then, then we leave. I'll meet you behind the stable. No one should be back there this late."

She paused for a moment, thoughtful. "Make it thirty."

"Why?"

She raised an eyebrow. "I thought you'd prefer a dividend of three." She gripped the hanjari tighter. "Thirty minutes, and you'd *better* not be late," she said. "Or I swear, you will *never* get this dagger back."

"Deal."

Koffi threw him one more skeptical look before darting down the hall like a shadow.

And then she was gone.

Ekon wove through the temple's hallways in silence.

In the distance, he could still faintly hear the cheers and whoops of the feasts' revelers, getting louder and more uproarious as it got later and the wine poured more freely. It was a strange contrast, almost unnerving. Down in that worship hall, Fahim and Shomari would still be celebrating. In another set of circumstances, maybe he would be too. Maybe, in another version of his life, he'd become a Son of the Six, follow in his baba's footsteps like he'd always envisioned. That plan was gone now, pages that belonged to a story he'd never write. He wasn't necessarily sorry for what he was about to do, but . . . the old want still tugged at him. If he was honest, there was even a small grief. He wouldn't be sad to leave the Temple of Lkossa behind, but he would be sad to leave behind what he'd once thought it was. Mama had left him by choice, Baba had left him by force, but this had always been home. This was the life he and Kamau knew best, and after tonight, he would never know it again.

He kept his ears pricked and his eyes sharp as he moved through its halls. Somewhere in this building Koffi was—hopefully—on her way to finding Adiah and getting out. Every time he thought about that, his stomach swooped.

Think, Ekon, a voice in his mind instructed. *Think. Where could Brother Ugo be?*

He checked all the usual places—the private prayer rooms, the memorial hall, even the kitchens—and found no one. Growing more desperate, he ventured into the western wing of the temple, where Brothers of the Order slept. Some of the rooms were occupied by sleeping old men—he peeked carefully into each one—but most were empty, rooms that belonged to members of the order still enjoying the festivities. Finally, he found the door he was looking for and knocked gently, keeping his voice at a whisper.

"Brother? Brother Ugo?"

No answer. Ekon nudged the door open and peered inside the room.

He would have felt better if the room had been destroyed, ransacked, indicative of any sort of struggle. What he saw instead disturbed him more. Brother Ugo's room was pristine. The small bed in the center of the little room was neatly made, its creases and folds perfectly aligned, as though no one had slept in it for some time. A stack of books was arranged near the simple cut-out window, and the few robes Brother Ugo owned were folded on his trunk. Nothing about the room was instantly wrong, but it held a distinct emptiness. In the back of his mind, Ekon thought of an old story, the tale of another old scholar of this temple who'd gone missing without a trace.

Satao Nkrumah.

Ekon went cold. What if someone had taken Brother Ugo against his will. What if they had him held prisoner somewhere now and were hurting him? His mentor was clever, but old, so it wouldn't take much at all to hurt him. He raked his fingers through his hair, trying to temper a growing panic.

Where? He asked the question over and over in his mind. *Where are you?*

He left the western wing and raced down a different hall. There was one more place he hadn't checked—the temple's library. Access there was usually restricted to Brothers of the Order and those given special permission by the Kuhani. It was a large enough place to hide someone, a place easy enough to block access to.

Please, please be there . . .

"Warrior Okojo."

Ekon stopped in his tracks and swiveled, an ice-cold dread running down his back. A figure emerged from the shadows of a doorway he had flown past without looking. The hair on his arms stood on end as moonlight filtered through one of the temple's massive bay windows and cast silvery light on one side of the Kuhani's face. Ekon swallowed hard.

"Father." Habit compelled him to bow and salute. The old holy man offered the faintest touch of a smile.

"I admit . . ." His voice was soft, but his eyes held a razor-sharp glint. "I am surprised to see you here."

Ekon drew himself up. "Surprised, sir?"

"Indeed," said Father Olufemi. In a matter of strides, he closed the gap between them. "I expected you to be in the worship hall celebrating the Shetani's capture, with your new brothers."

Brothers. The word repulsed him, but Ekon forced a small smile of his own. "I was, Father," he said cordially. "But I stepped away." He gestured to the worship hall, and then to the statues of the Six standing in silent observance. "I wanted to pay my respects, to praise the gods for this victory."

"I see." Father Olufemi nodded in approval. "That is quite . . . mature. Kamau has taught you well. I see the resemblances between the two of you more clearly than ever."

It took every bit of Ekon's restraint not to cringe at the mention of Kamau. He didn't want to see the images filling his head, but it was impossible not to recall his brother's slackened face, not to hear Father Olufemi's mirthless laugh. The smile faltered for a moment, just slightly. Ekon fixed it.

"*Thank you*, Father."

Father Olufemi looked over his shoulder a moment, as though deep in thought, before he spoke again. "I would like you to visit my study tomorrow," he said. "Now that you are a Son of the Six, there are confidential matters regarding the city's . . . *security* that you should be briefed on."

Ekon fought to keep his voice even as he bowed. "Yes, Father. Good night."

"Good night."

Ekon's muscles had started to relax as Father Olufemi began to turn, but without warning, he faced Ekon again. This time, he closed the gap between them, placing a wrinkled hand on Ekon's shoulder. At once the hasira leaf's saccharine scent filled the space between them. Ekon held his breath.

"I look forward to having you join our efforts," said Father Olufemi. "What we do is a duty, a righteous work." He walked away without another word, as slow and deliberate as he'd been before. Ekon watched him go, uneasy. Father Olufemi had seen him here, which meant they had even less time than before. He stared out the window and at the moon again. He and Koffi had agree to meet in thirty minutes exactly; more than half of that time was gone, and he was still no closer to finding Brother Ugo. He closed his eyes and tried to think of every detail, every place he'd ever been with his mentor. They'd gone on walks through the city, spent hours in the study rooms, they'd—

Then the realization hit him hard, stopping him in his tracks. Sweat snaked down his forehead as it finally clicked in his mind, and both panic and joy erupted within him as he turned and faced down one of the hallways.

He knew where Brother Ugo was.

CHAPTER 31

FIREFLIES

The smell of hay thickened in the air as Koffi neared the temple's stable.

Around her, she listened to the sounds of its inhabitants: the soft snores of livestock. Those sounds and scents both unnerved and comforted her—they reminded her of the Night Zoo.

She crept along the stalls one by one, peeking inside each and trying to discern their residents in the darkness. Ekon had said that Adiah might be down here, but he wasn't certain; she tried not to focus on the word *might*. She had half an hour to find the transformed daraja and then meet Ekon so that they could leave. It felt like a lot of time. She knew it wasn't.

Every shadow inside the stable seemed to grow longer as the seconds ticked by, moonlight trickling through gaps between the roof's wooden planks. She took a deep breath in and caught a new scent, ozone, the smell that always preceded rain. Monsoon season was coming, there was no doubt about that anymore; she hoped she, Ekon, and Adiah would be long gone by then.

A new wave of anxiety began building in her fingers; she tempered it by making a tight fist.

"Calm your mind," she whispered to herself as she rounded a corner of the stable. Calm, she needed to stay calm. She recognized this part of the stable—she'd once stood here with Jabir, right before they parted ways. She crouched down in the shadows, letting her fingers brush along the dirt floor. It was a different sensation; whereas the jungle's dirt had been warm and inviting, the stable's was cooler and distinctly less animate. Still, she was relieved to feel the familiar pulse of the splendor—not as powerful as before, but present. She coaxed it in a way she hoped was gentle. *I need to find Adiah,* she thought. *Help me find her. Help me save her.*

There was a moment's uncertain pause before the energy responded with a tug, somewhere near her navel. Automatically, she rose as tiny, familiar flickers of golden light formed near her fingertips, then ascended to bob almost playfully through the air before her. It took her a moment to recognize what they reminded her of, fireflies.

Help me, she urged. *Help me find her.*

The bobbing lights moved to form a chain. Koffi watched in wonder as they populated, illuminating a path down the hall to her right and around a corner. Perfect. From here, all she had to do was follow the lights, and—

"What the—?"

No. Koffi swore. She recognized the boy who had rounded the corner. He was the one she and Jabir had first encountered when they'd approached the stable; now he was staring at her with a mix of awe and horror. Koffi shrank back into a stall a few feet away as he seemed to pick the latter emotion to hold on to.

"Help!" he called over his shoulder. "Someone help!"

More footsteps sounded, and Koffi's heart sank. She started to reach for the splendor, to call it back, then froze. Would the flecks of light disappear, or would they float back to her and reveal her hiding spot? She wasn't willing to take that chance. Two more boys joined the first in the hallway. For a moment, they stared at Koffi's lights with the same sort of confused wonder before one of them spoke.

"What are those?" the second boy asked.

"Something bad," the first answered. "Looks like magic to me."

"The daraja's still in the prison, isn't she?"

"She's supposed to be, but—" One of the boys stepped forward and prodded the light with a finger. Koffi flinched in pain. "She might be trying to communicate with the Shetani and get it to free her. The Kuhani needs to be told immediately."

No. The lights sputtered. New anxiety rolled over Koffi as she thought about the Kuhani. If he went to check on her in the prison and found she wasn't there, her and Ekon's plan was ruined before it began.

"He was in his study, last I checked," said the boy, nodding to one of the others. "Go get him. We'll seal the exits, just in case."

He was closing the gap between himself and Koffi with each step. Koffi crept farther into the stall, withdrawing Ekon's hanjari from the sheath on her hip. She held it to her chest, remembering his words.

Do anything you have to do.

"Hey!" The boy's eyes locked on her. He opened his mouth, about to yell—

She lunged.

The movement came to her like an instinct. One of her arms extended and she turned on her heel, making a perfect circle. The hilt of the hanjari connected with the side of the boy's head, knocking him unconscious. He slumped to the ground. Koffi had barely caught her breath when she heard more footsteps.

"She's there!" one of the boys cried, running toward her. "Don't move, or—"

The light erupted.

It was sudden and consuming. Koffi's eyes went wide as pure light exploded from the once-tiny flickers and became magnificent auras of glittering gold. She rose from her crouch and stepped into the hallway. Her surroundings looked almost white, washed out and devoid of all color but that same constant white-gold. She looked down and saw that the boy who had been running was on his hands and knees.

"I can't see!" he shouted. "Someone help, I can't see!"

Koffi broke from her stupor. The splendor was still helping her. With ease, she ran in the opposite direction. The minute she left the hall, she felt its light begin to fade, heard the boy's disgruntled shouts, but she kept running with the sparkles overhead. They were guiding her forward.

She reached a large wooden door at the end of the hall, and the tug in her navel grew more pronounced, more insistent. Her heartbeat stuttered in her chest as she stopped before it, uncertain. There was no sound on the other side to indicate anything was there, but this was where the fireflies had stopped.

Please, she prayed. *Please be right.*

She wrapped her fingers around the door handle; to her surprise, it turned without protest. She stepped inside the room and froze.

It looked like an old storage closet, brooms and buckets pushed haphazardly to the side. A large bed of hay covered the stone cobbles in the center of the room, and there atop it was Adiah. Most of her body was bloody, latticed in an assortment of nicks and cuts, and the few parts that weren't cut were bound tight with thick rope. Just looking at them made Koffi cringe.

"Adiah!"

She crossed the room, dropping to her knees beside the creature at once. Adiah snarled, but it was half-hearted, a sound full of defeat. Tentatively, Koffi's fingers grazed her head, her back, and one of her cut-up paws. They'd abused her horribly. Furious tears filled Koffi's eyes.

"I'm getting you out of here." She held Adiah's gaze, hoping that could convey her message. "Just hang on, I'm going to get you out of these ropes. I just don't know…" She tugged at the biggest knots, near the beast's neck, with all her might, but they wouldn't budge; then she tried using the dagger without luck either. It would take too long to saw through all the knots. She sat back on her heels and swore.

"Any ideas?"

Adiah's eyes weren't on Koffi anymore, but on Ekon's hanjari. She looked from it to Koffi's face several deliberate times before Koffi understood.

"Oh. I've never tried that."

Adiah offered an encouraging nod, and Koffi looked down at the blade. Nausea was beginning to churn in her stomach, and she knew she was probably nearing the limits of how much splendor she could allow to pass through her body in such a short space of time, but she willed it anyway. At her beckon, warmth flooded her instantly, as though she'd swallowed a piece of sunrise. She focused hard on the hanjari until its silver blade illuminated gold. This time, when she pressed it to the rope, it cut through like butter, and in a matter of seconds the rest of the rope fell away around Adiah's body. The beast rose and stretched.

"Come on." Koffi jumped to her feet too and headed for the door. "We've got to get out of here!"

As quickly and quietly as she could, she steered Adiah back down the hallway. Her heart lurched when voices pounded from the other end.

"It was over here!" a familiar voice shouted, growing rapidly louder. "I can't explain it, Father, come quick!"

Koffi's stomach turned. Her muscles were spasming from the splendor she had already used, but she had no choice. She called to it yet again. This time, it came forth in a swell, surging through her so fast her knees buckled. Light filled the corridor and spread, growing brighter by the moment. In its luminance, four new figures were hunched on the ground, covering their eyes. One was wearing a deep blue robe she recognized. The Kuhani. His face was full of naked fear as he grasped uselessly at the light with eyes screwed shut. Koffi and Adiah skirted around him as he bared his teeth in a grimace.

"This is the work of the daraja!" he said. "She's gotten out and set the Shetani free! Find the Sons! Tell them to seal the city's front gates and send men to the borderlands, *now*!"

The boys didn't move.

"Now!"

"Sir, we can't—"

Koffi led Adiah down the hall at a sprint. She knew as soon as the light was gone and their eyes readjusted they'd begin their search, and she had no desire to be around for that. Her stomach somersaulted as Father Olufemi's words sank in. He was sending warriors to the borderlands, the city's exits were going to be sealed. Time was up. She, Ekon, and Adiah had to leave.

"Faster!" Every muscle in her body ached as she pushed herself to run down the last hallway, back to her exit point. It was getting harder to breathe, harder to see, and she knew she'd pushed too far. She would pay for it later.

They reached the back of the stable, and a tidal wave of relief flooded her body despite the pain. Now if they could just find—

She froze as she heard a scream.

It split the temple's quiet, long and agonizing. Adiah snarled, and Koffi stilled. She *knew* that voice and who it belonged to. She'd know it anywhere.

Ekon.

CHAPTER 32

THE MADNESS

By the time Ekon reached the corridor, he was drenched in sweat.

He'd run from the worship hall as fast as he could, but getting here had still taken what felt like an eternity. His heart rattled against his ribs as he ripped open the door to the old closet and barreled up its narrow steps, on edge. He wasn't sure why he hadn't thought of the sky garden before; perhaps it was because it seemed more dream than real. Perhaps he hadn't wanted to. Regardless, it was the last place he'd seen Brother Ugo, and it was his last chance.

Please, he prayed. *Please be right.*

He shouldered open the trapdoor, then pulled himself up and into the sky garden.

The moon above hung low, eerie as its light cast a silver sheen over the overgrown flowers. But Ekon ignored them, searching until he found a figure sitting on a stone bench in the garden's center. The person's back was turned away, but he recognized its shape.

"Brother Ugo!"

At the sound of his name, the old man turned. Pain lanced through Ekon as he took his mentor in. Brother Ugo's face was wrong—it had withered as though a whole decade had passed since they'd last seen each other. Ekon's heart lurched when the old man held out a frail, trembling hand and smiled.

"Ekon, my dear boy."

The words broke Ekon from his trance. He crossed the garden in what felt like only two strides and threw his arms around the old man as carefully as he could. It was disturbing to feel so many new bones jutting from Brother Ugo's body where they hadn't been before, but he didn't care. Brother Ugo was *alive*, safe.

"I thought they'd— I thought you might be—" He found he couldn't finish any of those sentences. He pulled away from Brother Ugo to look at him properly. Aside from the withered face and worn eyes, he looked generally well, and that was what mattered. "I'm glad to see you, Brother."

Brother Ugo offered a kind, albeit confused smile. "As am I to see you, Ekon. I admit, I didn't expect a visit so soon. If my information is correct, I'm now speaking with an initiated Son of the Six. Congratulations."

Guilt pricked in the back of Ekon's mind, but he brushed it away. "Brother . . ." The words came to him, then died in his throat. He'd known, from the second he and Koffi had gone their separate ways, what he was going to have to say to Brother Ugo if he found him. He'd gone over the words more than once as he'd searched the temple. But staring into the eyes of the old man who'd helped raise him and taught him everything he knew, he found what he had to say nearly impossible. He was going to have to break his mentor's heart.

"Brother," he murmured. "I've come because I need to tell you something."

"In good time, in good time." Brother Ugo waved the words away like tsetse flies. "I want to hear all about your heroic adventure into the Greater Jungle! I've already heard some of it, of course, but I want the details from *you*. How did you survive? How did you find the Shetani? Was it difficult to capture?"

"Brother." Ekon spoke more firmly. "Please listen to me. We need to leave this garden right away, and we need to leave Lkossa. It's not safe here. *You're* not safe here."

"Safe?" Brother Ugo's white brows arched. "Quite the contrary, Ekon. Lkossa is the safest it's been in nearly a century, thanks to you. I'm told the Kuhani is preparing to destroy the creature as we speak. There will be no more killings!"

"That's just it, Brother," said Ekon. "The Shetani *hasn't* been killing people." He swallowed. "It's been the Sons of the Six."

"What?" Brother Ugo clutched his chest as though there was a real danger his heart might fail him. "*What* did you say?"

Ekon's own chest ached at his mentor's disbelief, but he went on. "Earlier tonight, I overheard my brother and the Kuhani talking in his study. Father Olufemi admitted he'd ordered the murders himself. And Kamau admitted he'd been carrying them out. He implied other warriors were involved too."

Brother Ugo shook his head, his mouth still agape in horror. He looked so small, helpless. "I—I don't believe it," he stammered. His eyes were wet, terrified. "The Order wouldn't allow—our own warriors could never do such a—"

"I think it's more complicated than that it seems, Brother," said Ekon. "When I saw Kamau earlier, he didn't look . . . like himself.

447

Father Olufemi gave him something called hasira leaf to calm him down, then told him to keep his mouth shut. I read about it in Nkrumah's journal. It has all sorts of bad side effects, hallucinations and memory loss, to name just a few. When Kamau described the things he did, he made it sound like it was a bad dream, like it was something he didn't fully understand. If other warriors are having similar experiences, they may have been killing people for years under the leaves' influence without understanding it."

"Ekon—"

"You remember the way Shomari was that time in the temple," Ekon continued. "That time he randomly picked a fight with me and got irrationally angry? I think he was having a bad reaction to the hasira leaf. I think it makes people violent."

"Ekon." Brother Ugo had shifted away from him on the bench, shaking his head emphatically. "This is inconceivable, even by the furthest stretches of the imagination. The Shetani is a *monster*, and she has killed our people for years. Do you know how many bodies I've seen cremated, the marks I saw on those bodies? Those victims . . . their injuries couldn't possibly have been the work of a human being. No *person* could be that violent."

Ekon shuddered, remembering those bodies too. Those people hadn't just been killed, they'd been mauled, mutilated. The thought sent a fresh chill down his spine.

"I even remember the day your father died," Brother Ugo said quietly. There was pain in his voice. "It was a horrible thing to see, to watch the light leave his eyes. Believe me when I tell you that kind of violence was the work of a beast, Ekon." He met his gaze. "It was *not* the work of a man."

Something cold and unsettling seeped into Ekon's body then,

turning his mouth dry as paper. Slowly, he rose from the bench and stared down at Brother Ugo.

"I wasn't with my baba when he died," he said. "By the time the Sons had found him and brought him back to our home, he was long gone. The coroner believed he'd been dead for hours, that there was no chance he could have been saved." He held his mentor's gaze. "So how did you *see* the light leave my father's eyes?"

Brother Ugo frowned. "I—"

"And a second ago, you called the Shetani a *she*," Ekon continued, trying to keep his voice from shaking. "Why would you do that?"

It happened slowly. Brother Ugo's lips stretched into a nasty smile, exposing pink gums and broken teeth. Gone was the fright in his eyes, and when he spoke, his words were cool.

"You're so much like your father," he said, standing. "Attentive, astute, an *active* listener. It's what has made you such a good servant, Ekon, and it's what made Asafa weak."

Servant. The word struck Ekon as odd, *wrong.* Fragments from his memory stitched together, then came apart. He saw his father telling him to run, remembered what Brother Ugo had told him and Kamau later. Baba had been recovered at the jungle's edge; Brother Ugo had been the one who'd found him dead. Brother Ugo, who was now saying Baba *hadn't* been dead when he discovered him. Something tightened in his throat, a wave of nausea roiling inside him.

"He knew too much," the old man said quietly. "It was a tragedy, killing him, but a necessary one." He steepled his hands. "Certainly, he was more difficult to get rid of than Satao was."

Ekon focused on a singular word, felt it etch itself into his psyche letter by letter with the cruelty of a dagger's tip. *Necessary.* Words and stories blurred together in his mind, like hot tea poured over ink. In the back of his mind he had a thought. Scholars had said Satao Nkrumah had disappeared. They'd searched, but had never found him . . .

"I knew you would be different, knew you wouldn't fail me or ask too many questions," said Brother Ugo. He began to pace. "You were the perfect combination—young and athletic, smart and meticulous. Most importantly, you were *keen*, desperate for approval. It made you easy to mold into what I needed. I thank you for that, Ekon, for your *obedience*, your loyalty."

Ekon cringed.

"Our plan was almost foiled, though." Brother Ugo went on without looking Ekon's way. "When your foolish act of compassion forced the Kuhani to expel you from candidacy, I thought our hopes might be dashed." His eyes danced. "But then *another* idea came to me, better than the first. The rest was easy. You were already so eager to prove your worth, all I had to do was feed you a speech about destiny, set you on the path . . ."

Ekon felt as though he was sinking below some unknown surface as the words washed over him. The man speaking *looked* like his mentor, their voices were the same, but . . . none of this sounded right at all.

"You killed my father." He could barely speak the words. "You killed Master Nkrumah."

"Yes." Brother Ugo bowed. "I did."

"I—I don't understand," Ekon stammered. "I thought the Kuhani—"

"The *Kuhani*?" Brother Ugo actually stopped pacing to give

450

Ekon a considering look. "You thought Father Olufemi would be clever enough to orchestrate such things? You thought *he* could compel warriors to kill their own for nearly a century undetected?" He shook his head ruefully. "You overestimate him, Ekon."

"You—" Ekon struggled to find the words. He cast a look over his shoulder, at the garden's still-open trapdoor. It looked impossibly far away. "Where is the real Brother Ugo? What have you done with him?"

The old man's expression was almost pitying. "You stupid boy. Brother Ugo never existed."

Ekon's head swam. Instinctively, he stepped back, and the old man mirrored his steps. His outline was beginning to blur at the edges, eyes growing redder.

"It was a clever disguise," he said. "A kindhearted old man who kept largely to himself. Funny, no one ever *could* remember when I arrived here." He gave Ekon an almost-amused look. "I suppose people just thought I'd always been around."

Ekon was struggling to string words together to form a coherent sentence, let alone any kind of question. He stared at the old man with the familiar face but foreign voice. A terrible chill shuddered through Ekon's body. "Who are you?"

"You still don't know?" The old man cocked his head. "I thought it obvious."

And then it *was* obvious, so obvious Ekon hated himself for not putting the pieces together sooner. He whispered the name.

"Fedu."

The god of death nodded. "You have proven invaluable to me," he said. "I have been trying to get Adiah out of the jungle for years, and in a matter of days you not only retrieved her, but delivered her

451

to my feet. It is a shame you are not a daraja. I would have liked for you to be part of the new world I intend to create with her power."

Ekon's mind was racing, trying to make what he was hearing and seeing come together with some logic in his mind. A single question escaped him.

"Why? Why are you doing this?"

To his surprise, the grin slipped off Brother Ugo's—or Fedu's—face momentarily, and for the length of a single second, he saw something else in the old god's expression. Sadness.

"I don't expect you to understand," he said. "But as you've served me well, I *will* tell you. My brothers and sisters came together to create the world you know, a world you think is good. After their work was done, and they were content, each of them returned to their realms. Even at this moment four of them sleep, oblivious." The god's eyes glinted. "But *I* did not sleep. I remained awake, eyes open, and I watched." He gestured past the walls of the garden, as though seeing something far beyond them. "I saw the world produce things my own siblings could have never imagined—war, disease, famine. I watched darajas fight, and sometimes even sacrifice their very lives to maintain order among mankind, a terrible waste of skill and power.

"The others choose to look away from the brutal parts of what we have created, they choose to believe that what we have created is without flaw, is inherently *good*, because that was what they *wished*." Fedu continued: "But I do not see things as I wish they were; I see them as they *are*. This world is covered in filth, and the time has come for it to be cleansed."

"By killing people," said Ekon quietly. "By killing *millions* of people."

"Yes." The god nodded, solemn. "You will recall that, when you were a little boy, I once told you that the hardest choices often required the strongest minds."

"She won't help you," said Ekon. "Adiah knows what you are now. She'll never help you do this."

"I convinced Adiah once," said Fedu calmly. "I am confident that she can be convinced again." There was a dangerous undertone in his voice. "One way or another."

"She's gone." Ekon said the words as confidently as he could, moving slowly back toward the garden's entrance. It wasn't far; he could make it if he timed it right.

Fedu quirked an eyebrow, curious. "In all the years I helped raise you, I never took you for a liar, Ekon."

"I'm not lying." Ekon forced the words. "She and Koffi escaped, I made sure of it."

"Ah yes, the other daraja," said Fedu. "That is no matter. You will take me to them."

"No, I won't—"

There was no warning before the pain racked his body. Ekon fell to his knees, his back arching as pain pulsed through him in agonizing waves, like a thousand knives pricking every inch of his skin at once. Never in his life had he felt something like this; he wanted to die. As suddenly as it came, the pain disappeared. Ekon crumpled into a ball, half his face pressed into the dirt. When he forced one eye open, he found Fedu standing above him.

"A curious thing about the splendor," he said softly. "It *can* enter the body of someone who is not a daraja, though I've been told it is excruciating when it does so." He flicked his finger, and the pain returned tenfold. Ekon screamed. "I wonder how long it will

453

take before I break you, before you tell me what I want to know?"

Another wave of pain ricocheted through Ekon's body. This time, it wasn't like knives, but fire, burning across his skin, scalding him from the inside. Through the haze, he watched Fedu stoop beside him. His eyes were cold.

"And what I wonder most," he whispered in Ekon's ear, "is what will kill you in the end—the pain, or the madness?"

Ekon couldn't answer, couldn't speak as his lungs began to restrict, growing tighter as the pain enveloped his body.

The last thing he heard was the far-off thud of the garden's trapdoor.

CHAPTER 33

HEART AND MIND

Koffi heard another scream.

At the sound, Adiah swiveled, nostrils flaring. She raised her nose to the air to sniff, then let out a roar more terrifying than any Koffi had heard before. Their eyes met in the darkness for only a moment before a decision was made.

"Come on!" Koffi turned on her heels and pelted back into the temple. Adiah needed no further prompt as she stayed on Koffi's heels, snarling and snapping. Koffi knew they were being reckless, knew that at any moment they could run into more of the temple's workers or the Sons of the Six, but luck stayed with them. Somewhere far off she could hear the clink of glassware, laughter. Was there some sort of party going on? She didn't have time to think about it.

Ekon. Her eyes shot down each hallway, confused. *Where are you?*

She didn't know the layout of the temple outside of what Ekon had told her: The hallways and doors leading into darker passageways seemed endless. Adiah roared louder as another scream erupted from one of the hallways, this time closer still. Koffi followed the sound until she reached a door slightly ajar. She opened it more and saw a narrow set of steps leading up to what looked like a trapdoor above. White moonlight illuminated its outline. She charged up it, Adiah at her heels, and tried to push it open, but it held firm. She heard a low growl and barely had time to duck before Adiah's claws tore through the wood in one vicious motion. Koffi covered her head and closed her eyes as bits of the destroyed door fell all around them. There was a roar, and she felt Adiah push past her, and when she opened her eyes again, the end of her bottlebrush tail was already disappearing up the square opening above. Koffi hoisted herself up it, then stopped.

She knew the garden before her must have been beautiful at one point; there were old, dead flowers blanketing every inch of it. In another time, another era perhaps, it had likely been a sort of paradise, a haven. But she didn't care about the flowers; her eyes had fixed on the two people in the garden's center. One was standing with his back turned to her, and the other was on the ground. She focused on the latter.

Ekon.

Something was terribly wrong—she knew it the moment she saw him. In the silvery moonlight, she couldn't see any physical wounds on Ekon's body, but he was shaking, trembling as she'd only seen one time before. Tears streaked his cheeks, and his eyes were blank, as though she weren't there at all.

"Ekon!"

He winced at the sound of her voice, looking pained. Slowly, he blinked, and the gesture seemed to help him refocus his gaze. The muscles in his shoulder relaxed, and he looked up at her from the dirt. His eyes went wide when they found her.

"Koffi." He said her name in a dry rasp, audibly pained. In that single word, she heard an emotion; it took her a moment to name it: fear. Ekon sounded afraid. He began shaking his head, screwing his eyes shut.

"No . . ." A moan escaped him as he pressed his palms against his head, trying to block out something she could not hear. "No, you can't be here. You have to—"

"Ah, the darajas," said a thin, unfamiliar voice. *"Come at last, as I knew you would."*

Koffi started. She'd been watching Ekon so intently that she'd almost forgotten about the figure standing a few feet from him. It was unnerving; in the darkness, he was almost impossible to see, a silhouette she did not know. Behind her, Adiah snarled.

"Who are you?" Koffi's words echoed against the stone walls of the garden as the figure stepped forward, face still obscured. She pointed to Ekon. "What have you done to him?"

"After all this time, we are reunited," the voice said silkily. "It has been far too long."

Koffi paused, confused. That wasn't the answer to her question; those words didn't even make sense. It wasn't until another growl filled the air that she understood. The words didn't make sense because they weren't for *her*.

The figure took yet another step closer, finally illuminated in the moonlight. He was small and frail, with chestnut skin and wavy white hair. Wrinkles were etched deep into his features, and he looked old enough to be her great-grandfather. But something about him wasn't right. Koffi stiffened as he extended a hand.

"I see you haven't changed." He wasn't looking at her, but over her shoulder. "At least, not in any of the important ways. Tell me, Songbird . . . do you still sing?"

In answer, Adiah roared, but it wasn't like before. There was another audible emotion beneath the bellow, a terrible anguish. Koffi could practically feel the crackling splendor in the air. She didn't dare turn around to look at the other daraja; she wasn't sure what she would see. The name the strange man had called her was unfamiliar.

Songbird?

"I am glad you have finally come to your senses," he continued. "And that you have chosen a path of less resistance. You've even brought me something fresh, an assistant to aid in our efforts."

To aid in our efforts.

It hit Koffi then. She understood. Ekon had gone looking for his mentor, an old man he'd believed had been harmed. He'd found someone else instead, someone who wasn't his mentor at all.

"You're Fedu," she whispered.

"Clever girl." The god turned his gaze upon her with a chilling smile. "I believe thanks are owed to you too. My understanding is that you helped Ekon procure my daraja. You brought her to me."

"She's not going anywhere with you!" Koffi gritted her teeth. Beside her, she felt a hum of power as Adiah crouched low, understanding. For his part, Fedu looked between them, amused.

"I do not relish spilling daraja blood." There was laughter in his voice, though it didn't reach his eyes. "But make no mistake, child, you are but an ant in my path. Should you attempt to stand in my way, I will deal with you as such."

Koffi didn't answer, didn't wait. Her toes curled as she focused her mind and summoned the splendor, shuddering as it danced up her limbs and instantly warmed her. She heard a bellow and felt the ground beneath her shake as Adiah snarled.

Then they were moving in tandem, Koffi running to the left while Adiah moved right. She'd never done this before, never tried to use the splendor in a fight, but the power coursing through her seemed to understand what she wanted, as though it had a mind of its own fusing with hers. She spun on her heels and felt the thrum of more power enter through one hand, passing through her heart, then exiting through the other side. A golden ray of light escaped her like a ribbon, like a snake coiling in the air before it lashed across Fedu's cheek. He hissed, turning to face her, but before he could react, Adiah charged him from behind, headbutting him so that he went flying back, though he landed on his feet with un-nerving ease. He turned as Koffi came at him, raising one of his hands in a flick, and white-hot pain grazed Koffi's cheek. She felt herself flying backward. She groaned as she landed in the dirt, the wind knocked from her body. A dull haze clouded her vision, but through it she could just make out Fedu and Adiah. They were circling each other.

"Come now, Adiah," Fedu said softly. "You make this more difficult than it has to be."

The daraja snapped her teeth. She lunged at him, a flurry of claws swiping at his face, but he dodged her with ease.

"Look at what you have become after all these years, Songbird." He danced out of her reach easily as she swiped at him again, his lips splitting into a wicked smile. "Look at what holding in all of that splendor has done to you. You used to be the greatest daraja to walk the earth—intelligent, beautiful, and powerful. It seems you're little more than a fumbling beast these days—*stupid, ugly, and weak.*"

He's baiting her, Koffi realized. Adiah screamed; there was no other word for it. It was a sound of fury and violence, but also a sound of agony. She charged again, and Koffi understood a second too late what Fedu was going to do. Her lips tried to form the warning words, but not fast enough. There was a horrible crack as Fedu's fist connected with her jaw, striking her with an inhuman strength. The force of the blow sent her back, landing inches from Koffi. She did not rise again.

Fedu brushed the dirt off his clothes, unfazed. "If you will not give me what I want," he said testily, "then I will take it." He started toward her, steps slow and deliberate.

Adiah. Koffi didn't move—she didn't want Fedu to know she was still conscious—but she tried to meet the other daraja's eyes, to will them open. *Adiah, please wake up.*

Fedu was getting closer, only a few yards from them now. Koffi looked down at her own hand, inches from Adiah's too-still paw. For some reason, the longer she stared at it, the more clearly she heard Adiah's voice. She remembered the two of them standing in the Greater Jungle, the moment she'd looked into the eyes of a girl who was lost, tired, afraid.

I cannot endure this pain for another century, she'd said. *I am not strong enough to fight Fedu if he captures me, do you understand?*

Koffi *had* understood. They'd had a plan, and now it was gone. Fedu had won. He would take Adiah away, just as he'd always intended to, and use her for his own means. And Adiah would let him, not because she wanted to, but because she had nothing left, because she couldn't keep running anymore.

Once upon a time, another lifetime ago, she'd been someone else, a girl with hopes and dreams and loves and wants. She'd been a girl caught between her heart and her mind. In the end she'd chosen both, a scarier thing, but the braver thing. Koffi reflected on that. Maybe there was something to be said for learning how to do that, how to make the braver choice. In the back of her mind, she remembered the offhand words of an old woman in a marketplace, a lesson: *Anything can be bartered for, if you know its true value.*

In that moment, she knew what to do.

Her fingers extended, the smallest of movements, until they brushed Adiah's fur. They were barely touching, but that was all she needed. As soon as the splendor felt her touch, a new host, it came to her, tearing through as suddenly and powerfully as a storm surge. She watched in a haze as Adiah's body began to change again, morphed and reshaped into something more human. In the distance, a voice cried out.

"What are you doing?"

She didn't look at him, but Koffi could hear the bewilderment in the god's voice, his confusion. She ignored him. The rush of the splendor drowned the rest of the words as it overtook her, overpowered her. In the same moment she felt it fill her body to the brim, she knew that it was too much—far too much—but she didn't let go. This was her choice, her choosing, her barter.

She thought she heard the air shift when she finally let go of Adiah and sat up. The movement cost her something; her muscles ached, and her shoulders pounded. She felt . . . heavier.

"How are you doing that?"

She looked up and found that Fedu had stopped mere feet from

461

her, his eyes genuinely wide with shock. "How is your body able to hold so much of the splendor? It shouldn't be possible—"

"I want to make a barter." Koffi could barely keep her eyes open. "Leave Adiah and Ekon alone and take me. I'll go willingly."

"Koffi, *no!*"

Something ripped inside her as she looked in Ekon's direction and watched horror spread across his features. It was worse than she could ever have imagined. She made herself look at the god instead, waiting.

"Very well." Fedu was still staring at her, face full of surprise, but he seemed to be coming around to the idea. He was nodding. "You'll come with me, *now.*"

Koffi didn't argue. It took every fiber of her will to lift herself from the ground, to walk toward the waiting god. The splendor reverberated through her with every step. Her mouth went dry as Fedu's fingers fettered her wrists, no different from the ropes that had once bound her hands, but she resisted the urge to wince. She would not show fear, not here. She would not show anything. She glanced at Ekon a final time; he was the last thing she saw.

And then she was gone.

CHAPTER 34

BEASTS OF PREY

There was a flash of light across the garden, and then there was nothing.

It took several seconds for the ringing in Ekon's ears to abate. Even after it did, his eyes stayed shut. Seconds passed before he sat up, coughing through the haze of smoke and debris that filled the air. He looked around the garden a moment before his heart dropped.

"Koffi? *Koffi!*"

He jumped to his feet, ignoring the new pain. The entire sky garden was beyond recognition, burned and charred as though an unseen force had ravaged every iota of life there. Even the soil, once rich and brown, had turned brittle and ash gray. He stared at the place where Koffi had stood opposite Fedu just seconds ago while his mind tried to put together the pieces. She'd been there, *right there*. Now she wasn't.

No. The panic was instant, pervasive in Ekon's mind. For the first time in a long time, an old haze threatened his vision.

No, no, no.

He remembered the look on her face abruptly, the two emotions warring with each other in every inch of her expression. There'd been a terrible sadness in that look, but also something scarier still—resolve mixed with resignation, a decision being made. Koffi had made a choice to go with Fedu, but where had he taken her? Where had they gone?

His eyes cast over the sky garden again, then stopped. A small movement caught his attention. It took him a moment to understand what he was seeing, and when he did, his blood cooled. It was a body. Slowly, carefully, he approached it, muscles tensed. He came to a stop and stared down at it, confused.

The body belonged to a woman of an indeterminate age. She was tall and thin—with dark curly hair framing her face in a halo. Flower petals and leaves were littered across her naked body, and her eyes were closed in the gentlest way. Ekon supposed she could have been sleeping, but somewhere deep down he knew she was not. He also suspected he knew who this woman was, or at least who she'd once been. There was no hesitation as, carefully, he lifted her. Some of the flower petals that had covered her fell away, but others seemed to cling to her with a loyalty as he carried her to the once flower bed and lowered her into it. There wasn't enough dirt here to bury her, but something kept him from leaving just yet. He searched the ground around him until he found a rock with a sharp enough edge and kneeled beside her a second time. Every muscle in his body hurt as he traced the words in the dirt, but he made himself take his time anyway. When he was finished, he studied the letters.

Satao and Adiah

It was inadequate, he knew that as he stared at the tiny inscription, but it was all he had. With effort, he rose again, letting the rock slip from his fingers and clatter against the stone. Something in the air seemed to shift, but he kept still, waiting for a thing he wasn't even sure he could name. There was an irony to it; all his life, he'd been taught the ways of being a warrior and thought those were also the ways to be a man. Burying the body a young woman hadn't been part of that training, but in doing it, he felt distinctly older, like he'd paid a sort of quiet price. It wasn't the custom of his people, the act didn't follow the tradition, but he found he wasn't sorry for it. He gave the daraja one final look before heading for the garden's trapdoor. It felt strange dropping through it this time, landing on the stairs amid fragments of wood from the door Adiah had destroyed. Distantly, he heard the sounds of party revelers still in the temple's worship hall, but they felt like inhabitants of an entirely different world now, like something separate. Quietly, he emerged from the stairway and closed the door behind him. He knew, at some point, someone would likely find the trapdoor and the sky garden; by then, he'd likely be long gone.

He crept down the hallway, back toward the dormitories. A plan began to unfurl in his mind. He would grab supplies from his bedroom, food from the kitchens if he had time, then—

"Ekon?"

Ekon tensed, at once uneasy and afraid. He'd known, from the moment he heard the voice, who he'd see when he turned around, but that didn't make it any easier to meet Kamau's eyes. His brother was standing at the other end of the hallway. The skin between his brows was pinched hard in confusion.

"What are you doing here?" Kamau asked. His brow furrowed. "Why aren't you at the feast?"

"I'm leaving, Kamau." Ekon swallowed. "I can't . . . I can't be a Son of the Six."

"Leaving?" His brother repeated the word like it was foreign, then shook his head. He even gave a half-hearted laugh. "You wouldn't leave without saying goodbye to me, or Brother Ugo."

Ekon's heart drummed painfully in his chest. Even if, in this moment, he was horrified by his brother's actions, he didn't relish having to tell him the truth. He took a deep breath, then drew himself up to full height. "Kam, Brother Ugo is . . . gone."

It was as though he'd slapped Kamau across the face; his brother actually stumbled back as the words hit him. There was a sad moment as real horror crossed his face.

"Gone," he repeated hollowly. "What do you mean, gone?"

There was no hiding it. Ekon's voice trembled. "He's not here anymore."

"But *how*?" Kamau took a step forward, visible pain rippling across his face. "Why did he—?" He paused, as though something was dawning on him; then his expression contorted with rage. "You *hurt* him."

"What?" Ekon started. "No, Kamau—"

"I *told* you he was praying." Kamau stalked forward, teeth bared. "You weren't supposed to disturb him. Now you've done something to him."

Ekon's heart thundered wild in his chest. The words his brother was saying, the emotions, none of them were logical. A sliver of moonlight from one of the hall's windows illuminated Kamau's face as he came closer. In that fleeting moment, Ekon saw it.

Kamau's pupils didn't look right. They were wide—eerily dilated.

A sickly sweet scent filled the air then, stinging Ekon's nose as he tried not to inhale. He tried to keep his voice even. "Kamau, listen to me."

There was no warning before he charged. Ekon barely had time to brace himself before Kamau was upon him. Stars exploded in his vision as they collided, then crashed to the ground, bodies smacking against the stone floor. He tried to get free, to wriggle out of Kamau's grip as his brother grabbed his wrists and pinned him down. Up close, he smelled the remnants of the hasira leaf on his brother's clothes, saw the unnatural bloodshot quality of his brother's eyes. He kicked as hard as he could and sent Kamau reeling back, but it cost him. A stab of renewed pain lanced through one side of his body like fire without warning, and he winced. It was all Kamau needed. In seconds, he was back on top of him, this time with his fingers closing around Ekon's neck. Ekon gasped. Spots were forming in his vision, the world growing hazier by the second.

"Kam . . . ," he wheezed. "Kam . . . please . . ."

He didn't know exactly what did it, whether it was the quality of his voice or the way he said Kamau's name. But in that fraction of a second, past the hard glassiness of his brother's eyes, he saw something else—a flicker. It was infinitesimal, barely visible, but there all the same. That flicker, that tiny modicum in Kamau's eyes, was the part of him the hasira leaf's poison couldn't reach. Ekon held his brother's gaze and locked on to that something, pleading.

"Please." He whispered the word as his brother's grip tightened. "Please."

Kamau's fingers loosened slightly, only for a moment, but Ekon took advantage of it. He shot up abruptly, knocking heads with Kamau so hard his brother fell back and slumped on the floor, out cold. Slowly, Ekon rose, trying to ignore the hazy world around him and the new throbbing in his forehead. He stared down at Kamau's sprawled body and fought to temper the tightening in his throat. When the tears welled and fell, he didn't stop them; he was too tired. All his life, he'd been taught the same things. Men didn't cry. *Warriors* didn't cry. He'd wanted to a warrior, believed that the title and rank would give him something he wanted, needed. Emotion had been a thing to bury without remorse because that was how to show strength. So, he'd buried his pain. He'd spent years burying anything that made him uncomfortable, upset, or nervous, and he'd run from his own nightmares until they'd hunted him down like beasts of prey.

He was tired of running too.

Ekon knelt beside his brother, gently lifting until Kamau was propped against the wall. He squeezed his hand before he stood.

"Goodbye, brother."

Then he turned and ran.

By the time they reached the temple's back door, the starry sky was obscured in cloud cover. Every muscle in Ekon's body protested as he crouched low, but there was no choice; he couldn't be seen. He said a silent prayer of thanks as he crept under the Takatifu District's golden arches and found its posts abandoned; either the warriors usually stationed here had gone to the feast, or they'd been alerted that there was trouble elsewhere.

The city's streets were empty too, an indication of how late in the night it was. Ekon winced as the first drizzles of rain pelted his bare arms, slicking his sandals so that every step was harder and harder. He was close to the Chafu District, the city's slums, and if he could just get there and hide until he was rested enough to travel to the Greater Jungle . . .

"You there," a voice rang out. "All citizens have been ordered to their homes. State your business!"

Ekon's blood went cold as he picked up his pace.

He heard the crunch of someone else's sandals in the dirt, following him.

"Halt!" the voice rang out, its speaker starting to run. "In the name of the Six!"

Ekon broke into a run. He veered right, then ducked into a narrow alleyway as the sounds of more warriors neared. These alleyways weren't familiar to him. He wasn't sure if he was managing to lose the warriors or get himself more lost. He came to the end of one street and stopped. He was reaching his limit, his body still beaten from his encounter with Fedu.

"*Tsst!*"

Ekon jumped. The street around him was dark, empty, but the sound he'd heard was distinct. His eyes panned, searching.

"*Tsst*, boy," said a female voice. "In here, quickly!"

Ekon looked left. The door to one of the shops he'd thought was closed had abruptly opened, and a hooded figure was peeking out of it, beckoning frantically.

"*Come!*"

It was a dangerous risk, and maybe a stupid one, but Ekon was out of choices. He darted into the shop; the figure who had waved to him moved out of the way only long enough for him to get inside before shutting the door behind them both. They weren't a moment too soon; seconds later, the pounding sound of marching Sons of the Six warriors passed. When they were gone, Ekon took in his new surroundings.

It was impossible to discern what had once been sold in this shop. Slowly, Ekon looked to his savior.

"Who . . . who are you?"

The figure, still hooded, didn't answer.

"Why did you help me?" Ekon pressed, keeping his voice at a whisper. "Why did you help us?"

This time, the figure nodded. "You're hurt, and you need treatment."

Ekon frowned. "Not until you tell me—"

"I'll explain everything, I promise," she said. "But first, come with me, before you make things worse. I have a place you can lie down."

Ekon wanted to ask more questions, but his fatigue was growing. Slowly, he followed the hooded figure along a crooked hall until they reached what looked like the back of the shop, where usually inventory would be kept. But this was no inventory room. Its dusty walls were illuminated by a small, flickering oil lamp, and several sacks of what appeared to be flour were pushed together in one corner in a makeshift bed. The figure gestured for Ekon to sit. As soon as he did, the pain crept in. He'd never felt so sore in his life, and worse, there was still something throbbing painfully in his side like a knife. Involuntarily, he rubbed the spot, and the pain increased tenfold. He groaned.

"Lie down," the figure ordered. "Your injuries are severe."

Through his haze Ekon stared at the spot on his side where the pain was worst; there was nothing there. He stared back up at the figure, trying to find a face beneath the hood's shadow.

"I'm fine," he muttered. "There's nothing there."

"I'm not talking about your *physical* wounds, boy."

Ekon started to argue, but without warning the figure finally drew her hood back. Ekon started.

He'd only seen the old woman once before, but he recognized her. It was a strange sensation, and he felt something return to him like a half-forgotten dream. He saw short cottony hair, dark skin, and an amulet hanging from a leather cord around her neck. Up close and in better light, he saw a symbol was crudely carved into the metal, but he still didn't know what it meant. The first time he'd seen her, in the streets of the city's slums, she'd looked different, but . . .

"You. You're the one who—"

"My name is Themba." The old woman introduced herself matter-of-factly before pointing to the sacks. Bits of white cottony hair stuck out from her head wrap. "Lie down and stop moving, before you hurt yourself."

"I'm fine—" Ekon stopped short at the look she cut him, her eyes full of challenge. "All right."

Themba placed her knobby hands on Ekon's shoulders and pressed him down onto the flour sacks with surprising strength, then straightened to inspect him. After a moment, she sucked her teeth.

"Worse than I thought," she said, as though talking to herself. She cracked her knuckles and looked to Ekon, her expression wary. "I will try to do this gently, but I must warn you. It will still probably be painful."

Ekon barely had time to sit up. "What are you—?"

And then he was in pain, even more excruciating than what he'd felt in the garden. His back arched as he felt something pulled from him, something with a viselike grip. Just as quickly as the pain came, it was gone, but fresh tears still sprang to Ekon's eyes.

"That's the worst of it," said Themba. "You'll feel better in the morning. Now let's get you some sustenance."

Ekon tried to keep his eyes open as she moved to the room's corner, but it was a losing battle. He tried to move, and a groan escaped his lips. The old woman had been right, the worst of his pain was definitely gone, but he was still sore. He didn't know how much time passed before he opened his eyes and found Themba standing over him again. This time she held a small gourd of water.

"*Drink.*"

His body reached before his mind could, and he took several greedy gulps. The woman watched without saying anything until he finished.

"How do you feel now?" she asked quietly.

"Better," said Ekon.

"Good."

Ekon hesitated, then handed the gourd back to her. "Thank you," he said after a moment. "For helping me."

Themba nodded.

"How did you do it?" he asked. "How did you take that pain away?"

Themba offered a small, sad smile. "You might call it . . . a *gift*."

She flexed her fingers, and a small shimmer danced between them.

Ekon sat up. "You're . . . a daraja?"

"Very good, young man."

"But I thought . . ." Ekon looked from her to his hands. "Brother Ugo . . . I thought all the darajas were gone?"

"Many are," said Themba sadly. "But not all of us."

Ekon closed his eyes and shook his head, trying to make the pieces come together to form something logical in his mind. A second later, he opened them and met the old woman's gaze.

"How many more are there?" he asked. "Darajas, that is?"

"I do not know," said Themba. "I have not communed with another daraja in years."

"Why?"

"Because I've been hiding." She moved away from him, crouching to refill the oil lamp. "It has not been safe for my kind to be in this city for a long time. I fear it is still not."

Ekon swung his legs off the flour sacks, wincing. "I can't stay here," he said. "I have to go."

Themba raised one gray eyebrow. "*Lie down*, child."

"You don't understand . . ." Ekon forced himself to stand, ignoring the new stars that filled his vision. "I have to help my friend. She's a daraja too, and she's been taken, she—"

"I *know* what trouble Koffi is in."

Ekon stilled, the stars in his eyes temporarily forgotten. "You . . . you *know* Koffi? You've met her?"

"Only twice, though *she* would only remember the second time." Themba's eyes held a distinct sadness. "The time before that, she was only a baby."

Ekon stared at her a moment, confused. "I don't understand. Koffi didn't even know what she was until recently. How could *you* know?"

"Because I've known Koffi for a very long time," said Themba. "Even if she did not know me. Even if she was not *allowed* to know me."

"But—"

Themba stood, raising a hand to silence him, but her eyes were not unkind.

"Rest, child." She crossed the room and gently pushed Ekon back onto the flour sacks. "The important thing for you to do is *heal*."

There was something familiar about the woman up close, though Ekon couldn't put his finger on it as he fell back against the sacks. "I have to find Koffi . . ."

"*Sleep*," she insisted. "Tomorrow, when you are better, we will come up with a plan."

Ekon's eyes were closed and the words were fading. Themba spoke so quietly, he wasn't sure he'd heard what she muttered to herself.

"And then we will find my granddaughter."

AUTHOR'S NOTE

In May of 2015, while I sat in a bedroom surrounded by moving boxes, I started to write a story that would—many years later—become the iteration of *Beasts of Prey* that most know today. The story has evolved significantly over time, transforming from a vague, ambitious idea in my head to a fully realized fantasy novel brimful with all the trappings I both adored and longed to see in young adult literature. As I wrote and revised this story over the years, it became more than a creative outlet for me; it also became a device of catharsis, a chance for me to explore, reclaim, and celebrate a heritage that was violently erased as a consequence of transatlantic slavery.

I refer to *Beasts of Prey* as a Pan-African fantasy because—although Eshōza is not at all a real place—much of its influence and inspiration has been shaped by the very real continent of Africa. The decision not to focus on one region of Africa was a deliberate one; as a Black American woman, the reality is that I will never know exactly (or even approximately) where my ancestors lived and thrived prior to their capture, so this story honors cultures, mythos, and folklore from across different regions of the continent. It also explores the phenomenon of being the product of a forced diaspora. If you are familiar with African and African American studies, you may have caught some of the subtle and overt references included in the pages of this story, but I feel here it's my due diligence to lay things out in no uncertain terms for those who may have questions.

A prominent but largely unseen character featured in *Beasts of Prey* is the famed naturalist-scholar Satao Nkrumah. While he is not based on any real person, he is named after two distinct figures. The first is Kwame Nkrumah (1909–1972), who was a prominent Ghanaian scholar and political figure largely acknowledged as one of the fathers of Pan-Africanism, the ideology that encourages unity among people of Afro descent. The name Satao comes, incidentally, from an elephant. Those who know me well know that I am deeply partial to elephants. Satao the Elephant (1968–2014) was a Kenyan "tusker" best known for having rare tusks so long they nearly brushed the ground. In May of 2014, he was tortured and killed by ivory poachers in a devastating blow to East African wildlife preservation. Thusly, Satao Nkrumah is named after a revolutionary man and a beautiful elephant.

There are several small nods to anti-colonialists and Pan-African political leaders throughout the world. For me, it was important that Ekon—a young Black man who loves books—be surrounded not just by scholars, but by scholars who looked like him. Black scholarship, literature, and history have been historically marginalized, Othered, and otherwise diminished over time; simply put, I wanted Ekon to exist in a world where Black excellence was preserved and celebrated, as we see in places like the Temple of Lkossa's library. You'll note if you read that several of the masters of the temple where he lives are named after acclaimed

Black political leaders and revolutionaries like Nnamdi "Zik" Azikiwe (the first president of Nigeria), Julius Nyerere (the first president of Tanganyika, which is now modern-day Tanzania), Jomo Kenyatta (the first president of Kenya), Patrice Lumumba (the first prime minister of the independent Democratic Republic of the Congo), and Marcus Garvey (the founder of the Universal Negro Improvement Association and African Communities League).

The Zamani language used throughout *Beasts of Prey* is based on the Swahili language, which is spoken primarily in Eastern Africa by approximately 11 million people to date. It should be clear that I do not speak Swahili fluently, but I chose it as my base language because I've always found it to be a beautiful language, and it is where my own name—Ayana—comes from. Arabic-speaking readers may notice that some Swahili words are similar or the same in Arabic; this is because after years of trade and cultural exchange, Swahili has evolved and adopted some Arabic words. While I did at one point consider using a "conlang" (a constructed language) for *Beasts of Prey*, I ultimately decided that to do so was a form of Othering. Growing up, I saw many languages from the European continent used in fantasy, but never saw any languages based from the African continent, and I wanted to change that.

The mythological beings and creatures in this story are—for the most part—drawn from real lore across the African continent, and they are one of the things I most enjoyed while writing this story. While jokomotos aren't from any myth (I couldn't find a creature from folklore that fit the description I needed), the rest are. What Ekon once said about grootslangs is true—they come from South African mythology, and it's believed that gods split the grootslang into two distinct animals (elephants and snakes) to make it less fearsome.

Biloko (the plural of *eloko*) come from the Mongo people of the Democratic Republic of Congo in Central Africa. According to Mongo lore, they are vicious, dwarfish creatures who live in the thickest parts of rain forests and jungles. They are known to take the forms of innocent children, wear bells that can be used to cast spells on the unsuspecting, and have an insatiable taste for human flesh and bone. In many myths, it is often the "foolish" woman who is tricked by biloko, and so in *Beasts of Prey* I chose to subvert that trope and have Ekon be the one who is tricked by one.

Yumboes come from the Wolof people of Senegal in West Africa. There are inconsistencies about their origins and appearances, and evidence suggests myths may have evolved after the European invasion in West Africa, but generally speaking, they are known to be kind fairy-like entities who dance in moonlight and love lavish feasts. I wanted to include them in *Beasts of Prey* because I thought they sounded lovely, and I also wanted at least one of the beings that Koffi and Ekon encounter in the Greater Jungle to be friendly.

The umdhlebi tree (sometimes spelled *umdhlebe*) is another creation of Zulu lore in South Africa and has been called the deadman's tree in real life. Its Latin name is *Euphorbia cupularis*, and though it is not known to be toxic or poisonous in modernity, the oral stories of its power are terrifying.

The Six gods of Eshōza are not real, and the religion they come from is entirely constructed. While the African continent is brimful with fascinating and beautiful religions—including variations of Islam, Christianity, and more locally based religions—I did not feel it was appropriate to use a real religion that people adhere to and practice in a fantasy novel.

The Yabas and Gedes are not real peoples, but they do represent a small fraction of the diverse ethnic populations that often reside side by side throughout African countries and regions. Despite the fact that—to an outsider—many of these peoples look phenotypically the same, they often speak different languages, observe different religions and traditions, and sometimes don't even get along.

In *Beasts of Prey*, there is a chapter called "The Mamba and the Mongoose" that became one of my favorites to write based on its truth. In fact, the eastern black mamba *is* one of the deadliest snakes in the world; its venom can kill a grown man in approximately fifteen minutes, and most who are bitten by it die simply because they do not have enough time to receive medical aid. It's also true that the mongoose is the black mamba's mortal enemy. Fascinatingly, mongooses' cells have evolved so that they are essentially immune to the mamba's poisoning, and coupled with their own incredible speed, they are all but impervious to it. Watching a fight between them is one of nature's true wonders.

Lastly, the lore of the Shetani—which means "demon" in Swahili—was partially inspired by a real occurrence that took place in Kenya between March and December of 1898. As it happened, for several months, two brother lions systematically stalked and brutally killed construction workers who were trying to build the Kenya-Uganda Railway that was meant to bring the two countries together. Lions in the Tsavo area weren't an unusual occurrence, but the behavior of *these* particular lions was what made them strange (male lions usually don't hunt, and they certainly don't hunt together). At one point, the killings became so bad that the railroad was in danger of not being finished. Eventually, the brother lions—nicknamed "The Ghost" and "The Darkness"— were hunted down and killed, but the mystery of *why* they started hunting humans remains unsolved more than a century later.

ACKNOWLEDGMENTS

Beasts of Prey, or *BOP*, as I affectionately call it, is my proudest creative expression to date, a gathering of wishes and hopes come to fruition. There are so many people I want to thank from my heart for helping me realize this dream in all the big and small ways.

I owe my first thanks to my literary agent and fiercest advocate in the publishing world: the extraordinary Pete Knapp. Pete, what you do every day for the world of children's literature is nothing short of pure magic. Thank you for believing in this story with your whole heart, and for believing in me. Thank you for answering every single one of my questions, for turning *RuPaul's Drag Race* into an important lesson in character development, and reminding me to never be afraid to ask for the moon. A sincere thank-you as well to Emily Sweet, Andrea Mai, and the fabulous team at Park & Fine!

My second thanks is to my sensational editor, Stacey Barney. Stacey, from the start you shepherded *BOP* through the publishing world with unrivaled care, and I know I am a better writer because of your keen editorial eye (speaking of eyes, you were right; there were far too many!). Thank you for being a kindred spirit on this journey, and for our enthused discussions of food processors and T-Pain. Most of all, thank you for not "letting me out the house with my slip showing." (I remembered!)

Beasts of Prey simply wouldn't be the book it is without the incredible teams at Penguin Young Readers and G. P. Putnam's Sons Books for Young Readers, who showed it so much love and enthusiasm from the beginning. A heartfelt thanks in no particular order to Jennifer Loja, Jennifer Klonsky, Felicia Frazier, Emily Romero, Kim Ryan, Shanta Newlin, Carmela Iaria, Alex Garber, Venessa Carson, Summer Ogata, Lathea Mondesir, Olivia Russo, Ashley Spruill, Cindy Howle, Caitlin Tutterow, Shannon Span, Bezi Yohannes, James Akinaka, and of course Felicity Vallence (Aussie! Aussie! Aussie!). I truly hope this story makes you all proud.

A tremendous thank-you to Ruth Bennett, Natalie Doherty, and Asmaa Isse of Penguin Random House UK for bringing *BOP* "across the pond" and introducing it to new readers in the United Kingdom and greater Commonwealth. It is a joy to know my book will find a home in places I myself have not yet been.

Thank you so much to my dynamic film agent, Berni Barta, for championing this book in the film industry with such genuine passion and fervor.

I'm so grateful to Theresa Evangelista, the brilliant mind who transformed *BOP* from a messy document on my laptop into something so beautiful. Theresa, thank you for your care, vision, and talent! Thank you to Marikka Tamura for bringing the pages of this book to life with such thoughtful and perfectly-rendered design. I owe a heartfelt thanks to Virginia Allyn for the incredible hand-drawn maps seen at the beginning of this book.

Not least of all, I am indebted to Chandra Wohleber, who probably (definitely) saved me from utter embarrassment multiple times during copyedits. Thank you, Chandra.

There is a special group of people who have been friends to me throughout *BOP*'s publication journey. They've been critique partners, confidantes, and an irreplaceable support system that I couldn't have made it through without. Thank you to Lauren Blackwood, Lane Clarke, Natalie Crown, Alechia Dow, J. Elle, N. T. Poindexter, Emily Thiede, and Amélie Wen Zhao. A special thanks to Maiya Ibrahim, who has read *BOP* more than anyone else and been a true friend.

To Roshani Chokshi, my trusted Virgil on this voyage: I'm so glad the universe brought us together in the throes of a pandemic. "Thank you" will never quite encompass how grateful I am for all you are, but I am thankful for the advice, the endless support, and the reminder to "always hide my fangs so they never see the bite."

Thank you to the authors of my favorite stories: Some of you wrote works that changed my life, and some of you graciously reached back to encourage a fledging author full of nerves and silly questions: Sabaa Tahir, Renée Ahdieh, Leigh Bardugo, Shelby Mahurin, Brigid Kemmerer, Adalyn Grace, Kate Johnston, Samantha Shannon, and Shannon "S. A." Chakraborty.

I would not have reached this milestone without the support of so many friends in the online writing community: Daniel Aleman, Veronica Bane, Rena Barron, TJ Benton, Kat Cho, Becca Coffindaffer, Tracy Deonn, Brenda Drake, Ryan Douglass, Sarah Nicolas, Kellye Garrett, Stephanie Jones, Allie Levick, Lori Lee, Taj McCoy, Cass Newbould, Molly Night, Claribel Ortega, Tóla Okogwu, Tómi Oyemakinde, Jamar Perry, Ryan Ramkelawan,

Irene Reed, Jesse Sutanto, Jeida Storey, Brandon Wallace, Catherine Adel West, and Margot Wood. Thank you to the bloggers, book reviewers, librarians, booksellers, and educators who supported and championed this book from the start. I'm also so grateful to the Black influencers and creatives who really rallied behind me on social media as *BOP* debuted—your voices are truly powerful.

To Corey and Ashley: Thank you for every adventure—good, bad, and otherwise. Thank you for your love and support, and for always being the reason I want to do good in the world. I hope every single one of your dreams come true, and that I'm always there to see it.

To Mom and Dad: Thank you for the Yellow House, for Big Top Circus, for always doing my hair no matter how old I get, and for mac 'n' cheese and sweet potato pie that always tastes like home. Thank you for letting me borrow as many books as I could carry from the library, and for pretending not to notice when I kept writing under the covers after you told me to go to bed. Thank you for teaching me to "push through" and to be kind. I love you both.

To Grandma Elezora, Grandma Geri, and Grandpa Ronald: Thank you for your love and for giving me small pieces of yourselves to make me who I am. To Grandpa George, Grandma D, and my beloved Grandpa Aston: I'm so sorry you weren't here to see this moment, but I hope it makes you proud. I miss you terribly all the time.

To my many aunts, uncles, and cousins: Thank you for raising me, for uplifting me, and for watering a little flower so that she could grow. Thanks also to my Aussie family for reminding me that I am loved all over the world. To Paul, Gail, Matt, Natalie,

Brett, Michael, Tarek, Huda, Medina, and Latifa: mahalo nui!

To Aunt Meredith and Aunt Rhonda: Thank you for so many laughs and beautiful moments, and for reminding me that God did not give me a spirit of fear.

To my two lifelong best friends, Adrie and Robyn: You are irreplaceable. Thank you for always being there for me and for blessing me with two beautiful friendships that have spanned decades and continents alike. I've grown better with and because of you.

There are so many incredible friends and mentors who've shown me unending kindness. Thank you to Bates, Bricker, Brumett, Jarret, Billie, Akshay, KI Fall '12, Daniel, Katie and Sterling, Chris, Kim, Michelle, Kris, Alison, Stacey, Joan, Mackenzie, Ronetta Francis, Erin Hodge, Jon Cannon, Dr. Angela Mosley Monts, Dr. Janine Parry, Dr. Calvin White, Jr., Mr. William "Bill" Topich, Ms. Megan Abbott, Dean Todd Shields, and especially Dr. Jeff "Jefe" Ryan and the Class of 2013 Polvios, who changed my life.

And to my Puddin': You have been with me every step of the way, even when life was cruel and kept us miles apart for a whole year. Your fierce love for me and adamant faith in me know no bounds; what an honor it is to call you mine and to be yours. Here's to road trips across the Outback, cliffside picnics, a New Orleans park bench, and a beach in Hawaii. Our story is my favorite of all.